Praise for
IF I BRING YOU ROSES

"Rich with fascinating detail and engaging characters."
—Rosellen Brown, award-winning
author of *Before and After: A Novel*

"A stunning novel of love and longing between deeply affecting
characters . . . Marisel Vera immerses readers in mid–twentieth
century Puerto Rico and then Chicago with the same eloquent
ease that she draws us into the richness of her characters' lives.
This is a moving story, an amazing debut by a gifted author, and
a book to keep for reading again and again."
—Lorraine López, award-winning
author of *The Realm of Hungry Spirits*

"Marisel Vera is a gifted storyteller with an eye for the subtle
motions of the human heart . . . Vera understands her characters
and brings them to us with lyric intensity, humor, and perfect
pitch so that they live in us long after the last page is closed."
—Jonis Agee, award-winning
author of *The River Wife*

"A richly told tale of obsessive love . . . deeply sensual and
mysterious."   —Cristina García, award-winning
author of *Dreaming in Cuban*

"Brilliant . . . With this amazing debut, Marisel Vera has burst
onto the literary scene. I am eager to see what she writes next."
—Tayari Jones, author of *Silver Sparrow*

If I Bring
You Roses

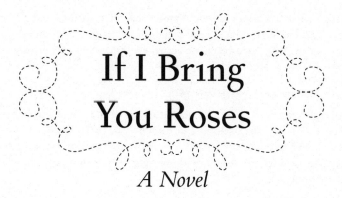

If I Bring You Roses

A Novel

Marisel Vera

GRAND CENTRAL
PUBLISHING

NEW YORK   BOSTON

Copyright © 2011 by Marisel Vera

Grand Central Publishing
Hachette Book Group
237 Park Avenue
New York, NY 10017

www.HachetteBookGroup.com

Printed in the United States of America

First Edition: August 2011

10 9 8 7 6 5 4 3 2 1

Grand Central Publishing is a division of Hachette Book Group, Inc.

The Grand Central Publishing name and logo is a trademark of Hachette Book Group, Inc.

Library of Congress Cataloging-in-Publication Data

Vera, Marisel.
  If I bring you roses / by Marisel Vera.
    p. cm.
  ISBN 978-0-446-57153-1
  1. Marriage—Fiction. 2. Puerto Rico—Fiction. 3. Chicago (Ill.)—Fiction. I. Title.
PS3622.E7I36 2011
813'.6—dc22
                        2010041017

Para los jíbaros

Acknowledgments

I couldn't have written about los jíbaros without the help of the two most important women in my life: my mother, Maria R. Vera, and my godmother, Rosa Vera Tarafa, who were always ready to answer questions and share their stories about growing up on the mountain in Puerto Rico. Thank you to Gina M. Pérez for generously sharing her doctoral dissertation about Puerto Ricans on Chicago's near northwest side. Mi compai Larry Starzec, favorite teacher and reader, believed in my talent from the beginning. Thank you to Jane Cavolina, mentor and friend, and to my teachers Paulette Roeske, Jonis Agee, Rosellen Brown, and Cristina García, who encouraged my writing. A big thank-you to my agent, Betsy Amster, who didn't let me give up when I just couldn't rewrite the ending one more time and to my editor, Selina McLemore, for believing in the story and supporting my way of telling it. I am grateful to Constance Alexander, Stephanie Kegan, Leah Griesmann, Lauren Jiles-Johnson, and Tayari Jones for reading various drafts and providing valuable insight.

Many friends and relatives cheered me on throughout the years and I am so grateful for their support. My sisters, Maria,

Enilda, and Ivy, babysat so that I could write. Thank you, sisters! My daughter, Alyssa, advised me on grammar while her brother, Freddie, charted routes through the Puerto Rican countryside. My two Gails—Gail Vanderster-Zwang and Gail Roemer Montenegro were always ready to help and have coffee. Mi comai Sandra Ryan saw me through two difficult years with love and generosity as only one's best friend can. My love and appreciation to my husband, Wilfredo Ramos, for making my dream his.

Thank you to The Ragdale Foundation and a heartfelt gracias to the Chicago Public Library, especially to the now-defunct Humboldt Park Branch on North Avenue and California, where I made a weekly pilgrimage all the years of my childhood.

Felicidad

Chapter One

June 1942

Felicidad's dress stuck to her thin frame, and her bare feet felt the burn of the sunbaked road. She clutched her books against her stomach. She'd had no breakfast except for coffee and had refused lunch: a lump of peanut butter plopped down directly on a tray. The Missus had been angry at her ingratitude and had mocked her, saying maybe she thought herself above the others, Felicidad with the made-up name, a name that wasn't even Puerto Rican because she certainly had never heard it before. Felicidad, ha! She wasn't likely to find much happiness because she was going to die of starvation first.

Felicidad longed to tell the teacher that her name was a wish, a hope her parents had for her life to be a happy one. Instead she stood under the almácigo tree, as the teacher directed, while the other children, even her brother Ruben, ate the school lunch, glad to ease their hunger. She picked at the copper-colored bark that peeled off in papery flakes before plucking a few leaves, intending to give them to her mother. When her sister Isabel was alive, Felicidad would bring the leaves daily for Mami to brew tea to cure Isabel's terrible itching. How she hoped Mami would be cooking in the kitchen. But sometimes when Felicidad came home from school she would find her mother lying on her bed clutching her head, murmuring words that didn't make sense, the baby crying.

Papi decided the children and all the housework were too much for Mami and decreed that the girls would take turns going to school. This was Felicidad's lucky year; next year would be Leila's. The girls knew it could be worse; they could be like the Martinez Gutierrezes up the mountain who kept the daughters at home and the sons in the fields. Even Felicidad's older brothers had some schooling.

Her younger brother had run home ahead of her when the school day ended, but she lingered under the spell of the blue sky and the lush green of the mountain. The air was still with the heat of the afternoon and heavy with the fragrance of the wildflowers that grew abundantly along the country road. She made a game of walking under the shade of the light green leaves of the eugenio trees, glancing up at the brilliant blue sky through the large, broad branches. But she should hurry; she was liable to get a little slap for dawdling.

Felicidad saw a man walking toward her. Maybe he was a vagabond, a mendigo like Mami's cousin Primo Samsón.

She wished it might be Primo Samsón, although it was unlikely since they had had a visit from him only last year. Mami had shared their dinner with him, lamenting that she didn't have any rice because it was scarce since the war, but at least there were a few beans and codfish and always cornmeal.

Felicidad's mother had given Primo Samsón a sheet from her own bed; Papi had said, Mujer, are you as crazy as your cousin? Who knew what kind of fleas or disease Samsón carried with him. Mami had said, Do unto others as you would have them do unto you. After all, he knew that pobre Samsón hadn't been the same since he lost his land and his wife left him. While she cooked, Samsón had sat on the stoop of the lean-to kitchen, the inside of which was black with smoke.

Felicidad's father had built the house, only thirty feet by twelve feet, from pieces of salvaged wood that had served other houses and showed the years of beatings from the tropical climate. The house rose on stilts among mango, panapén, and orange trees. Granada bushes and banana rhizomes grew in the shade of the large mamey trees. El batey, a yard of pounded dirt typical of the campo, surrounded the house. Felicidad's father had anchored a hollowed-out limb from a bamboo tree to the roof to drain rainwater down into a barrel. Mami and the girls used it to sponge-bathe at night while Papi and the boys went down to the river. Alongside the house was the pen where the family kept pigs when they had them.

Down the slope was the barraca, a thatched-roof hut, built low to the ground from plant fiber to store crops and to shelter the family during hurricanes. Felicidad's father had cut and tied reeds into bundles to fit the barraca's wood frame. A chicken coop built from scraps of wood and mesh wobbled on narrow posts like a tiny ramshackle house. A rooster with his harem of hens pecked the ground.

Mami had fluttered about listening to Primo Samsón tell stories about Puerto Rico and what he had seen in his travels, about how the island wasn't what it had once been. Felicidad had taken up her mother's piecework and sat in Papi's chair so that she, too, could hear the fairy tales without happy endings.

The mendigo passed her and said, Buenas, niña.

She turned off the road into the brush and walked uphill on a narrow dirt trail strewn with stones and broken branches. She stubbed her toe on a rock and walked on tiptoe the rest of the way. All she could think about was the pain in her stomach; Mami was sure to have saved something from her own lunch, even if only a cucharón of cooked cornmeal. Harina, beans, something.

The shouting frightened Felicidad out of her languor and jarred the tranquil afternoon. She stared up at the sky as if expecting Papa Dios to appear and reassure her, saying, Little Daughter, do not worry. She heard children shrieking over the howl of a wild animal.

She ran toward the sound, her feet kicking up dust and dirt and rocks and pebbles. When she reached the ravine that led to her family's home, the shouting became louder and she ran faster, half sliding down the path that led to the house. She tripped over a large twig and grabbed it, thinking in her fear that somehow she might use it to beat back whatever it was that was making that hideous sound and scaring her brother and sisters, most likely one of the mangy dogs that scavenged around in the countryside eating the eggs that the hens laid and sometimes the hens as well. She wondered where Mami was and why she didn't chase off the dog herself.

Felicidad came to the clearing. The sun glistened on the roof cobbled together from pieces of zinc that Felicidad's father had picked up here and there. Stones and large rocks littered the area surrounding el batey, where she found her siblings shouting up at the sky. Why were they doing that? Where was Mami?

And then she saw her. Her mother crouched on the edge of the roof, howling a high-pitched cry that did not belong to a human being.

Felicidad was confused. Why was Mami on the roof, why was Mami wearing that strange pink shirt and pair of pants with those black patches? And then her brother and sisters were upon her, clutching at Felicidad's dress and legs, and it came to her that her mother was naked, her skin burned by the Puerto Rican sun.

"Felicidad, why is Mami on the roof?" Five-year-old Juanita was crying.

"She won't get down." Eight-year-old Leila, a year younger than Felicidad, cradled the sleeping baby.

Felicidad dropped her books on the ground. "Take Juanita and the baby to Hilda's." She lowered her voice so that her siblings stepped closer. "I'll go get Papi."

"I'll come with you." Ruben was seven and would rather work in the fields with his brothers than go to school.

"Stay and watch over Mami," Felicidad said. "Pray she doesn't jump."

Chapter Two

Felicidad ran. She didn't notice her favorite mango tree, which always hid a juicy mango just for her between its leaves. She didn't breathe in the perfume of orange and lemon blossoms from the cluster of citrus trees. She ran past the tomatoes and onions and green peppers that her father had planted and tended by moonlight. *Mami naked on the roof.*

She ran past the fields of malanga and yuca and yautía and calabaza and sweet potatoes, past the little patch where Papi grew tobacco, which he shared with his brothers. *Mami naked on the roof.* Somehow, she put one foot in front of the other, running toward the field of corn that she could see at a distance. She ran without thinking how she would tell her father when she found him. Her throat was dry. What she would do for a little tazita de café. Her heart beat the refrain: una tazita de café, Mami naked on the roof, naked, naked on the roof, una tazita de café, Mami naked on the roof, naked on the roof.

She spied an obreo hidden among the tall stalks of corn.

"¡Miré!" She stopped to catch her breath. "My father, Juan Vicente Hidalgo. Have you seen him?"

El obreo was hand-hoeing the ground and didn't pause in

his work. Like most farmworkers, he wore a hat, a long-sleeved shirt, and long pants despite the heat. His feet were bare. He nodded to the left.

"Over there. Your father and your brothers."

Felicidad ran between the rows of corn, moving through the airless tunnel of tall, green stalks. The leaves of corn brushed against her arms and legs and she felt her breathing constrict as she ran faster toward the end of the rows, finally bursting through the stalks and colliding into her older brother Vicente. In his threadbare shirt and too-short pants, Vicente was tall and bone-thin as they all were, including their parents. Only Don Agostos's wife was plump, and everyone said that was because he owned the country store and she could eat from the jars and tins as she pleased. Why was that jar of olives that Pancho Pacheco bought last week not quite full?

Vicente caught her by the elbows and shook her.

"Mami," she said, but it was indistinguishable from a croak.

"Felicidad, con calma." Vicente was missing his four front teeth and he pressed his lips together into a straight line, imitating their father. He relished his authority over his siblings because he was the oldest and a boy.

"Mami is on the roof, Mami is on the roof naked," Felicidad said.

"This better not be a game you little kids are playing." Vicente's fingers tightened on her elbows.

"I swear it's true." Felicidad struggled to get free. He had forgotten he was holding her.

Vicente called out to their father; Papi came running.

He pushed back his hat from his eyes. "Your mother?"

"She's on the roof, Papi," Vicente said.

"Get the boys." Papi disappeared into the stalks.

Felicidad wondered why her brother hadn't told their father

that their mother was naked, but he would find out soon enough.

They ran in a little pack, father first, elder brother next, and Felicidad lagging behind the twins, Julio and Eduardo. She wished that this day was just another day when she would wake in the dark, trembling and calling out to her mother to protect her from the Spirits that roamed restless in the night. She often dreamed of Spirits running in these very mountains on this very same path. Felicidad heard their footsteps pounding the ground as they ran in the moonlight, rustling the leaves of the banana and plantain trees.

Now she listened to the footsteps of her father and brothers and Felicidad prayed that somehow she had been mistaken about her mother on the roof, naked.

She heard a woman's voice, normal as the afternoon sun, and thought, Mami, that's Mami. The others reached the clearing to the house before Felicidad and stopped, so she knew without seeing that her mother was still on the roof.

"Get the rope," Papi told Vicente. "Felicidad, get your mother's dress. Julio and Eduardo, come with me."

In el batey stood Hilda la mulata, midwife and nearest neighbor.

"Ay, Don Juan Vicente, la señora is very bad." She was toothless like most poor country folk. "I sent my Berto with Ruben for the priest."

"Why did you do that? This is family business," Felicidad's father said.

"It was either the priest or the curandero," she said.

"¿Curandero? Witch doctor!" Papi said.

"Forgive me, but your señora is obviously possessed by an evil spirit." Hilda pointed up to the roof of the house where Felicidad's mother perched precariously on the edge.

"Son of a bitch!" Papi spat in the dirt.

Felicidad wanted to hide behind her mother's skirt as she had done as a little girl. She ran to get her mother's dress.

Inside the house, a kerosene lamp sat on the table covered with a dingy oilcloth. Two machetes with their blades pointing down were wedged in the wall behind Papi's chair. Next to it was the requinto guitar that Papi had carved out of roble wood. He hadn't played it in a year. Felicidad and her siblings fought for the chair on the rare occasions when Papi was away, but Mami would cede it to Vicente as the oldest male. Papi had built a wood bench, but the children preferred to eat outside on tree stumps in el batey or perch on a favorite branch, taking turns climbing and holding plates for one another.

Tin cans and cups made from the inner shells of coconuts and plates of higüero wood were stacked on a shelf. Spoons, also from higüero, along with Papi's silver knife and fork, rested in a box. Three frying pans of varying sizes, a small strainer, and a large ladle hung on hooks nailed to the frame of the house. A pair of seamstress scissors dangled upside down on a nail. Draped over a beam to keep it dry and clean was a colador to strain coffee: a piece of cotton fabric, permanently stained brown, stitched around a circle of wire.

Felicidad's mother stored each day's portion of coffee beans in a tin that once, long ago, held caramels. Two empty bottles without labels were wedged between the wall and frame. A sack of root vegetables sat on a makeshift shelf. Next to it was a stone molino for grinding corn into flour.

A bunch of bananas not quite ripe hung suspended from a ceiling beam. Beneath it was the massive mortar and pestle for grinding coffee beans that Papi had sculpted out of a tree trunk.

Nailed to one wall was an elaborately carved Jesus on a large wood crucifix, a gift to Mami on her wedding day. A picture of the crucifixion drew one's attention from the bed. On the wall Papi's good shirt, pants, hat, and various pieces of clothing hung on nails, which served as the family's closet.

Papi had partitioned part of the house with a faded piece of cloth to make a family bedroom. In the main room the twins rolled out a catre while Vicente slept on old clothes or whatever he could find. Felicidad and her sisters and Ruben slept two by two, head-to-toe, on top of a quilt spread on a casoneta, a frame with springs; over their heads hung the baby's coy, a sling with a flat base that dangled from the ceiling like a hammock. Across from the casoneta was her parents' bed, with its mattress of dry plantain leaves and pillows stuffed with corn husks. On the floor, between her parents' bed and la casoneta, was an escupidera, which the family used at night as a latrine. The enamel basin was large enough to squat over and had a handle for carrying. Felicidad, as the oldest girl, emptied it out and rinsed it every morning.

A bird flew in the open door. Felicidad looked up, afraid that it might be a bat. Last year a family of bats had settled on the rafters of the house, and Papi had beaten them with a broom to get them out. She shooed the pretty blue bird out the window.

Vicente untied the rope from the coy.

Mami had folded her dress on top of the wood trunk that held her prized possessions including the porcelain figurines from Spain of various holy saints.

Felicidad heard footsteps on the roof, her father shouting, her brothers calling out, and a deep growl that, by now, she knew came from her mother; then she felt a weight flinging itself off the roof. Mami. Felicidad's hands shook as she picked up the dress.

"¡Felicidad!"

She hurried outside, her mother's dress in her outstretched palms as if in offering.

Felicidad couldn't understand how her mother could be standing in the yard, kicking at Felicidad's father with her bare feet, clawing at him with her fingers.

"¡Condenada mujer!" He cursed a few more seconds and then wrestled his wife to the ground.

"Bring that goddamn dress!"

Felicidad scurried over. She didn't realize she was crying.

"Stop that goddamn whining and dress your mother," he shouted at her. He turned to Felicidad's twin brothers. "Boys! Get some water."

Papi pinned Mami down between his knees and braced her elbows against the ground. Felicidad's mother moved her head side-to-side, saliva leaking from her mouth; her legs thrashed beneath him. Tears welled in Felicidad's throat and she coughed.

She wanted to recite to her mother all the prayers that she had murmured to them each night, phrases that merely reassured Felicidad of her mother's presence. But for Mami, they were blessings, reaffirmations of her faith, of her surety of God's pledge to them, that somehow he would take care of them.

But all Felicidad could say was Mami, Mami, please. With Hilda's help she managed to tug the dress over Mami's head and pull her arms through.

"Vicente," Papi said. "Tie the rope to her wrist."

Vicente knelt on the ground and did what he was told. He already had the hands of a man and the quick, deft fingers of one accustomed to field labor. He had worked alongside Papi since he was old enough to follow behind him, dropping seeds in the holes his father dug in the ground. He had spent a total of three years in school. He could read and write a little and that would need to be enough.

"¡Ay!" Vicente yanked his hand away. Blood streaked down his wrist in a thin line from where his mother had scratched him.

Papi gave his wife a little shake. "¡Mujer, por favor!"

There was a note of sadness, a tinge of exasperation in his voice, the tiniest hint of a cry that betrayed all the days of working under the punishing sun, the disappointment of backbreaking effort for so little yield, the fear that despite how hard he tried, he wouldn't be able to fill his children's bellies.

Her mother lay sprawled in the dirt, her father's strong farmer's hands gripping her fragile wrists. Her brother's jaw was clenched so that he wouldn't cry, dirt streaked down one pimply cheek.

Hilda whispered to Felicidad, "Go get a wet cloth to pass over your mother's forehead."

Felicidad ran back to the house and removed a rag hooked on the wall in the lean-to kitchen. A large green coconut husk filled with water was set aside for cooking. Her mother took special care that the cooking water should always be clean, but Felicidad stuck her dirty hand in the shell and cupped water twice to her lips. She wanted to cry with the guilt of it, from her fear of her mother's irrational behavior, of her father's despair, her brother's pain.

She dipped the rag into the water and hurried outside, water dripping on her skirt. Hilda took it from her and gave it a good wring.

"Pass it over your mother's forehead." She handed it back to Felicidad.

She didn't want to touch her mother, this screaming woman, this crazy woman naked on the roof, this wild animal lunging at her family.

Hilda gave her a little push.

Felicidad wiped Mami's brow with trembling fingers, but rather than calming down she began thrashing and screaming again.

"Vicente, we're going to tie her to that tree," Papi said.

They stared at him, sure that they had misheard.

Papi was already half dragging, half carrying her. Mami pulled at the rope, digging her heels into the dirt, but Papi kept his grip on her arm, walking with the firm determined strides of a man in control. Vicente wrapped the rope around the tree trunk; Papi tied Mami to the trunk, her back against the bark, arms outstretched like Jesus on the cross.

Her brothers hurried up the hill carrying lard cans filled with water on their shoulders. They didn't question why their mother was tied to a tree.

Papi sent Eduardo to the house for a cup, filling it with water from one of the cans. He pinned back his wife's hair and poured water into her open mouth. She sputtered, wetting the collar of her dress.

"Rosario, why are you behaving this way?" Papi let go of her hair.

Surely, their mother had heard the pain in her husband's voice, the plea to his beloved Rosario? In that moment Felicidad believed that life would ease back to the sameness of yesterday, with Papi working the land and Mami caring for home and children.

Mami reached out a bare foot and kicked Papi hard in the shin.

"¡Coño!" He limped away.

"Felicidad, you'll have to manage dinner today. Boys, go back to work," Papi said. "I will stay here with your mother."

Vicente gave Felicidad's shoulders a little squeeze then tilted the five-gallon can to pour water down his throat. He passed the can to his brothers before heading back to the cornfield.

★ ★ ★

Hilda was sitting in Papi's chair peeling malanga and yautía with a knife. Felicidad carried in the can of water, bending at the waist from the weight. She poured water into a tin can that had once contained tomato sauce.

"Give me some, too," Hilda said.

Felicidad offered hers and got herself a cup made from a coconut, refilling it twice.

The midwife stared at a piece of salted codfish soaking in a pan of water on the table. She talked over the howling from the yard.

"These hard times are bad enough, but to have a baby born dead? Oh, how I hated my job that day. Of course, your mother got pregnant with Raffy right after, but then your sister Isabel died. What woman wouldn't go a little mad?" Hilda glared at the codfish as if it were responsible for all the trouble.

Felicidad tucked the lard can of water under her arm and went through to the kitchen. A pot of beans was on el fogón— the poor woman's stove. Stones were set on a tabletop in a bed of ashes. On the smoke-blackened wall was a square cut into the wood, which served as a window; the matching square of wood was hinged to one side. It was opened in the morning and closed at night to keep out the harmful night air. Hammered to the base of the window was a wooden shelf sloping down into the yard, supported by more wood anchored into the ground. Lard, drained from the last time the family smoked a pig, was stored in a large earthenware container. A galvanized pail used for dishwashing or bathing sat on it.

The howling became louder. Felicidad and Hilda crossed to the open door of the lean-to. Her father had loosened the rope so Mami now sat on the ground. He squatted down, passing the washcloth over her forehead. They couldn't hear what he was saying to her.

"He's a good man, your father is," Hilda said. "Up the mountain a ways, Pedro Maldonado abandoned his family. Six children."

Felicidad turned to look at Hilda. The sun had baked her skin the color of bark and left it with as many wrinkles.

"Why did he leave his family?" Felicidad had to know.

"Because a man can or because sometimes the responsibility is just too much." Hilda's glance acknowledged that while Felicidad was still a child, soon the day would come when she, too, would learn the ways of men.

Felicidad wondered about this Pedro Maldonado. How was he different from her father? Perhaps his wife wasn't a helpful mate, perhaps she was sickly or didn't have sons, although girls sometimes worked in the fields. Maybe this Maldonado was just a bad man.

A ligartijo sprinted up the smoke-blackened wall and out of reach before Felicidad could get the broom to sweep the small lizard out.

In the evening they brought her into the house; Papi and Vicente held her up between them. Felicidad looked away from her tear-streaked face.

Father Manuel Cortez wore a long black cassock and a black hat and kept a silver rosary handy in his pocket. He glanced around the room. He had not often gone into the mountains. It was difficult to see in the dark house after the long ride in the bright sun, but he didn't need to see to smell. He took out his handkerchief from the pocket of his cassock and dabbed his nose. What was it? It wasn't a single odor in particular; it was the smoke of the fogón, it was the jíbaro habit of shutting himself up from the dangers of the night air. It was the stink of human beings living in a tropical climate, it was the escupidera, it was sweat and bacalao and the coffee beans crushed by maceta and pilón. It was living.

He had arrived on the island from Spain only six months before, on the eve of Pearl Harbor. His parishioners made fun of him behind his back for the thick brows that met over the bridge of his nose. Other than that, his congregation agreed that he could be worse looking.

Not even in Spain, in the country towns where he had served his first years as a priest, could he remember such malnutrition, such sheer impoverishment as he had seen on this beautiful island of Puerto Rico. The priest blamed the Americans who now owned most of the farming land. He had heard from many of his older parishioners how life hadn't been so desperate when Mother Spain had been in possession.

In town it was not unusual to find children sleeping on the cold steps of buildings or a mendigo huddled in a doorway with his child in his arms. On this very ride up the mountain, he had seen children whose protruding potbellies were incongruous with their bone-thin frames. There was not much that he could do about food. There was little rice on the island: Supplies from the good Christians of his sister church in Spain were impossible with the war and the German submarine blockade. Much more was needed from the United States. He would appeal to the governor, American or no, about whom he had heard good things, and to the bishop. Sometimes, in the dark of night, he despaired of being so far from his home country and of his growing certainty that what the island people needed most were food and shoes, not religion. And then he would kneel and beg God to forgive him for his human frailty.

Father Cortez saw children in the little house; a child lurking in that corner, another in that one, a few bunched up on a wooden bench, two leaning over the table there. A chair.

"We'll need a chair," the priest said.

"The chair," Papi said.

One of the twins set it where the priest pointed.

Papi sat Mami in the chair.

The rope was still tied to one of Mami's wrists. Vicente looped it through the chair's ladder back and handed the end to Papi, who tied her hands.

Mami began to curse and yell with renewed energy. She called the priest an hijo de puta and her husband the king of all hijos de putas. Her children, she said, were motherless bastards and she, the motherless bastard of them all.

Ashamed, Felicidad looked away. Leila carried the baby on her hip. She slipped her hand into Felicidad's. Juanita, crying, hid behind her sisters.

"Your mother's behavior is a sign that an evil spirit has taken possession of her," the priest said.

"She prays every night," Papi said. "How could that be?"

"Even the faithful are fallible," Father Cortez said. "We humans are all of a weak nature."

Papi, resigned, moved away from his wife. "If you can alleviate her suffering, I'll say nothing more."

Father Cortez pulled at his collar. He could not get used to the heat of the tropics and envied the barefoot children their clothing, which, although tattered, must at least be cool. His shame at such thoughts added harshness to his instructions.

"We must have water," Father Cortez said. "And a large bowl."

Eduardo brought forward the second lard can of water, Julio the bowl.

Felicidad thought now there wouldn't be enough water.

"Do you have candles? We must have candles, at least two or three," the priest said.

Her father nodded to Felicidad, and she went to the trunk to get her mother's precious candles.

Papi and Vicente each took a candle. When she tried to give the third to one of the twins, her father gestured for her to keep it.

Felicidad whispered in Leila's ear. "Put Raffy in the coy. Have Ruben take Juanita to get avocados then watch the vianda and bacalao."

"Do I have to?" Leila whispered back.

Father Cortez's solemn tone in the darkening day was as terrifying as Felicidad's dreams.

"Do not be afraid, children of God, the almighty Father will protect our good sister," he said.

Felicidad's brothers looked at her.

"Now let us pray." Father Cortez began to recite in Latin. Felicidad's father stared unwaveringly at his wife as if by sheer will he could rid her of whatever sickened or possessed her. Her brothers slouched forward like the tired laborers they were. Felicidad, handmaiden to the men, stood apart. She could hear Leila at the fogón. She hoped Ruben would find enough avocados. The wax of the candles dripped on the wood floor; she would have to scrape it up.

She thought she might faint. Men stank when they came in from working in the fields. Felicidad tried to identify another odor, worse than the male smell. Then she realized it emanated from her mother. Mami had relieved herself on Papi's chair. Ay bendito, if only somehow she could have gotten her mother on the escupidera. Felicidad dared a glance at her father. Yes, he had noticed. She hoped Mami's dress wasn't soiled; she only had one other dress, which was for her yearly trip to Mass and for weddings and velorios.

Father Cortez placed his hands on Mami's head, holding it steady with his fingers.

"Save your daughter, Lord, from this evil that has found its way into her mind, this evil that has stolen her soul. This woman is a good wife, a good mother, a good Catholic. Bring her back to your fold, dear Lord, I entreat You."

Father Cortez bade them to join him in praying the rosary. Each night, Mami knelt by her bed and said the rosary, for which she was named. Felicidad would take up her embroidery and watch her through the gap between the wall and the cloth that was the bedroom curtain. She liked to hear her mother murmur the prayers in rapid succession and had learned to distinguish the periodic up-and-down chants that signified the next decade of Hail Marys. Felicidad murmured what words she could recall. Her father's praying surprised her, and her mother quieted down at Papi's voice reciting Santa Marías.

Father Cortez poured water from the lard can into the bowl and made the sign of the cross over it. Felicidad had seen him do this during the blessing of the palms.

"Begone, Satan!" The priest splashed Mami with water. "In the name of the Father, the Son, and the Holy Spirit, begone!"

Mami began to murmur softly. Juanita's singsong voice filtered up through the floor's wood planks from beneath the house, where she liked to sit on the ground filling tin cans and glass jars with dirt as the chickens pecked at her feet. Outside the wood box of a house, the world lived on in the caw and trill of birds, the ceaseless hum and buzz of insects, the scampering of small critters, the breeze filtering through the trees. Inside the house, a group of people stood entranced by a little girl's reedy voice, by candlelight, by the mysteries of God and Spirit.

"God is all-merciful," the priest said.

Papi carried Mami to the bed and Leila tended to her. Felicidad carried the chair into the lean-to and scrubbed it with the hot ashes from el fogón.

Father Cortez was now able to pay closer attention to physical matters and he took note of the sackcloth curtain that hid the beds in the cramped room, the single chair, the sad children all impossibly thin. He was moved by pity as he often was with these campo people. He wrote monthly reports to his superiors in Spain, letters he did not mail because of the war, about the abject poverty, the urgent need for nourishment for the physical body in addition to that of the spiritual. The island poor were at the mercy of the German submarines patrolling the ocean and upon the charity of the American government and the island's rich businessmen. He had seen members of this family before— certainly the older girl with the fanciful name, and he wondered what it was about her eyes that made him remember her. Some of the other children, too, had been to church, the blond girl and the twin boys. He remembered the twins because one had green eyes, the other brown, and both were missing their front teeth.

"You must be hungry," Papi said.

Father Cortez was a man as well fed as one could be on a tropical island during wartime and he could not take food away from these children, for whom he feared it was their one and only meal this day.

Felicidad's father insisted. "It would be an honor."

Leila went to help Felicidad, who was peeling one of two large avocados by el fogón. She told Leila to place a piece of bacalao and yautía and malanga on each plate while she added slices of golden avocado.

"Do I give the knife and fork to Papi or the priest?" Leila held up the knife and fork.

The knife and fork were relics from Papi's previous life; the rest of the set had been sold somewhere along the years of his marriage.

Felicidad considered the problem. Their father used the utensils every night, but the priest was a holy man and used to a proper table. Besides, how could one offer him a spoon that their father had carved from wood? It wasn't as if he were a jíbaro.

"Give them to the priest," she said.

When her father nodded, Felicidad knew she had chosen correctly.

Papi sent Vicente to lead the priest's horse down the mountain. They agreed that the priest would send a car in two hours' time. Father Cortez assured him that he would send a woman to accompany la señora. Felicidad heard: "...Not to worry... rest...the dedication of the good Sisters...one month, perhaps longer..."

She stood looking at her mother, who seemed to sleep without breathing: only the heat of her body reassured her that her mother was not dead. Felicidad lifted the skirt of Mami's good dress and eased her into the panties with the modesty that her mother treasured.

Felicidad took her mother's hairbrush and tied it up in the faded blue dress she used for a nightgown. She waved a mosquito away from her mother's forehead then squatted down beside her. Felicidad recalled her mother's tenderness, the way she put her husband and children first, how she never seemed to sleep, always working: caring for the children, grinding corn and oats and manioc into flour as the base for many of their meals, then cooking, serving, washing, ironing, mending, never quite finishing one chore before there were two or three or four others requiring her attention. One thing Felicidad was certain of was that as long as she lived, she would never utter a word of this day to a single human being.

She wondered how Mami got an evil spirit inside her. Felicidad knew that at night, when it was so dark that the mountains and the sky were one, the Spirits felt empowered to walk the countryside. They were all around them, her mother had said. They wandered through the dark night, searching for what would quiet their restlessness, an indiscernible something that would bring them peace. One had to take care not to tempt a Spirit, not to be doing what one shouldn't be doing. Wanting something desperately was dangerous, her mother had warned her. It made one vulnerable to Spirits. Remember that, Felicidad.

I'll remember, Felicidad had said.

Papi came in and stood over the bed, staring down at the ghost that was his woman. Her father's face was dark with the shadow of a beard; her mother liked him clean-shaven. Some nights, before Isabel had gotten sick, Felicidad would glance up from embroidering roses and see her parents standing together in el batey. Papi would be doing some kind of odd job like repairing the chicken coop by moonlight and Mami would bring him his coffee. They would be talking, her mother laughing softly. Felicidad would wonder what her father had said to make her mother laugh in that peculiar way. If she asked her, Mami would smile and say, "One day you'll have a husband and you'll know."

Felicidad watched Papi press his fingertips against his temples.

"Is Mami going to be all right?"

Her father looked away. "God willing. She just needs a rest. What with the baby that died...and then Isabel...It's a hard life..."

They stood for a few minutes in silence, Papi lost in his thoughts and Felicidad engulfed in a sense of foreboding that, being so young, she did not recognize as such. She only knew that she wished her mother would wake and sit up in the bed and that all would be as it had been before—before the stillborn baby, before the death of Isabel, before her mother on the roof naked, before.

"We need to wrap her in something so that she won't catch cold from the night air," Papi said.

Felicidad considered the problem; her mother had so little. Then she thought of Mami's silk mantilla woven into a flower garden and brought from Catalonia by a long-dead ancestor.

"Mami's wedding mantilla," Felicidad said.

"Get it," her father said.

The mantilla gleamed white in her father's brown farmer's hands. He handled it gingerly, careful not to snag the silk.

"She was just eighteen when I married her. I knew her older sister, your tía Prudencia, and my parents told me that it was time I got myself a wife," Papi said. "I was already twenty-five years old and they had heard...that's not important. I went to see Prudencia and your mother opened the door. I knew that moment that she was the one for me."

"Was Mami very pretty?" she dared to ask.

"She was the most beautiful girl I'd ever seen," Papi said. "You favor her, Felicidad."

Felicidad stared up at her father in wonder. He had never talked like this before.

Papi draped the web of flowers over his wife's head and shoulders. It was so long that he was able to wrap it around her and bind her arms to her body. If she awoke before reaching town, she would cause little trouble.

He lifted his sleeping wife into his arms and buried his face in the lace.

"Rosario," he said. "What will become of us?"

The children watched their father carry their mother into the night until they could no longer see the white speck that was their mother's mantilla. Felicidad prayed that the Spirits that roamed the mountains would stay away from her parents and that Mami would return the same as before. She prayed, too, that their father would not abandon them as Pedro Maldonado had abandoned his wife and six children.

Chapter Three

Felicidad woke before the sun unveiled its face. The room was hazy with shadows, and she wished that she didn't have to leave the casoneta she shared with her siblings. Her parents' bed was empty. Papi was already up and tending to one of the many farm chores. She went to el fogón and saw that there wasn't enough kindling to start a fire. Why hadn't she thought about this the night before? She had to start thinking more. Felicidad ran outside to hunt for twigs or scraps of wood. Her bare feet became cold and wet with the morning dew. She was glad there was beginning to be light enough for her to see because she was afraid of stepping on a spider or a slumbering snake. The rooster crowed. She climbed a little way up the hill, worrying that she was taking too long, that the coffee would not be ready for her father.

The family's day started and ended with coffee; in fact, there were some nights when the children were already asleep and Mami would shake them awake to drink their café. A cup of coffee filled the belly and kept away the hunger. Except for Papi and the older boys who worked the land, there was no breakfast. Evenings, Mami roasted the coffee beans in a cast-iron pot on

el fogón and ground them in the tree-trunk pilón. Now it was
Felicidad who took the tin from the shelf and poured coffee
beans into the pot. If only she had thought to roast them the
night before.

She went to start a fire. The twigs were damp. Felicidad
rubbed them dry on her skirt, then broke them into pieces. She
prayed that they would catch fire on the first try, but when they
did, she forgot to thank God. She hovered over el fogón taking
care that the beans not burn. She set them to cool on a plate,
then poured them into the coffee mortar.

Felicidad lifted her arms and crashed the maceta into the
pilón again and again. Soon she began to tire and her shoulders
to ache, yet she kept pounding the pestle into the huge mortar. Papi became angry when he found pieces of the beans in
his coffee. This wouldn't be the morning to annoy her father.
While Papi woke her brothers, she heated water for coffee and
porridge. She stirred ground up oats into the boiling water to
make avena, then served her father and older brothers. Felicidad spooned ground coffee into the colador and draped it over
the blue enamel coffeepot, then poured the water through it.
The boys swallowed the coffee in quick gulps so as not to keep
their father waiting.

The baby woke crying for his mother and Felicidad mixed
powdered milk with warm water and poured it into an opaque
bottle.

When Felicidad went to remove her father's empty bowl, he
looked up at her.

"Don't forget the lunch," he said.

Watery excrement leaked out of the baby's bowels, and she held
him over the escupidera. Then she gave him to Leila to wash
while she carried the escupidera by the handle and emptied it

away from the house. It was heavy and awkward and she needed two hands to carry it. When she came back, Leila was using a leaf to clean Raffy. Felicidad rinsed out the escupidera with the dirty bathwater.

She had forgotten to send Ruben for water so she told Leila to find some kindling. Felicidad carried the empty lard can under her arm, stopping by the quenepa tree. Birds picked the green limes off the tree, where they grew in grape-like clusters, then dropped the fruit on the ground after only a bite. She picked a half-eaten quenepa off the grass, tore out the bitten part, and peeled the thin, tight skin with her fingernails. Then she ate it, making a face at the tart melon-like pulp.

Felicidad walked on. The forested countryside did little to lighten her spirits. She could think only that her mother was gone.

She took refuge from a light shower under a coconut palm. The old Felicidad would have brooded over her only dress getting wet, but the new Felicidad worried whether Leila had gathered twigs before the rain. She wouldn't be able to cook lunch if the kindling wasn't dry.

Felicidad thought that if she and Leila tried very hard, they might be able to do Mami's work while she was away. Perhaps their mother just needed to rest and eat lots of good food and drink plenty of milk. She couldn't remember the last time she and her siblings had drunk real milk. Not since Papi had to sell their cow.

The rain stopped and she continued on to the well her father had built onto a rocky shelf of the mountain. He had laid a small tank of cement to catch rainwater that coursed between the rocks flowing in and through a six-foot pipe that Papi had rigged with a valve to open and close. It was a lot better than going to the river. Once the five-gallon can was full, she lifted it onto her hip and hurried up the dirt road, her bare feet splashing in the puddles.

Leila was feeding Raffy sugared water. She was undersize for her age, but with the same capacity for mothering as their mother.

"Tell me that you found kindling before it rained," Felicidad said.

"It's by the fogón," Leila said.

Felicidad went inside and set the can of water on the table. She broke some twigs and went about lighting el fogón. It took numerous tries, even with praying, to get the fire started. She set water to boil before peeling the yautía and ñame. Leila put the baby down and Felicidad tied one end of a rope to the coy and the other to her ankle, so she could rock it while she went about her chores.

When the twins came for the fiambreras, enamel pots with lids nestled on wire hangers, Felicidad measured out portions of bacalao and vianda into the individual containers.

"Did Papi say anything about Mami?" Felicidad asked.

Julio pointed to his red ear. "This is what I got when I asked him about her. Maybe we should share it," he said.

"No thanks," she told him.

Felicidad's arms and shoulders strained to lift the can of water to fill the palangana. She looked out the ledge for a leaf with spiky edges. She called out to her sister, who sat on the ground staring out into space.

"Juanita, pick me an hoja de fregar," she said.

Felicidad scrubbed the pots and dishes with the spiky leaf and set them on the ledge to dry. Then she poured the dirty dishwater out the window into the yard. Leila came in with the naked baby, who was squirming in her arms, his arms and legs red with prickly heat.

"Maybe he's just hot," Felicidad said. "Let's wash him."

Felicidad poured clean water into la palangana and wiped his face with a clean leaf, murmuring indistinctly as her mother had always done when one of them was sick. The words had never been important, only their mother's soft voice and gentle touch, cool and calming.

"Mami puts aloe vera on rashes," Leila said.

"Go pick a leaf while I dry him," Felicidad said.

They cut open the aloe vera and scooped out the gel, which they smoothed over the baby's skin with their palms. Leila put Raffy down for a nap and covered him head-to-toe with an old sheet to protect him from the mosquitoes while he slept. Some families had mosquito netting to drape over the beds and coy, but they didn't have that luxury. A black spider the size of her palm crawled up one wall and Felicidad knocked it down with the broom and swept it out the door. On the shelf where Mami set sacks of beans and vianda and what food they had, she found a nest of cockroaches, and she set to boiling water. Then she did what her mother always did—poured the water over the cock-roaches and killed them.

While the baby slept, she sent her two younger sisters to gather more kindling. Felicidad rinsed her hands with water and used a spiky leaf to scrub them well as her mother had taught her. In Mami's chest she found the package containing the pieces of a blouse: front, back, collar, sleeves. Each piece was precut and marked where one piece was to be hand-sewn to the other. Mami usually worked on the blouses—which required more skill—while Felicidad embroidered the handkerchiefs, but she had begun to teach Felicidad how to embroider the large hibiscus on cascading vines or the blossoms of the flamboyant tree. Both were very popular in American stores. Even Doña Claudia, the woman in town who represented the American store, had marveled at Mami's flights of fancy, at the gardens come alive in embroidery silk.

That evening Felicidad saw that her mother had started to embroider red hibiscus on the sleeve of the blouse and had sketched the size of the flower on estraza paper. She set the piecework on the table along with her mother's sewing scissors and embroidery thread, which she kept in the large tin that had once held perfumed soaps from Spain.

Sometimes she had gone with her mother to deliver the finished pieces to Doña Claudia, who would pay Mami a dollar or two and give her more work. How her mother would stretch those few dollars! They would stop at la panadería and admire all the pretty pastries on the shelves as some women admire diamonds and rubies in a jewelry store. Mami would tell of her brother who had married a woman whose family had negocios. They had a good business with their panadería because even in these hard times, everybody had to have bread.

"Too bad this isn't the uncle's panadería," Felicidad said. "We could eat bread and not have to pay."

"Oh, we would have to pay," Mami said.

Bent over in her father's chair, Felicidad could have been any girl or any woman doing piecework with strands of embroidery silk draped over her shoulder. Her mother put her to embroidering when she was five. She had been so happy to see her daughter's talent with a needle, telling her that she was following in a long Spanish tradition. Often when they sat together on the bench, Mami would correct Felicidad's posture. Hadn't she noticed that most of the seamstresses they knew, young and old alike, were slump-shouldered? She must think of her spine as the trunk of a tree. Wouldn't she rather grow up straight enough to reach the sky than drooping over on the ground like a vine? Having a straight back was just as important for a seamstress as for a dancer,

her mother said. When she had been about Felicidad's age, a traveling troupe of flamenco dancers from Spain had visited and she
had gone to see them perform. It would be hard for Felicidad to
believe, but there had been a time when she hadn't been quite as
poor as she was now. ¡Ay, Felicidad! The dancers! The women so
beautiful. The men so handsome. All the flounces on the dresses.
She and her sisters had counted seven on one dress alone. She
dreamed that one day she, too, would become a flamenco dancer.

Felicidad had looked up at the wistfulness in her mother's
voice, at her face with its hollow cheeks, the pinched mouth
with its missing teeth, and the sadness that never seemed to
leave her dark eyes, and she wondered how it could be possible
that she had once dreamed of flounces and music and handsome
men sweeping her off her feet.

Once or twice as the weeks passed, while Felicidad was
embroidering in the evenings, she felt her father's gaze. She
expected him to say something, to comment in some way on
one of her chores or ask her to get him something, a tin of water
perhaps, but he would only nod and go back to sharpening his
machete or repairing a tool. Some evenings he would call for
Leila to bring him Raffy and he would bounce the baby on his
knee to all his children's delight. On these occasions Felicidad
remembered the happy days when Mami was home and Isabel
was alive. She laughed along with the others, hoping that her
laughter would ease the loss of her dead sister and her absent
mother.

Felicidad's father shared the land with his brothers and, on his
portion, he planted root vegetables like yuca, malanga, batata,
ñame, apio, and yautía. Corn. Equally important were the beans,
rosadas and blancas, rojas, pintos, and also garbanzos and gandules. Felicidad and Leila often helped Mami crack open the

slender pods, their mother keeping a watchful eye on their work so as not to waste a bean. The family relied on the fruit from the trees he had planted: the coconut palms, mamey, mango, quenepa, quama, lemon, lime, guanábana—from which Mami would make a favorite drink if the children didn't eat all the ripe fruit—panapén, sweet orange, and sour orange trees. Also different varieties of banana trees like plantains and the sweet, tiny-fingered niños or the mansano, its fat-fingered cousin. He even grew a delicious banana with a black skin. He planted papaya, chayote, aguacate. He grew pepinos because Mami had a particular liking for them. He planted oregano and cilantrillo bushes. Recao grew wild. And then there were the tomatoes and peppers and garlic and onions and corazones. Papi grew tobacco for his own use and coffee for his family's consumption and to sell, along with legumes, to neighbors or in town. He planted everything and anything; any seed or root he could find, he planted. He liked to tell Mami that he was a man with many mouths to feed and he couldn't afford to be choosy.

Mami had been gone a month and try as she might, Felicidad didn't know all the things necessary to feed and care for the household of a large family—her father and eight children including herself. Daily she foraged for leña for el fogón and root vegetables and ripe fruit, but somehow there were never enough dried pieces of wood or fruit and vegetables. She didn't quite know how to measure and mete out the beans and dried codfish from their meager stores. Sometimes there was enough for their meal; other times, not. One day, after she portioned out the lunch for her father and brothers, there wasn't any food for her and her sisters. She was so hungry that she made casabe although she never liked the flat, dry cakes made from grating the roots of the yuca plant and adding water to make dough.

Her sisters waited eagerly while she roasted the cracker-like cakes in a pan. She yearned for her mother's guidance, for her patience in teaching her all that a young girl should know.

Felicidad could cook beans and boil green bananas, ñame, malanga, batatas, any root vegetables. Cooking harina de maiz was easy—you boiled it in water, stirring constantly—but grinding the corn was man's work. From this corn flour, Mami's magic fingers would shape surullos, delicious sticks of cornmeal, which she wrapped in banana leaves and roasted directly on top of hot charcoal. Mami wasn't afraid of the fire. Her fingers danced around the flames, flipping the surullos until the bananas leaves were brown. Nothing tasted better with a cup of café con leche than freshly made surullos.

One evening there wasn't any bacalao or rice for dinner. Felicidad had cooked a pot of beans. Papi came home from the fields and said, "Felicidad, come, we are going to make surullos."

The twins went to the barraca to get a sack of corn and another of charcoal bricks that Papi made from burning green wood. Felicidad used the big knife to slice the kernels off the cob. One of the twins poured the kernels into a small opening in the molino while the other turned a pole like a crank. The top stone of the molino rotated on an axis anchored on a metal rod and ground the corn into a fine powder.

"You see how red the charcoal bricks are?" Papi's fingers seemed to touch the fire and dart between the flames. "Where are the banana leaves?"

Felicidad hurried to the shelf to get the stack of green leaves.

Papi placed the leaves on top of the coals to soften before picking them out and laying them on a plate to cool. He showed Felicidad how to add water to the cornmeal flour and shape the dough into rectangles.

"Now you wrap the leaf around the surullo so it won't crumble in the fire," he said, before placing one on top of the charcoal. "You try."

"Papi, I can't," Felicidad said.

"This is woman's work," he said. "Do it."

Her fingers trembled over the flames. The heat warmed her fingertips.

"Don't drop it," he said. "Place it on the brick."

The slippery banana leaf dropped from her fingers into the fire.

Papi shook his head. "Well, at least the fire was fed."

"I'm afraid," Felicidad said.

"Try again," Papi said.

Her father was getting irritated; he was tired and hungry. She wished Mami were here making surullos and not she. Felicidad placed another on top of the charcoal and when her father directed, she reached in to flip it over. Later that night it hurt to hold the embroidery needle between her fingertips.

Felicidad brewed the evening coffee and took a cup out to Papi, who was under a mango tree weaving banana leaves into an aparejo, a plaited pack saddle for horses or burros. Known for the intricate tapestry of his aparejos, Papi would weave one for a horse that would span six feet over the animal's back and three feet on either side. He wove the quilt into a three-inch-thick layer, tying the leaves in place every six inches with rope that he made from emajagua rushes. Felicidad waited by the wood-frame loom staked into the ground while her father drank his coffee.

They watched the sunset wash over the mountain and listened to the evening breeze rustling the leaves of the trees. They heard the drone of the night insects and the lullaby of the coquís. She imagined that this was how it would be for her one day, how she would make the evening coffee for her own husband. Felicidad recalled her mother's soft laughter when she brought Papi his coffee. She wondered if Papi was thinking of Mami now, if he missed her as much as she did. She thought the answer was yes and it made her heart ache in a way that she didn't quite understand.

As if from far off, she heard her siblings in the house where she had left them drinking their coffee. She felt removed from them by more than just mere distance, but by the responsibilities she had inherited because of her mother's absence. The girl who had dawdled on her way home from school, who thought of her mother saving her a spoonful of beans, was no more and she didn't have time to think about that girl or mourn her. That girl had been but a child.

Felicidad was still afraid of the Spirits that roamed the mountains at night, but her father's presence gave her courage. She knew without thinking that her father would protect her and, with the passing of each day, she grew more confident that her father was not like Pablo Maldonado up the mountain who had abandoned his family. Papi expected complete obedience from his children and he liked things done in a particular way, yet Felicidad and her siblings would say he was fair. Her father was a proud man and not one for railing against fate or lamenting misfortunes. He had a reputation as a hard worker equally dedicated to the land and to his family. Everyone said that he was like his grandfather, who, in the late 1850s, had arrived from Spain as a young man determined to make Puerto Rico his home. Grandfather and grandson were known for having carácters— a fierce temperament, a strength of character, a single-minded determination—attributed to the Spanish blood. They were men respected and even a little feared by family and neighbors alike; they were men one thought twice about offending.

She turned to watch him drink his coffee, which she had

served in a porcelain cup. The family had two, which were reserved for the parents and guests. Mami would drink from a tin cup as the children did, but she always served Papi's evening coffee in one of the porcelain cups. Felicidad had often pondered the history of the cups, thinking of the great care Mami must have taken for them to survive. The children knew not to touch them. Mami, herself, had always washed the cups, and now Felicidad had taken on that duty too.

Felicidad plucked a dama de noche flower, breathing in the heavy scent of the pretty white blossom named the lady of the evening because it showed its face only at night.

Her father handed her the empty cup.

"Sunday, I will go see the priest. I'll need my good shirt," Papi said.

"You'll go to Mass, Papi?" Felicidad looked down at the piles of shiny brown leaves at her feet, thinking that would make their mother so happy.

Papi's laughter reminded her of that fateful day. She shivered in the dusk.

Felicidad left the baby with Ruben while she and her sisters went down to the river. Monday or Tuesday was the usual wash day for the women of the campo, but Felicidad found it impossible to keep up with her mother's schedule. Felicidad had liked helping her mother with the laundry because after they had scrubbed the dirty clothes clean and stretched them out to dry on bushes or rocks, she played in the river with the other children. She glanced up at the huge breadfruit tree by the river bank, recalling how she and her sisters had had so much fun running around picking up all the ripe fruit they could find. Back at home Mami would boil the breadfruit and the seeds, which resembled chestnuts. They could barely wait for the seeds to cool to eat them.

Today they were the only ones at the riverbank. She and Leila carried the burlap sacks of clothes and Juanita carried the precious blue soap that they bought by weight at the rural store. The girls scrubbed the clothes with large stones. The scabbing blisters on Felicidad's fingertips tore as she scrubbed. It seemed to her that her body always ached, that she was always tired. Was this what Mami had felt?

Papi looked like a young man in his well-starched clothes. His eyes were a startling blue in a face tanned as brown as the coconut shells from which the family drank. His hands were brown, too, up to the wrists, and then they were the color of coconut milk. When Papi laughed, one noticed his missing teeth.

Felicidad was to come with him that Sunday morning to attend to her mother. Ruben would help guide the neighbor's burro, which was laden with sacks of charcoal and corn to sell in town. Mami would ride the burro on the way back.

Papi tied the laces of his shoes in a knot and swung them over his shoulder. Felicidad and Ruben followed their father down the mountain. Tiny rocks and pebbles dug into the soles of her feet.

Felicidad examined the burns on her wrist from ironing. Her father liked the cuffs of his shirtsleeves doubled over, and she had struggled to get them just so. There were many things that she didn't know how to do, things that Mami would know.

Last night Felicidad woke to find Leila leaning over her.

"Felicidad," she'd whispered, "what if Mami never comes back?"

"She'll come back." Felicidad tried to sound as certain as a whisper allowed.

"I hope she comes back. I'm tired of doing all the work," Leila said.

★ ★ ★

Papi squatted on the side of the road while he put on his shoes. They weren't work boots or fancy shoes for show, just an ordinary pair of shoes that he saved for town or to talk business. He had once told Mami that a man was at a disadvantage while barefoot because he could never be anything other than a peón. Poor man, rich man, a man had to have shoes.

The sun beat down on them. It was warmer than on the mountain, and the pavement was hot under the children's bare feet. Small frame houses with balcóns lined either side of the main street. Most had small yards; some people kept chicken coops under their houses to supply their families with eggs and poultry.

Papi sent the children off to the church, where he would meet them after he sold the charcoal and corn at the general store. Felicidad and Ruben hurried past a cafetín that sold bebidas—coffee, tea, fruit drinks—and paused in front of the window of la dulcería, staring openmouthed at the sweets, the trays of dulce de coco, guava squares, lechosa, and pudín. They remembered the time Mami had made the delicious bread pudding studded with raisins: it was a year ago, perhaps, before their sister Isabel had died. Then again, maybe they had dreamed it.

They passed other negocios. A fonda with half a dozen tables had a sign that read WE SERVE RICE AND BEANS, MEAT. Someone had crossed out RICE. They saw one or two clothing stores with fairy-like dresses in the windows, and a hardware store with machetes stacked next to metal basins. There was the alcaldía where Felicidad told her brother the mayor lived and the church across from la plaza. Built in the Spanish style, the windows of the white building were shuttered against the sun and heat.

Felicidad liked attending Mass because she could rest. She pinned a piece of white lace that she took out of her pocket to her hair and slid into the back pew that their mother favored because Mami was ashamed of their bare feet and threadbare clothing. There were other families as poor as they and others worse off, yet there were also people in well-fitting clothes and new shoes. How Felicidad envied them! When Felicidad had asked her mother for a pair of shoes, red shoes would be nice, Mami said that someday she might have a pair of red shoes, but she would have to pray hard for them. After months of praying and no shoes, red or otherwise, Felicidad gave up.

While Father Cortez said Mass, elderly ladies in black with their hair covered with Spanish mantillas prayed the rosary. The murmured Our Fathers and Hail Marys and the clacking of the rosary beads reminded Felicidad of her mother. A bird flew in through the open window and she watched it fly across the altar. She wished on it that her mother would be the Mami before her sister Isabel's illness, before the troubles. Then she could go back to being the old Felicidad.

They went outside after Mass to wait for their father. The priest passed them still dressed in his holy vestments, cocking his head to hear what one very short lady had to say. Felicidad, at nine, was taller.

"Doesn't he know us?" Ruben asked.

"He must have many parishioners." Felicidad knew it was something that Mami would say. She decided to speak to the priest. Papi might be upset with her, but she had heard the priest accept an invitation. What about her mother?

"Pardon me, Father Cortez, I hesitate to trouble you," Felicidad said.

The priest looked down at the girl. What clear enunciation. True, not Castilian Spanish, but a nice pacing to her words spoken in a charming little-girl voice. Not what he had expected in ragamuffins.

"We would be in your debt, if you could tell us where our mother is," the girl said.

"I know you?" He took a good look at the girl and her brother. She was a pretty thing with delicate features and dark hair that looked as if someone had set a pot on her head and trimmed the hair beneath it. Her brother had gone to the same barber. The townspeople laughed at the jíbaros for things such as these.

"You came to help our mother." The girl pointed up in the direction of the mountain.

He looked into her dark eyes and remembered.

So these were the children of that poor, unfortunate woman. At first he had been too preoccupied to notice the children who came out of the shadows. He recalled how he had taken deep breaths on the ride home, uncaring of the islanders' warning about the dangers of the night air. When he had arrived at the rectory, he had ordered his servant to fry him some eggs and he had eaten three with four pieces of toast slathered with papaya preserves.

"Where is your father?" Some things were better for a father to relay.

"He had to run an errand, but he'll be back soon," the girl said.

Father Cortez thought of the lunch that awaited him at Doña Flores's table, such delicious arroz con pollo with peas and carrots even that it reminded him of his mother's paella. Still, the work of God must come first. The good woman would be sure to hold lunch for him, and he could thank her with a story of children searching for their mother.

"Wait here," he said.

The priest entered the church and was swallowed up by the dark coolness of the vestibule. Felicidad looked down at their feet and wished they weren't so dusty. Father Cortez had worn shiny, black shoes without a smudge. Where was Papi? Surely, he knew when Mass ended. If he didn't hurry, he might miss the priest and then when would they get Mami back?

Father Cortez came out dressed in his black cassock with his hat set on his head at a jaunty angle.

They followed the priest down the cobbled walkway behind the church, past lush flowering bushes heavy with perfume. He led them up the steps to a wood-frame house with a small porch.

"¡Ignácio!"

A dark-skinned elderly man hurried down the hall.

"There must be a cracker somewhere or other you can feed these children," he said. "I will be in my study."

Ignácio instructed them to wipe their feet on the bamboo mat outside the door. They entered the rectory with bowed heads. Cool ceramic tiles soothed their sore feet. They had never seen anything so grand, and Felicidad wished that she had checked Ruben's feet to be sure they didn't shame their parents by leaving footprints in their wake.

They followed Ignácio into a kitchen gleaming with a large white cabinet. They stared openmouthed when he opened it and took out a glass pitcher of milk.

"Sit down." Ignácio pointed to the table and chairs.

Surely, he didn't mean for them to sit down at the table? Ignácio pushed Ruben toward a chair.

"Sit, sit. Are you children dumb? Can you not hear?"

They sat, afraid to risk the treat of a cracker. Ignácio busied himself in the pantry. The children would have been stunned to learn that not only did some people stockpile sacks of rice and beans and cans of peaches and tins of chocolate even during the war, but that these stores had their own special room. They waited silently, Felicidad hiding her feet under the table and gesturing to Ruben to do the same.

Ignácio gave them each a chunk of cheese and some crackers, but not the Marías from Spain, as those were only for the priest except for the one or two he himself could sneak. He went back to the pantry for a block of guava paste and cut a few pieces.

"Eat," he told them. "I don't have all day."

While her brother washed the pasta de guayaba down with his glass of milk, Felicidad lingered over the sticky square and admired its redness, surely the color of hibiscus.

They heard the servant's returning footsteps and Felicidad plopped the square into her mouth, afraid that Ignácio would yell or that he would take away her plate before she was finished.

Ignácio surveyed the children at the table, milk drunk, food eaten, no talking.

"Uh-huh, that's the way I like it." He waved them up from the chairs. "Your father is with the priest."

Felicidad and Ruben followed him down the hall again, wiping their sticky lips with the backs of their hands.

The white floor tiles continued into a sparsely furnished room with a huge wood crucifix on one wall. Their father sat on a wooden bench, holding his hat between his legs. The priest wrote at a desk in front of a bookcase filled with leather-bound books. A small burlap sack like the kind their father filled with coffee beans sat among framed pictures of a blond Jesus Christ, one of the Holy Father, and another of a woman whom Felicidad did not think was the Virgin Mary.

Ignácio closed the door behind them. They stood awaiting instructions from either their father or the priest, but none came.

Padre Cortez addressed their father. "And that matter that we discussed...you agree that it is for the best?"

"The best." Their father inspected the brim of his hat.

"The most important thing is that the evil spirit is out of her," Father Cortez said. "Sometimes we have to make difficult decisions for the right reasons. God likes to test us."

At this, Papi looked up at the priest. Felicidad had never seen such an expression of despair on her father's face before and she was afraid.

"Don't worry, señor, those doctors up in San Juan have seen cases like this before. All she needs is a little rest, a little food, some sleep," the priest said.

"A little food, some sleep," repeated their father.

Father Cortez got up from his chair. "Well, if you'll excuse me, I have an appointment with a certain arroz con pollo."

Felicidad thought of her mother's arroz con pollo, how she chopped the chicken so that everyone got a piece of meat, dicing fresh herbs and steeping annatto seeds in oil for the rich orange-red color. For these occasions, Papi or Vicente killed one of their chickens. Or her mother would wring its neck right there at el fogón. Mami told Felicidad that a woman must be prepared to do anything.

Leading the burro, the children hurried down the road after their father. His shoes were slung over one unyielding shoulder. They stared without speaking at the back of Papi's white shirt, now dabbled with sweat.

Felicidad wished she dared to ask her father what the priest had said about their mother, but she was afraid of what he might tell her.

In time they would learn Mami's fate. That was the nature of secrets in the mountains. The heat of the day kept them suppressed inside the wood and zinc houses, but the night air released the secrets into the countryside, blowing them in gentle breezes and sifting them through the leaves rustled by the Spirits wandering restlessly through the mountain nights.

That evening, Papi sat in his chair rolling tobacco into a scrap of paper. He cut the cigarette into three pieces and tucked two into his shirt pocket. He smoked the third piece in deep contemplation. Now and again he looked up at Leila, who was tending to the baby, and at Felicidad, who was embroidering. When he spoke, the children were quiet; even the baby stopped making gurgling noises. He told Felicidad that she would have to go to the medical center to get some milk for Raffy. Even Juanita understood that Mami wasn't coming back home anytime soon.

When Felicidad went to bed, she thought of her mother somewhere out there listening to the coquís. She felt a rush of air. Spirits? We are all Spirits, her mother had once told her. Felicidad dreamed of Mami floating over the mountain and knew that her mother protected her.

The days awaiting news of her mother passed slowly for Felicidad. Sometimes she dreamed of that terrible day. Felicidad would be standing alone in el batey, holding the wedding mantilla like a tarp, calling out "I'll catch you, I'll catch you," as Mami perched on the edge of the roof, arms outstretched. Felicidad always woke up trembling at the image of her mother suspended in midair.

Whenever she could, Felicidad embroidered, her fingers cramping as she strove to copy Mami's minute stitches, hoping that the day would come when her mother would hold up a blouse and say to her, Felicidad, I am proud of you. It looks like mine!

One day Ruben brought home two letters for their father.

One was a business-like envelope, return address San Juan; the other was written in a firm, unadorned hand.

"I think that one must be from Mami's relative. The one who owns la panadería," Felicidad said, proud to know more than her siblings.

They stared at the envelopes as if they would be able to divine their contents. That night Papi read the letters to himself then tucked the envelopes in his shirt pocket, the two pieces of cigarettes a bump against the fabric.

The day came when Papi told Felicidad to prepare his good shirt and pants. He would need to leave before sunrise and wouldn't return until night. Felicidad should save him his dinner.

That next morning he stood by the open door, a tall man dressed in his good white shirt and pants with his Panama hat in one hand, dangling his shoes by the laces in the other.

"I am going to get your mother," Papi said.

They asked him questions all at once. Could they go, too? Was she well? Would she be the same mother as before, before la tristeza? He held out his hand for silence.

"We have to be very careful not to say or do anything that could upset or agitate her in any way," he said.

"Will she have to sleep all the time?" Felicidad asked.

Papi looked at her. "I hope not," he said.

One afternoon after her mother came home, Felicidad sat at the table granando gandules, cracking open the black-eyed pea pods with her fingernails and dropping the empty pods into the lap of her dress, while Mami told her stories about Spirits. Felicidad's great-uncle had encountered a Spirit while walking his cow down the mountain. He had run away in terror and broken his leg. Felicidad's grandfather, her own father, may he rest in peace, was tormented by the family of cats he said lived under his bed. At night, while everyone slept, the cats called out to him, shrieking his name. Pobre hombre, it got so that he would get up in the middle of the night and bang his head against the wall to make them stop.

"My father wasn't quite right in the head during that time," Mami said.

"Were there really cats living under his bed?" Felicidad glanced across the room at her parents' bed, imagining the family of cats.

"No cats. Mamá sent for the curandero who prayed over him and rubbed him with special herbs for two days," Mami said. "I was afraid of Spirits then."

"I'm afraid of them, too," Felicidad said.

Felicidad's mother stared out through the open door. "When your sister Isabel died, my heart hurt so bad, but I felt her spirit," Mami said. "I would stare out at the mountains and think my little girl was still with me."

Felicidad tried not to think of her older sister, of the terrible itching inflaming her vagina, causing her to cry with shame and desperation, or of the day when she had been taken away to the hospital and returned home in her coffin, which had been set down for the velorio on the very same table at which they now sat shelling beans.

"We are all flesh and blood, but Spirits, too. It is difficult for you, a child, to understand. I, too, am sometimes confused. My family believed in Spirits and we would often pray to them and call on them to help us. Yet the Church tells us that except for the Holy Spirit there is only what you can see. The sun, the trees, this table, you, these beans," Mami said.

"We must follow the teachings of the Church." Her voice

quavered. "Yet I know what I know. Spirits are everywhere, even in this room. At night, I hear their whispers."

"Mami?" Felicidad wished her mother would stop talking about Spirits. She was afraid to look around the house, afraid she would see a Spirit.

Her mother stared into the bowl of gandules as if she hadn't seen it before.

"We are only human," Mami said.

Felicidad stared at her shadow of a mother, so thin that her bones poked out beneath the collar of her dress, and she believed.

Chapter Four

The aunt came for her on her tenth birthday. It was a season of much rain so that the aunt's shoes sank in the mud and her stick legs with them, sloshing in and out, in and out of the mud. Mami gave her a parcel with two pairs of panties she had sewn and closed Felicidad's hand over two caramelos, telling her not to forget to pray. Felicidad followed the aunt on the long walk down the mountain where a público stopped for passengers. She clutched the package to her chest and felt the coolness of the mud squishing between her toes, splashing on her ankles. The mountain was alive with the caw of the birds and the rustle of its fauna, but Felicidad was deaf to her childhood home. Felicidad stopped to look for her father among the rows of bean plants. She fell behind and the aunt chided her to keep up—she didn't have all day.

Felicidad imagined Papi striding through the fields, sweeping her up onto his shoulders and carrying her down the mountain as he had when she was a small child. He had pretended to be a paso fino horse, she, a Spanish conquistador.

Her father had told her that morning of her birthday. Felicidad was grinding the coffee beans in el pilón, using two hands to lift the huge maceta.

Papi said, "Felicidad, your attention."

He never asked so formally. He spoke to them and they knew enough to listen. She trembled to think what she had done wrong.

"How would you like to live with your uncle? Mami's brother. Wouldn't it be nice to live in town?"

"A visit?" Was this a birthday surprise? A reward for how she had taken over her mother's work? The things she would have to tell the others when she returned!

Papi took up la maceta and began to pulverize the coffee beans. Felicidad was so surprised that she didn't realize for a moment that he hadn't answered her question.

He looked at her then. "You will live with them, Felicidad."

She stared into his blue eyes that were so startling in his brown face and thought it must be some kind of joke.

"But Mami can't do everything," Felicidad said, smiling a little.

"One of your aunts, my own sister, Imelda la jamona, is coming today," Papi said.

Felicidad looked at Mami to tell Papi that it wasn't nice to tease her on her birthday, but she was still lying in bed and her father wasn't smiling.

The thump, thump, thump of the maceta echoed the thump, thump, thump she began to feel in her head.

Perhaps there was something that she could do better, maybe if she worked harder. Just yesterday she had run after butterflies with Leila and Juanita, time better spent embroidering. She had felt guilty even as she chased them, knowing that people said that seeing mariposas meant someone would soon die.

"Have I done something wrong?"

Papi looked at her with those light eyes of his and she wondered, Why do some people look like they want to cry yet not a tear would dare to leak out?

"No, niña. You've been a good little mother, but you're still a child," he said. "Soon it will be time to cut the cane, and when I go to la safra, we must have another woman in the house."

She would stop asking to attend school. She would grind the coffee beans finer, she would cook surullos and not complain about burning her fingers.

"I can do better, Papi. I promise I can do better," she said.

Papi gave her back la maceta, a glossy mound of fine brown powder at the base of the pilón.

"You will live a good life and have everything your mother and I wish for all of you," Papi said.

She didn't want all that. She wanted only to stay with her family.

"I don't want to go," Felicidad dared to say.

"You must. Vicente will work for my uncle Praxtor and Ruben will stay home from school to bring the lunches and help in the fields."

"But, Papi…" Felicidad made to go to Papi.

Her father turned away. "El café, Felicidad."

The aunt had sat by the window instructing Felicidad to keep her hands on her lap and an eye on the man next to her. She was to let her know if there was any falta de respeto. Not that she expected any—after all, it was broad daylight and in full view of others—but you never knew with men. Felicidad was embarrassed; the aunt spoke loud enough for everyone to hear.

The caramelos melted into a glob that made a squishing sound when she opened her palm so she held it closed, afraid that the aunt would make her throw the candy out the window. Once the aunt turned her back, Felicidad planned on eating it and licking her palm clean. Caramelos were only for birthdays. She wasn't going to waste them.

El público, by nature of its business, made what seemed to be random stops on the single-lane road to pick up or drop off passengers. Going around the mountain, they fell behind a team of oxen. The man next to Felicidad asked the driver to stop just for a moment so that he could buy one of those coco fríos from that stand up the road because, ay bendito, it was as hot as Ponce in the car.

"That's the problem with these públicos. It takes all day to get you where you want to go," the aunt said. "One day I'll have my own car and I won't have to put up with this tontería of stopping for coco fríos in the middle of the day when I have things to do."

Felicidad was thinking that she would like a coco frío, too. She had never had one and she had already eaten the caramelos.

She said to the aunt, "Today is my birthday."

"Humph." The aunt turned away.

The driver and the thirsty passenger went out to the stand, an aluminum tub on top of a rickety card table. The vendor dug into the tub for a large green shell, slicing off the top with his machete.

Felicidad looked down at her hands and tried to think of other things, of how her fingernails really were very dirty, as the aunt had pointed out, and not what her mother was doing or her brothers and sisters or if Tía Imelda la jamona had already arrived and taken her place and she, forgotten. Especially, she tried not to think of her father's eyes.

The driver came back and so did the passenger, carrying two coconuts.

"Niña, a coco frío for you on your birthday," he said. "Con su permiso, señora."

Felicidad waited for the aunt's permission.

The aunt nodded at his good manners. "Thank el señor," she said.

Coconut water eased down Felicidad's throat and helped soothe the ache that had settled there ever since Papi told her that she was to live with her uncle. She wondered if her parents had ever drunk cold coconut water. She wished she could say to the aunt, Tía, have you ever had coco frío because, if not, then why don't you try it, and, if so, why aren't you drinking it? For Felicidad, the car was no longer hot and musty with the odor of passengers past and present, or with the lady-like perspiration of the aunt seeping through layers of perfumed powder. She didn't feel the hot stickiness of the seat beneath her thighs or smell the stink of cigarettes. Everything was wonderful, everything was coco frío.

The aunt glared at the driver when he stopped for a passenger. Felicidad wondered why she couldn't trade places with the aunt. She would have liked to sit by the window. She wanted to stare at the people chatting in the dusty town plazas, she wanted to look out at the land, at the wood houses perched precariously on hillsides, to wave to the people they passed, often obreos working the land or skinny, barefoot children, to memorize their faces and everything she saw, so that she could describe it to her brothers and sisters upon her return.

When finally they reached the aunt's town, she indicated to Felicidad to follow her. They hurried past pastel houses with wrought-iron gates, curtains fluttering in the open windows. From a street cart, a man sold linbergs—flavored ices of coconut or tamarind or pineapple. Another sold fried yuca fritters called alcapurrías. Laundry women balanced baskets of clothes on their heads. Two well-dressed men rode horses, one of which defecated on the street as it passed. The aunt said to no one in particular that they should ride their horses en el campo and let the animals take care of their business out in the countryside where they belonged.

Felicidad clutched her mother's package to her chest, thinking she didn't know there were so many cars in the world. They reached the plaza where merchants had set up sheds. Ceramic basins, large and small, pots and pans and fiambreras hung on hooks or were stacked on shelves or on the ground. Handkerchiefs and ladies' slippers dangled on nails. She wanted to stop and look over the items for sale, preferably with a tamarind ice in one hand and an alcapurría in the other. The aunt chided Felicidad to walk faster, it wasn't her business to be looking around and what did she have to look at, she was the one who would be looked at with her rags and dirty bare feet, like any peasant from the mountain.

The aunt's home was a neat frame house with a porch. The aunt pointed to the burlap sack used for a doormat, a sack that had once held rice, and Felicidad wiped her feet before following her inside.

"Wait here," the aunt said. "I'll go get your uncle from la panadería."

She stood; she had been taught to wait until invited to sit. When her tío Pablo came, he saw a skinny little girl with a haircut like his own father had given him and eyes dark and shiny as coffee beans. Her trembling hands clutched a parcel wrapped in the estraza paper he used en la panadería.

"Ay bendito, you look like Rosario." He was overcome with love for his sister and pity for her child.

"Bendición, Tío," Felicidad said, asking for his blessing.

"God bless you." Tío Pablo kissed her cheek.

"Well, it seems she has some manners," the aunt said, grateful for that, at least.

There were three bedrooms, each smaller than the other, each filled with more furniture than the other, but to Felicidad it was one of those haciendas that her mother had told tales about, that their Spanish ancestors had owned before the Americans came, before sugarcane plantations, before the great hurricanes of 1899 and 1928, before so many children, before Felicidad.

She would share the smallest bedroom with seven-year-old Adela and have mosquito netting and the privacy that was impossible in her one-room house, which not even her parents enjoyed. She thought of her tía Imelda la jamona having to share a bed with children, caring for another woman's family and home, and never having a moment for herself. Felicidad pitied Tía Imelda la jamona and took note that her fate was the result of not having a husband and home of her own and being dependent on the charity of others.

That first day was the worst day of her life, worse even than the day her mother had her breakdown or was possessed by the devil or a Spirit or whatever it had been. Immediately upon her arrival, she felt the urge to relieve herself. Felicidad walked around the back of the house looking for a letrina, sure that a house as grand as the aunt's must have one; even her family had one as poor as they were. Why, she could recall the day when they got their very own letrina! Papi and the boys dug the hole and the town's municipality delivered a brand-new letrina gratis. People along the way stopped whatever they were doing to watch the tiny wood shed strapped to the cab of a truck driving up the mountain. The children drew lots to see who would use it first. Felicidad stood outside the door with the others, calling out to Leila and asking her to tell them how she liked it.

She searched the back of the house in vain. No letrina. It made her think that the aunt and her tío Pablo weren't as civilized as their house implied. Oh, she did not want to have to go back to squatting on the ground! Back home on the mountain there were tall trees and bushes and lush vegetation providing some measure of privacy. Here in town, the houses were close together. How about if some neighbor were to see her? The shame she would bring to her uncle. But Felicidad didn't see what else she could do, so she squatted down in a corner of the yard under a lemon tree and peed.

Felicidad stood by the table while the others sat at their meal. When Tío Pablo asked her why she didn't sit down, she told him that at home she usually ate outside with her siblings sitting on tree stumps or perched in their favorite trees. The aunt ordered her to sit and pointed to the way Felicidad held her fork, telling the girl that she held it like a monkey, but what else could one expect from a girl who ate in a tree. Her cousins, twin boys a year or two older than she, giggled and called her Cousin Mona until their father admonished them for calling her monkey. Adela smiled, too young to understand. Felicidad had never seen a monkey, but she knew enough to be embarrassed. When she tried to eat, her rice fell through the tines. Look, such a jíbara the girl is! It was impossible to cut off a piece of her green banana with a knife, as the aunt demonstrated. She wished she dared to pick it up with her fingers or at least to ask for a spoon.

She had a plate of food—viandas, chicken, and rice—that would feed three of them back home. Yet Felicidad could only pick at what was on her plate.

The aunt asked her questions. How many brothers and sisters do you have, Felicidad? Two dead, seven living! That many? Pablo, did you know that your sister had that many? How does your father support them? How many brothers did you say? All work in the fields? Hmmm. What grade are you in? You didn't go all last year? Stayed home to help!

Felicidad answered in between her few bites of food. She wondered why only the aunt spoke and not her uncle. Was he not interested in his sister's family? Eventually, she would learn that her tío Pablo was a man of few words and an easy nature and that the aunt liked him that way. The aunt said, Tell me about your mother, what is her condition? Felicidad knew it was a falta de respeto not to do as the aunt asked. Before Papi had left for la finca, he had admonished her to do as she was told. Naturally the aunt only wanted to know out of familial concern, but she did not want to remember that day.

The aunt grew frustrated at Felicidad's brief answers. She thought the girl was either disrespectful or just plain dumb. After dinner, the aunt led her to the basin. "This is a sink, Felicidad. Have you seen a sink before? I didn't think so. How did you wash dishes at home? A palangana! In which you added water? From el pozo? ¡Hoja de fregar! How primitive! Soap? You didn't have any! Well, that's not the way we do things here. By the way, we don't expose our dirt to the neighbors." The aunt shook her head in exasperation. "No, muchacha, it is just an expression. What goes on in this house stays in this house. You don't go about telling my business, your uncle's business, your cousins' business, the family's business, to anybody. Understand?"

"I understand," Felicidad said.

The aunt nodded in satisfaction. "I appreciate how you protected the privacy of your family. It isn't right to bare your troubles to the world, but I am not the world. I am your aunt, part of your family, and you can tell me anything. Understand?"

"I understand," Felicidad said.

The aunt grimaced in what Felicidad would learn passed for a smile. "Now let us go over your place in the house.

"Adela's clothes are your responsibility. You used to wash down in the river? Well, lucky you. In this house you soak the clothes in the tub and scrub on a washboard using plenty of soap, mind you. Let me see your hands. Hmmm, your hands are small, but they must be strong. You have to wring the clothes before you hang them on the clothesline. Clothesline? In the back of the house. See these little wood things? Clothespins. Tomorrow Lucinda will show you how to wash. The sheets, I send out to a washerwoman. It's only for now because I ordered a washing machine from Sears, Roebuck. Mala suerte that I have to wait until the war is over to get it. Lucinda? Lucinda is the woman who helps your uncle and me in the fonda. You didn't know we had one? Yes, muchacha, we have la panadería next door and the fonda. Really, more like a cafetería, just a few tables and a kitchen for now, but respectable. I have the talent for cooking. I could make even rats taste good. We're hard workers, your uncle and I, and we expect you to earn your keep. Your father wanted to give us one of the others, Leila, I think. She's the blonde? But I knew that you were the one for me when I heard how you cooked and cleaned and took care of the children when your mother had her breakdown. That's what happened to her, right? There is a saying: If the pot of rice is burned black then the pot of rice is black. I've heard of such a thing happening to women before. I think it comes from having so many babies. Something happens when a woman gives birth, and often, it's not good. Take my advice, Felicidad, and don't have too many babies."

Felicidad stood at the sink, thinking soon it would be time for Mami to make the evening coffee. Maybe she would take coffee out to Papi. They would stand in el batey like the old days, before the sad times, whispering to each other.

The aunt continued. "I've heard of plenty of women who lose their minds when they have babies. I think it's something in their blood that makes them like that. One woman banged her head

against a palm tree until finally her husband took to tying her to
her bed before he went out to la finca. It seems to me that most of
the women who get sick like that are campo women. I think it's
the primitive life and the running back and forth to el curandero
for this and that instead of going to the doctor."

Felicidad thought of her mother standing on the roof, naked.

"Muchacha, are you listening? In the mornings I work en la
panadería and then I go to the fonda. You are to watch Adela
after you come home from school."

Felicidad held her breath, ay bendito, if she had heard correctly, if only she could have this one thing to live for.

The aunt had certain thoughts on what made for a happy
marriage and letting a man think he ruled the household was
one of them. The girl's uncle had promised Felicidad's father
and she let her husband have his way, against her will, true, but
still, he got his way. On another point, the aunt was firm: She
didn't believe in squandering affection. Each night before bed,
she held out her cheek for her children's kisses and willingly
granted her blessing with each petition for Bendición. As for
love and affection? In her opinion, there was too much kissing and loving going on. Look at all those brothers and sisters
of Felicidad and all those mountain people with half-starved
tribes of twelve or sixteen children with protruding stomachs,
all those barefoot children haunting the mountains like spooks.

Felicidad would prepare the children's breakfast along with her
own while the aunt tended to customers en la panadería. Once
the aunt taught her, she would cook dinner. Sometimes the aunt
might bring food from la fonda depending on what was left over.
Leaving food on the plate, the way Felicidad had, was not permitted in her family, not when some people like Felicidad's own

brothers and sisters were wasting away due to a lack of rice and beans, was that right?

"Yes, Tía, that is right," Felicidad said.

The aunt scrutinized her to make sure she wasn't being disrespectful and, satisfied that the girl wasn't smart enough to be sarcastic, told her, "You watch your step, young lady, and we will get along fine."

She told her to call her señora always, no aunt this, no aunt that, because next thing she knew Felicidad would be calling her by her first name and she wasn't having any of that. Felicidad never considered not following the aunt's instructions.

Was it her fault Felicidad didn't have shoes? What would the townspeople think of her with a relative shuffling down the sidewalk in her bare feet? She had given the girl an old pair of her own flats, now she had to suffer the noise of the too-big shoes flapping all over the floor. Tomorrow, she would buy the girl a pair of proper shoes and a dress or two, nothing fancy, tú sabes. She couldn't let it get around that the new girl in school who was barefoot and dressed in rags was her niece. The lengualargas in town would love that! Was it her fault her husband's sister lived in a one-room shack? With a dozen children? Oh, why did everything have to be so difficult for her? She even had to show the girl how to use the toilet.

The first nights Felicidad knelt at the bedroom window listening to the coquís, imagining their familiar chanting lulling her family to sleep. She wanted to call out to her mother and know that she would comfort her. She missed her brothers and sisters. They had never been intimate, talking and sharing their thoughts and feelings, but they had the same parents, lived the same life. She helped Adela with her homework, caring for and dressing her as one would a favorite doll, but often she thought of Leila and Juanita and how pretty her sisters would have looked in Adela's frilly dresses. She hoped that Leila was able to go to school now that Tía Imelda la jamona was helping their mother.

She reminded herself that her parents wanted her here and that one day she would return. She imagined the day when she would again embroider with Mami by the light of a kerosene lamp and listen to the screeching owls and other night creatures. Her mother would turn to her and say, It's just the creatures of the night. We are together and all is well.

Felicidad wasn't sure, but she thought there was a Spirit in the house with her. She felt the Spirit in the moments when she was most lonely, when she wanted to cry out for her parents and home. She thought of that day when Mami had talked to her of Spirits and believed that her mother had sent one to watch over her, and she was no longer afraid because the Spirit's presence was steadfast and reassuring in the manner of her father. The Spirit stood beside Felicidad during her aunt's reprimands; he accompanied her through the town's streets in the early days when everything was new and intimidating in its unfamiliarity. At night, the Spirit sat at the foot of her bed until Felicidad fell asleep dreaming of how it would be when she returned home.

Her twin brothers would run down to the road to help the driver unload the presents that she would bring. They would have a party because it was Three Kings Day, feasting on roast pork and pasteles and arroz con gandules. Papi would pass the jug of cañita to the neighbors come to celebrate. One neighbor would produce a guitar, another maracas, the third a güiro, y entonces, se formo! Singing! Dancing! She would show Tía Imelda la jamona how to grind the coffee beans in the grinder with the handle that was another present. Café con leche. Did she forget to mention the cow? Mami would serve arroz con dulce, which Felicidad had cooked on the aunt's stove and brought in a dozen of her fanciest plates. Her uncle would provide the cinnamon and fat juicy raisins. The singing! The dancing! The food! Ay bendito, God was good, Mami would say. After everyone was asleep, Felicidad would dart about, setting down a present or two by each pair of brand-new shoes, just like the Three Kings.

It warmed her heart, the way they would beg her forgiveness for sending her away, telling her that they had been miserable every single day and that it was better to be without rice and beans than without her, their precious Felicidad.

That first night Felicidad wrote her mother. The aunt admonished her not to write her business and to remember that once a woman had un ataque de nervios as her mother had, anything sad would make her sick again. Felicidad tore up her letter begging to come home and wrote instead to her father: They are good to me here. I drank a coco frío. Tío Pablo sends this dollar. Felicidad.

From then on, she wrote only when she had a dollar to enclose. She couldn't put her yearning to return in her letters and the details of her comfort would be cruel to her siblings, so what was the point?

With the passing of the days, Felicidad settled into the aunt's household. She slept on a real mattress instead of a box spring; coils didn't jab into her back. When she turned her head on the pillow, a piece of straw didn't poke her in the eye. She wore shoes and ate well-prepared food so she didn't need to drink a laxative to rid her intestines of hookworms. Even the work she did for the aunt was easy compared with her old chores. She cooked on an electric stove. She didn't have to hunt for firewood. There was no going to the river to wash clothes or el pozo for water. The aunt had a toilet so she didn't have to go out to the letrina or empty out the escupidera every morning. She didn't have to roast the coffee beans or mash them with a mortar and pestle. When the aunt discovered Felicidad's gift with the needle, she ordered a Singer sewing machine from the Sears catalog and put her to making Adela's dresses from Simplicity patterns, which Felicidad enjoyed. She did her schoolwork without worrying abut completing piecework to make a much-needed dollar. Now she embroidered because she wanted to and because it reminded her of the happy days.

Felicidad struggled with her guilt over her comfortable life, but what was worse was that the hardship of her childhood began to fade from her memory.

She thanked God every night for all her blessings and especially for her cousin Adela, who treated her like a big sister, holding her hand to and from school those first years, insisting that Felicidad share her bed, and begging her cousin to let her help with the housework until she grew old enough to realize it was work.

All this, yet Felicidad yearned for more.

Except for school, the aunt allowed her out only long enough to walk from one place to the other. She kept her skin white for she was never out in the sun long enough for it to imprint its love on her. Not that the much-prized white skin did her any good.

She was a servant in the aunt's home and even with Adela's companionship, she was lonely. She didn't belong to anyone and no one belonged to her. Despite the warning that she would not see her family for a very long time, she hadn't believed it would be so.

In those first days it was the hours that Felicidad counted, hours when she believed in her heart that her father would arrive in a público or on a borrowed horse or even a burro to take her home. When the days became months and still no Papi, she thought her mother's Papa Dios and her Papa Dios couldn't be the same God.

The first year away from her family was the hardest because she ached for her old life. The morning of her eleventh birthday, Felicidad put on her best dress and sat en la sala with her hands folded on her lap, back straight, the way Mami taught her. She waited all day for her father.

That night at dinner her uncle promised to take her for a visit as soon as business permitted.

"You're sure to see your family very soon," Tío Pablo said. "Either your aunt or I will take you. Isn't that right, mujer?"

"It's half a day's ride in a público," the aunt said.

Tío Pablo squeezed Felicidad's hand. "I'll take you. I'll get to see my sister again."

Her uncle's promise at first gave her hope, but the years passed and still no visit. First, Felicidad was too young to travel alone and the aunt was always too busy and secretly disinclined to give up a day to travel up a mountain to see people she didn't care to see. Felicidad's uncle was a man of good intentions; he always planned on taking his niece back for a visit. Such a sweet girl that Felicidad was, so capable and helpful that it was the least she deserved, but her uncle, when the day approached for the visit, had forgotten his promise or he hadn't planned properly for taking the time off from la panadería or it was the year when he had advanced to the second round of the domino competition en la plaza and that didn't happen often! He was so sorry. He promised he would take her soon.

Always, her uncle looked a little ashamed when giving his excuse. It pained Felicidad because Tío Pablo was always so nice to her. Eventually she resigned herself to not seeing her family. She meant to go as soon as she was old enough, but she didn't count on growing into doubt and fear. By the time she was fifteen and could travel alone, too much time had passed. What if her family didn't want to see her? What if they didn't remember her—or worse, what if they didn't care? She was a different Felicidad from the one she had been and they were a different family from the one she had known; a spinster aunt had taken her place and her older brothers had been scattered to different parts of the island. She would be going alone to a family of strangers.

With the passing of the years, she eased into the routine of living with the aunt and her uncle's family and did her best not to pine for the family she'd left behind. Only the infrequent letter in her father's hand or the sighting of a country mother and young daughter with paper parcels tucked under their arms inflicted a quick stab of pain for what she had lost.

Felicidad would close her eyes and seek comfort in her Spirit Father: she was a little girl again being carried on her father's shoulders, Papi galloping down the mountain making her squeal with frightened delight. And for a little while, she was happy.

Chapter Five

When she was sixteen the aunt took her to the country to care for her invalid mother, Doña Carolina. The aunt had stayed just long enough to kiss her mother hello and good-bye. La viejita wouldn't remember a thing. What was the point?

Felicidad was used to the activity of a town, to hearing the laughter or voices or footsteps of passersby or the crunch of car tires from the street floating through an open window. She had grown accustomed to sleeping in the glow of a streetlight instead of in the shadow of a mountain. True, she couldn't deny the campo's magic—the infinite greens of the trees and foliage, the flowers that grew in every color and type, the birds that cawed and sang and whistled and crowed and were anything but silent, the abundance of fauna and the glorious shock of color everywhere testifying that God had been there—but by night-fall it was obvious that He had become bored and moved on someplace where there was something to do other than stare out into the black mountain night.

Felicidad couldn't muster anything stronger than pity for this viejita whose own daughter shunned her. Felicidad fed her spoonfuls of chicken soup and rubbed mashed avocado and banana onto her toothless gums. She held a porcelain cup with tepid coffee up to the old lady's lips, waiting for what seemed like an eternity for her to swallow.

Every morning, Felicidad dipped a clean washcloth in the warm water she heated on a kerosene stove. She washed the furrows on la viejita's forehead and dabbed at the crow's-feet and the deep hollows under the brown unseeing eyes.

As often as necessary, Felicidad changed her cloth diapers. She gagged over the excrement smeared over the flaccid buttocks. Felicidad chattered on to hide her distaste at touching the wrinkled, flabby flesh. Was the water too hot? Too cold? Wasn't it a hot day, ay bendito, not as hot as in town, she was sure. Always hotter in town. No mountains to block the sun. And the avocado yesterday, wasn't it heaven? She always did like a good avocado. Especially a generous slice with a bowl of rice and beans. Nothing as good as that. Yesterday she had eaten a mango as sweet as any of the pan dulce the aunt sold at la panadería. She was sure that with the mangoes that grew around the house, la doña had eaten her fair share. In the aunt's bakery there was a customer who would always say that she would choose the smallest piece of mango over her husband's kiss any day. Felicidad was exhausted from talking by the time she got to the old lady's feet.

With the passing of days she learned to bathe la doña in silent concentration, communicating with her hands respect and compassion for the old lady's age and condition. She wiped la viejita's decaying buttocks and dried the sparse white hairs of her pubis. Twice weekly she washed the old lady's hair, unwinding the tight bun and letting it fall in wispy gray ropes at her ankles. All the while Felicidad combed it, la viejita murmured on about her amor Ramón, taking delight in the musicality of the words, each joyous repetition making her young again.

Mi amor, Ramón. Ramón, mi amor. Take down ay bendito, Ramón. Felicidad marveled at it, knowing the aunt's father had been named Fausto. She was curious to hear more, but mala suerte, the old lady was senile.

Every day she put Doña Carolina down for a nap when the sun was its hottest. In the small room that the aunt had assigned her, she lay in her slip staring up at the ceiling through the mosquito netting. She wondered about la viejita's Ramón. *Ramón* was a name sure to belong to a lover. Felicidad thought that it would be nice to have a lover. She wasn't quite sure what a lover might do other than the obvious, but if a little old lady who couldn't remember her own daughter could remember a lover from at least forty years past, it must be something better than she could imagine. Felicidad closed her eyes, ready to dream of a prince come to teach her what Doña Carolina knew. She enjoyed a delicious shiver. Her Spirit Prince was handsome. And tall. She reveled in the strength of his arms as he held her and she didn't protest when he thrust open her legs. A sensation that was new to her—a warmth—tingle—thrill—tremor—seeped languorously throughout her body. Her breathing quickened, she began to moan. Ay bendito, thank God the old lady was deaf.

Except for the occasional barefoot peasant passing through Doña Carolina's field, she had only the daily visit of Margarita Silva, a neighbor, who delivered supplies. She brought a small bag of coffee beans or pieces of a freshly killed chicken, its blood soaking a rag. A pitcher of milk. Once she brought a hunk of pork that Felicidad chopped into small pieces to fry, saving a few chunks to season the rice. Margarita brought tomatoes, a green pepper pointed at the tip like the old lady's nose, potatoes that Felicidad added to a chicken fricassee.

Margarita was a woman the aunt's age who confessed to

Felicidad that she and her husband rented their house and patch of land from the aunt and were being forgiven past debts plus a bit more on the side for helping out Doña Carolina. The old lady had had a nurse from town caring for her, but the poor girl had lasted only six months. It was hard getting someone to stay in the country. She herself often stayed with the old lady, the nurse being so frightened of a mountain night. Most likely, the aunt would find someone to stay permanently. Not Felicidad? School? She was to stay only two months? Well, she couldn't blame her. Maybe a widow who had already experienced life or, better yet, a jamona, who had no one to live for, would be best.

Margarita hoped la Doña Carolina would last for a long time, years, if God was merciful, because her husband could barely feed their family of five; things were so bad for everyone and they were one of the lucky families with only three children. Not ten or twelve like others around these parts; those Vegas up the mountain had sixteen. Three children, none of her own. Not from her body, anyway. A boy from her husband, that maricón. A son by that woman, that Lucy. Surely, she had heard? No?

She had problemas de mujeres. Since she became a señorita she had bled like someone had taken a machete and cut her up good. Blood that stained like achiote oil, so hard to scrub from her sanitary rags and then she had to drape the darn things on top of the bushes to dry. Her brothers loved to play tricks on her and hide them or hang them on sticks and wave them like flags. One of those maricónes buried a pair in el batey. She was a poor girl; she had only one or two cloths, maybe three.

Did Felicidad have brothers? She hadn't lived with them for many years? Lucky girl.

Her husband had brought her back Lucy's child wrapped up

in a towel. He said Lucy had enough children; this one is mine and now yours. That maricón. Later her sister died and her husband's new wife didn't want her girls. So that was how she got her children.

Another visit, Felicidad learned that she had known Felicidad's aunt as a young girl, was Felicidad aware of that? That aunt of hers had always been stingy. (Here Margarita knocked her elbow against the porch's wood banister.) Forgive her for criticizing a relative. She didn't mean to give offense.

Margarita was sure the aunt owned several houses in addition to the one she lived in. The Rodriquez Vélezes down the mountain lived in another of the aunt's houses. Her house wasn't the greatest house, not made from cement and stone, but still, it wasn't a bad house for a poor family like hers although over the years it had fallen into disrepair. Her husband did what he could, that maricón, but really, wasn't that the province of the aunt? It was her property, after all.

Felicidad only needed to nod and murmur something indistinct for the woman to continue; she gave her a cup of coffee and let her go on. Talking seemed Margarita's only pleasure and what did it hurt to listen?

She found that she welcomed the neighbor's chatter; she looked for any details that she could glean to help her understand the aunt's character. Margarita supplied a few. The aunt's family had money, enough to give to each of their children to start their own business. Ah, the stories she could tell Felicidad, how the family didn't think the aunt would ever marry, twenty-nine and no man until one of the brothers brought home Felicidad's uncle. No money, true, but so handsome. They had a happy marriage? It seemed so, Felicidad answered. It was none of her business to tell the aunt's story. Felicidad had the common sense of a middle-aged servant. She hadn't lived six years in someone else's house and not learned to keep her mouth shut.

Felicidad recalled clearly the lesson of the aunt's: A woman had two fates—that of a wife with her own home or that of a spinster on sufferance in someone else's home. She didn't want to be like Tía Imelda la jamona taking care of a home and children not her own. Felicidad decided that she would very much prefer to be a wife.

During the day the hours passed slowly, the heat compressing the sounds and noises of everyday living so that all was in a state of slumbering, her young life included. Felicidad, instead of feeling rejuvenated by the splendor of nature, imagined her youth leaving her body in the red shoes she had dreamed of as a little girl. What would become of her in a few years when she finished school? Felicidad recalled her father holding her mother's wedding mantilla and talking about how Mami had been the most beautiful girl he had ever seen. Would any man ever feel like that about her? Felicidad wished for a man like her father, but where could she possibly meet such a man? Probably not at la panadería under the aunt's watchful eye and probably not at school. Mala suerte, she couldn't count on her brothers to bring her a handsome stranger.

In some ways Felicidad felt she was on holiday, because after she took care of the old lady and her chores there wasn't someone to assign others. The aunt was always ordering Felicidad to make coffee or draw a bath or mop the kitchen floor, she hadn't special-ordered the linoleum from the Sears catalog to have it buried under dirt, for that, she would have a dirt floor like some people she knew. At Doña Carolina's she could rest when the old lady rested or flip through one of the old magazines she found under la viejita's bed.

How amusing to discover such a frivolous cache: *Vanity Fair,*

Vogue, Redbook, Glamour. She wondered why they were there and to whom they belonged. She was happy to have them. She spent hours staring at the photographs of beautiful girls in dresses and suits so lovely that her stomach ached as in the days before she had gone to live with the aunt, days when she ate only one meager meal a day, when the only water she drank was what she lugged back from the well.

How she coveted the shimmering silks and satins and gauzy chiffons, dresses as impossible for Felicidad to possess as rubies, emeralds, sapphires, and diamonds. Envy made her feel ugly, poor, and unloved.

Only when she was in bed, with her Spirit Prince loving her, only then did she feel beautiful, only then did she dare to believe that someday, some man would love her, too.

Now Felicidad was twenty years old and still living with the aunt and working en la panadería. She was waiting: waiting to gather the courage to visit her family after all these years, waiting for a summons to return home, waiting to learn that she was wanted. She was waiting for a miracle or at least a sign of some sort to show her what to do with her life. En la panadería she saw people and exchanged a little conversation, just enough to live through another day without having to decide to do something, anything, to ease the loneliness, to escape the drudgery, the complete monotony of her life. She ached to be someone different, to see somewhere different, do something different, even if it was only to eat meals without rice and beans.

She wrapped flaky pastelillos filled with guava paste for the older women, the lengualargas, who interrogated her daily. Is it true Tito Alvarez came into la panadería for a coffee and stayed half an hour? How many cups of coffee did he drink? What did he have to say to her? What was she doing talking to that boy?

She knew he didn't make more than a few dollars a week selling vegetables on the roadside and it wasn't even his own truck. And listen, Felicidad, he wouldn't ever make much more than that, not with spending half the day drinking coffee. Why hadn't her aunt swept him out along with the dust? Her aunt and her tío Pablo, did they know about this man monopolizing her time?

"No, doña, the aunt doesn't approve of young men spending time in the shop," Felicidad would say.

Did Felicidad realize she would never get anywhere in life wasting her time talking to men who hang around in shops?

"Sí, Doña María, Cristina, Guille, Rosa, Teresa, Anita, Nilsa…"

All those nights she spent at the aunt's house leaning out the window and staring up at the sky, she drew hope from the stars glittering their brilliance on her skin. When she marveled at the constellations whose names she never could recall, Felicidad saw herself wearing a gown that she had embroidered with roses, floating in the arms of her prince.

Every day she looked for him in the sun-wrinkled faces of the farmers, in the bashful eyes of the stoop-shouldered cane workers, in the furtive glances of the married men who parlayed indecent offers out of earshot of their wives. Only at night, when Adela was fast asleep, did the man she yearned for make his appearance in her Spirit Prince. Sometimes, when she couldn't tolerate another moment without a loving touch, she let him love her, oh so quietly, so as not to wake her cousin. Afterward she fell asleep to dream of her future husband.

When Aníbal came into la panadería one afternoon, cocky and assured in clothes that marked him from out of town, Felicidad had taken a good look at his hands, at the long fingers, at the clean, carefully clipped nails so different from the cracked, dirt-filled ones of the farmers and laborers who came into the aunt's panadería, and, she knew, if only he wanted to, he could make her feel beautiful. That first day Felicidad looked into Aníbal's eyes, the brown of caramelos, and thought that maybe God cared after all.

Aníbal

Chapter Six

1950–1952

Aníbal Acevedo had always been attracted to dark-skinned women, much to his parents' dismay. In his first years alone in the States, his mother wrote him monthly: long letters warning him not to give in to the lures of las negritas Americanas, to remember that Alfónzo Lizardi, who had lived on the mainland for many years, had been a victim of racial segregation. She reminded him that even in Puerto Rico, it mattered if a girl had pelo malo or skin el color de café. Wasn't it better to marry a girl with white skin than not? Let her eyes be el color de café, if he liked dark brown so much. (Here was the only time his mother alluded to her son's preference.) If he couldn't find himself a puertorriqueña blanca then she and his father would find one for him. His father's brother, Tío Placido, knew of a girl who worked in her family's business with skin as white as the flour her uncle used to bake bread. She was a pretty girl that one, everyone said so. And respectful of her betters. She wasn't one to go traipsing around with men and, if she were, it wouldn't be a secret, the chismosas being what they were on the island. Why don't you come soon? A good woman will keep a man out of trouble; just ask your father if this is so, she wrote.

Aníbal would smile at his mother's entreaties, thinking how she still had the old-fashioned way of mountain people. The last thing he wanted was a wife. That was for men who were established, who had money in the bank, who were afraid to die alone.

He fingered the fragile envelope stamped POR AVIÓN in blue ink and admired the beautiful penmanship that his mother had labored over as a child, her parents being Españoles of a certain class who put much stock in such niceties. Aníbal momentarily remembered the warmth and love he had felt in her presence, and then he tossed the letter and went about his business, forgetting her until the next letter or until the first of the month when he sent her a few dollars.

His mother was persistent. It was his third year on the mainland and she wrote of how she was physically ill with the hunger to see him, her firstborn, again, how she prayed a rosary for him every night. It was true that there weren't any jobs in Puerto Rico for able-bodied men let alone decent women, at least not any paying more than a pittance. She could remember her grandfather talking about the old days when he had paid his laborers enough so that they could eat a full plate of rice and beans, and now her son had to leave the finca to eat who knew what in a foreign land. What was the world coming to?

Did he remember Simón, that clubfooted boy who was the son of Rosa Galvez? Bueno, esa pobrecita Rosa Galvez suffered such a tragedy with her only son, thinking he was working in a factory in Nueva York, but in fact pobre Simón, along with many other Puerto Ricans, was being held captive in a labor camp in someplace called New Jersey. Did he know of such a place? She and Rosa Galvez agreed that New Jersey was someplace near Chicago where he, Aníbal, was. His mother went on in her letter that she had been about to write him to see if he could look for Simón, maybe after work, but then Rosa Galvez had received a letter from her son. Did he know what those American sinvergüenzas had done? They had forced Simón and the others to work seven days a week, from sunup to sundown. If Simón had wanted to be a burro, then he would have stayed in Puerto Rico and worked the cane. Somehow, Simón had managed to escape, but his mother wasn't clear on the details except to say that when he first went to the American authorities with his complaint, they asked to see his papers and wrote down his name under PROBLEM ALIEN WORKER or so Rosa Galvez said. They weren't quite sure what *alien* meant. Aníbal thought it was another way of saying "Puerto Rican not wanted."

Mamá insisted on seeing him. If he didn't have the money, although that was impossible because everyone knew how rich one became in the United States, she was determined to save what he sent her until she had enough for his fare.

If only Mamá knew how difficult it was to keep a dollar in a man's pocket. He had enough money to rent a room and to put aside for his dream of owning his own business, a men's clothing store. A tienda where he could sell both long- and short-sleeved guyaveras to the Puerto Ricans and flannel shirts for those customers trying to be Americans. Men had to buy clothes, why not from him?

Other days he wanted to sell records. Music to dim the ticking of his heart reminding him of the months and then years of not getting ahead, believing he was disappointing his parents, music for those nights he missed his family and the island, music reminding him of his orgullo of being Puerto Rican, music to ease the humiliation of working like a mule, of hearing the whispered "Pig, spic" from strangers on the bus, of being told to get back on the boat and go back to Cuba or South America or Mexico. Few in 1952 had heard of Puerto Rico, fewer still knew of the shame of stuttering over the English words when he tried to explain he wasn't Cuban or South American or even Mexican, but Puerto Rican and therefore American, too. Since he couldn't explain and usually the name caller didn't care to listen, he ended up saying what he had to say with his fists.

Aníbal yearned to sell music for dancing—hip-grinding merengues and two-step cumbias and faster, sassier guaguancós and, always, the sexy mambo—but especially, he wanted to sell sweet boleros to recall island breezes and the beat of his mother's heart as she hummed away the sting of his father's belt.

Slow boleros to remind him of his first kiss, his first groping of a girl's breasts, his hands over her blouse and then under, her soft no, no, Aníbal, no, her laughter tickling his ear, his penis pressed against her thigh and staining the fabric of his pants. Sexy boleros hot like his first forbidden taste of fruit between a woman's legs, those sturdy brown legs of the wife of his neighbor, the elderly Don Carlos. Forty years old, but still caliente the woman was, the heat of her pussy branding his fifteen-year-old penis so that from then on, always, he would rather make love to a woman de color than a pale one.

Ay, those first encounters. Her plump thighs and big ass squeezing him until he thought he would die, but, oh, death would be sweet even at such a tender age. Why hadn't anyone told him? His father? The older boys? Had they ever experienced the same pleasure? Why hadn't anyone told him that sticking it into a woman's pussy was better than anything he could do for himself?

Instead of school, morning lovemaking in the neighbor's house, the hurried removal of clothing, the lifting of a skirt. His palms, already developing into rough farm laborer hands with calluses on all the fingers, gripped her ass while he pressed himself against her still-soft stomach that had never experienced childbirth.

El bolero. You couldn't be a living Puerto Rican man, at

least not a young, horny man, and not know how to dance it. Why, Aníbal had gotten half his women that way. Fifty percent pussy.

He was one of those men lucky with women. Always a woman to screw when he wanted one. Female lips and tongue and legs and ass to remind him he was young and alive and he had his future ahead of him; soft breasts to make him forget that he worked in a factory where the foreman assigned him and los morenos and all the other people of color all the shitty jobs. He needed a woman to make him forget that his mother's wish that he become a great man was more fantasy than dream. A girl to help him believe in himself, that he could sobrevivir, that he would prevail.

These women could be found everywhere. She was whomever to Aníbal: an older woman he met on the plane up from some-place, PR; a girl in a tight skirt walking down the street, her sweet young ass swinging, Fuck me, Fuck me; various women he sat next to on the bus; an unwed mother with young children he met at the grocery store; another young mother whose husband was a traveling salesman; an assortment of married women who pressed against him at parties while their husbands tossed back shots of rum; the teacher of his compadre's little daughter who smiled at him when he had taken her to school, and that teacher's room-mate. (Ay, that was something he had never dreamed he would have when he was in Puerto Rico, two American girls at the same time. Dios, but he loved America.) The waitress at the diner where he sometimes ate dinner, the barmaid at the cantina he and the boys from work frequented Friday nights, a woman who cleaned the factory. Puerto Rican, Mexican, Cuban, Negro, Italian, Irish, Polish women.

It didn't matter that he couldn't speak much English, it wasn't as if he were going to be carrying on any long conversations.

Still, he lived by his own personal code: He didn't touch the female relatives of his friends and he tried to avoid screwing virgins, not because he was so respectful of a young girl's treasure, but because virginity was a gift for her future husband and he wasn't going to be a maricón and ruin some young girl's life. He wasn't going to be responsible for some pobre muchacha being treated like an Elena he had known, no señor. The scandal when her husband of one night took her back home and tossed her at her father's feet and no amount of explaining, about how she had fallen off a horse as a child, how she couldn't be held responsible for an accident, doing any good. The father had to send her off to relatives in New York to be able to hold his head up at the country store when he went for his nightly shot of rum.

In his first years in the United States, Aníbal yearned for the weekend, for two full days free of overseers and bosses and the lackeys of overseers and bosses, two full free days with nothing to do except fuck women and eat and sleep, days when he wasn't obligated to do a thing except seek his own pleasure. Lazy days, unless he chose to fill them with overtime or odd jobs like working for a friend of a friend, earning a little money under the table lifting cases of beer onto trucks or moving furniture for Ramírez Mueblería over on North Avenue and Rockwell.

When Aníbal wanted to buy a bed for his new apartment, he went over to Ramírez Mueblería thinking to give his money to fellow portorros, para cooperar, to keep the money en la raza, be good for all like everyone always said. But what a cheater, that Miguel Ramírez.

Aníbal wondered why was it always the tiny men with mustaches who, when they got a little power, everyone had to pay? Miguel Ramírez charged 32 percent interest to his fellow

Puerto Ricans, more if they didn't have permanent jobs, and 15 percent to everyone else.

Aníbal said, "Pero brother, no es justo."

Miguel Ramírez said, "You know how many puertorrique-ños sell my beds and sofas and tables to their compadres, furniture still on my books? So, brother, por favor, dame un breakee. But for you, Aníbal, because I know you, you used to work for me, your mother knows my mother, you have a job and are a man of respect, for you, I make a deal: You pay half now and half on delivery. You can deliver it to yourself." Here that mar-icón Miguel Ramírez had a good laugh.

Aníbal's fist itched to smash his face, to give him a little brea-kee, but it was true Miguel's mother knew his mother. Aníbal hid his fist in his pocket and went over to Meyer's Department Store on Chicago Avenue and bought his bed.

In Aníbal's opinion this was the nucleus of the Puerto Rican problem, the demon in the pit of the businesses of his fellow countrymen and the reason few Puerto Rican negocios on the mainland prospered: They hiked up prices so a poor man came out of their stores feeling like a peón with his straw pava between his legs. It was as if he were still on the island petition-ing el patrón for a job breaking his back working the cane, and then he had to be grateful, too, for the privilege of walking like a hunchback for the rest of his life.

At Meyer's it was all business, no pretense that the customer was getting a deal because his father shared a jug of cañita with your father. Where you work? How much you make? What you want? How much you pay? When you want it? Straight busi-ness. No disrespecting a man by talking like you were doing him a favor and wasn't he lucky? Aníbal left Meyer's with his receipt and contract in his pocket feeling proud that he could go into an American store and buy a bed as if he were Rockefeller. That was the problem with the Puerto Rican businessman: He didn't know how to make a man feel like Rockefeller.

Most days Aníbal was glad to be born a Puerto Rican; he was proud of his country, his culture, his island. How much worse to be one of millions and millions of Chinese or to be born in Russia with that cold weather and what everyone said was food so terrible, gracias a Dios, they had el vodka. He couldn't imagine a day when he wouldn't enjoy a plate of rice and beans with a pork chop fried a crisp brown the way he liked it, or when he wouldn't want to stand on his father's land and look out on the mountains that were his country and thank God for it.

There was something about the island that called to him. He couldn't name it, but probably the blood and sweat of his land-toiling ancestors had seeped into his skin when he himself had tended to the coffee trees and stood for what seemed like days picking coffee cherries.

He felt himself to be a fairly fortunate man. Suerte had rubbed itself onto his skin when he was born just like the crushed garlic Mamá had massaged on him once when he developed a rash that no one, not even the curandera, had ever seen before. How he had screamed. Later Mamá said a voice had spoken to her and told her to use ajo. Whenever her husband or her brother Hernán or one of her boys was sick, she gathered up spices and herbs and concocted a cure. Natural herbs and prayer were better than anything a doctor could do; it had been good enough for her own mother and, besides, the priest didn't need to know. She was willing to take her chances with God. After all, she would have the Blessed Virgin to intercede for her because she was a mother, too, wasn't she?

Aníbal was luckier than most of his friends, whose parents raised them with whippings instead of tenderness. He had a

mother whose gentleness tempered her husband's flashes of violence. Papá had always been quick to break off a twig or yank
off his belt, but Aníbal could count on his fingers the times his
father had resorted to such beatings since he became a man.

Aníbal yearned to be the kind of man his father was, one of
those men whom everyone respected, who was master of his
home, his wife, and his sons. A man who was servant only to
the land. If Papá said, Aníbal, fill the thermos for we will be
gone from morning until night, Aníbal would go to el pozo and
fill containers carved from higüero wood with cold water. If
Papá said he wanted coffee, Mamá ran to roast the coffee beans,
waving her hand to cool them faster. She poured the beans in
the grinder, cranking the handle as fast as she could, the water
and milk already boiling on el fogón. When he said, Mujer, this
sopón is too cold, didn't she know it should be served hot, his
wife reheated the chicken and rice soup, sorry she had failed to
please him, hoping that he would forgive her and that the piece
of pudín she had saved for him would restore his good humor.

One of his first memories was of being five years old and
Papá sending him to Tío Hernán's little hut.

"Take your brother. Stay there until Mamá comes for you,"
Papá said.

Mamá protested, saying it was Sunday, and what if a neighbor stopped by for a tazita de café?

Aníbal left his brother with Tío Hernán and ran back to peer
at his parents through a crack in the wood door. He saw them in
fragments—Papá's shoulders, his strong back, his mother's hair
flowing down to her waist, his father's tongue lapping up the
milk from her breasts, milk meant for his little brother Diego.
He didn't understand why Mamá didn't push him away. Later
Papá found him sitting on the ground watching ants crossing
under the bridge of his legs.

He knelt beside him. "What are you doing there?"

Aníbal knew he was risking a beating. "Did you hurt Mamá?"

Papá laughed. "Were you watching us? I should take the belt to you, but you're lucky, I feel too good. What your mother and I did makes us happy. Keeps me strong. You've seen the dogs and pigs do it, right? Mamá and I are just like the animals."

Papá looked so young and so happy, just like when he drank and played dominoes with the uncles. Aníbal wanted to be just like him.

"Will I do it, too?" he asked.

"You're my son, of course you'll do it," Papá said. "One day, many years from now, you'll have a wife, too. You must love other women first, the way I just loved your mother. Now forget about all this and go get your brother. And Aníbal—" Aníbal remembered the stern look he was accustomed to seeing on his father's face.

"Don't tell Mamá you saw us," Papá said.

That day Mamá hummed while she cooked their dinner and when her husband rubbed her ass as she stood at el fogón, she didn't squirm or admonish him to remember the children. Aníbal never saw his parents making love again, but he never forgot Papá's good humor or Mamá's carefree mood. Since that time, sex had been a happy thing for him, a way of celebrating— or when he was unhappy, a way of squeezing a little joy out of his rotten circumstances. If he felt sick, sex could cure his cold or cough or sore throat better than a whole bottle of aspirin or cough medicine. If the asshole foreman started talking his shit about spics, fucking lessened the pounding against his temples.

Aníbal recalled one Friday in particular when he was working his first factory job in Michigan and he was so homesick that he was thinking of going back to the island with a whole fifty dollars in his pocket. He happened to meet up with this little blonde named Suzy Roberts who worked in the office. He had never messed with her because he was only an assembly-line man. Plus, she had a boyfriend, one of the business types. But suerte, the guy was out of town and she was in the mood for some Puerto Rican sausage. When morning came, he swore the bushes looked like palm trees.

It was like that still. If that asshole Mackie assigned him to Area B, where it got so hot that he got flashbacks to when he worked in the ovens up in Michigan, he would get pissed off and need a release. Some other guy might exchange his paycheck for a row of shot glasses filled with rum or pick on some guy to beat up until his knuckles were chafed and bloody enough to prove to himself he was a man. But not Aníbal. He got himself a woman and when he was done, he could play guitar in the church choir (even though he never learned) and give glory to God. Sex was the best thing God created, after woman that is. Forget the birds and trees and flowers and oceans. Forget even Puerto Rico.

Chapter Seven

The night he quit his automobile job to move to Chicago, Aníbal traded a carton of cigarettes for a little slip of paper with the name and address of one Chago Vargas. He got it from Jujú Hebrón, who was related to Chago by marriage—or was his father's uncle a cousin of Jujú's mother—or maybe it was the other way around? It wasn't important. Jujú was Puerto Rican, Chago was Puerto Rican, and Aníbal was Puerto Rican, and that's all that mattered. It was all part of the Puerto Rican system of dando la mano, of helping one's fellow portorro out because the day would surely come when you would need help, too. Aníbal went over to Chago's apartment the same day he came in from Michigan, which was the same day that Aníbal decided two things: He would never again work in a hot oven or pick crops for anyone other than himself.

Chago said that since Jujú had referred him, Aníbal could wait until he got a job to pay room and board, but his wife, Ana, loosened the bills from his fingers. Aníbal had no complaints. He had his own cot with clean sheets each week and two bedspreads for winter. He didn't mind the noisy dinners with Chago and Ana and their kids. The louder it got, the harder it became to hear the restlessness that hummed inside him. Ana liked to joke that she had two husbands, Aníbal to fix the leaky faucet or rearrange the living room furniture the way she liked it—never complaining—and Chago to give her esa cosa. (Here she was in the kitchen talking to her girlfriends, marking off her husband's instrument at her elbow.)

Aníbal couldn't help but envy Chago's bounty. His apartment, his wife, Ana María, with her peasant's body: short, hipless, and heavy-breasted, dedicated to fulfilling her husband's needs and to caring for their children, Chagito and Anita. Every night Ana served her husband's plate of rice and beans and meat first, and then Aníbal, before she served the children and, finally, herself.

Chago told Aníbal his sad story: He had just returned to the mainland after burying his only brother, who was killed over a woman. One of those putas who hung around the bars in San Juan sucking the life out of a man as well as his money, he told Aníbal in a voice destined never to go above a whisper, the result of a childhood infection that, gracias a Dios, had spared all major bodily functions. And, brother, things are bad back home, a man can't get a decent-paying job—not unless he's American. The only thing the fucked-up Puerto Rican can do is work the cane and, hombre, I ain't doing that shit again.

"Me, too, hermano," Aníbal said. "I'm fucked if I ever work the cane again."

Chago became Aníbal's brother, but he could never think of Ana as a sister. He hadn't any sisters and couldn't forget that she was no relation to him, a woman who with the fragrance of her rose-perfumed bathwater drove him to the solitary respite of his bed.

On Friday nights he and Chago went drinking after work. Lately Aníbal found it took three beers to quiet the ache inside him. Four were even better. Only fucking a woman could make it disappear, at least for a while. The one time he had gone over his limit, he and Chago had tumbled down five steps, waking the neighbors, two drunks singing country songs, crying for the beautiful island that had failed them.

One Friday, Ana refused to allow her husband in her bed, so Aníbal dropped Chago onto the living room sofa. Chago's legs hung over the armrest, his work boots dripping muddy water on the floor. Ana stopped cursing only after Aníbal pulled off the boots and set them on an old towel used as a doormat. When Ana bent over her husband with a blanket, Aníbal's gaze traveled up the length of her bare legs, taking in the flimsy cotton of her nightgown. He put his coat back on and told Ana he was going to visit a friend.

"A friend? At two o'clock in the morning? I know what these friends are," she said.

After that night Aníbal knew his time was up at Chago's. Maybe Mamá was right. He found himself dreaming of having his own home and his own wife. In his dream, his wife had Ana's peasant's body. Three years of sixty-, seventy-hour workweeks, cautious expenditures, his only extravagance a '45 Oldsmobile, seven years old but new to him, had allowed him to save some money—not a lot. Not thousands like his mother thought, but still, enough to rent his own place.

Ana helped him find an apartment. You couldn't just look in the papers under APARTMENTS, not if you were Puerto Rican. She knew someone in the building—the landlord was a polaco who didn't mind renting to the race for a price—who told her of a one-bedroom apartment more than big enough for Aníbal and for the wife that he should get himself, because, after all, what was a man without a good woman? It was fine for Aníbal to have himself a little fun, but after a while he needed to settle down with a nice girl or la gente would start talking about him, you know how people are, saying there must be something funny about him. Funny about him? At this Aníbal laughed, as did his friend's wife. Still, Aníbal, do yourself a favor and get yourself a good woman who can cook and take care of you. Chago lent him a cot until he bought himself a bed, saying, That should be good enough for two, brother. Aníbal didn't need much for he didn't intend to do more than sleep there. He arranged to go to Chago and Ana's for most of his dinners. Ana gave him a pot or two and a couple of cups and dishes, plus some coffee and a colador, and he slipped her a few dollars.

"Let's knock on the door downstairs," Ana said. "I know la doña who lives there. I'll introduce you."

He was too polite to say, Por favor, no doñas. He didn't want any little old lady spying on him through her peephole, noting when he came home drunk or had him a woman.

Pero, ay bendito, the woman who opened the door was his ideal: dark and full-breasted, like none of the little old doñas that he had ever known.

"I didn't know you moved in with your mother," Ana said.

"I didn't," the woman said. "A daughter can visit her mother without announcing it to the world, can't she?"

Ana said something else, but Aníbal wasn't listening.

So this wasn't Doña Petra. He could have guessed it by her breasts.

"Mami is out. Come in and wait for her," the woman said.

"I can't," Ana said, with that smugness a woman has when she has a husband and the other woman doesn't. "My husband is waiting for his dinner. Dios libre that he serve himself!"

"Don't let me keep you from your chores." The woman smiled, flashing the gap between her front teeth, and Aníbal imagined brushing his tongue against it.

Her name was Marta Muñoz. Aníbal would learn it later from her very own lips in between his kisses. He had driven Ana home, declining to stay for dinner, insisting that he had another compromiso. Ana had scoffed, saying, I know what these compromisos are.

Aníbal stopped to buy Coca-Cola and rum. He had turned the landing leading up to his apartment when he saw her sitting in the corner with a brown grocery bag on her lap.

Marta held a finger to her lips then pointed down. "My mother is downstairs."

"I'm surprised to see you," Aníbal said.

"Are you?" she asked.

He smiled.

"I thought you must not have any groceries." She stood and picked up the bag.

"You're a good cook?"

"I'm better at other things," she said.

Aníbal dug in his pocket for his key. It slipped between his fingers. Finally, he opened the door and took the groceries from her.

Marta walked into the living room. She stopped in front of the cot Aníbal had set up in the middle of the large empty room. "The bed's here. That's good."

"Why?" He didn't give a shit why, only that her blouse had three buttons and he could have it off in as many seconds.

"My mother is a light sleeper. Her bedroom is under yours," she said.

He stared at Marta, not comprehending. Tonight Aníbal was a little dense, a little like the stereotypical jíbaro, the country bumpkin just off the plane, not understanding the language and out of step with mainland city ways.

She laughed at him, smoothing his shirt with her fingers. "We wouldn't want to wake her."

Aníbal set the grocery bag in one of the bookshelves built on either side of the fireplace. He didn't have a table and the pantry was all the way in the kitchen. He stuck his hand up beneath her skirt.

"The windows," she said. They looked at the windows, without shades or curtains.

"It's dark," Aníbal said.

"Still," Marta said.

"Don't worry, we won't be standing long," he said.

Chapter Eight

November 1952

Two months: sixty nights of Marta, Marta, Marta. Coño, but that woman could suck the juices out of a man and leave him wondering if he were still alive. It was too much fucking togetherness. Every night when he came home there she was, sitting on the landing waiting for his ass, waiting to get into his pants. Hombre, but in the beginning, yes, in the beginning it was fucking good. The best he ever had, but after a while, even the best gets damn boring when you have it every single day, ¿tú sabes? With a regular woman he could take a break, Fridays, at least, and go drinking with his compais as God wanted man to do. Pero, no, that condenada Marta had to meet him at the bar—the woman fucking drank, too. Bueno, he could admit it, he was of that class of man who didn't think it looked right to have his woman clutching a beer bottle. Some things were for the man to do and some things for the woman.

The problem was that Marta didn't see things like that, divided like that, this for him and that for her, no, Marta didn't see that. She wasn't the kind of woman a man brought home to Mamá, no, not Marta. And that was good in some ways and bad in others. Still, maybe he should do what his compais told him to do and just shut the fuck up, every man wished he had it so bad, doing it regular to a woman like Marta, so jugosa. He should just go about his fucking business and shut the fuck up.

He was almost relieved when Mamá wrote him two letters in one month asking him to come home.

"Hijo, when are you coming home? If you come now you can help with the coffee harvest. Your father is not the young man he used to be and what with your brother Diego working elsewhere, it's difficult for him and your tío Hernán to pick the coffee beans in time. Tío Hernán isn't a young man, either. While you're here, you can see the Hidalgo girl. I'll expect you."

Aníbal knew one thing for sure, he wasn't planning to visit this girl, what was her name again? The Hidalgo girl. He was satisfied with things just as they were. Sometimes, after they had sex, Marta and he would joke about the little Hidalgo girl his mother was so keen on.

"Do you think she has a big nose?" Marta asked. "I've seen plenty of those Puerto Rican Españoles and they all have long, pointy noses."

"Better than long, pointy feet," Aníbal said, pulling on her toes.

"Seriously, are you going to see her?"

"Who?"

"This Hidalgo girl."

"I'll be too busy picking coffee cherries," Aníbal said.

"That better be all you'll be doing," Marta said.

"Same for you," Aníbal said.

"You won't see her?" Marta said.

"Not if I can help it," Aníbal said.

Chapter Nine

Puerto Rico was the way Aníbal had left it, the poor man's heaven on the ocean. The sun zapped his skin of any moisture he had brought with him. Tío Hernán had driven three hours to the San Juan airport to pick him up. His uncle gathered him in his arms with the same ease he lugged heavy crates of vegetables onto his truck. Aníbal hadn't given his uncle much thought in the years he had been away and now the times Tío Hernán had carried him as a little boy on his back through the fields, the sweets he had always kept in his pant pockets, all these memories came back. Even now Tío Hernán pulled out Aníbal's favorite butterscotch. Aníbal realized how much he had missed Puerto Rico.

"You're so pale," Tío Hernán said. "Is there no sun allá fuera?"

"Only a few months of the year," Aníbal said.

"You've never been dark like me, but you used to look like you had some blood in you, man," Tío Hernán said.

Aníbal was glad that he had left behind the brick buildings and bungalows of his Chicago neighborhood in the middle of November. He imagined that the palm trees cooled the sweat dripping onto his collar and that the sun dried the perspiration from his armpits before it could stain the fabric of his shirt.

"You're going the wrong way," Aníbal said, pointing to the street behind him.

Tío Hernán was never without a cigarette stuck in the right side of his mouth. "María Lucía said to drive you into el pueblo. There's a girl she wants you to look over at la Panadería Velásquez," he said.

He'd written his mother that he had only a week in Puerto Rico and unless this Hidalgo girl was going to help him pick coffee beans, he wasn't going to have time to see her. He should have known that she wasn't a woman to waste time when she had a mission.

"Que calor. Can't I go home first and take a bath?" How could he have forgotten that Puerto Rico was like his mother's caldero of boiling rice?

"Doña Santiago says she is the prettiest girl in the town and, even better, she don't talk much." Tío Hernán's grin showed off the few tobacco-stained teeth he had left.

"You're sure she's pretty? It's too hot for an ugly girl." Aníbal unbuttoned his shirt.

"¡Coño!" Tío Hernán laughed, and his cigarette dropped onto his lap. He tucked it back between his lips. He slowed down to a crawl and pointed to a blue-frame building.

"La panadería," he said.

"Where's the girl?"

"Inside?"

"How am I supposed to see her?"

"Go inside."

"Like this?" Aníbal looked down at his wrinkled clothes.

"No?"

"Take me home."

"But María Lucía said—"

"Don't worry, I promise you Mamá wouldn't want my future bride to see me like this." He winked at his uncle.

Tío Hernán laughed, jabbed Aníbal's arm.

"¡Coño!" he said.

Aníbal had his uncle pull over so that he could drive. He drove slowly through the town with the eyes of an outsider. Many of the houses and businesses were wood-frame and dilapidated and in desperate need of refurbishing and fresh paint. The town looked beaten down by lack of money and the ceaseless sun and the harsh rains and wind inevitable in hurricane season. The people, too, seemed weather-beaten. They walked slowly, either because they had nothing urgent to do or because in the sun and heat it was prudent to expend energy only as needed. Young men and old men alike stood on street corners or leaned over once-pretty verandas smoking cigarettes or just passing the time of day. Women balanced bundles of laundry on their heads, walking with the dignified grace of their African ancestors to wash in the quebrada that flowed alongside the town, their little children skipping behind them. Shabbily dressed mothers and daughters carried packages wrapped in papel de estraza under their arms, which he thought might contain piecework or embroidery or some other type of stitchery. He had known girls who did that type of work at home for pennies.

All the people were thin, even the round-hipped laundresses. On the very rare occasion of a sighting of a fat man or woman, people would stop whatever they were doing to stare and speculate on the lucky one's life and fantasize about the meals consumed to achieve such glorious girth.

When he turned the corner down a side street, the houses were poorer, shacks really, laundry flapping on clotheslines hung in the small bit of space between the houses. Mulato and negro children played in the dirt beneath dresses and pants and sheets. These were the homes of the laundresses who washed for the big houses in town, for the wealthy with money to travel or to study in Paris and Madrid or in the States. (This, Aníbal had only heard, not being of the class to know someone with such good fortune.) He considered driving past where these anointed people lived, but decided against it. Why wake up any buried envy or sense of injustice? Better to go home to the mountain.

Aníbal drove out of town without regret. At this point of his journey, the road was paved and wide enough for two cars, but once they reached the foot of the mountain, it would turn into a single lane. Aníbal recalled the thrill of driving down the mountain at night with his brother Diego. He marveled over the well-constructed road that one would not expect on an island full of poor people, but then again the Americans—or had it been the Spaniards?—had their priorities.

When Aníbal reached their mountain, he pulled off the road and parked the truck in the brush.

"What are you doing?" Tío Hernán asked.

"Looking," Aníbal said. How could he explain to his uncle that he needed to immerse himself in color, to breathe in the mountain air and the fragrance of the trees and flowers of every variety and color in the rainbow growing on his island; to feast on the limitless vista of blue sky and green mountain, to listen to the insects and birds; that he wanted nothing more than that the splendor that was the mountains of Puerto Rico, his Puerto Rico, might seep into his very soul? This was his Puerto Rico, not the island's fabled beaches or the tourist hotels or Viejo San Juan that he had seen only in pictures, but this mountain, this view, his uncle, his family, his mother awaiting his arrival, this was the Puerto Rico he had carried in his heart the years he had been away. Beautiful Puerto Rico that had failed him and thousands of other jíbaros like him, too. He let the vibrant hues of the countryside, the reds, oranges, yellows, pinks, magentas, greens, and sun-bleached whites of the island, sink into his skin. This was his Puerto Rico. He was home.

Tío Hernán handed him a cigarette and he smoked it, although it was one habit to which he had not succumbed.

"What's wrong with Papá?" he asked his uncle.

"Is something wrong with him?" Tío Hernán stared at him through the wisp of cigarette smoke.

"Mamá said he wasn't well," Aníbal said.

"He's getting old. We're all getting old," Tío Hernán said.

Aníbal drove up the mountain and immediately felt cooler, the heat of the day and the sadness of returning to Puerto Rico as an outsider fading away. The truck's tires kicked up the gravel from the road. He drove with speed and daring, which is the only way one should drive on a narrow road cut into the curves of a mountain. When making a blind turn, he honked his horn. Twice, when he pulled over to let an oncoming car pass, the driver and passengers waved to him as if he were family. This was the way of Puerto Rico. When the paved road turned into a dirt one, he knew he would soon be home. The family's finca was up the mountain, its steep slopes making it ideal for coffee growing. Aníbal drove to the clearing on which his father and Tío Hernán had built their house from madera del país in the traditional cuatro aguas style with a pyramidal roof of corrugated zinc sloping down on all four corners. He recalled how the ping ping of rain on the roof had lulled him to sleep and he realized how much he had missed it without knowing that he had. It was a shock to him to see how the house stood surrounded by coconut palms and citrus and mango and mamey trees with the mountains behind it. There were his mother's pink roses on one side of the house, tarps for drying coffee on the other. He could see the window of the room that he had shared with his brother, the one he used to climb out of to visit a woman, some fulana or another. There was the barraca and farther away from the house the pigpen and chicken coop. He heard the cow but didn't see it. Alongside the house was a small shed where Aníbal's father kept tools like machetes and hoes and baskets for gathering coffee berries and the washtub-like machine he used to remove the pulp of the berries.

He saw all that he had taken for granted when he lived in the countryside and that he had forgotten when he left it. Here, in this house, in this campo, on this island, was his past and the Aníbal he had been. He worried that he had lost that Aníbal and replaced him with another man unsure of where he belonged.

She was waiting for him, standing outside the door in her blue housedress with the polka dots, the same dress she was wearing, the same place she was standing when he left three years ago.

"¡Mamá!"

Aníbal lifted her into his arms. His mother was the sun that woke him in the mornings with the fragrance of coffee just brewed; she was the warmth that drew the family home at night with the promise of something delicious to eat and an ear to hear their troubles. She was the coolness of the mountain nights and the moonlight that wove around them while she told fables of times past, histories of his grandfathers and great-grandfathers, tales of los Indios and los Españoles and the Americans and of great hurricanes, stories of what it meant to be Puerto Rican.

He asked for her blessing and she gave it. He was home and nothing else mattered, certainly not what came before this moment. Later, he said to all her questions, later, he would be glad to tell her much, but not all (because she was the mother of a normal young man and therefore should not be told all), of what she wished to know of his life in the States, of what had occurred since she had seen him. Later.

"Where is Papá?" He knew the answer already.

"The harvest won't wait, hijo," Mamá said.

"Make me a plate of something or other and I'll go help him," Aníbal said.

Mamá didn't say, No, hijo, you must be tired, rest. Help your father another day. Aníbal didn't expect her to and she didn't. He let Tío Hernán carry his luggage into the house while he went to the side where the coffee beans were spread out on a number of toldas made of canvas, the shiny red cherries drying in the sun. Aníbal picked up a rake leaning against one of the stilts that served as the house's foundation. The wood handle was smooth and comfortable between his palms. He gazed on greens so vivid that he had to shade his eyes. He admired the canopy of trees on the mountain and it came to him suddenly that he missed being a farmer. Perhaps he should come back to the island and work alongside his father. He would grow coffee and beans: white beans, pink beans, red beans, pintos, garbanzos, and gandules. Perhaps he should talk to his father about coming back. Aníbal turned the coffee berries over so that the sun could dry the other side. He remembered as a small boy the very first time Papá had poured a handful of the freshly harvested cherries into his little palm.

"Do you know what these are, hijo?" Papá had asked.

"Beans!" Aníbal said.

"Coffee beans," Papá said.

"Coffee beans!" Aníbal said.

"This is food for you and me and Mamá and your little brother," Papá said. "This is rice and beans and milk for our family."

Aníbal popped one of the red cherries into his mouth.

His father's hand squeezed his jaw, forcing him to spit it out. He swatted his buttocks.

"Pay attention. It's not to eat," Papá said.

Aníbal began to cry. He was confused and his jaw hurt.

"Boys don't cry," Papá said.

Aníbal had learned to mind his father's look.

"Now, watch me and do what I do," Papá said.

His father showed him how to pull out the toldas from beneath the house; how to move the coffee-laden tarps out in the sun.

"Mamá will help you until you are older and can do it yourself," he said.

The next day when his father and Tío Hernán left for the finca, Aníbal waited anxiously while Mamá finished nursing the baby and placed him in the coy. Together they pulled the heavy toldas out from under the house and shifted them into the sun.

When Papá came home in the evening, he was satisfied with his son's work. Aníbal felt his first happiness at not only having done a job well but also for his father's praise.

The next morning, after the men left for the fields, Aníbal didn't wait for his mother to help pull the tarps out from under the house. While she nursed Diego, he toddled outside on his little legs. Wouldn't Papá be proud of him when he proved that he could do it all by himself? He went under the house and grasped the edge of a tolda and he pulled with all his might, his little arms pulling and yanking at the canvas. He was able to shift it some and then he gave it one great big yank. Hundreds of berries flew off the tolda and scattered on the ground beneath the house. Aníbal fell back and banged his head against a wood beam. His mother came running at his scream, the baby still on her breast.

He was crying, a great big boy of four. He knew his father would be angry, but he couldn't help it. His head hurt; worse, he had spilled the coffee cherries, for which he could expect a whipping when his father came home.

Aníbal was so ashamed that he came out only when he heard the exasperation in his mother's voice. He knew he wouldn't be able to expect any sympathy if he tested her patience much longer.

He huddled at her other breast, breathing in the smells that were his mother: the slightly sour odor of spilled breast milk, the salt of dried sweat, that smell of woman as yet unknown to Aníbal, and always, the aroma of coffee that clung to her skin.

"Hijo, now you have to be a great big boy and pick up all the cherries, every single one you can find, and put them back on the tolda," she said. "You understand? If you search hard, you can find them all."

"Mami, there are spiders." He was terrified of spiders.

"Better spiders than your father's belt," Mamá said.

"But Papá—"

"Papá will never know. I'll help you after I put Diego down," she said.

After they had gathered the cherries, they pulled out la tolda into the sunny yard and she picked out the clumps of dirt that Aníbal in his ignorance had tossed in with the coffee berries.

After they had dusted all the beans and spread them out in a field of red, his mother hurried to catch up with her housework. Aníbal followed her around the side of the house where she kept a small garden of plants that she used for medicinal purposes such as to cure emapacho, the jíbaro's stomachache. She clipped off a bit of yerba buena for a warm tea to settle Aníbal's anxiety and picked a head of garlic to make a salve for the bump on his head. While Aníbal drank the sweet mixture, he thought of all the coffee cherries glistening in the sun like red pebbles.

Aníbal turned over the beans with the rake. His father had

devised a way to stack the toldas in layers and store them under-
neath the house at night to protect the coffee beans from dew
and rain. In the past, Aníbal's father had talked of a building to
house the coffee beans. He had imagined trays to lift in and out
of the shed on coasters and moved outside to sun-dry and then
rolled back inside just like in the big coffee plantations. Papá
dreamed of the day when he could plant more coffee trees and
reap a bigger harvest (if God was good and didn't send any more
hurricanes) to provide for his sons' future and their families.

The clothes Aníbal had left behind, his farmer's uniform of cotton pants and long-sleeved shirt, were there on the bed under
the mosquito netting, freshly washed and pressed. He and his
brother had long teased their mother about why they needed
clean clothes only to get them dirty again working on the farm.
And why did they need to be ironed and starched? It wasn't as
if they were going to a dance. Mamá would shake her head and
say that it gave her satisfaction and even pleasure to send out her
men in clean clothes. Papá and the boys learned to let her be and,
perhaps, to themselves, they might concede pride that they were
so well cared for.

Mamá had the gift for healing. When they were children,
Mamá took them to the Americans' free clinic for vaccinations
against malaria and tuberculosis, but for common illnesses she
looked outside to her plants. Diego had once suffered from an
eye infection that caused his eyes to be swollen shut and she had
gathered herbs from her garden and crushed them en el pilón,
adding a few drops of Spanish olive oil. She massaged the concoction into his forehead and soon Diego could open his eyes
again. When her boys were teething, she brewed tisanas by
steeping grama blanca or alumbre in boiling water and coax-
ing the suffering child to drink the cooled liquid from a spoon.

She plucked the pink petals of the passionflower that grew on a vine to brew parcha juice to lower Tío Hernán's blood pressure. For fevers, she made a variety of teas from quinio del pasto and menta leaves or applied compresses to feverish skin made from eucalyptus or camphor leaves. A drink made from salvia was said to draw the blood to the feet. She mixed coconut milk with special healing herbs to break up a neighbor's gallstones. Jenibre amargo was good for arthritis. When Papá's cow gave birth, Mamá boiled tautua, using it to apply warm compresses to the cow's teats to draw out the milk and ease inflammation. Garlic eased toothaches and earaches and cured fungus and even impotence.

But Mamá's specialty was the healing of stomachaches and diarrhea, which were common in the countryside, with its propensity for hookworm and dysentery. Aníbal and his brother were always complaining of stomachaches and Mamá would cure them with té and juice made from mint leaves or rose petals or ginger or majorana, which had a sour taste. Mamá also added pasote to warm water to rid her sons of parasites. She would boil the roots and leaves of recao and make them drink the cooled water to fight flu or pneumonia. Before Aníbal worked the cane, his favorite remedy had been a guarapo of yerba buena steeped in warm milk and a little sugar.

When Aníbal and Diego walked barefoot through the fields and cut their feet on rocks or scratched their legs against bushes or branches, Mamá would swab the wounds with mercury or iodine, which she bought in small bottles from the town's pharmacy. Sometimes they scratched a bee or mosquito bite and infected it with their dirty fingers, and Mamá cleansed the bite with salt water or rubbing alcohol. One day while helping Papá plant gandules, Aníbal had stepped in an ant nest and the ants had crawled up his pant leg. Mamá had picked leaves from the annatto tree, removing the tiny seeds and boiling them in lard to draw out the red dye. She mashed the seeds with a spoon, staining the lard an orange-red, then used a leaf to smooth the cooled mixture over the bites on Aníbal's skin. How everyone had laughed at his red leg.

Aníbal had grown up thinking Mamá could cure anything.

When he went into the kitchen, the table was a garden of herbs: heads of garlic; piles of green, red, and aji peppers; and bunches of cilantrillo, recao, oregano, and Spanish onions. He moved aside the jars of salt and black pepper and sat down. "Mamá, it looks like you're cooking for the whole countryside," he said.

"Or maybe for a special occasion?" She gave him a knowing smile.

Mamá stood at the kerosene stove exactly as he had imagined her, especially those first lonely days away from home. He had sent her gifts from the States: a pair or two of shoes, a handbag for Mass. The first time he had entered a Sears department store was to buy a few yards of cloth for his mother. Intimidated by the well-dressed salesladies, he was about to leave when one spoke to him. He looked into her kind eyes and told her how he wanted something pretty to send to his mother, something with flowers. He left the store with the package of blue fabric under his arm, thankful that there were other women on earth like his mother.

Mamá brought him a plate of rice and beans and empanadas de bacalao.

He looked up at the shelf at the half dozen glass jars filled with dark brown liquid—mabí bark fermenting. Mabí was a refreshing drink and good for the kidneys.

Mamá poured beans into the coffee grinder and turned the handle, the beans rattling in the grinder. She pulled out the little drawer with ground coffee, filled the cotton colador then poured boiling water through it.

"You still don't drink sugar with your coffee?" She smiled at him, sure of his answer, wanting only to hear her son speak even if it was a single word.

"Never," he said. Since the first time that he had cut sugarcane, he had not had sugar in his coffee. With the taste of sugar, he was in the cane field, tall stalks looming eighteen feet high over him and rats scurrying about his feet. With the taste of sugar, he was breathing cane dust; his lungs became constricted and he would start to wheeze, the weight of the machete heavy in his hand. With the taste of sugar, his back ached from constantly stooping to grab the cane, sharp pain stabbed his shoulders from swinging the heavy blade, sugarcane stalks pricked and cut his palms and wrists, cane silk threaded beneath his fingernails. With the taste of sugar, the sun beat down on his head, his shirt stuck to his sweaty back, and Papá's old shoes chafed his ankles.

With the taste of sugar, he was twelve years old again with Papá waking him up before dawn saying, "Today we work the cane."

"Now listen, son. You follow behind me and you go only as fast as I go. There is a rhythm to cutting the cane," Papá had said. "You have to pace yourself. You don't want to faint among the stalks."

Aníbal had sat on the edge of his cot while his father used plant twine to tie his shirtsleeves to his wrists and his pant legs to his ankles.

"It's so tight," Aníbal said, thinking he would soon wake from the nightmare.

"Better tight than a snake crawling up your leg," Papá had said.

Mamá cut a piece of bread for him, telling him, that it was the very last loaf and that if he wanted to eat more bread while he was in Puerto Rico then he had to go down to town and get some at la panadería. This time he should go in instead of driving by. Of course, Hernán had told her! How could he buy bread unless he entered the shop? And while he was there, he might as well get himself a wife, save him time and her worry.

He laughed. "Mamá, por favor, I've been home five minutes. Besides, why do you worry? I can take care of myself."

"Oh, yes," Mamá said, "I know how you men take care of yourselves."

Perhaps Mamá had heard something here or there from people they had in common. Of course, she couldn't know about Marta and that thing she had done to him so that he wouldn't forget her. He felt himself get hard thinking about her tongue, how it had burned his skin, how he had gushed into her mouth. He shifted in his chair. He worried that his mother could read his mind.

Standing outside his parents' house, Aníbal filled his lungs with the scent of Puerto Rico, his Puerto Rico. He plucked a mint leaf and brought it to his nose. He remembered the time a pig had gotten loose in Mamá's garden, trampling what it didn't eat. Mamá had been so furious that she had taken out her anger in the machacando of garlic and herbs in the mortar and pestle and, later, in the slashes she made in the pig's skin to tuck in the fragrant mixture. That had been one delicious-tasting pig.

He stood in his mother's garden, entranced by the distinct aromatic fragrance of the herbs and the sweetness of the roses and mesmerized by the mountain vista. How could it be that only hours ago he had stood in front of the sidewalk of his brick apartment building waiting for Chago to take him to the airport, shivering from the cold?

"¡Aníbal!" Mamá leaned out the kitchen window. "Why are you standing in my garden? Your father is expecting you."

Aníbal picked coffee cherries and swatted mosquitoes and other insects in the shade of a plantain tree. He tried to ignore the ache in the back of his head from tilting his head up to reach the branches.

Papá glanced in Aníbal's basket, judging the quantity of berries. "What do you think, Hernán?"

"Not bad for a gringo." Hernán slapped Aníbal on the back.

"Let's go home. Hernán will take care of the beans," Papá said.

Aníbal thought how Papá didn't seem as tall as when he left. They walked down the mountain in silence, stopping to survey the coffee trees, the cultivated patches of beans and corn and root vegetables and tobacco. This was Puerto Rico, his Puerto Rico. He swallowed; his throat hurt. Maybe he was catching cold.

Chapter Ten

He saw the Hidalgo girl through the glass waiting on a customer. No one who knew him, thank God, or by midafternoon busybodies would be adding their own conclusions along with sugar to their coffee. He gripped the brim of his hat. He was a grown man who had been with his share of women, a few more than allotted to the average man, some of his compadres might say, yet here he was uneasy about buying bread. He didn't understand his nervousness because all he had promised his mother was that he would buy bread. He had even warned Mamá that if he didn't like the look of her, if her teeth were rotting or missing, as was often the case with these malnourished girls, or if she had that pinched or sour look that sometimes these poor little jamonas developed from years of deprivation and not much expectation, well, then he would just buy the bread and go about his business. Was that understood, Mamá? His mother agreed that he was doing all she could expect or even want and then she kissed him. Yet she didn't fool him. She could be a determined woman, but Aníbal meant to resist her entreaties. After all, he was not in need of a wife.

Aníbal pushed open the door. A little bell announced his

entrance, but the girl was counting change into a customer's hand and didn't look up. Aníbal examined her as if she were a thing to be bought. She was less delicate than she appeared at first glance and didn't look like she would break when he made love to her; her limbs were long and her shoulders wide like a girl used to fetching and carrying. Two fans whirled on the counter losing their battle with the heat escaping from the ovens in the back room. The customer left, but not before she took in Aníbal's crisp shirt and the knife pleats on his pants that his mother had ironed only that morning.

The girl's shiny forehead put him in mind of Vaseline. She tucked a curl into the blue-and-white scarf she had wrapped like a headband around her forehead. Aníbal's gaze followed the line of her bare arm to the perspiration mark on her white blouse. The dark stain of an old burn marred her wrist, and he felt an unexpected longing to press his lips against it. He knew the urge to scatter the tiny buttons of her blouse among the trays of cookies and pastelillos like sugar beads. That was when he decided a pretty girl was like any other and he could at least ask her name.

"¿Señor?" The girl looked down at the counter, her cheeks flushed.

Aníbal ordered his mother's loaves of bread, but when ¿Qué más? came out of her lips, he asked for a pound of galletas and another of the little pastelillos de guayaba Tío Hernán loved. He set his hat on the counter and dared a finger on her palm as he counted money into her hand. His words were rushed, unlike the smooth, teasing words he had perfected on a long line of chicas. He needed to hurry, another customer was sure to interrupt them.

"You're so beautiful, señorita. You like movies? I'll take

you to one. Or we could drive to San Juan. We'll go dancing. Whatever you want," Aníbal said.

The girl laughed, giving Aníbal a glimpse of her tongue.

"Dancing in San Juan? That's another world. Are you crazy?"

Aníbal leaned on the counter, his arms crushing the soft loaves he had just bought.

"I'm crazy," he said. She smelled like fresh bread.

She stepped back, wary of his closeness, but he took her hand and curved the fingers into his palm. "Spend the day with me."

"I don't know you," she said.

"You will," he said.

She looked at him with dark brown eyes the color of freshly brewed café, eyes that said to him, Convince me.

He smiled, his nervousness vanished. She wasn't much different from any of the other women interested in his wavy hair, his good looks, his strong body, and the money in his pocket.

"We can drive to the beach," Aníbal said.

"Ay bendito, the beach! I've never been to the beach," she said.

"Never?" Aníbal thought of making love to her on the sand.

"I don't have a bathing suit," she said.

"You don't need one," he said.

"¡Señor!"

He laughed at her flushed face. "Excuse me, señorita. I mean we don't have to get in the water. We can just walk on the beach."

Felicidad thought about walking in the sand with this good-looking stranger. For once, she wouldn't mind walking barefoot. She knew that she shouldn't go with him. She didn't know a thing about him and he looked too confident, too sure of himself and her answers, but, ay bendito, how she wanted to do something! How she wanted to leave this stinking bakery far behind her and shed the skin of the responsible, reliable, hard-working Felicidad and do something different from the ordinary, something rash, something!

She busied herself while she thought it over, rearranging the pastries, the white iced doughnuts in one tray, in others chocolate doughnuts, cinnamon cucas, thick speckled squares of dulce de coco, and guava-filled turnovers with the red filling leaking out in tiny puddles.

"Is it true what they say about snow?

"Why are you asking me about snow?" He hadn't told her anything about himself.

She pointed to the new shirt he had bought over on Chicago Avenue. "Your clothes. They're American."

He'd forgotten how he was a marked man.

"Tell me about snow," she said.

Aníbal wanted to kiss her. "Snow lands on your tongue like cold sugar crystals." For once, words didn't fail him. He was a poet. "Snow would glitter like a blanket of stars in the night of your hair."

She stood there, lips parted, dreaming of snow.

"I finish in an hour," she said, "but I have to ask the aunt if I can go." Felicidad looked down at the crumbs on the counter. She thought of the ocean that she would never see, because she was certain that the aunt would refuse permission.

Aníbal was not accustomed to waiting for a girl to ask her relatives. He looked into her café colao eyes.

"Come with me, I mean you no harm." Aníbal meant it when he said it.

She smiled at him. "It's not that. The aunt is very strict."

"Don't tell her," Aníbal said. It was so easy for him to read the longing in her eyes. He knew that his mother would say that enticing this innocent girl to disrespect her family was mal hecho, that he should know better—but right now he didn't give a shit what the aunt thought, or even his mother.

"I'll be waiting for you outside," he said.

The bell chimed. A woman dressed in black paused in the doorway, assessing Aníbal with eyes that had endured seventy years of bad luck and expected a few more before she was finished.

Aníbal gathered up the loaves of bread and bags of galletas and pastelillos.

As if Aníbal weren't there, the old woman started her inquisition. "And who is that young man? ¿Tu novio?"

"I don't have a novio, Doña Tasio," the girl said.

"Uh-huh. Does your aunt know of him?" The old lady took in the girl's pink cheeks.

Aníbal was outside when he realized they hadn't exchanged names.

Chapter Eleven

Felicidad climbed into the truck. Aníbal got a glimpse of her thigh. Tiny roses embroidered the hem of her skirt, and he wanted to touch them.

"I like what you're wearing," Aníbal said.

"I made it," she said.

"You made it?"

"I like to sew," she said.

He drove. It was curious that she didn't seem to care who he was. She pressed against the door of the truck, giggling as the breeze ruffled her hair through the open window. He glanced at her and started to laugh, too. He felt foolish, laughing over nothing. For the first time in years, certainly since the time he left the island for the States, he felt young and carefree and thought twenty-three years old wasn't so old. There had been times when he had wielded a machete or worked in one factory or another that he had thought himself an old man like his father. Now this girl who probably hadn't had such a difficult life—after all, here she was living in town in a comfortable house—this girl brought out the boy he had forgotten.

She didn't ask him questions and so he didn't answer any.

They listened to the radio. Some woman had given birth to a baby in a público while on the way to the hospital and he looked at Felicidad and she blushed.

"Those públicos stop every five minutes," Aníbal said. "No way in hell could she make it to the hospital in time."

"Especially if the público got stuck behind a pair of oxen carrying sugarcane," she said.

"Now the woman's famous," Aníbal said. "That kid is going to be miserable growing up."

They drove out of town and onto a country road. They laughed when they fell behind a público.

"When I was a kid, I said I was going to drive a público. All you need is any old car and you hang out in the plaza with your friends. Somebody needs a ride, you say fine, take a seat, and then you wait for the next passenger," Aníbal said.

"Did you ever do it?"

"Nah, you could spend all day waiting for passengers, maybe not even make gas money. Plus, you need a car," he said.

"You have this truck," she said.

"I borrowed it to take a pretty girl to the beach," he said.

"Gracias, señor," she said. "No matter what happens, I'm glad."

"What could happen?" He glanced at her, noticing how she kept her face turned to the open window.

"Look! There's a man selling coco fríos." She pointed to the roadside quiosco.

Aníbal pulled up behind a público. He helped her out of the truck, and they stood at the side of the road waiting their turn. Aníbal bummed a cigarette. He offered her half.

"I don't smoke," she said.

"Neither do I, really." He could have told her that he only smoked when he was anxious, but that would have been ridiculous because why in hell should he be anxious?

They admired the vendor's skill with the machete, how he sliced off the top of the hard green shell with only a slight flick of the wrist. Aníbal joked that the vendor must have spent some time cutting the cane. The vendor and his customers reminisced about the sugarcane harvest, of the days when they got up before dawn with their fathers and brothers to walk to the cane fields. Except for the público driver, every single one of them at one time or another had worked the cane.

Aníbal and the men lamented about how there was no work in Puerto Rico, how the Americans and the high-class Puerto Ricans were the only ones making any money, like that wealthy rum family living up on the big hill in town, who drove identical fancy cars so that the men cutting their sugarcane would think it the same car. They didn't want to flaunt their wealth over their workers earning twenty-five cents a day and that paid in script. Aníbal said, Hey, you own one fancy car in a land where you work from sunup to sundown and still can't fill your family's belly with rice and beans, then you're rich, no two ways about it. Yup, the men agreed, these American companies worked hand in hand with the rich Puerto Ricans and they had the people by the short hairs, pardon the expression, señorita. Was it better on the mainland, they asked Aníbal, who said that the Americans still had the Puerto Ricans by the short hairs even up there. The Puerto Rican governor, was he doing any good? The men shrugged. It was all in the way one looked at it, they guessed.

Aníbal handed the girl a coco frío and led her back to the truck. He honked at his compatriots who were still discussing the government, the greedy American businessmen, and, worse, the Puerto Ricans who were traitors to the race, getting rich off their fellow countrymen. Aníbal joked that maybe he had started a revolution or something.

She drank coco frío the way his mother prayed, eyes closed, and with a look of complete transcendence. He shook his head, wondering what was so great about it. Yes, it was cold, yes, it was coconut water splashing down your parched throat, but it was just liquid, and too sweet at that.

He stared at her lips glistening wet and thought that he would like to be a coco frío.

Felicidad opened her eyes and wiped her lips with the tips of her fingers.

She turned to Aníbal and held out her hand. He took it.

"Felicidad Hidalgo," she said. "I'm happy to know you."

"Aníbal Acevedo," he said. "I never knew a Felicidad before."

"It was wishful thinking on the part of my mother," she said.

"Wishful thinking?" He thought it a strange thing for her to say.

"She meant it as a blessing," Felicidad said.

When they got to the beach, she carried her shoes in her hand. The sand was white and pristine and burned their feet. They ran to the edge of the water to cool them. Felicidad pulled up her dress to her thighs, laughing as the waves splashed against her legs.

"Ay bendito," she said, "was there ever such a day?"

"Ay bendito," he said, staring at her legs.

They sat under the shade of a coconut palm tree, their feet buried in the white sand, their clothes drying in the sun. Aníbal felt the sting of salt water on a scratch on his arm, but he welcomed it as proof he was not dreaming. The beach was deserted except for an American family with young children collecting seashells.

"The family went to the beach once on a school break," she said.

"You didn't go?" Aníbal was thinking that every pretty girl should wear a white blouse and that it should get wet.

"Someone had to stay at the panadería." She untied her scarf, and her hair fell down to her waist.

Aníbal wanted to push her down on the sand and take her right then. He would swallow her protestations with his kisses, caressing her until she came to like it. She looked at him with those trusting eyes and he woke up from his reverie. What had he been thinking? He wasn't a brute.

He went back to the truck to get an old quilt and a loaf of bread.

She shook her head when he offered her some. "I don't eat bread."

"How can that be? You work en la panadería," he said.

"I can't stand the smell of baking bread," she said.

"It's like me and sugar," he said. "I hate anything that reminds me of working the cane."

Felicidad moved closer to him. "Is it so bad, working the cane? Every year during la safra, Papi and my older brother would leave us to go cut the cane. I hated when they did that. I was so scared up in the mountain, so afraid of the blackness of the night, and of the Spirits that roamed the countryside," she said.

"Spirits?" Aníbal laughed. "Spirits are a myth passed on from jíbaro to jíbaro. They're part of the past. In this life there is only what you see, what you can eat, what you can touch, what you can buy. There is only the physical and the pleasure that you can get out of it."

"I believe in Spirits," Felicidad said.

"I believe in making love," he said.

Felicidad shifted her hair so that it hid her face.

"Do you like working en la panadería?" he asked.

"They're good to me there," she said. "Tell me about the United States."

He shrugged. "It's a place to live and work like any other. I eat and sleep and make love there like in any other place."

Her fingers played in the sand. Damn, but he wouldn't mind her fingers playing with him.

"How come a pretty girl like you isn't married yet? What is your story?"

She looked up at him then. He felt a little jolt. Damn, she was beautiful.

"There's not much to tell. I'm just a girl who bakes bread," she said.

The sun began to set and they walked on the edge of the water. Aníbal took her hand in his, and she let him hold it. He was beginning to feel as if he were under some kind of spell, something that was binding him to her, this girl without a story. He got a queer feeling in his stomach and thought he still must be hungry. He wished he had thought the day through and brought with him a fiambrera filled with Mamá's rice and beans and maybe some fried pork. The girl must be hungry too, since she hadn't eaten the bread he offered her.

"I wish I had thought to bring a fiambrera filled with my mother's good cooking," he said.

"I used to fill the fiambreras for my father and brothers," she said.

"Maybe we should find someplace to eat," Aníbal said.

"Don't worry, I can go a long time without eating."

They held hands throughout the sunset and then she said that they had better go back.

"Not yet," he said, kissing her.

When they broke apart, she moved away.

"I have to get up early to open la panadería," Felicidad said.

He drove fast, honking at any drivers who got in his way, swearing at a cow loitering in the road. He didn't speak to her and she didn't speak to him. When they reached the town, she began to finger-comb her long hair and he pretended not to notice. He stopped in front of la panadería and she told him not to bother to get out.

She leaned through the open window.

"When do you go back to the United States?" she asked.

"In a few days, after I help my father with the coffee harvest," he said.

Felicidad held out her hand.

He kissed it.

"Thank you, Aníbal Acevedo, for the best day of my life," she said.

She ran into the house next to la panadería. He could see her speaking to a woman whom he assumed was the aunt. He made a U-turn and drove toward the mountains.

Felicidad y Aníbal

Chapter Twelve

The aunt was waiting for her. She examined Felicidad from head to toe, noting the tangled hair, the sun-burned nose, and, especially, the defiant look in her eyes that had never been there before, not in the ten years that she had been so kind as to have the girl in her home. It added to her displeasure. Felicidad's absence had caused her much trouble. She came home to find a note from Felicidad—two sentences, mind you, saying how she had gone to the beach with a friend—friend!—instead of Felicidad in the kitchen preparing the family's meal. She had to send her boys over to the restaurant to procure their dinner, when the boys should have been studying. Her boys were going to be doctors or lawyers, and doctors or lawyers had to study, not run around doing women's work.

"What have you to say for yourself, young lady?" The aunt stood with her hands on her hips.

"I left a note," Felicidad said.

"I read it," the aunt said.

"I apologize for any trouble," Felicidad said.

"Who was he?" the aunt asked.

Felicidad didn't question how the aunt knew she had been

out with a man. "His name is Aníbal Acevedo and he's visiting his family."

"You went out with a stranger?"

"Yes."

"He's from around here?"

"The United States."

"An American! What kind of girl does that make you?"

"Aren't we Americans, too?" Felicidad dared to ask, but she saw that the aunt wasn't amused.

"With your permission, I'd like to go to bed. I have to get up early."

"Not so fast, young lady. Let us go and speak to your uncle. I'm sure he has something to say." The aunt led the way to the living room, where Felicidad's tío Pablo sat soaking his feet in Epsom salt. Felicidad felt like gagging at the memory of drinking water with Epsom salt to rid herself of intestinal parasites.

"Here she is, Pablo," the aunt said. "Your niece just back from who knows where, doing who knows what, with who knows who."

Tío Pablo raised his eyes from his newspaper. Felicidad's uncle looked like what he was: a tired businessman. Long forgotten were dreams of being a musician and going about the island playing el cuatro and singing jíbaro songs.

"Señora, I left a note," Felicidad said.

"A note!" the aunt said.

"It was all perfectly innocent and proper, señora, I assure you," Felicidad said.

"No, *señorita*," the aunt said. "Proper would have been if you had a chaperone. Or had at least introduced the man to your uncle."

"I'm sorry, señora, but it all happened so quickly," Felicidad said.

He thought how much like his sister the girl had grown to

be. He recalled how as a boy, when his mother had spoken of angels, he had imagined them with his sister's sweet disposition.

"Tío Pablo, I'm sorry if I inconvenienced you and la señora," Felicidad said.

Long ago he had given up on getting the girl to call his wife aunt. For some reason it suited them both for her to use the formal and distant señora.

"Inconvenienced us! Young lady, Adela came home to an empty house," the aunt said.

"Señora, Adela is almost seventeen," Felicidad said.

"It's not up to you to run the household, señorita," the aunt said. "Or are you still a señorita?"

At this, both her husband and Felicidad stared at her.

"¡Señora!" Felicidad said.

"¡Mujer!" Tío Pablo said.

The aunt turned to her husband, demanding that he stand with her against Felicidad.

"Do we know what she was doing all those hours with this man? She writes a note and then she takes off just like that? After all the years of feeding and clothing and schooling her same as our own children, and all that we have done for her and her family? What kind of gratitude is that? What respect does she have for this family, for our standing in the community? What will the neighbors think?"

Felicidad wished she could sit down but neither had bidden her to do so.

"What did you do?" The aunt's tone demanded a full confession and no less.

"We drove to the beach and we talked," she said.

"Is he an honorable man?" Tío Pablo asked.

"I think so," Felicidad said. It was better not to think of the way he had looked at her.

"You think so!" the aunt said.

"What is his family name?" her uncle asked.

"Acevedo. His name is Aníbal Acevedo and his family lives in the country," Felicidad said.

"Acevedo," her uncle said. "I think there is a family of Acevedos who are coffee farmers."

"Yes, he said they grew coffee," Felicidad said.

"Well, at least you know something," the aunt said.

"Are you going to see him again, Felicidad?" Tío Pablo asked.

"I don't know," Felicidad said.

"So you risked your reputation for nothing?" asked the aunt, nodding as if, yes, she knew it would be so.

"I don't think it was for nothing," Felicidad said. "I've never been to the beach before."

She knew her answers were irritating the aunt, but, ay bendito, she was so sick of her.

Tío Pablo looked at his wife. "Mujer, have we never taken Felicidad to the beach?"

Felicidad turned to her uncle, thinking she didn't want to dredge up any slights real or imagined. All she wanted was to go to bed.

"Tío Pablo, with your permission, I'd like to go to bed. I have to be up early to open la panadería," she said.

He waved her away with his newspaper. She felt the aunt glaring at her back, but for once she didn't care.

The room Felicidad shared with Adela was pink and white with splashes of blue in the bedspread and curtains. Her cousin Adela was sitting on her bed reading one of the romantic novels that she smuggled into the house between her schoolbooks. So far, she had avoided her mother's detection.

"Tell me everything before I die!" Adela bounced on the bed.

"Tell you what?" Felicidad gave her cousin a sidelong look.

Adela jumped off the bed and grabbed her by the shoulders. "Let me look at you," she said. "He kissed you! How was it?"

Felicidad smiled. "How do you know, you little brat?"

"Remember when Efraim kissed me in the school yard? When I came home and looked in the mirror, I had that same look in my eyes," Adela said.

"You're such a fast little thing! If only your parents knew," Felicidad said.

"Enough about that! Start at the beginning." Adela pulled Felicidad onto the bed. "Wait, first let me lock the door."

The cousins lay together on the bed as they had since Felicidad had come to live with the family. They were more like sisters than cousins and when she thought about Leila and Juanita, she felt guilty and sad.

"I was en la panadería and María Cruzita was telling me about—"

"Stop!" Adela tickled her cousin.

Laughing, Felicidad told her how Aníbal had come in and bought bread and cookies and told her about snow.

"That's a line the guys around here can't use," Adela said.

Felicidad didn't say how he had leaned on the counter, his arms crushing the loaves of bread, or how she had shivered when he touched her palm. Or the way he had looked at her when he called her beautiful.

"He has a car?"

"His family's truck. They're farmers. Coffee," Felicidad said.

"Farmers? Humph." Adela had her mother's disdain for men who worked the land. "All that dirt and those smelly cows and pigs and—"

"Anyway, he's visiting from the United States," Felicidad said.

"Hmm, that makes him more interesting," Adela said. "Is he good looking?"

"Most women would say so," Felicidad said, thinking about how her legs had trembled.

"How does he kiss?" Adela reminded Felicidad of the aunt.

Felicidad got up from the bed. "I'm sticky from the beach. I'm going to sneak in a bath." Bathing at night was disturbing to the boys, who were studying, or so the aunt said. Felicidad, unlike the aunt who chose to delude herself, knew that the boys were men now and that they often went out at night to do the things that men do.

"When you come back, I want to hear about that kiss—and don't think you're sleeping until I know everything, young lady," Adela said.

As she lay in bed, Felicidad's legs ached, but it was a delicious tiredness that recalled her walking barefoot in the sand, the sun on her skin, the sheer joy of being like any other girl. Usually she liked her Spirit Prince holding her until she fell asleep, but tonight she could only think of Aníbal. Her stomach hurt; she realized she was hungry. Not since coming to live with the aunt and her uncle had she ever gone to bed without eating. It reminded her that she was at Tío Pablo and the aunt's mercy for her income, plus room and board, and, therefore, her family's well-being. It took some of the pleasure of the day away. Yet whatever happened, she would remember this day with Aníbal. She didn't know if she would see him again because she didn't have anything to offer him but the obvious. That thought kept her awake for hours.

Chapter Thirteen

Aníbal drove up the mountain much slower than he had driven down. He had to get up early to help harvest the coffee beans, but he was in no hurry to get home. He was young; he could go a day without sleep. For the first time that he could remember, he was in a quandary about a girl. He didn't know what to do about this Felicidad, this Hidalgo girl. It wasn't like in the States, where he could take the girl out once or twice and if they liked each other or even if they didn't like each other, they could have sex and then go about their business. She certainly wasn't a woman like Marta, who chose to have an affair and damn the consequences.

Felicidad was a virgin waiting for marriage and what need did he have for a wife? None. Chicago had plenty of restaurants where he could buy a meal, or he could eat at Chago and Ana's place, and he had Marta—and others, if he liked—for his other needs. He was all set. Aníbal decided that it was only the sadness of her situation that drew him to her. When Felicidad looked at him with those eyes that were as deep a brown as any roasted coffee bean, he wanted to keep staring into them. Oh, he wanted to caress her breasts, too, that went without saying.

They were a good size, not too big, but large enough so that each would fill the palm of his hand.

There was something of the blackness of the night that reminded him of her belief in Spirits. Silly girl to believe in them. So childish. So backward.

He stuck his arm out the truck's open window, and the night breeze pushed against his hand. She had giggled when the wind ruffled her hair. He shook his head, trying to get her out of his mind. The nightly clamor of the crickets and cicadas and the two-note chirping of the coquís accompanied him up the mountain, but instead of the usual ko-kee, ko-kee, they chanted su-cker, su-cker.

Aníbal remembered the culture of the mountains and, despite her living in town, Felicidad was a girl from el campo. He knew that people would talk, that he shouldn't take her out again, not unless he had serious intentions toward her. He parked the truck en el batey, which was far enough away from the chicken coop that he didn't wake the rooster a few hours early. He dropped the bread and cookies onto the table. His mother had left a plate of rice and beans and corn on the cob for him and he ate it. Then he went to the bedroom he had once shared with his brother. It amused him to think that he had often crept into the house just so before he went away.

He fell asleep thinking of Felicidad, oblivious to the wet fabric of her blouse clinging to her skin. He could make out the shape of her nipples through her bra. He'd forced himself to look away and concentrate on what she was saying. He awoke with his hand sticky on his penis, the sheets soiled. Shit, he thought, Mamá is going to give me hell.

By midmorning Felicidad knew much of Aníbal's story. Women who normally sent one of their children to buy bread came in themselves to tell her what they knew about the Acevedo family and to find out what they could of the girl's escapade. How did they know? Oh, Celita Guzman was walking her little Mónica to catechism and there was Felicidad getting into the cab of a truck! You can imagine her surprise, and how she couldn't rest until she had fulfilled her obligation to Felicidad's aunt to relay what she had seen.

The questions! Where had Felicidad gone? Did she know this Aníbal, this Acevedo from before? No? No! Well, she should know that he was a picaflor, always one for the ladies. There had been some story of a Sonia and also some Doña something or other he was rumored to have romanced right under the husband's nose. Some say that was why he had to leave the island, because he was running for his life, although it's true that others say that he went like many others seeking employment. Felicidad didn't have any serious plan for this young man? Not that she wasn't pretty and fair enough to catch the eye of any campesino, but there are men who can't be caught, just like some fish. Don't worry, Felicidad, you're a sweet girl, someday a young man will come in and take you right out of la panadería the same way you take loaves of bread out of the oven. But this Aníbal Acevedo, no, they didn't think so, not from what they had heard.

Felicidad served las damas and kept her placid expression firmly in place. When the first one had come in and rendered her opinion about Aníbal's intentions, or lack of them, she had discounted it, for she was an acquaintance of the aunt and Felicidad expected little better. But after an entire morning of such predictions coupled with the aunt's "I told you so," she fought self-pity. She told herself that Aníbal had made her feel like a beautiful woman and that was worth all these bochincheras and even the aunt's smug satisfaction. She went about waiting on the customers, but while she boxed half a pound of pastelillos de guyabana with their red paste oozing out, she couldn't help recalling how for a minute, just for a minute, she had dared to hope for more.

Chapter Fourteen

Mamá was waiting with his coffee and a big piece of bread. Aníbal kissed her cheek. Papá and Tío Hernán were already eating porridge made from cornmeal. The men looked at each other and nodded; it was too early for conversation. Aníbal was grateful that he drank his coffee black in the mornings.

"Speak!" Mamá said. "The Hidalgo girl. You saw her?" She was almost sure he had because of the baked goods, but with Aníbal she couldn't be certain. He was as likely to have gone to another panadería before visiting some woman or another.

"She is one very pretty girl." Aníbal hoped that would satisfy his mother.

The men looked up with interest.

"And?" she asked.

"Does anything else matter?" Aníbal ate his bread quickly. Mamá was likely to take it away if she wasn't satisfied with his answers.

"What else?"

"Her teeth are good. I was afraid she would be missing a few like a lot of the girls around here." Aníbal winked at the men.

Tío Hernán laughed, squirting some of the golden harina over his shirt.

Mamá rapped her knuckles on Aníbal's head, giving him a cocotazo. Her son tried to duck.

Tío Hernán laughed harder.

"Stop that," she ordered.

Tío Hernán hid his smile behind a cupped hand.

She poked at Aníbal's shoulder with her finger. "Don't think you're leaving this house until I hear more. The coffee beans can rot on their branches."

"¡Mujer!" Papá said. "That's our livelihood."

"Shhh," she said. "Aníbal was about to say something."

"Mamá, there isn't much to say. She was very pretty, but I'm not in need of a wife," Aníbal said.

"You're not in need of a wife? Hummph! That's what *you* say," Mamá said.

"It was all perfectly innocent. I took her to the beach, we walked and we talked. That's it. I swear," Aníbal said.

"What kind of man would let a stranger take a señorita to such a place? Maybe they're not our kind." Mamá folded her arms across her chest.

"I convinced her to come with me and leave a note." Aníbal hoped to reassure her.

"Mal hecho, hijo, mal hecho," Mamá said.

He could see from his mother's stunned expression that she considered such news much worse.

Papá pushed his chair away from the table. "Mujer, this is all well and good, but today we have more need of Aníbal's fingers than he has of a wife, so no more."

Aníbal stole another hunk of bread before making his escape.

María Lucía sat in her kitchen long after the men left the house. She was disappointed in her son, in her Aníbal. Here she had found a young woman who would surely make him a good wife and what had that sinvergüenza done? Nothing of which she was proud, nothing that was good. Most likely, he had put the girl in a bad situation by whisking her away to the beach without her family's permission.

She wished she could do something to help her plan along. Finally she set to wash the dishes and put her kitchen in order. She prayed to la Virgen and the saints for guidance. She wondered what type of herb would be useful as a concoction to bring Aníbal to his senses. María Lucía decided that they would attend Mass and that Aníbal would drive her. She wanted to take a look at this Hidalgo girl herself and see what could be done about the situation. If Aníbal returned to the mainland, then he would go back with a wife.

Aníbal agreed to placate his mother. "I'll go to Mass, but I'm not buying bread," he told her.

His mother smiled. "La panadería will be closed on Sunday."

"Why doesn't that comfort me?" her son asked.

She sent him to get his good shirt so that she could iron it.

Mamá had already been up for hours before Aníbal came into the kitchen. He had woken to his mother's humming and the clattering of pots and pans.

Aníbal went to the hand pump at the side of the house. He filled a small pan with cold water to use for shaving. A mirror hung from a tree branch, and he set his shaving things on a wooden crate that Mamá had set up just for this purpose. She was not having one of her men mess up her house.

He walked into the kitchen, dressed in the suit that he had purchased back in Chicago at the Sears department store on Irving Park and Cicero.

"Look at you, you could run for governor." Mamá offered her cheek for his kiss.

"You could get three wives looking like that," Papá said.

His wife shushed him. "Don't be silly. What does a man do with three wives?"

"Same thing he does with one wife, only times three." Papá winked at his son.

Aníbal appealed to his father to intercede with Mamá.

Papá shook his head. "I told her to leave you alone, but you know how she is when she gets excited over something."

Mamá refilled his coffee cup as his reward.

"Isn't your father nice to come with us? But we only go to church once or twice a year," Mamá said. "It's not that much of a sacrifice, is it?"

"It is for me, mujer," Papá said.

"I'm warning you, don't expect a wedding out of it," Aníbal said.

She laughed. "Hijo, don't be ridiculous."

"I know your ways," her son said.

His mother ignored him and turned to her husband. "Now go wash up and put on that nice blue suit Aníbal brought you. It wouldn't do for Aníbal to be more handsome than his own father," she said.

Aníbal drove the truck down the mountain with Mamá squeezed between her two men. Papá pulled his hat over his eyes. Aníbal was annoyed with his mother's high-handedness, but he was home for only a week. He didn't want to spend it fighting with his mother.

"That dress is pretty," he said.

"I made it from the fabric you sent me," Mamá said.

"Felicidad was wearing a dress she sewed herself." Aníbal

spoke without thinking. As soon as the words left, he wanted to retract them, but Mamá had to make a big deal of it.

"¿Felicidad? Is that the Hidalgo girl's name?"

"Yes." He decided to speak very little.

"Felicidad. Hmmm. What kind of a name is Felicidad? I never heard of anyone called Felicidad. It's not a Puerto Rican name. It must be a made-up name. It says so much about one's parents. You were named after your grandfather. My tío Claudio died of tuberculosis and I was named after his wife because she never got over it. Your grandmother thought that if she had a namesake, it might ease the pain of losing her husband and not having children. It didn't work. The woman hated the sight of me, especially after I gave birth to you," she said.

"What about the name *Felicidad*?" Aníbal was unable to help himself.

"Perhaps for this girl, this Felicidad, her parents wished happiness, and so they named her," she said.

Aníbal thought of what Felicidad had said about her mother's wishful thinking.

"Is she?" Mamá asked.

"Is she what?" Aníbal asked.

"Happy?" Mamá asked.

"I don't think so," he said.

Mamá nodded as if to say, yes, she had thought it to be so, that the girl was unhappy, for how could it be otherwise with a name like *Felicidad*?

Chapter Fifteen

María Lucía and her men sat in the fifth pew, where she was close enough to hear the priest above the cries of the children and infants, and far enough from the altar to show she didn't think herself so much better than everyone else. The first pews were for the nuns or the women dressed in black: the widows and the old maids, those pobrecita jamonas, reciting Our Fathers and Hail Marys throughout the Mass, their nervous fingers clacking rosary beads. Also in the front pews sat those come mierda people who thought themselves special or better than most because they lived in big houses and bought their household goods mail-order from the Sears catalog or their clothing from Saks Fifth Avenue.

Sitting between her husband and son, María Lucía stared straight ahead like a good Catholic woman whose only thought was on the Mass (never mind it was in Latin, which she didn't understand), not the fact that she had left a pot of rice and another of beans on the stove and she hoped Hernán would replace the lids on the pots so that the flies and the flying cockroaches wouldn't feast on her food.

Every time Aníbal turned around his mother dug her elbow

in his side as if he were a little kid. He fantasized about taking off with Felicidad to the beach again. This time he would bring two blankets, one to lie on, the other to pull over them while they made love. He would go again to la panadería and he would say to her just one word, "Come," and they would disappear. It would be just like with Lolita Chacón, a girl he had gone to school with and whom everyone said had a secret lover. He would be Felicidad's secret lover. Lolita went out to feed the chickens one morning and never came back, making "feeding the chickens" a running joke.

When it was time for communion, Aníbal stepped aside to let his mother precede him. He saw Felicidad. She wore a pale yellow dress, her hair spilling out from under her mantilla. When she raised her gaze to his, he swam in café colao eyes. He wanted to stand right there in the middle of the aisle, taking inventory of her in the manner of a teenage boy: high cheek-bones, red lips, soft breasts.

Felicidad lowered her head as if in prayer, lace shielding her face. He felt his penis press against the fabric of his pants.

Oh, shit, he thought, and he held his hat just below his waist in the casual move he and his brother had perfected as teenagers. Aníbal walked past the communion line and into the church-yard where he adjusted himself under the flamboyán tree.

His mother came out after Mass shaking her head. As a woman surrounded her entire adult life by men, she didn't ask why he had left.

"So you saw her." Papá was grinning.

"What are you going to do about it?" Mamá asked. "Hang around in the churchyard like a teenage boy?"

"I told you, Mamá. I'm not buying bread," Aníbal said.

His father laughed.

His mother wasn't amused. "Let's go greet the priest so we can prove that we know how to behave."

They walked to the front of the church, where various small groups had congregated. Several people called out greetings to Aníbal's parents while María Lucía waited her turn to talk to the priest. The men watched the pretty damas and señoritas walk by. Aníbal was like his father; neither could understand why a man would devote himself to things of the spirit and become a priest when there was so much luscious female flesh that deserved and needed attention.

Aníbal kept an eye out for Felicidad, but didn't see her. For the first time, he gave serious thought to whether she had gotten into trouble for going out with him the other day. His mother would have liked it if he had gone to Felicidad's uncle, hat in hand, and declared his intentions before sweeping her away, but really, that was for ancient times. His mother waved Papá to come and join her little duet with the priest. Aníbal, thankful she hadn't called him, too, leaned against the trunk of a poinciana tree, grateful for the shade of its feathery leaves.

He contemplated when his mother's letters had begun to change, when their tone became more insistent. Here he had been in Puerto Rico a few days and no one had mentioned his father's health. And why wasn't his brother Diego helping with the harvest, too? Diego was working on the island. It would have been easier for him to come home. Aníbal suspected that it had all been part of a ploy to find him an adequate wife. His mother must have heard something about his life in the States, perhaps something about Marta.

To passersby Aníbal was so still he might have been asleep, but his mind was busy. He felt that the answer as to why his mother was so anxious for him to marry was readily available and it annoyed him not to grasp it. By the time his parents came up to him, he was irritated with his mother and unwilling to placate her.

"Aníbal, your father and I are going into the church," Mamá said.

"Why?" He pushed his hat back and saw her pleased expression and it added to his irritation.

"To wait for the priest," she said.

"Don't be getting any crazy ideas," he told his mother.

"Do you want to know why we're waiting for the priest?" she asked.

"Not at all." Aníbal knew she wanted to tell him. Maybe his lack of interest would make an impression where words had failed.

He tilted his hat over his eyes. What did his mother think, that she could get the priest and then all she had to do was to say to him and the girl, All right, now get married?

Aníbal was determined to get his father alone and to express his concern for Mamá's sanity. Maybe she was working too hard. It was a difficult life for a woman out in the country with no female companionship for weeks or months at a time. He would send a little more money so that Papá could hire a woman to help Mamá, a skinny jamona who was too old or too ugly for his father or Tío Hernán to fool with.

The longer he waited under the sun, the more irritated he became. He was a man, after all, and he could handle his own love life. And what about Papá? Shouldn't his father put his foot down and tell his wife to leave their son alone? Their son who was a man and independent as well: in fact, a son who regularly sent money home. He wondered why he hadn't noticed before that his father left housekeeping and the raising of his sons to his wife, yet did what he wanted when it came to the farm or to his dalliances with other women. Mamá could complain and argue all she wanted, but his father declared that he was the man and had a man's privileges and it wasn't up for discussion.

He heard voices drawing near. He pushed back his hat and

saw his mother flanked by his father and the priest. Shit, he thought, it's really happening.

"Padre Ocasio, this is my firstborn, my Aníbal." Mamá placed a calming hand on her son's arm. "Padre Ocasio knows the Hidalgo girl."

"¡Mamá!" Aníbal could only stare at his mother.

"I don't know the girl personally, but the aunt is very active in the church. She is responsible for the flowers on the altar," Padre Ocasio said to María Lucía.

"So lovely," she said.

"My predecessor's parish spanned many of these little towns and mountains. He kept meticulous records. I think he had some dealings with the girl's family up in the mountains. Yes, Padre Cortez wrote down every little thing. I expect I'll catch up on my reading one day when I have nothing else to do." Padre Ocasio chuckled as if he couldn't imagine wasting his time so.

"The good father is going to be so kind as to introduce us to the family of the Hidalgo girl," Mamá said. "I'm sure you would like to present yourself, Aníbal."

"We'll be able to see la panadería from the corner," the priest said.

Aníbal wondered how something as simple as taking a pretty girl out to the beach could become so complicated. Then he remembered that this was Puerto Rico and when it came to a certain class of señorita, nothing was simple.

He thought of Felicidad's reluctance to talk about herself. He had not given her any indication that he would ever even see her again and yet here he was arriving at her home with his parents and the priest. He worried that once he stepped over her family's threshold, anything could happen.

"Wait." He stopped on the sidewalk. "I'm not sure as to why we're going to force ourselves on a family of strangers."

His parents and Padre Ocasio turned to look at him. "Aníbal, you're attracting attention," his mother said.

He saw that it was true. Whole families sat in their iron-gated marquesinas or on their balcóns, enjoying a favorite pastime of watching people go by. Some called out greetings to the priest, inviting him to come in for a glass of cold limonada or a tazita de café, and to bring his friends in, too. Aníbal's father tipped his hat in thanks, the priest waved, his mother smiled, proud to be in the priest's company and wearing her finery. And so Aníbal walked on. Just one block but, damn, it seemed so much longer than the miles he had once walked to his country school. How was he going to get out of it? Another time he might have given thought to how he, a man who never prayed, was now praying. He would have laughed at himself and, maybe in the future, when he reflected on this day, he would do just that— call himself names like fool, coward, Mamá's boy, and pendejo, which he was, for obvious reasons.

Any stupid maricón would have known that with a girl like Felicidad and a mother like his, today was inevitable.

And that is why he found himself on a Sunday, hat in hand, on the steps of the house in which Felicidad lived, waiting for the priest's knock to be answered.

Chapter Sixteen

When Felicidad herself opened the door, Aníbal realized that she was one of the help rather than a member of the family. He felt protective of the Felicidad he had taken to the beach and angry that he should feel it.

The priest spoke to her. "Good afternoon, señorita, we have come to call on your uncle."

Aníbal felt her gaze flicker on him as she invited them to come in. He wondered what she could be thinking and then realized there was only one thing that she could be thinking.

His parents and the priest entered, but Aníbal paused in the sunlight. He was sure that it would be as warm inside as it was out, as most Puerto Rican houses tended to be. He didn't want to be sweating in his new suit while being looked over by the girl's family for a position for which he didn't want to apply. Once in, he knew it would be difficult, if not impossible, to extricate himself without embarrassing his parents and, what he thought mattered more, humiliating an innocent girl involved unwittingly in his mother's marital game. Felicidad stood in the open doorway, not speaking, a questioning look in her eyes, those dark eyes that stirred something in him beyond his penis.

He looked into those eyes and saw that she didn't expect anything from him, that he could go away if he pleased.

Aníbal heard a woman's voice call out, and he knew it was the aunt. He came up the steps and Felicidad closed the door behind him.

"Why are you here?" she asked in a hurried whisper.

"It's my mother's idea," he said.

"Ay bendito," she said. Her gaze comprehended all. "Listen, while I get the drinks, make an excuse and go."

"I think it's too late for that," he said.

His parents and the priest were sitting in a room squeezed with enough caboa wood furniture to fill two houses. A ceiling fan with bamboo blades swirled the hot air about the room, its motor clicking away the seconds. A man he took to be Felicidad's uncle faced the priest and his parents. A tall woman in a housedress stood next to the uncle, and Aníbal thought, *Here* is the master of the house.

Everyone shook hands and expressed enchantment and pleasure at meeting, as was the usual custom of civilized people, but he saw that the aunt took special note of him. He was left with the impression that he came up wanting.

The priest was saying how these good Catholic people, la familia Acevedo, had expressed a desire to get to know them, how Señora Acevedo had admired the flowers in the church and he had told her how the lady of the house was dedicated to good works. Did they know that the Acevedos also found the bread of la panadería delicious, as he himself did? Here the priest patted his stomach. It was obvious, wasn't it? Chuckle, chuckle. The Acevedos had sent their oldest son, este gran macho, Aníbal, all the way down from the mountain to get some, now didn't that say a lot about their bread? Polite laughter from the Acevedos, genuine from Felicidad's uncle. The aunt? Nothing.

Aníbal thought his mother fortunate in her choice of intermediary. Who better to speak for the family than the town priest?

Felicidad's uncle asked where they lived, for he had never seen them before, and when they said that they farmed coffee, he became nostalgic about his childhood. He told how he had never slept better than in the mountains, with the cool breeze easing the heat of the day. And the nights, ay bendito—excuse me, Padre—nowhere were the nights as black as in the mountains. He still had family where he had been born and raised. In fact, the girl's mother still lived on the mountain.

"What a pretty girl your niece is," his mother said to the aunt. Aníbal was grateful to her. Maybe he wasn't as angry with her as he had thought. "I think she favors you."

The aunt made a face, as if to say Felicidad wasn't beautiful, as anyone with eyes could see. "She is my husband's niece. I am her tía política."

"Ay, I see," his mother said and Aníbal saw that she understood Felicidad's position in the household. For once, he would be interested to hear what she had to say about one of his women. Now that he saw Felicidad again, he thought of her as somehow his—not in the physical way of a man and a woman, naturally— but in an older brother, younger sister way, or maybe as a cousin. Yes, a cousin.

While Aníbal was mulling over how he considered Felicidad, his mother saw that the aunt had little affection for the girl and María Lucía was curious as to why. It was very true that it was dangerous to have a beautiful young woman living in the same house with one's husband and sons. Yes, she would never have permitted such a girl in her own home. She believed that it was asking for trouble. It was normal for a man to want a fresh, young thing, unsoiled and untouched; after all, weren't all women unsoiled and untouched before they became wives? Of course, a husband should keep his hands to himself and so should the sons, married or unmarried, but she had lived long enough to know that wasn't always the case. Why, look at her own cousin, pretty Soledad, who had sheltered her very own sister, the baby of the family, when their parents died, and look what happened: Soon her husband, Oscar, was setting up another household down the mountain for the young girl and his new family. No, it was no good to have another unattached female in the house, girl or woman, relative or not.

Felicidad brought in a tray of tall glasses of limonada. Aníbal took the tray from her. She looked at him, surprised. He saw again that Felicidad was the servant girl. She hadn't brought a glass for herself, but before he could offer his, the aunt sent her back to the kitchen for something else.

María Lucía looked at the girl's uncle to see if she could detect any interest that was nonfamilial, because that could explain the aunt's coldness and, of course, that was important to know if she was interested in acquiring the girl for her own son. The uncle had seemed genial and neither unfriendly nor too friendly with Felicidad.

Aníbal's mother pitied Felicidad more because she was young and fine-boned and didn't seem made for hard labor, but then again, that was the lot of all poor girls. María Lucía had noticed that the girl's hands were red with a number of small scars, most likely burns from working en la panadería. Yes, she pitied any girl who didn't live with her own parents.

While her husband and the girl's uncle discussed the coffee harvest and the priest asked Aníbal about the States, she turned to the aunt and spoke in a voice that welcomed confidences.

"You have children of your own?" María Lucía doubted it. La señora appeared to lack maternal instinct.

"Oh, yes. Twin sons. They returned to the university only

this morning. They're going to be doctors or lawyers," the aunt said. "And a daughter, too. She'll be home in a little while. She's visiting a neighbor."

"Has the girl lived with you long?" María Lucía looked at the aunt with the sympathy of one woman to another who could only begin to understand how difficult it must be to have to shoulder such a burden.

The aunt gave a sigh and, seeing that María Lucía understood her plight, came and sat next to her, knees almost touching.

"Señora," she said, "you have no idea what I had to teach that girl. Why, when she came to me, she was only a child. Just ten, can you imagine!"

"Ten! So young! Are her parents dead?" María Lucía thought that of course they must be. But, no, the girl's uncle had said his sister still lived on the mountain. She touched the aunt's arm as was natural in a conversation between speakers, especially those of the same sex. A touch conveyed attention, sympathy, empathy, shock, surprise, amusement, any and all emotions: It was the Puerto Rican way.

"Dead? No! But irresponsible, I should say," the aunt said. "They're one of those country families who have a dozen children without thinking how they will feed them."

"Such a shame." María Lucía pitied Felicidad and her family.

"You don't know the half of it," the aunt said. "Why, when I went to get her, I couldn't believe that my own husband's sister could live in such a way. Ay bendito, señora, a ramshackle house that her own husband had built, obviously from bits and pieces of wood he found here and there. A small house, no, a very small house—I'm sure you've seen these houses that the jíbaros build in the mountains—just a few planks of wood and a scrap of corrugated zinc. And inside! A piece of tattered cloth separated the beds from the rest of the house. They all slept in the same room; the parents and the children."

María Lucía nodded. She herself lived in a house made of madera del país and corrugated zinc.

"The woman cooked in one of those lean-tos. ¡En un fogón! Probably, her own husband made the charcoal. No chimney, of course, so the smoke shifts back into the house, making everything all smoky and black. I couldn't breathe to tell you the truth and could not even force myself to stay for a cup of coffee, if my sister-in-law had been able to provide one." The aunt raised her eyebrows as if to add, Which is doubtful.

María Lucía thought how she had cooked on a fogón until Aníbal had begun to send money and they could buy a kerosene stove.

The aunt went on, relishing the sad tale, telling it as if it were only yesterday when she had gone to pick up Felicidad rather than ten years before. "The only thing worse would have been if the house was one of those straw-thatched ones, a bohío, it's called, like in the time of the Indians."

The aunt smiled, happy that she had found a kindred spirit, someone new to whom she could relay her hardships. "I had to set out very early in the morning to get the girl, but my husband had promised his brother-in-law. The sacrifices one makes for one's family."

"Such trouble." María Lucía again touched the aunt's arm, giving her a look that applauded her kindness toward the girl and her family.

In reality, María Lucía felt for the girl and whatever had happened to her family that they had been compelled to send her off. She thought most likely it was la pobreza, the acute poverty that was an affliction, if not an incurable disease, for many island families.

"Tell me, señora, what could possibly have induced the girl's parents to send her away? Was it the lack of food for so many children?"

This time the aunt touched María Lucía's arm. "Well, they didn't eat three meals a day to be sure, but it was more than that." The aunt pointed to her head and twirled her index finger in a circular motion.

"Pardon?" María Lucía said.

The aunt's voice dropped to a whisper. "My sister-in-law became possessed by an evil spirit," she said.

"Dios mío." María Lucía made the sign of the cross.

"The priest had to come and everything," the aunt said with some glee. "Her brother, my husband, thinks that she just had un ataque de nervios. She had an older child who died and at least one stillborn baby. Of course, some women are delicate and have nervous breakdowns after childbirth, but I don't think that was it," the aunt said, as if she were a medical doctor. "Not every woman climbs on the roof"—she paused for effect—"*naked.*"

"Naked?"

"Naked."

María Lucía was too shocked to continue her part in the conversation and was able to respond only with "ay sí," "ay no," and "no me digas" to the aunt's monologue. She was glad la señora didn't need much response. If she weren't still in a daze over the girl's background, the girl she had intended for her firstborn, she would have marveled at how la señora, who had been so distant at first meeting, had become a gregarious windbag full of her own importance.

Aníbal's mother glanced at her son, now in conversation with the priest, who, it seemed, had once traveled to a country called Wisconsin on a religious retreat and was comparing his journey with Aníbal's, although how he could when Aníbal had only been to the United States, María Lucía didn't know.

She was being punished for choosing a wife for Aníbal when that decision was best left to the Almighty. It pained her to learn about the girl's miserable past, but sorry as she was for the pretty girl, she wasn't the wife she wanted for her son.

When her own uncle had told her of the Hidalgos, he had mentioned all the children, and after her own female troubles María Lucía had seen such a large family as an indication she would have many grandchildren. Now she hoped that Aníbal would stand firm in his determination not to marry. María Lucía knew one thing: They had to leave as soon as possible.

The girl came into the room and stood next to the aunt, not speaking, but waiting for acknowledgment as a young lady should. María Lucía noted the proper Spanish upbringing and wondered if it was the mother's or the aunt's doing. She regretted again that the girl's background was so unacceptable because otherwise she would have done very nicely for her son.

The aunt gave her permission to speak.

"Señora, the meal is ready," the girl said.

María Lucía realized belatedly that she must have been in the kitchen cooking. As was the custom, the aunt invited them to eat and neither she nor her husband would accept the expected protests of it being too much trouble or the denials of hunger. María Lucía wished more than anything that she could leave the house and go back to the sanity of her own mountain where no woman had ever stood naked on a roof for all to see, but most of all she wished that she had never heard of the Hidalgo girl.

At the table, la señora introduced her daughter Adela, a pretty little thing with her father's good humor and her mother's keen gaze.

Aníbal's mother picked at the arroz con pollo with

habichuelas rosadas that the girl had cooked, thinking about how Aníbal had jumped up to help her carry in the food, this son of hers whom she could not remember bringing his dirty plate to the dishpan. The girl said that she had to do something in the kitchen so to please excuse her and Aníbal had followed her. Adela and the men laughed while María Lucía and the aunt exchanged glances.

Aníbal sat at the kitchen table while Felicidad made herself a plate.

"You don't have to sit with me," she said.

"Everything tastes better when I'm looking at a pretty girl," he said.

She stared down at the arroz con pollo.

"Why didn't you eat with the others?" Better not to tease her or she might never eat her meal.

Felicidad shrugged.

"You're a member of the family, not a servant. It's not right," Aníbal reached for her hand.

"Why did you come?"

He let go of her hand and picked up his fork. "My mother thinks that you would make a good wife for some man."

She slid her fingers up and down her glass. "Do you think I would make a good wife?"

Aníbal pushed aside his plate. He wasn't hungry anymore.

Chapter Seventeen

As was customary, the Acevedos issued an invitation for their kind hosts to visit them in el campo. Aníbal's father promised coffee fresh from the mountain. María Lucía wished that she had not had to invite them, for she thought that the less they saw of the girl and the family, the better. She told herself that la señora would be unlikely to want to visit a mountain home without running water and a proper bathroom. They walked back with the priest, who called out "Que calor" to people sitting in their marquesinas cooling themselves off with their Spanish fans, but Aníbal knew that, more than an evening breeze, his fellow countrymen liked nothing better than knowing their neighbors' business.

María Lucía went inside the rectory saying that the priest had something for her.

Aníbal took her arm when she returned. "Mamá, thank you."

Her stomach hurt. "For what?"

"Felicidad will make some lucky man a good wife," Aníbal said.

"Are you that man, hijo?" she asked.

"I might be," he said.

Her stomach hurt so much that she wondered if the girl had put something in the arroz con pollo, for now that she thought about it, the chicken had had a peculiar taste to it.

On the drive home, María Lucía clutched her stomach, thinking God was punishing her for the things she was about to say of an innocent girl. Still, she had to say them. As a mother, she could not condone her son marrying into such a family. She listened to Aníbal talk about the girl, how she was treated like a servant, how she was expected to sleep in a cot in her cousin's room, how she had completed school and earned good grades, how her eyes were such a deep brown, they were almost black, did Mamá notice that? He could look into her eyes all day. Mamá, why aren't you saying anything? Did you find out anything from the aunt?

Papá said, "Padre and I had a little thirst for some rum, mala suerte that we weren't offered any. El señor could have used some himself, what with that woman for a wife."

"Aurelio, it's Sunday! Have some respect," María Lucía said.

"Respect for what, mujer?"

"My stomach hurts," she said, "and you and these curving roads are not making it feel any better."

Aníbal said it wasn't Felicidad's food that was the cause of her stomachache. Wasn't she a good cook? Yes, she would make some man a good wife.

"You?" his father asked.

"Maybe," he said.

"Pull over," his mother said.

Aníbal drove off the road. His mother threw up in the brush.

On the drive up the mountain, his father slept and his mother was unusually quiet. Aníbal mused that the aunt, that cold stick of a woman, could make anyone's stomach hurt, and his poor mother had been stuck talking to her all that time. Still, he would have liked to hear all that his mother had learned from that woman;

Mamá was one for acquiring information. He never knew how she did it, living on a mountain.

The truck bounced in a dip of the road. His father murmured a few indistinct words, but didn't wake up.

Mamá clutched his arm. "Be careful, son," she said.

He glanced at her but wasn't able to see her clearly without a full moon.

"When we get home, I will brew some rose tea. That's all I need," she said.

"She's beautiful, isn't she?" Aníbal asked.

María Lucía didn't answer.

The men went to tend to the animals and the coffee beans. María Lucía walked to her garden and plucked a rose from a bush. In the kitchen, she found the pots of food covered and with plenty left over. She went to the shelves that lined one wall to get the stone carafe filled with drinking water. She lit the stove, setting water to boil. When it was ready, she plucked a few petals and dropped them in the water. María Lucía stared at the floating petals. She knew what she must do.

Aníbal sat at the table. His mother bustled about in silence. He imagined that he was back in his own Chicago apartment, in the kitchen without a table or chairs. It had come unfurnished and except for a stove and refrigerator and the bed that he shared with Marta, he hadn't bothered too much with it. Marta. Seeing Felicidad again couldn't help but fuck up his life. He would have liked to put all the blame on his mother, but he was ready to admit to himself that he had wanted to see if she was as beautiful as he remembered and if she still smelled like the freshly baked bread she hated.

He thought of Felicidad in the aunt's house waiting for permission to speak, not looking her uncle or the aunt in the eye.

She had the manners of a girl trained the traditional way, the Spanish way. Aníbal had wanted to ask her why she didn't just go back home and live with her family. Living on a mountain wasn't so bad. In many ways, it was more pleasant than the town in which Felicidad lived, with its hot and humid weather and its poor, dilapidated areas. In the mountains one had forests and pristine air to breathe and lush vegetation and cool, moonlit nights to fuck one's wife. One had the best coffee in the world and every kind of plant growing practically at one's doorstep. When Mamá wanted to make achiote oil, she stepped outside to pluck a few leaves from the annatto tree. He could walk a little way and pick mangoes and peaches and oranges in season. Banana and plátano trees shaded the coffee bushes while lemon and lime trees grew outside their door. He fantasized about living in a house like this very one and waking up with Felicidad in his arms, her hair smelling of coffee. She would make a good type of wife for such a life; days would be spent tending to the land and the children, nights with making love.

Marta would hate it because she was too American, too citified, too used to the luxuries of nightclubs and television and radio and mambo records. She liked the fast life that she could get in a big city, the free-spending men who took her dancing and drinking and bought her presents like red chiffon nightgowns.

If he compared the two women to a drink then Marta would be like a shot of rum going down a man's throat so hot that it burned him, giving him a temporary jolt of well-being and strength that he could get no other way. Felicidad would be like the coco frío she so loved, a beverage that was a little too sweet for his taste, but that would refresh him after a long day, reminding him of where he came from and why it still mattered.

His mother came to the table with two steaming cups of rose tea; she handed one to him.

"I wish you didn't have to go back," his mother said. "If only things were better in Puerto Rico."

Aníbal shrugged. He had been over that when he'd decided to leave the island.

"Do you like it over there?" she asked.

"You get used to it," he said.

"You haven't drunk all your tea," Mamá said, sipping hers.

He would have rather had a shot of rum or some coco frío, but he drank the tea with petals floating in it, just to please his mother.

Chapter Eighteen

Aníbal plucked a coffee bean, thinking it was as red as Felicidad's lips. He worked automatically picking berries, stopping every now and then to slap away mosquitoes from his face and arms and legs. The basket around his waist was almost full. He stopped to pull his hat lower on his forehead and then tilted his head to search for more ripe berries. The back of his head ached. Damn, he'd forgotten that it wasn't any fun to pick coffee. He stripped another branch and then another. It was hot. The sun filtered through the leafy shade of the banana and plantain trees. Another damn mosquito bite, this time on his cheek. Coño, what was he going to do about Felicidad? He had been thinking about her since her uncle's house a few days ago. It was ridiculous that two innocent meetings had caused him so much anguish and he hadn't even gotten anything out of it. He plopped another cherry into his basket; life was a son of a bitch.

Aníbal's mother went about her daily duties without the joy she always felt when tending to her home. After Aníbal had first left for the States, she had cried for weeks, worrying about her son. The years he was away, she dreamed about the day when he would return, when she would cook for him and clean for him and feast upon his handsome face enough so that she could store the image of it away to get through the next three years, if that was how long it would be until she saw him again. She had heard various rumors about Aníbal's goings-on in the States; they knew other families with young men on the mainland. It seemed that Aníbal had been up to his old ways, but this time worse: This time the girls were Americans and who knows what. She was terrified that he would marry one of them. Both she and Aníbal's father could trace their families back to the Spanish and she wanted nothing less for her two sons than that they marry their own kind. Felicidad came from a similar background and breeding, but it was just unlucky that she had the problem in her family.

María Lucía wished that she had dared to make him drink a second cup of the tea, which would have guaranteed forgetfulness, but he was sure to suspect that she was up to something. She had been known to sneak an herb, or a drop of this and a pinch of that, into their drinks to cure this or ease that. She hoped that he had slept well without dreaming of the Hidalgo girl. She herself had slept fitfully, worrying about whether she should tell Aníbal the girl's story, but she hesitated. He might pity her enough to marry her.

That evening, María Lucía called Aníbal to her room on the pretense of seeing to the mosquito bites on his face. She hoped he would offer his plans without her having to ask.

A crocheted runner covered the top of María Lucía's bureau, on which she kept little wood statues of her favorite saints. She had lined candles around them as in an altar and, each night, she lit them. Now she said a special prayer to each saint petitioning for her son to forget the Hidalgo girl. Aníbal had given her a few tonterías from the States, such as a snow globe, and these, too, she had set on the bureau. The iron bed that had been the marriage bed these twenty-five years took up most of the room. At one side of the bed was the rocking chair that her father had made for her upon Aníbal's birth. She kept their good clothes in trunks made from higüero wood and hung their everyday pieces on hooks on the walls.

Aníbal sat on the bed. "I remember how I used to scoot under the bed when Papá came looking for me to give me a pela. He always found me."

"Maybe because you always hid in the same place," Mamá said.

He laughed. "I was a stupid little critter, wasn't I?"

"Mosquitoes can always tell fresh meat." She dipped a cotton ball in a salve of aloe vera that she had made.

"Mami, what do you think of her?" Aníbal asked.

"Who?" María Lucía dabbed at a mosquito bite on Aníbal's nose.

"Who do you think? The girl you would have married me to yesterday if you could have arranged it," Aníbal said.

María Lucía looked across the room at the saints. Which one would grant her wish for Aníbal to forget the girl? "I was wrong to pressure you to marry her."

He tapped her hand. "Let that be a lesson to you. Don't be so pushy with my brother."

"Maybe I was too hasty," María Lucía said. Saint Joseph, Saint Barbara, why are you silent?

"What? Is this the same woman who marched me up in my Sunday best to my intended's house with the priest in tow?"

Aníbal didn't seem to be taking the Hidalgo girl seriously. The saints had granted her prayer, she thought, but her relief lasted only a moment.

"I don't like the thought of her living with the aunt," Aníbal said.

María Lucía recalled the Hidalgo girl's quiet demeanor, the glint of sadness in her eyes, the burns on her hands, and she pitied her, but her son came first. (It was better not to think of the girl by her name. It made her decision less personal.)

"That's her business," Mamá said.

"I've come around to your way of thinking," Aníbal said.

She looked at him, trying to decide if he was teasing her.

"Doesn't that make you happy, Mamá?"

María Lucía dabbed at another mosquito bite on his cheek, trying to decide what to do.

"There's something about her that makes me want to help her. And it doesn't hurt that she's beautiful," Aníbal said.

María Lucía went to the bureau and took out a small bundle from a drawer. She paused in front of the altar and with her fingertips pressed a kiss on each saint. Maybe now one of the saints would come through for her.

"Aníbal, I learned something from the aunt. About Felicidad," she said.

"I won't believe anything that woman said," Aníbal said.

"Do you remember that I went to the rectory with Padre Ocasio after we left their home?" She held out a packet of paper tied with string.

"What are these?" Aníbal turned it over in his hands.

"Letters from the priest. About Felicidad's family," Mamá said.

"Isn't that sacred?" Aníbal looked down at the yellowing pages. Everything on a tropical island got old quickly.

"I think that's only if it's confession," she said.

He looked at the date of the first letter. "Mamá, she was only a child then. What could I possibly learn that would matter now?"

"It's better that you read them for yourself." She untied the string.

He glanced through it. "It's about her mother, not Felicidad."

"Don't fool yourself. These things run in families," his mother said.

Aníbal shuffled the pages in his hands and swallowed hard. He could understand his mother's worry—he forgave her for intruding on Felicidad's past—but Padre Ocasio he couldn't excuse or forgive. What kind of man of God lets the secrets of his parishioners slip through his fingertips? And Father Cortez was no better. These priests, these so-called men of God, who can decide if a woman has or hasn't an evil spirit inside her, they did more harm than good, he was sure.

Felicidad's mother was probably depressed about her daughter's death. Times must have been very hard for the family what with the lack of food and the passel of kids. Who wouldn't go a little crazy? That would drive any normal person on top of a roof. Hell, just the thought of having a dozen kids and having to feed and clothe all of them made him want to climb on the roof himself. He dwelled on this a few more moments, trying not to think about Felicidad, about a skinny little girl watching her mother tied to a tree. Instead he thought about the priest's letter describing how he had gone to Felicidad's uncle and aunt, petitioning them to help their own flesh and blood, and how the aunt had taken the girl and made a servant of her.

He got up from his parents' bed and paced the room. Something must be done! He had to save her from the aunt and uncle, he had to release her from her prison, he had to feed and clothe and love her. Until this moment, he had been undecided on what to do with Felicidad; as much as he wanted to take her to bed, he wasn't sure he wanted to be a husband. He had been teasing his mother about marrying her. Now he thought it best that he should marry her. It wouldn't be so bad, he told himself. She was young and beautiful and capable. She would make him a good wife. She was used to doing what she was told. She would be grateful to him, and every man knew that there was nothing better than a grateful woman.

Aníbal had to act quickly to arrange his marriage before his return to the States. It was necessary to help with the coffee harvest for a few more days and then he and his mother would leave very early in the morning and pick up the girl at her relatives' home. Having his mother with him would ease any difficulty. They would take her straight to the priest. Luckily, María Lucía had already spoken to Padre Ocasio about such a possibility. His mother was nothing if not efficient. Aníbal would bring her back to his parents' home before they had to depart for the States. He had just enough money to buy her plane ticket. Not for a second did he think that she would refuse him.

María Lucía cursed herself for meddling. She hoped the saints knew what they were doing.

Chapter Nineteen

On the way to town three days later, María Lucía advised her son on the treatment of a wife. You must take her gently in hand and treat her with the kindness and respect a wife deserves, but you must never forget that you are the head of the house. You wear the pants. A woman will wear them if you let her. Just look at me, I am a perfect example. Whenever I start thinking that I can tell your father what to do, he gives me a little slap, just a slight pescosa, and I am back to knowing my place. And that's the way it should be. A family can have only one person who heads it. It would shame me if it weren't you, she told him. Aníbal asked her why she was telling him all this, didn't she think he could handle his own wife? His mother said, You have always been one to have your head turned by a woman.

When they arrived at the rectory, the priest was taking his breakfast and they left word that they would be returning shortly for a wedding. Then they went to la panadería, where customers were waiting for Felicidad to take out the freshly baked bread from the oven. She almost dropped the tray when she saw Aníbal and his mother. When it was their turn, Aníbal reached for her hand, which was dusty with flour.

"We came for you," he said.

"Ay bendito." She covered her mouth with her free hand.

"We're getting married right away," he said.

"I can't," she said.

"What?" The nerve of the girl! María Lucía could not have imagined such a girl rejecting her son. Still, maybe the saints had decided to grant her petition.

"You don't want to marry me?" Aníbal was surprised to feel more disappointment than relief.

"I have to work today," Felicidad said.

"It has to be today," Aníbal said.

"Where are your uncle and aunt?" María Lucía peered toward the back of the shop. Surely this girl wasn't expected to do both the serving and the baking.

"I don't think la tía has left for the fonda yet. I will get Emilio to watch the counter." She hurried to the back. Felicidad returned with an old man limping behind her. He shook Aníbal's hand, telling him that he should take very good care of Felicidad because she was as sweet as any of the cookies he had ever baked.

María Lucía turned to Aníbal, who was looking at the Hidalgo girl as if she were his breakfast of hot coffee and fresh bread. She didn't think that her son was taking this step as seriously as she would have liked. A few days ago, she would have been happy with his rashness, but now she could only pray that he wouldn't be sorry.

Felicidad invited Aníbal and his mother to sit in the sala while she went for the aunt and uncle. They could hear Felicidad's excited voice and the aunt's shrill tone and the uncle's deeper one. Mother and son looked at each other with raised eyebrows when they heard the aunt shouting. Aníbal made to get up, but his mother stopped him with a shake of her head.

Make as little trouble as possible, she told him, better for the girl's family back on the mountain.

The aunt and uncle followed Felicidad into the room. The men shook hands and the uncle offered his congratulations to la señora Acevedo, assuring her of her son's fine choice for a wife. He was glad to give his approval on behalf of his sister, but he had one request.

"We must insist that Felicidad visit her family before she leaves the island," Tío Pablo said.

"Aníbal must leave in a few days. I don't know if that is possible." María Lucía didn't think it such a good idea for her son to consort with crazy people, but she should have known that Aníbal wouldn't listen to her. All it took was one little plea from his bride-to-be.

"Please, I so want to see my family again," Felicidad said.

"If that's what you want, Felicidad," he said.

"Now the wedding, when is it?" the uncle asked.

"The priest is waiting." Aníbal dared to look at the aunt, who was standing with her arms crossed.

The uncle laughed. "You are certainly a man in a hurry," he said. "I beg half an hour. I'll run to the school and get my daughter. Adela wouldn't forgive me or Felicidad if she missed the wedding."

"I need to pack," Felicidad said.

"Let me help you," María Lucía said. "It would be my pleasure. I haven't any daughters of my own."

"Mamá, why don't we wait in the church?" Aníbal wouldn't put it past his mother to try to persuade Felicidad to change her mind.

"It would be an honor to have your mother help me," Felicidad said.

The uncle turned to his wife. "And you, mujer, what have you to say?"

The aunt looked at the group with narrowed eyes and pursed lips as if to say, No one asked my opinion so I will keep my mouth shut, but it won't turn out well in the end.

Felicidad's uncle urged his wife, "Go put on your prettiest dress. You're practically the mother of the bride."

It was a pretty little room, exactly the kind of room María Lucía would have wanted a daughter of hers to have. Shutters opened out to the street during the day and closed at night, as was the custom. Mosquito netting swathed a large canopy bed. In a corner was a folding cot, which she assumed was Felicidad's.

"Such a lovely bed." María Lucía sat at the foot.

"It's Adela's," Felicidad said. "We share it. Don't tell the aunt."

María Lucía saw that her son's future wife was a girl really, although no younger than she was when she married Aníbal's father, and she worried for Felicidad. The poor girl was ignorant of what marriage would entail, especially marriage to a man like Aníbal, who had many of his father's entojos. The girl searched for her things in a lighthearted manner, as if she were going off on holiday. Aníbal's mother wanted to ask her for assurances that she had at least affection for Aníbal and gratitude for his choosing her. Her son was somebody, a prosperous man in America, and she, his mother, desired for him a wife in the traditional manner, one who would willingly be commanded by her husband and who would consider herself fortunate to be his wife.

She looked at Felicidad flitting around the room, packing up her possessions, and thought that it was all in God's hands now.

Chapter Twenty

That first night as man and wife, Aníbal had taken her back to his parents' house, where his father had slaughtered and roasted a pig on a spit between two poles. His mother served arroz con gandules to the neighbors. There was rum and there was dancing. People brought musical instruments: guitars—the requinto, the tiple, and the cuatro—and güiros, maracas, and drums. As was tradition, the musicians sang about the jíbaro's love for his heritage and his woman.

Felicidad heard how lucky she was to get Aníbal, such a hardworking man, and successful, too. Felicidad was sure to have her own house, a closet of beautiful dresses that would shame the rainbow, and maids. Maybe Aníbal would give her a young girl to clean her house and wipe the behinds of their children. Was it true that Felicidad had been a criada herself? Pobrecita. Of course, they would never have allowed a girl like her to work in their homes, no offense, but if they could have had one, they would have chosen one of those little ugly ones. One of those girls whose collarbones poked out of her dress and whose stick legs swam in her dead mother's shoes, if she was lucky enough to have shoes. A girl like that praised you to God for every plate of rice and beans you passed her way. Not one like Felicidad with hair that fell to her waist like rainwater. Get one of those girls, Felicidad, but maybe in America they don't have girls like that. No one is hungry in America.

After all the guests were gone, her mother-in-law shooed her from the kitchen. Leave those dishes for me, muchacha. Another time you can be a good daughter, tonight your duty is to serve your husband. The older woman insisted that Felicidad and Aníbal take her bedroom, don't worry, she and Aníbal's father were happy to vacate it for the wedding night. Maybe their first grandson would be made that very night, only God knew. Perhaps Felicidad would turn out like her mother, always with a baby on her breast. Better to be like that than to have woman problems after your second like she had. Ah, well, God's will.

Felicidad lit the candles on the dresser, dipped her fingers in the saucer of holy water, and made the sign of the cross before the wood statuette of the Virgin Mary. She wondered if she should change out of her wedding suit with the pink rose she had embroidered on the lapel.

Where was her husband? When he didn't come, she entertained herself picking up objects from his mother's dresser: half a dozen small wood saints, including Santo Geraldo, whom she recognized because of the skull in his hand; a porcelain figurine of a young shepherdess carrying a baby lamb; a silver thimble; a Bible, her fingers lingering over the smoothness of the leather cover. There was a snow globe that fit into the palm of her hand. She curled up on the bed and shook it so that snow drifted down onto the roof of the brick house, with its circle of tiny evergreens enclosed in a white picket fence. She wondered at its ingenuity, grateful for its beauty. It made her forget her apprehension of a wedding night with a man she barely knew. This is how Aníbal found her on his mother's pale blue bedspread, a pile of white—skin, suit, snow—with flashes of fire—shoes, flower, hair.

She never wore her nightgown because Aníbal didn't give her a chance to change. That night, she had bitten her lip to stop from shouting to the whole countryside the pain of her bridegroom trying to break her in two. She was conscious of her in-laws on the other side of the wall. They must know everything. What else was possible in these wood-and-zinc houses?

Her new in-laws might as well be sitting in their kitchen chairs along the foot of the bed, watching as their son undressed her, smiling their admiration over the way Aníbal sucked her breasts, her father-in-law peeking at her vagina, his head nodding to the rhythm of his son's hand moving over the black curls, her mother-in-law approving when Aníbal entered her, tearing away her virginity, gratified to hear her cry of pain.

Later, when Aníbal buried his head between her legs, Felicidad was torn between pushing him away and crying thank you. She held on to the bedpost and tried to banish Aníbal's parents from the room's shadows, but they stayed, unwanted, in the manner of poor relatives, as the aunt liked to say.

Her mother-in-law shook her head at her son's animal behavior, which he must have picked up from allá fuera, everyone knew how those women on the mainland were eager to open their legs to any fulano with a dollar in his pocket, women who were ready to take those foul things in their mouths or even jammed into their asses like four-legged bitches.

Her father-in-law grinned, feeling the blood gush hot into his penis, imagining his lips replacing his son's, his hands kneading her breasts, her ass, thinking he knew a thing or two more than his son. He would have her nails scratching her name on his back so he wouldn't forget her, pleading, Papi, Papi, por favor. He recalled many a woman who had begged him not to stop. Aníbal was just starting out, and he was proud of his boy, sí señor, he was doing his father proud—but naturally he was the better lover, with more years of fucking than his son had been alive.

And the next day? The next day was como nada. Everyone was respectful of Felicidad. Her skin was sore from her husband's caresses, she ached between her legs, and she had to force herself not to walk with her thighs apart as if his penis still lurked inside her. She caught Aníbal's gaze on her with that satisfied smile a man got when he had been with a woman. I could eat you right now, he whispered. She was ashamed to feel her juices trickle down her panties.

His mother gave her Aníbal's shirt to iron before they set out to her parents' home. Aníbal's mother still ironed in the way of mountain women and Felicidad went out to the yard and heated the flatirons on the logs. When they were hot enough, she wrapped the handles with rags and brought them back inside, setting them on the cloth-covered table. She wiped off the soot. It was unnerving to have her mother-in-law watch her, but Felicidad was used to the aunt standing over her. She felt that la señora's attention was not malevolent, but a test of her wifely abilities.

"It's a miracle that you still remember how to do it," her mother-in-law said.

"I remember a lot of things," Felicidad told her.

She sprinkled her husband's shirt with watery starch. La señora handed her a faded pillowcase like the one that had covered Felicidad's mother's pillow. Felicidad's fingertips caressed its much-washed softness, thinking of how she had prepared for what they thought would be her mother's homecoming, the day they went down the mountain to speak to the priest, how she scrubbed her mother's pillowcase in the river and ironed it while it was still damp. She and Leila had taken turns propping the pillow on the bed until they were both satisfied that it was inviting, that their beloved mother would notice it immediately upon her entering the house and praise their housekeeping and attention to detail.

"Felicidad. You take the pillowcase and spread it over the shirt so that the hot iron doesn't burn the fabric," María Lucía said.

"Yes, of course." She had to pay more attention to what she was doing or la doña would surely think that her son had chosen a woman who couldn't take proper care of him.

Chapter Twenty-one

It wasn't very romantic driving with her new husband to visit her family. For one, Aníbal's tío Hernán had to go, too, because after the one night with her family, there was still the drive to the airport in San Juan and then Tío Hernán would drive back home. It was a lot of trouble, but that was the nature of the jíbaro life. Everything took great effort.

The men anticipated a long drive over the mountains in the Cordillera Central. Aníbal's father recalled how, as a boy, he had traveled with his father on horseback to visit family in Ciales, or was it Morovis? He couldn't remember, he had been so young and it was so long ago. María Lucía packed a large cardboard box with foodstuffs—bananas and oranges and cans of evaporated milk and small sacks of rice and beans and coffee beans—for Felicidad's family. And for the children—plates of arroz con dulce that she had made special for the wedding. She added sandwiches made from the bread bought at la panadería and yesterday's lechón; she knew how much Aníbal loved roast pork sandwiches. Don't forget to give your family our regards, she reminded Felicidad. I hope on some future occasion we will have much to celebrate, she said with a meaningful look, causing her daughter-in-law to blush.

In the truck Felicidad sat between the two men, ay bendito, she felt so uncomfortable. Her skin was so tender after last night, if she closed her eyes she could still feel the imprint of Aníbal's lips, of his fingers gripping her ass, easing himself into her. She was not going to think about last night anymore. Better to concentrate on the present. Soon she would see her mother and her father.

God help her, Tío Hernán stank. His skin emitted the sweat of field labor and the odor of manure mixed with roasted coffee beans and home-grown tobacco. His scent filled the cab of the truck and she was surprised that Aníbal didn't comment or that he didn't stop by a stream and say, Tío, take a swim. She wondered how she could suggest it. Felicidad was used to taking a daily bath. She had forgotten that in the country when one wanted to bathe, one went down to the river or, if fortunate and ingenious, showered in a little wood shack with a pipe rigged up to catch rainwater. Aníbal's family had that option but it had been impossible to shower last night. She had done no more than pass a wet cloth over her skin. Even now, she blushed to think how she had waited until her new husband fell asleep to tiptoe to the basin and wipe herself between her legs.

She didn't want to arrive hot and stinky after not seeing her family for years. Yet they were mountain people, without toilets that flushed and lovely bathtubs that one could sit in and dream until the inevitable banging on the door began.

Aníbal smiled at her. "You comfortable?"

"Very." What could she do but lie to her husband, this stranger.

He stuck an arm out the open window. "It's so pretty, isn't it? You never see so many different shades of green in the United States. Although I once picked tomatoes and lettuce up in California and it was green, but not as pretty."

"Is California a country?"

"A campo in the States. They have a lot of them up there."

She wondered if that was where they would live, this California. As a child, she hadn't had any doubt that one day she would be a farmer's wife.

"Did you like it? Picking tomatoes in California?"

He shook his head. "It's not good for a man to pick any crops but his own."

Tío Hernán fell asleep on Felicidad's shoulder. She tried not to gag. After a while she dared to ask Aníbal if they could stop by a stream or river so she could bathe.

He knew of a river and he parked the truck off the road, alongside the brush. They left Tío Hernán sprawled out on the seat and headed down the dirt path to the river. Felicidad had brought a cake of soap wrapped in a towel, luxuries that she had used daily at the aunt's house. They followed the rushing sound of water and the cawing of the birds to the riverbank. Wildflowers perfumed the air and embroidered the grass. They stood transfixed by a family of pink flamingos tiptoeing across the bank, their stick legs gliding noiselessly in and out of the blue water.

Aníbal held his arms out to the countryside. "This is my Puerto Rico."

"You miss it," she said.

He turned to look at her. Felicidad glanced down at the soap in her hands, suddenly nervous.

"I'm going to bathe now," she said.

"So bathe." He unbuttoned his shirt. She backed away from him.

"Someone might see us."

"Only the birds." Aníbal reached for her. "Querida," he said.

She couldn't help smiling at him for calling her beloved, for wanting her in daylight, at herself for being so brazen as to be unafraid of him, at being married, at going home, at such a day.

They had to stop twice on the mountain road to ask directions to her parents' house. She could only recall that her family lived farther up the mountain and that the house had to be reached on foot. After all these years of dreaming about coming back home, all the nights of praying for it, she was apprehensive now that the time had finally arrived. Aníbal stopped one barefoot jíbaro carrying a tree branch on his shoulders like a pole with a huge bunch of green bananas suspended at either end. The man pointed them farther up the road. Two more miles and they found a boy skipping rocks in the dirt.

"Hey, that's my house. I'm Hidalgo," he said.

Felicidad looked into the boy's blue eyes and screamed. "Raffy, you're Raffy!"

Tío Hernán woke up. "Don't tell me that you hit your wife already," he said to Aníbal. "Chico, you could at least wait a few days."

Raffy climbed onto the bed of the truck, saying how he couldn't believe that this was his big sister Felicidad that he had heard about. He forgot why Felicidad had gone away. How was it living in the big town, had she come to live with them again? Did she know that he had little brothers? And a baby sister? Ay, Mami and Papi were going to be surprised, yes, they were. Tía Imelda la jamona was getting pretty old now. She could hardly hear. Yes, Leila was home, and Juanita, too. Vicente? He had gone to the war. China, maybe. Korea? Yes, that's where. The twins? He wasn't sure where they went. Working someplace or other. Ruben helped Papi on the farm. He helped, too, taking them the lunches and bringing water. There, there was the house. It was hard to see it from here. Better park here. Park here. Right here on the edge of the road. By those trees. Boy, wait until the others see the truck, wait until he told them he had gotten to ride in it, boy, would they be jealous. He jumped off and ran down a little dirt path.

Tío Hernán carried the box of foodstuffs and followed Raffy. Felicidad hesitated. No one knew that they were coming. Everything had happened too quickly for a letter and there weren't yet telephones or telephone lines on the mountain. What if her mother and father didn't want her here? How could she bear the pain of it, the shame of it? What would her new husband think of her? What would her mother-in-law say?

"What's wrong?" Aníbal asked.

She faced Aníbal in the cab of the truck.

"What if they don't want me?"

He took her hand. "I promise you that they will be happy. Your father is probably killing a pig right now."

"You think?" She couldn't help smiling, thinking what a homecoming that would be, if only Papi had a pig to slaughter.

"We'll send the boy for our things later." He kissed her palm and helped her out of the truck.

Felicidad led him down the path of her childhood.

Sky and mountain framed the downtrodden house that seemed to grow in a garden of flowers: orchids, hibiscus, and roses. The straw hut that was the barraca crouched down a way from the house. Chickens pecked about the children playing in the dirt of el batey.

Aníbal put his arm around her. "Look, Felicidad. That lady. Is she your mother?"

A tall, skinny woman stood in the open doorway, a baby on her hip. Felicidad wanted to run to her, to throw herself upon her mother, but she waited for a smile, a wave, some signal that Mami recognized her and was glad she was home.

They had almost reached her when Mami cried out.

"Is that you, Felicidad? Could it be?"

Her mother's bone-thin shoulders shook as she held the sleeping baby. Felicidad embraced her.

"Bendición, Mami," Felicidad asked for her blessing as customary.

"Santa María," her mother said. "It's a miracle."

Chapter Twenty-two

He was lying on the floor of his in-laws' house, straw from his pillow poking into his face every which way he turned, while in the parents' bedroom his wife shared a bed with her sisters. Tía Imelda la jamona slept on a catre only a few feet from him. Aníbal stared at a ligartijo crawling on the ceiling. How had it happened that he wasn't with his wife? The coquís and other night critters serenaded him and moonlight flickered in through the cracks in the wood. Aníbal thought pobre gente, they must dread a good aguacero. He listened to Felicidad's old aunt and father snore, thinking Felicidad's parents were sharing a bed. He thought of Tío Hernán sleeping on a blanket outside and Felicidad's brothers in the bed of the truck. He wished he was making love to his wife al aire libre under the stars. He was one horny bastard, but he had a right to be one. After all, he'd just gotten married. What the hell was he doing all by himself in the fucking mountains?

He opened his eyes and there she was, kneeling by his pallet.

"Are you a dream?" He reached for her, touching her here and there to make sure she was real.

She lay down next to him. "We can't do anything. They'll hear us."

Aníbal turned her on her side and pushed up her dress.

"We can't," she said again.

"How do you think the country people do it? Your parents had ten children." He unbuttoned his pants.

Thirteen, ten plus the last three her mother had while she was away, Felicidad thought, but she was too distracted to correct him. She tried to turn toward him.

"Besides, your Tía Imelda la jamona is deaf." He pressed himself into her back.

"Please don't," she said.

She was surprised that he stopped and just held her close to him. She fell asleep in his arms, forgetting that she had come out to ask him if she could stay a few weeks with her family, if he would leave her on the island.

Two days after his marriage, Aníbal got off the plane in Chicago without his new bride. He felt disoriented, uprooted from his native soil. Just hours before, he had been a married man, making love to his new wife in his island home, and now he was a man alone in this cold steel-and-concrete world. All around him people called out to their loved ones, kissing relatives and friends as if they were long lost and helping to carry beat up or makeshift suitcases and sacks of fruit and root vegetables like malanga and ñame. It seemed to him that everywhere he looked couples were embracing, but not he. Tonight, just weeks before Christmas, he was as miserable as he had ever been since he first left the island.

Chago picked him up at the airport.

"¡Maricón! You got married?"

"Can you believe it?"

"Who to?" Chago whispered as loud as he could to be heard above the car's heater.

"The girl my mother found." Aníbal huddled inside his coat.

Coño, it was cold. He wished he was back on the island in bed with Felicidad.

His friend shook his head. "What about Marta?"

"What about her?"

"Don't tell me you're going to see her?"

"I'm not going to fuck her," Aníbal said.

Chago laughed because they both knew that that was all a man did with a woman like Marta.

"Better stay with us. Save yourself for your bride," Chago said.

"Don't worry, compai," Aníbal said. "I can take care of myself."

The last thing Aníbal wanted was to be in the next room while Chago was making love to Ana, not when his own wife was at home with her mother. It wasn't that he felt different or married, just that if he had a wife, then she should be with him. Wasn't that what marriage was all about?

Aníbal waited on the dark street until the taillights of Chago's car disappeared. His suitcase knocked against his leg. He looked up at the building; lights were on in every apartment except his. He recalled Felicidad's café colao eyes begging him to understand her need to stay behind. Shit, it wasn't that he missed her or anything like that, but how was he going to get through the night with her scent still on his body?

Here he was, pitiful like any man alone.

"Hombre, get some control," he told himself.

Aníbal had turned into the unlit landing leading up to his third-floor apartment when he saw the glow of her cigarette.

Marta stood up from the top step, blocking his way. "You going to kiss me?"

He kissed her cheek.

She stepped aside. "Open the door, you fool."

"What are you doing here?" Aníbal dug in his pocket for his key.

"You haven't been over in the old country that long," Marta said.

Her hand was on his belt. He pushed it away. He was a married man. "Marta, stop."

She laughed. "That's the first time I ever heard you say that."

"We have to talk."

"Let's talk later." She unbuckled his belt.

"I have something to tell you," he said.

Her fingers paused on the zipper. "The Hidalgo girl?"

"Felicidad," he said.

"What?"

"Her name is Felicidad. I married her."

"¡Maricón!" She gave his crotch a smack.

"¡Coño!" He dropped the suitcase on the floor. Doña Petra would probably come to investigate in a second.

"You fucked her?"

"Marta, she's my wife."

"I saved myself for you!"

"Marta, be reasonable."

"Where is she? Your little wife?"

"Puerto Rico with her mother."

"That's convenient." Her hand was back on the waistband of his pants.

"You sure?" He knew he should send her home, but he didn't want to be alone.

She shook her head. "I'll worry about it tomorrow."

Aníbal reached under her skirt. "No panties, Marta? Ay bendito."

Inside the apartment they tried not to bang too hard against the door.

Later Aníbal fed Marta slices of juicy mango with his fingers. They didn't talk much.

Chapter Twenty-three

Upon her arrival, Felicidad had been horrified to see that each of her sisters was missing her front teeth. Leila told her that they had fallen out by age twelve. Didn't she remember that the same thing had happened to Vicente and the twins? It was sure to happen to Raffy and the others. Felicidad wanted to weep for beautiful Leila, who splayed her fingers over her mouth like a fan, and for sweet, feeble-minded Juanita, who still cried for every little thing. Before Aníbal left, he had whispered in her ear telling her not to worry, that they would send the girls money for false teeth.

Next to her sisters, Felicidad felt ungainly and out of place with her good shoes and clothes, and she gave away some of her things. Leila mocked Felicidad's town manners, envious that her sister was a married woman. She was too uppity for them now, Leila told her. When she asked for a fork and knife with which to eat her dinner, the family laughed at her. Didn't she remember that there was only one set, and that was for their father? Felicidad sat at the table while her siblings went outside to eat.

★ ★ ★

One day Felicidad took up her mother's embroidery while Mami shelled beans into a bowl, dropping the empty pods into the lap of her dress.

Felicidad recalled the evenings of her childhood when she would sit on the bench with her mother, embroidering roses and dreaming of troupes of Spanish dancers. She wanted to ask Mami if she remembered, too.

Her mother stared out through the open door into el batey where Tía Imelda la jamona carried the baby on her hip, scattering corn for the chickens with her free hand.

"I don't think I will have any more babies. I'm getting too old," her mother said.

Felicidad did a quick calculation. Mami had turned forty-five on her last birthday.

"It's your turn to have babies," her mother said.

Felicidad didn't look up from her needlework. She couldn't help blushing, thinking it was possible that she was already pregnant.

Her mother examined her work. "I'm glad you still embroider; you're the only one with the gift for the needle," she said.

"I remember how we used to embroider together." Felicidad yearned to ask, Mami, did you miss me? She wanted to tell her mother how she had wanted nothing more than to be back home sitting on this bench and embroidering with her. Felicidad waited for her once-beautiful mother to say more, to talk about the years Felicidad had been gone and ask her how she had borne it, or maybe to tell her how she regretted sending her away. If not that, then at least Felicidad wanted Mami to tell the stories of her childhood, stories about flamenco dancers and dresses with flounces.

Instead they worked together in silence until Tía Imelda la jamona brought the baby to his mother to nurse.

Felicidad took a big gulp of air before entering the latrine, trying not to breathe until she was done. She was careful to hold her dress up while she squatted. She learned to keep her hair in a tight bun, because flying cockroaches and other insects liked to make a nest of it. One day she saw a snake coiled where the family kept the pile of corn husks and discarded paper scraps they used instead of toilet paper. Another day she got her period and she was surprised to feel relief rather than disappointment that she wasn't pregnant.

When Felicidad couldn't sleep, she stared out through the cracks in the wood at the countryside lit by the moon and stars. She heard the rustle of the leaves and thought of the Spirits roaming the mountains, how her Spirit Father had been her companion those first years away from home until she had grown up. Then she had the Spirit Prince to love her. He was here with her now, but she sent him away. She didn't need a Spirit Lover because she had Aníbal, a man in the flesh to whom she belonged and who belonged to her. She hoped that he was thinking of her and that he couldn't sleep, either.

Felicidad yearned for the old camaraderie that she had once had with her siblings, especially Leila, the connection that develops only with the sharing of circumstances and daily routine. Felicidad was determined to reach out to her sister, to reestablish the companionship that they had once had.

She went with her sister to the river to wash clothes. She recalled how it had been one of her favorite chores because after spreading the clothes on bushes to dry, she played in the water. Leila was glad that she had thought to bring pieces of blue soap because they had run out. Felicidad used a rock to scrub dirt from a collar. She worked as fast as she could, but Leila finished two pieces to her one.

"You're soft," Leila said.

Felicidad laughed. "I guess."

Leila sat back on her haunches. "It should have been me wearing that pretty dress and going to America with my handsome husband."

Felicidad pushed back a lock of sweaty hair. She wasn't used to working beneath the hot sun anymore. "What are you talking about?"

"Papi wanted to send me to live with the aunt, not you," her sister said.

Felicidad tried to think if this was true. Had anyone ever told her this?

"Why do you say that?"

"I heard them talking." Leila jerked her head in the direction of the house. "The aunt asked for 'la trabajadora.' And that was you—always cooking or something."

"Do you think I wanted to do Mami's work? I wanted to go to school," Felicidad said.

"Well, you did go to school, didn't you? Papi saw to that," Leila said. "You were always his favorite."

Felicidad looked down at the stone in her palm. Papi *had* loved her, *had* wanted to keep her home with them. For the first time she saw how sending her away—and her brother Vicente, too—must also have been difficult for her parents. Perhaps, especially, for her proud father, because it was an admission that he couldn't provide adequately for his family. Yet he had done it because he thought it best, however much it must have pained him. Leila said that she had been her father's favorite. Something lifted from her heart: a weight that had begun to settle there those first days away from her family, and had gradually calcified throughout the years of waiting to return home. Felicidad saw that what had been a terrible thing had also been good.

She had helped her family and, unlike her siblings, had lived a comfortable life. She had also met Aníbal, which would never have happened in this remote countryside.

Leila put her hand to her mouth and turned away.

Felicidad went to her, but her sister stood rigid in her arms.

"I wanted to be here with you," Felicidad said.

Leila said through her fingers, "It's not fair."

The day Tío Hernán came to get her, Papi stood in the dirt batey of the small one-room house. Felicidad wanted to embrace her father, to speak of the sacrifice that she now understood that they had both made, but her father was not a man to show emotion and was unlikely to welcome a mention of the past. Instead she kissed his cheek in parting, the rough bristles scraping her skin. She closed her eyes, wanting to etch the feel of her father's cheek into memory.

"This is no place for you," Papi said. "You belong with your husband."

Felicidad nodded. She belonged with her husband.

Felicidad y Aníbal in América

Chapter Twenty-four

December 31, 1952

Felicidad came to her husband on New Year's Eve in her wedding suit with the rose she had embroidered on the lapel and sandals with ribbons tied into bows, her toenails painted red to match. She was a jíbara, a country hick, just off the plane with her toes frozen like ice chips to the soles of her sandals. When she took them off that night, the lining stuck to the bottoms of her feet. Ay bendito, shoes that cost ten dollars. She hadn't allowed herself to think about how long it had taken her to earn that money or how her mother could have fed her brothers and sisters on it, only that the shoes were red and open-toed and made her feet look elegant, the way she was sure the feet of all Chicago women looked.

She felt lost in the crowd of people calling out to relatives and friends, many wearing silly party hats and waving HAPPY NEW YEAR and 1953 banners. The airport in San Juan was like a marketplace, hot and humid, with palm trees growing tall around it and seemingly through it, with loud people laughing or crying, and mangoes, avocados, and papayas spilling out of bags to sneak into the United States, where people said fruit was scarce. Here in Chicago the people were quieter, weighed down by their heavy coats and galoshes and the cold air that followed in their wake, filtering in through the glass and concrete.

At first she didn't find her husband in the crowd of families. Felicidad couldn't have imagined so many Puerto Ricans off the island, the new arrivals carrying tattered suitcases or cardboard boxes tied with twine. It reassured her to hear people speaking Spanish; it lulled her into believing that the worst was over. The pain in her head and the ringing in her ears were her own fault. She had chosen the cheap flight that only the poor Puerto Ricans flew. The plane wasn't pressurized; it had to fly at a lower altitude and at a slower speed, lurching and bumping through the sky, causing suitcases to fly about the cabin and people to throw up.

On tiptoe Felicidad searched for Aníbal. "Felicidad," he would say, just her name, as he had said it to her before he left. "Felicidad," and it would be enough. He would gather her up in his arms as if it had been years since he had last seen her, long years deprived of her laughter and voice and body, instead of just weeks.

She saw him hurrying around the old ladies making the sign of the cross on the foreheads of little children, the fathers swinging their sons up in the air, the men and women, all of them thin, celebrating their reunions.

"There you are." Her husband stopped three feet away from her.

Felicidad trembled in her light suit and sandals.

"I should have borrowed a coat." Aníbal took off his gray overcoat and gave it to her. He didn't help put it on. Instead he picked up the suitcase and headed out to the street. She had to hurry to keep up with him.

Felicidad paused to marvel at the falling snow. She lifted her face up to the night sky, snowflakes landing on her face and hair like kisses.

"Snow," she said, but she meant thank you.

She shivered in her husband's coat. She should have felt warm and protected, but she was lost in the folds of fabric. Felicidad stared out of the car window listening to the swish of the wipers. Now that she was alone with her husband she didn't know what to say to him. Seeing him again had not been what she had dreamed. He hadn't taken her in his arms and kissed her. Instead he had rushed her out of the airport and into the car as if afraid he might meet someone he knew and have to introduce her.

This new place was flat. She stared in awe as they passed houses and buildings blinking red and green lights. There was not a single palm tree in sight, no flamboyant red trees or wild-flowers growing haphazardly along a winding country road or pastel-colored houses crammed among lush vegetation. Her nose began to run, and she dabbed at it with her cold palm. She pulled the coat over her knees and her fingers brushed her stock-ings. At the airport she had seen women with smooth, hairless legs. A child had pointed to Felicidad's legs, telling her mother, "Esa mujer tiene las piernas belluda." She had been embarrassed at the dark hair obvious even through her stockings.

Streetlights loomed over the car as it passed. The trees she saw were leafless sculptures spawned from the cement sidewalks. Here and there a pedestrian trudged through the street, ghost-like. There weren't any coops beneath the buildings or houses, no chickens squawking for freedom. The island was never quiet, not even at night, when the coquís and other critters held their symphony. Here there was only the crunch of the car tires on the snow-covered streets, the hum of the car's engine, wind-shield wipers jeering jíbara, jíbara, the silence of her husband.

Aníbal drove with the nervous concentration of someone who has never driven in snow. In the weeks since he had left Felicidad on the island, her beauty had faded in his memory and he had begun to think that he should have heeded Mamá's advice. Now that he saw her again, he thought, Coño, the girl is beautiful. He had planned to treat her like any woman whom he might have to pick up at the airport, like somebody's old or ugly relative, but then he had seen her shivering in the cold airport and he couldn't do it. He couldn't go up to her and kiss her on the cheek like she was just any fulana or another, as if they'd never made love, not when she looked at him like he was every dream she'd ever had.

He had to say something and so he pointed out places of interest. This neighborhood, here? Lots of Puerto Ricans live around here. That building there, my friend Chago lives there. You'll meet him sometime soon and his wife, Ana. You'll like Ana. She always has women friends around. Over there? See that building? Second floor? Last week, I went to a party there. A baby's baptism. I swear there was a whole band playing merengue until like two AM, when somebody called the police and there went the party. It's not easy having fun in America. Somebody is always calling the police on you.

What would he do with Felicidad if the snow turned into a blizzard? He was still of the same opinion as before he went to Puerto Rico. He had decided before her arrival that he didn't want the responsibilities of a wife. He had gotten all sentimental and sad for Felicidad and had wanted to rescue her. It had nothing to do with how she looked. Why, he probably would have married her even if she had been one of those ugly, toothless girls. He just had a big heart. His problem was that he was too kindhearted. It was a curse.

Felicidad felt her husband's unease. She hadn't spent ten years living and working in the house of her tía política without learning what every good servant must know: how to read one's employer. She wasn't sure what she had done to displease him.

She had tried to make herself beautiful for her new husband. Tío Hernán's body odor had been so pungent that on the way to the airport, Felicidad had asked to stop at a drugstore to buy perfume. She had prepared herself for her husband as best as she could in the airport restroom, washing her face and dousing herself with scent.

Aníbal needed time to figure out what to do with Felicidad. He didn't want to hurt her but he wasn't really to blame. These things happened. Sometimes a man got carried away with his good intentions.

She wondered why Aníbal had spoken as if he were a polite stranger rather than the man who had transformed her from a timid girl waiting for life into a woman living it.

He glanced at her, saw her hands folded on her lap like a little girl. Marta wanted him to tell Felicidad tonight that he had made a mistake marrying her. But where could the girl go? Back to the aunt and uncle's house? Damn, she couldn't go back there, even if the aunt would take her back. Which she probably would, so that she could gloat over Felicidad's misfortune. He couldn't do that to her, not to that girl from the island. It all came back to him, how she had felt in his arms, how she blushed when he undressed her, the way she had giggled when he chased her at the river. Would it be so bad if he turned to her right this moment and said, Felicidad, I'm glad you're here, if he reached for her hand and kissed it? He *had* married the girl and paid for her ticket and here she was expecting to be a real wife to him. Why not just say Welcome home, mujer, and step into the role of a husband?

He was driving so slowly. Ay bendito, if she got out of the car she could probably walk faster, although maybe not in her beautiful sandals. She tried to wiggle her toes but couldn't feel them. The snow reminded her of an American movie she had seen where a very tall actor ran down the snow-covered street yelling and laughing. She wanted to run down the street yelling and laughing. Maybe Aníbal would run after her, yelling and laughing, too, as he had that day at the river.

"Is it very far?"

"No, the snow makes it slippery."

"You're shivering. You shouldn't have given me your coat."

"I'm fine, it's just the heater doesn't work so well. Neither does the radio."

"You'll get sick without a coat," Felicidad said.

Aníbal wished that she would stop talking. If she spoke again, he would tell her that he had to pay attention to his driving. Damn, he was so confused. She was so beautiful, so trusting, it would be so easy to make love to her tonight. But then, what about tomorrow? What about the day after that? Or six months from now when he tired of her? Because that was what he did. What then? What would he do with her then? Send her away after living with her as man and wife? Abandon her in the apartment? He couldn't do that to her. Ruin the rest of her life like that. Felicidad was different from the other women and she trusted him.

Aníbal stopped the car in the middle of the street alongside two chairs. He got out and moved the chairs onto the snow-covered grass.

Felicidad couldn't help wondering what kind of place she had come to, where people left perfectly good chairs outside in the snow. One day she would buy her family a chair, two chairs even, so that when a visitor came her father wouldn't have to give up his own.

He opened the door for her. She reached her hand to the ground and touched the snow.

"It's cold." She laughed at the shock of it against her fingers.

Aníbal looked at her playing with the snow. This was the beautiful girl his penis remembered.

"My sandals will be ruined. They're new!"

He put the suitcase on the roof of the car and reached for her. He carried her into the silent night, in the wondrous stillness of black and white, snow descending on his hat, her hair, his shoulders, her legs. Snow falling like blessings or incantations, his footsteps vanishing behind him.

Aníbal set her on her feet in the entry and she looked at him with those dark eyes of hers that expected so much of him, and he knew then that he couldn't tell Felicidad on the same day she arrived that everything had changed. He just needed a little time to figure out what to do, but first things first. He had to get through tonight and the next couple of days until he came up with a plan. Until then he would think of her as a relative. Yes, she was like a cousin to him, a younger cousin, no, a sister who had come to stay with him for a while. A sister. Yes, that was how he would treat her, that's what he would tell Marta, that's what he would tell Mamá when, months from now, he wrote.

"We're on the third floor." He followed her up the stairs, wincing at the loudness of their steps. His overcoat dragged on the floor, white and black, snow and her hair on the gray cloth. He wanted to say, Mujer, pull up my coat, but it would be treating her like a child and right now, when he had held her in his arms, he had wanted to fuck her like any woman. It made him angry that he couldn't hold his resolve for five minutes.

"Who lives here?" She paused on the second landing.

"Doña Petra, an older lady." ¡Diablo! The girl had been in the building only seconds. Did she already have to start with the questions?

Felicidad waited patiently while he unlocked the door and wondered why he was so annoyed. What had happened to the charming, brash young man who had taken her away under the aunt's disapproving watch, who had made love to her under the waterfall?

Aníbal stepped into the tiny hall. "This is it."

He switched on a light. The bathroom faced the apartment door; a porcelain bathtub sat on its clawed feet.

"Aníbal, a bathroom with a tub and a toilet! Ay bendito, tell me there's water," she said.

He laughed. "Yes, there's water, mostly cold."

Felicidad thought he must be laughing at her for being such a jíbara. Some of the pleasure left her. Still, she didn't care if snow came out of the pipes; she would boil it in a pot. She ran her hands over the top of the toilet tank. Never would she have to use a letrina again. Dios, but America was great.

"Show me the rest of this palace," she said.

He turned on another light. Aníbal told her that la sala was called a living room in American. The room had large windows and was bigger than her family's entire house.

"No curtains?" Of course, they were on the third floor, but curtains made the house a home, she had learned from the aunt. In her parents' house the window was cut into the wood with a shutter that was closed during heavy rains and at night. The aunt and uncle, of course, had pretty, floral curtains with ruffles trimming the edges. She yearned for a home with curtains.

"Curtains cost money," Aníbal said. What the hell was it about not having curtains that bothered women so? "Besides, I haven't been living here long."

She was shocked that Aníbal might not have pockets stuffed with dollar bills. Since he had come from America and his family was better off than hers, she had thought it so.

A bed was the only furniture in the room, and she felt the mattress for plantain or corn husk stuffing and the pillows for straw.

Felicidad wondered if she would be lucky enough to have a kerosene stove or if she had to go back to cooking on a fogón. Certainly she wouldn't be rich like the aunt and have an electric one. Shelves with a few books lined either side of a fireplace. She wasn't curious enough to read the titles. A lamp topped with a pink shade stood on a box in a corner.

"What's that?" Felicidad pointed to the fireplace.

"It's called a fireplace. I think they used it in the olden days to heat up the place. Maybe to cook. I don't think it works," Aníbal said.

"I don't see el fogón," she said. "Where will I cook?"

"¡Fogón!" He laughed. "This is America."

He led her into another empty room which she thought was meant to be a dining room just like the aunt's, but she didn't want to ask.

He pointed to a closed door. "Tomorrow I'll move the bed in there. I'll get my compai to come help me," he said. "And this is the kitchen. See here? Here's the stove and this is a refrigerator. I'm paying for both on time. I borrowed the table and chairs from Ana, my compai's wife."

Felicidad stared at the refrigerator, stunned by its gleaming beauty. It was turquoise.

He opened yet another door. "This is the pantry."

"El pántry?" She stared at the containers of oatmeal and coffee on a shelf and remembered another pantry from long ago when she had gone to get her mother. She reached out a hand to steady herself. Suddenly it all seemed too much: the airplane ride she thought would never end, the passage of one world into another, the miracle of snow, the weight of Aníbal's heavy coat, the coldness of her husband.

"Here, take off the coat. We'll see if we can borrow one for you until payday," Aníbal said.

She followed him back to the living room and watched him drape his coat over a towel on top of a silver thing.

"Ra–di–a–dor," he said. "The heat, when we get it, comes out of it. I try to keep pots of water on top of them. It makes it easier to breathe."

Felicidad wanted to ask so many questions. Did the heat come out of the ground? But how could that be when they were on the third floor? Did it come from the floor below it? She determined to always keep pans of water on top of the radiador, if that was what it took so that they could breathe. Were they the same pans that she would use for cooking? Was this whole apartment just for the two of them?

Aníbal had placed her suitcase on the bed and asked her if she wanted to take a bath. Yes, she wanted a bath, warm water over her skin as she hadn't enjoyed for the last month she had been with her family, soapy water to wash away the memory of the letrina without proper toilet paper and the flying cockroaches nesting in her hair.

Her husband sat at the foot of the bed, turning the pages of a newspaper. She fumbled through her things. She wondered if she should wear the nightgown made of gauzy fabric on which she had embroidered tiny roses. She placed her hand on it, then she chose a homely bata, a simple cotton nightgown that the aunt had deemed respectable in a house with young men, a bata of the type favored by middle-aged women who had flaws to hide and little expectation of revealing them.

Felicidad glanced at her husband. Why was he just sitting there? Why didn't he kiss her? What had she done to offend him? He seemed more like a stranger than even on that first day when he had come into la panadería. She would never have thought that the Aníbal from the island could be so cold.

She locked the bathroom door, hoping that he wouldn't hear the click. When she flushed the toilet, she cringed at its loudness. The tile floor was like a layer of ice, the faucets chilled. While the tub filled, she looked in the mirror, trying to discover how the month in her parents' home had changed her so that her husband now found her repulsive. She sat on the edge of the tub and pressed her forehead against the cold porcelain sink. She would not cry. Instead, she imagined how her Spirit Prince would welcome her to such a lovely place. He would take her in his arms and twirl her through the apartment, their laughter and dancing echoing through all the empty rooms.

She stepped into a tub of lukewarm water and hurried with her bath, washing her hair and dipping her head back in the water to rinse away Puerto Rico and the painful silence of her husband.

Aníbal had to stop himself from laughing at the nightgown she wore. He was sure that he had seen his grandmother up the mountain wearing one of similar style. Then he thought that she wasn't wearing anything under the nightgown. It was all coming back to him, how she looked naked, the way her body responded to his. Would it be so bad if he made love to her? Stop, he told himself. He went to the sink and filled a glass with cold water. He gulped it down. He was a grown man and he should be able to exert some willpower if he needed to. After she ate her bread and ham with a nice big piece of queso blanco that Marta had left behind, he would order her off to bed. He would lie down in the farthest corner of the bed, leaving plenty of space between them, and maybe then he might be able to stop thinking about reaching under that nightgown.

"You must be hungry," he said.

He does care, she thought. It's just that meeting me again

after being married only a few days is so awkward. Soon he'll ask me about my family, about how it was without him, if I missed him, and it will all be like before.

"I haven't been truly hungry for years, not since I went to live with the aunt and uncle. Besides, a nice woman shared her rice and beans with me. She actually brought a fiambrera on the plane," Felicidad said.

"Here we have steel lunch boxes, but I don't think anything works as well as those fiambreras," he said.

She wanted to ask, Why were they talking about fiambreras when they hadn't seen each other for a month? Why didn't he say he was glad to see her, that he'd missed her? That it was hard for a man not to have his wife with him?

Felicidad counted on her fingers. "We had four. One for Papi, one for Vicente, and one each for the twins. We were lucky if we could fill two containers. My brother Vicente said that he always opened the third container first because if there was something in it, then he knew that that day his belly would be full."

The subject of fiambreras exhausted, they finished their meal in silence, listening to the scrape of the chairs against the floor, their cups clinking against the saucers, suddenly aware of how much noise chewing bread and ham made.

After Felicidad went to bed, Aníbal washed the cups and saucers, something he normally didn't do, at least not until there wasn't another cup to be used. His father and brother were sure to laugh if they saw him at the kitchen sink when he had himself a wife. He doubted that sleep would come easily that night. He knew what he wanted to do, what he had felt like doing when Felicidad had walked into the kitchen all fresh and clean smelling after her bath, all that cheap perfume and Puerto Rican sweat washed down the drain.

Tomorrow he would get Chago to help him move the bed into the bedroom. Better yet, he would take it apart himself rather than have Chago asking questions. He didn't need his friend going home and telling Ana his business; Ana knew everybody's business. If you had a secret, you didn't drink any beverage that she offered you because she was sure to put something or other in it to loosen your tongue. He knew it to be true. Why, one time when he lived with them, he drank her coffee—which he swore was brewed with the coffee beans from his father's farm it was that good—and next thing he knew he was talking about some girl he had met when he had first left the island and picked lettuce in California, some migrant woman with three or four kids whose husband had abandoned her. That wasn't very unusual, him picking up a strange woman, only that he was telling Ana about it.

He sat on the edge of the bed. Felicidad's hair fanned out on the sheet, black against the white. Marta's hair was short and kinky, pelo malo as the island people say. He liked to clutch it in his fingers during sex. He was ashamed to admit that the last time was just that morning. Even his father might shake his head at one woman out, another in. He had to go wash the sheets. It didn't feel right doing woman's work, but he wasn't the kind of man who didn't have respect for his wife, who would let her lay down in another woman's soil; his mother had raised him better than that.

Felicidad was breathing softly. That night they had spent in her parents' home, in that little wood place more shack than house, he had also listened to her breathing and pitied the little girl who had witnessed her mother's breakdown, who had taken that mother's place in the family and then been sent away. He held her through the night, willing her to dream of what was to come, instead of nightmares from the past—and here he was now, thinking how to get rid of her, how to send her away without shaming her, without hurting her.

Aníbal wanted to make love to her, but, fuck, it wouldn't be right. Felicidad wasn't just any girl. She was like an angel or maybe a princess. A little jíbara princess. So unspoiled, so eager and content with whatever he could give as long as she had running water and a toilet. He couldn't resist touching her hair, recalling how at the riverbank she had untied it and it had fallen in waves around her shoulders. He yanked back his hand as if it had been burned. He went to take a shower. For the first time in his twenty-three years, Aníbal Acevedo chose a cold shower over a flesh-and-blood woman. How his compadres would laugh at that.

Chapter Twenty-five

When Aníbal woke, Felicidad was at the stove. She had put on a black mantilla over her nightgown. He went to get a flannel shirt and she smiled when he gave it to her. He wondered why he felt so foolish.

He sat at the table. It rocked and he reminded himself to shove something under the leg later.

"Did you sleep well?" Ah, black coffee ready the moment he sat down. He breathed in the aroma. There were some good things about having a wife.

"I must have. I don't remember a thing," she said. "I made some avena. Is that all right? I found a container in the pantry. I never saw such a beautiful thing as that pantry. I can't believe I have a whole room for food!"

She placed a bowl of hot oatmeal in front of him. "I know you don't like sugar, but I thought you might not mind a little butter."

He swirled the butter into the brown mush. "You found the stove easy to use?"

She fingered a dial. "The aunt had one. I can cook anything on this magic thing."

They stared at the stove as if it were a deity worthy of worship and Aníbal finished his breakfast in silence, listening to the wind rattling the kitchen window. He had taped plastic sheeting over all the windows to keep out the cold and wind and to contain what heat there was inside. This window, as all the others in the apartment, also lacked curtains, but if Felicidad noticed, she didn't say, and Aníbal was grateful.

Aníbal thought maybe he could take her for a ride, show her around a little. That would get them out of the apartment. He would drive slowly.

"When you're ready, I'll take you a dar la vuelta," he said.

He went to the living room and began to dismantle the bed, thinking it would have saved a lot of trouble if he had put it in the bedroom where it belonged in the first place.

Felicidad wore Aníbal's coat again, turning up the collar and breathing in her husband. She smelled rice and beans and rum and the brilliantine he used in his hair and something else that she couldn't place. The wool scratched her face and made it itch, but she didn't mind. She felt protected from the cold, from the world, from the future. Felicidad told herself that that little tug at her heart when he put his arm around her to help her push through the wind meant that he cared about her, the way he had back on the island. She was glad that she had changed into the shoes she had worn to work en la panadería. The best that she could have said about the ugly things was that they were serviceable and had protected her toes from many a falling tray. They were better for snow than the pretty red sandals and would do until Aníbal bought her something called galoshes.

Dark oil stained Aníbal's brown jacket, which had a torn front pocket and a sleeve slashed from elbow to wrist. Felicidad planned to mend it. She remembered her brothers in their tattered shirts, stained brown with dirt and sweat and speckled here and there with grass and dried blood.

There was so much for her to learn, so much that he could teach her. Aníbal pulled away from the curb then stopped the car. He got out and picked up the chairs in the snow, placing them in the space he'd just vacated.

He had laughed at her astonished look. "I'm holding my spot. You shovel your parking space and save it with chairs. No one touches it. It's a matter of respect."

Aníbal drove slowly. Side streets hadn't been cleared of snow and the main streets were slippery. Besides, what did it matter when he had to kill time? He pointed out a few things here and there, like the diner where he sometimes ate. There, there was the famous Sears, Roebuck department store. Had she heard of it? Oh, yes, the aunt ordered many things from there, had he noticed the linoleum in the kitchen? No? Well, the aunt had ordered it from Sears, Roebuck. One day, when he had the time, she would like to go inside so that when she wrote her cousin Adela, she could tell her how she had been in the actual store. Did he like her cousin Adela? She was sweet, almost like a sister, but of course she had sisters and none were like Adela.

Over there, see that building? It's famous for something, he said, but he couldn't remember what. He had to be honest, he didn't know that much about the city. He knew only what most of the Puerto Ricans knew, where to work and shop and where to live where people left you alone—people who weren't Puerto Ricans, that was. It was an easier thing living on the island because everyone you knew was a Puerto Rican just like you except for maybe the Spaniards and the big shots in the town or the hacienda owners who were American ricos and didn't have anything to do with you because they were rich Americans and bigots, too. Here most people weren't Puerto Rican, and that was a problem.

Bigots? Bigots are people who don't like you just because you're Puerto Rican. He could tell her that it could be ugly living with people not of your race, but why, when she would learn soon enough? When you were with a fellow Puerto Rican, you didn't have to explain a thing. With someone who wasn't Puerto Rican, you had to justify who you were and how, although you couldn't speak English very well, you were still an American. And then there was the skin color dilemma. In Puerto Rico, you might be black, white, or Indio, but you were Puerto Rican first, then black or white or Indio. Here, everybody except the blacks and the Mexicans and Puerto Ricans was white; sometimes even the Orientals were white. Yes, it was a problem when you weren't white. He wished that she didn't have to learn it, but la vida was la vida and he had no control over it.

Felicidad was wondering why he hadn't kissed her since her arrival, why he hadn't said a single thing a man might say to a woman let alone a husband to his wife. Felicidad stared at her breath suspended in air and wished that he would say something to make everything easy between them the way it had been in Puerto Rico. Her feet were very cold. She had been told on the island that people who had returned from the States complained about a cold so icy that it was like her favorite frozen ices and so she had packed a mantilla. Now she thought she could imagine what it would be like to live inside her turquoise refrigerator.

He explained that it was too cold to work on the heater. His compai Tony had a shop and he was going to take the car there and work on it, he was sorry, he hoped she wasn't too cold. Felicidad said no, although she wished that she had thought to ask Aníbal to borrow a pair of his socks. Her legs were tinged red and she rubbed them gently through her stockings, careful not to snag them.

Aníbal stopped the car. It appeared to Felicidad that he parked in the middle of the street. The snow was piled a foot high against the curb.

"There's Comacho's Grocery," Aníbal said. "Coño, I think it's open. That Comacho will sell his mother for a buck. Let's go in and do a little compra."

Comacho's was on the corner and sold a little bit of everything. His customers who had cars bought their groceries at the A&P, but when it came to the rice and beans, the links of chorizo and morcilla sausages, the tubs of manteca for frying, the pieces of pork with the skin still on to sizzle in lard for the delicacy called chicarrones, all this could be bought only at Comacho's or a place like Comacho's. A Puerto Rican yearning for a bit of home went there to buy a coconut to make Mamá's arroz con dulce, to crack it open and scoop out the fleshy white meat to grind and cook with rice and sugar, a little bit of cinnamon, some cloves, and lots of raisins. Then a little drink of rum, and back to the island it was. Or he could buy a pound of gandules, half a pound if that was all that was possible. Especially around the holidays, every portorro had to have gandules. And what did that Comacho do but increase the price by ten cents, saying that gandules were hard to come by during the holidays and everyone knew that was when they were most wanted. What was a Christmas without arroz con gandules?

Today it seemed as if half Chicago's Puerto Ricans were at Comacho's. Aníbal was relieved not to bump into Ana or one of his compais. He introduced Felicidad to Comacho and to Lupe, his mujer. It was rumored that Comacho had left his legal wife and children back on the island.

Then there were the island men who congregated in small grocery stores to relive their youth or to get away from their families, jíbaros who once worked the land, men from the pueblos who had escaped the futility of unemployment and slum dwelling for factory work, island men too old or ill to work. They loitered around the store, four or six men, stepping like dancers out of Comacho's or a customer's way, always with a cheerful word, a helpful hand to reach a high shelf. They bought their cigarettes from Comacho's and a shot or two of rum from the bottle he kept behind the counter.

In the summer these island men stood outside the store basking in the sun and reminiscing about those days on the island when they were working the cane or putting their children to bed with a hunger eating their insides so fierce that sometimes they cried themselves to sleep. They showed each other their scars from cutting cane or burning wood for charcoal and bested one another with tales of who had suffered most and eaten least. One learned of Ismael Gonzalez, of the day when he could not swing his machete one more time and it had fallen from his hands to the ground as if it were burning steel. He had left the machete languishing among the stalks of cane, a sliver of silver amid the green, and then he had abandoned his wife and nine children, God help him, that very day. Gonzalez had heard that two or three of his children were living somewhere on the mainland and, on a day like today, when it was the beginning of a new year, he thought he might ask around and try to find them.

And then there was Valentín Vega, the handsome viejito with green eyes and skin turned coarse from the Puerto Rican sun. The elderly gentleman with the erect carriage and courteous manners would only say that before the Americans, before the great hurricane of 1899, his family had owned a large coffee plantation, and then they hadn't.

José Lopez also had nine children, two of them born while he picked crops in the States. He had been gone three years and had come back to eight kids instead of six. There were lots of stories going up and down the mountain about how this could be so, but he had chosen to believe his wife, who said that his own spirit had visited her while he was away. His wife was a curandera and she had powers that others didn't, tú sabes.

Alfónzo Pérez was proud of his black mustache, which was as thick as he was bald. He had come to Chicago with the first wave of Puerto Ricans from the island in the 1940s. He liked to tell of how he had met his wife, his Carmen Luísa, climbing out of a second-story window escaping the life of an indentured servant. If he hadn't been there to catch her, she would have broken a leg or two, if not her skull. Carmen Luísa's story was not so unusual. Families let their daughters come up from the island, families desperate to eat rice and beans, the government assuring them of their employers' good character. True, his own sister Mónica had worked as a domestic, too, and had been treated as a servant should be, but his wife, his Carmen Luísa? Now, that was another story.

In good weather they stood outside smoking cigarettes and nodding to the passersby, Puerto Rican and non–Puerto Rican alike, averting their gazes respectfully from the women, Don Valentín pressing penny candy into the soft young palms of his grandchildren sent for a gallon of milk, proud that his daughters were raising them to be respectful, but lamenting the loss of the Spanish language in these children living in the States.

When Aníbal brought Felicidad, these island men were inside Comacho's, bemoaning the cold and the snow that they had shoveled from the walkways of their buildings, and the buildings weren't even theirs, mind you. Those dueños living out in the suburbs, they sure knew how to stick it to the Puerto Rican. But, diablo, it was a cold day.

And then in came Aníbal with his new wife, a sight as unexpected as a Christmas bonus from the factory. Here was this beautiful young girl with hair streaming from her scarf like ribbons and they breathed in their island radiating from her skin.

"Your wife?" Lupe asked. "No me digas."

"Pero muchacho, when did this happen?" Comacho was weighing a pound of jamón polaco and forgot to put his thumb on the scale.

When Aníbal told Felicidad to buy what she needed, she and Comacho went down the aisle like in a dream. He, to carry her selections and to savor the youth and freshness of Puerto Rican womanhood and, she, to satisfy her appetites. The shelves were crammed with canned goods, beans, creamed corn, creamed spinach, green beans, evaporated milk, condensed milk, boxes of cereal, pancake mix, syrup, cake mix, sacks of rice and beans, cornmeal, rice meal, sugar, flour—more food than she could ever have imagined. In the very back of the store, a butcher in a bloodstained apron cut up huge slabs of meat and Lupe filled sausage casings with the rice-and-blood-sausage mixture for the morcillas that she sold by the pound. Never had Felicidad bought food: Always that was the aunt's domain, and she bought in bulk for the house and the fonda. Not too many hours ago Felicidad had been a nobody on a tropical island, wilting in the heat, and now, here, in an urban tundra, she was a bona fide ama de casa outfitting her own pantry.

She chose small sacks of beans, every variety Comacho had, garbanzos, rosadas, pinto, rojas, white beans, and when she asked about gandules—after all, it was the holidays—Aníbal bought her half a pound. And then she needed another pot and a mortar and pestle. Was that all right? And a knife. She wanted one with a wide sharp blade. Oh, a large frying pan. And lard. To fry pork chops and chicken. Eggs. A dozen, por favor. Salt. Sugar. Bacalao, too, for a nice fricassee. Señor Comacho, do you have viandas? And annatto seeds and alcaparrados. Recao and cilantrillo. You have both? And garlic and onions. Peppers, both red and green. Ají peppers, too. Aníbal, am I spending too much? Would it be possible to buy a small bottle of olive oil? From Spain? And some saint candles? When she was done, one of the men helped Aníbal carry the bags to the car.

"Now, that's what I call a compra," Lupe said to Felicidad. "I can see you know your way in the kitchen. It's good that you're here. It's hard on a man being left alone to his wild ways. A man needs a good woman to take care of him whether he knows it or not, and whether he likes it or not." Lupe nodded at Aníbal as if to say, Just so you know.

When they left, Comacho shook his head and told the men, "I predict un gran revolú. You men have seen that Marta?"

Grunts. Nods. Murmurings. Yes, they had all seen Marta. What, were they blind men? Only a dead man or a eunuch, maybe, wouldn't be aware of Marta. She was the juice of the pineapple, the sauce of the beans, the ajo en mofongo. But that wife? That Felicidad? Aníbal was one lucky maricón. That Felicidad was like rice, tender yet filling, without which a man still felt hunger, a Puerto Rican man anyway. A man needed to eat it every day to feel strong and contented. One might think that rice was bland, but no señor, not if you knew how to make it. There was a technique to it, you see. You couldn't use too much water or it would be soggy. Too little, and it would be hard and you would think you were eating pebbles. And salt. Very important was the salt when it came to rice. You wouldn't want to eat rice without salt. It would taste like nothing. And the oil. You needed the oil. There were no limits to what you could do with rice: arroz blanco, of course, asopao, arroz con pollo, arroz con gandules, arroz junto, arroz con sarchichón, even arroz con dulce. Majarete prepared from rice flour. Rice was mother's milk and fincas and palm trees and what came before and was now and would be hereafter. Rice was Puerto Rico.

Yes, you're right, Comacho, it's going to be un gran revolú.

The groceries they bought at Comacho's were what Felicidad imagined Christmas presents to be. She refused Aníbal's offer of help. Such a pleasure as organizing her very own kitchen and pantry and foodstuffs she didn't want to share, and besides, he was the man of the house. She prepared coffee and fried eggs with longaniza sausage because he said he was hungry after such a compra and when he told her that he was going to go out for a little while, somebody somewhere he had to see about something, she promised him a fried pork chop for dinner. She tried to remember if Aníbal had seemed restless before. Was he annoyed with her? Perhaps she had spent too much money at Comacho's, but when she had asked Aníbal if she should stop, he said no, that they needed to eat and that she was only doing what he should have done.

After her husband left, Felicidad was lonely, but she wasn't alone. She felt the Spirit Prince watching as she stacked the small bags of beans, one on top of the other. Next to them, the large tub of lard and the small package of annatto seeds. Then the salt and pepper and the precious bottle of Spanish olive oil. Felicidad resisted turning around. The Spirit Prince would be sitting in the chair that Aníbal had recently vacated, the dirty coffee cup and saucer still set at his place. She had been too eager to put away her cache of groceries to wash them.

She lifted the ten-pound sack of rice with trembling fingers and placed it on the bottom shelf. How she loved this pantry. There was even room over in the corner for a broom and mop, dustpan and bucket, even an ironing board. Why hadn't she thought to ask Aníbal to buy them? Maybe she could borrow them for now from the neighbor downstairs, this doña.

Yes, if she glanced over her right shoulder she would see the Spirit Prince. Felicidad knew it was foolish to be nervous. He was here because she so desired it, because she so desperately wanted a companion, because she needed him. She wanted him to be sitting in Aníbal's chair.

Felicidad surveyed her beautiful pantry, its shelves stocked with more goods than she remembered in the country stores of her childhood, and she was grateful to her husband. And along with gratitude was love, delicate and floundering, but love just the same, and the loyalty due a husband from a wife. And so, when she turned around and glanced at the table, she saw only the dirty dishes, and she stepped lightly to clear them.

She wished her husband was home.

Chapter Twenty-six

Aníbal had left the apartment looking over his shoulder like a man on the run. He was running away from both his wife and his woman, from the decisions he had to make, the actions he had to take, from the cans of evaporated milk in the pantry that Felicidad bought to bake a flan. He ran out of the building into the cold and took in great gulps of air even as the coldness cut into his lungs. He welcomed the sharp pain as proof that he was free from the child-like trust of his beautiful wife. He had felt his breathing constricted in the apartment. He stuck his hands in the pockets of his work jacket. Already out of habit he had left his good coat for his wife. Ridiculous. As if she had anywhere to go. He hurried to his car. He sat in it, warming up the engine, watching the wisps of heat defrost the windows like a devouring nebulous being crawling up the glass. That was one of the first things he had learned from his fellow Puerto Ricans, you always warmed up the engine. Aníbal tapped the steering wheel with his gloved fingers. He would go over to Chago's house, see if Ana could lend him a coat for Felicidad until payday.

Ana answered his knock. "Muchacho," she said. "What's gotten into you? You look like the devil's following you."

"¡Diablo!" Chago whispered, shocked at his friend's wild look. "¡Ana, café!" He pushed Aníbal onto the sofa.

Aníbal stared without seeing at the coffee table set against one wall that Ana had turned into an altar, with plastic statuettes of her favorite saints and bottled candles, complete with a dish of cookies and small bowl of water in offering.

"Coffee won't do it." Ana hurried out of the room.

"I'm not ready to be a husband," Aníbal said.

"It's a little late to be thinking that." Chago lit a cigarette. Aníbal took it.

"I couldn't leave her there on the mountain." Aníbal didn't even want to think about the other alternative of sending Felicidad back to the aunt.

"You're tenderhearted." Chago sat next to Aníbal.

"She wanted to spend a Christmas with her family. Is that too much for a person to ask?" He took a drag of the cigarette.

"Have you been drinking?"

Aníbal didn't hear his friend's whispers.

"They're so poor, worse than we ever were. So desperate," Aníbal said.

"You're babbling." Chago patted his friend's arm, hoping to calm him.

"And her mother. That's one sad story."

"Everyone has a sad story." Ana came into the room with a bottle of rum and three shot glasses.

"Let's drink to sad stories." Chago took the bottle of rum.

Ana eyed Aníbal; her eyes were heavily outlined in black. "You need to get rid of that woman."

"Which one?" Chago asked, chuckling a little at his own joke.

"Don't be an idiot". Ana stood with her arms folded, shaking her head.

"It's not that simple," Aníbal said. "Marta's got some kind of encanto over me."

"Don't be a child," Ana said.

"Why didn't you marry Marta when you had the chance?" Chago poured the rum.

"Who said anything about marrying Marta?" Aníbal downed the rum and motioned for another.

"He's not that stupid." Ana's voice was doubtful.

"Then what's the problem?" Chago whispered.

Aníbal looked down at the empty shot glass in his hand. Yes, what was the problem? He had juggled two women before and he needed to do it only until he could figure out a plan. Why did he keep thinking of Felicidad's eyes?

"New Year's Day and you left her all alone." Ana clicked her tongue in that way women do, women Puerto Rican or otherwise: *tut, tuts* that said, You idiot, shame on you, stop feeling sorry for yourself and be a man.

"Go home," Ana said.

"Go home," Chago said.

Aníbal drove through the snow-covered streets abandoned by man and beast, time suspended by streetlight. Brick buildings and bungalows festooned in red and green lights glowed eerily white. He drove slower than he ever had on a mountain curve, slow enough to see into the lives of the buildings, into the living rooms of people sitting down in front of televisions or reading by lamplight. But eventually, he still arrived home.

Aníbal climbed the steps to his apartment. Maybe his friends were right, maybe the solution to his problem was the simple one, the honorable one.

She was on the second-floor landing.

"Marta," he said. Coño.

"The one and only," she said.

"What are you doing here?" She wore a tight white sweater. He could see the dark nipples pushing against the fabric.

"My mother lives here, don't you know." She pointed to the open door. "Why don't you come in?"

He needed only to reach out and hold her breasts in his hands, their familiar shape and weight a perfect balance in his palms.

"My wife—" What did Marta think? That he was the kind of man who could be enticed by a pair of tits, big tits chocolate brown in the palms of his hands?

"Your wife?" She put her hands on her hips. "Not that again."

"My wife." He didn't like the way she talked to him.

"Now it's your wife this, your wife that? That didn't take long," Marta said.

"It's none of your business." He was glad that she was making him angry. It distracted him from her tits, those big, chocolate-brown-in-the-palms-of-his-hands tits.

"Ha! Maybe you forgot that I'm not one who sits around night and day embroidering handkerchiefs like those girls from the island," Marta said.

She was agitated now, breathing a little faster; her breasts shook under the tight sweater.

Aníbal thought, One more time, if he could only see and hold them one more time, he would be satisfied, just to say good-bye to them even, those big chocolate tits, Marta's tits, his. Hombre, what was he thinking? If she would only stop talking, if she would only go back inside her mother's apartment, if she would only let him think a little. Maybe after dinner, after a good night's rest, maybe then he could figure things out.

Marta stepped in close so that her breasts skimmed his shirt. "Mami won't be home for an hour."

"I can't," he said.

"Oh, I know you can," Marta said.

Felicidad had a banquet waiting, the pork chops fried until the edges were just on the right side of burned, rice and beans, lettuce and tomato salad, and boiled malanga and yautía with olive oil for dipping. She kept the pork chops warm in the oven while he took a quick bath. He didn't want to come to the table stinking of what, he didn't say. She apologized for not having his bathwater ready. Felicidad didn't ask him where he had been or why he seemed so jittery, but served him first as his position as man of the house dictated. She watched him eat his dinner and yearned to speak to him, to have him speak to her. Felicidad wanted to reach across the table and touch his hand and say Thank you—for bringing her to America, for letting her buy everything she desired at Comacho's, for the lovely new home, and even for his shirt that she wore in the cold apartment. But his moodiness checked her. Instead she glanced at him for a moment and thought the words she would not voice, Thank you, Aníbal, for my new life.

They finished their dinner without speaking. Felicidad felt incredible sadness for the loss of conversation that she imagined should be between a man and a woman, a husband and a wife. She had thought that she and her new husband would have much to say. That they could be different from her uncle and the aunt, who rarely exchanged a word. At home Felicidad's mother never ate dinner with her husband. She was too busy meting out what food there was to the children, who took their plates outside. Papi, too tired from a day working on the farm to carry on a conversation, ate with the same efficiency of movement with which he planted corn or picked beans.

She had been trained to wait to speak until her elders or her betters spoke to her. Well-bred children, young adults, and young wives waited for permission before speaking (Dios libre that they interrupt!). Felicidad remembered how she had once stood at the aunt's elbow while she chatted with a customer, waiting to tell her that one of the ovens in la panadería was overheating, but the aunt had ignored her until she smelled the burning bread.

The aunt had tutored Felicidad and Adela in the proper way of a wife. She wasn't going to have anyone saying that the women in the family were brutas. She had taught the girls by reciting anecdotes. Remember that Clarita Pérez who used to come in and buy pancitos? Well, she interrupted her husband while he was speaking and he gave her a nice slap right in front of her mother, who told her that she had brought her up to know better. And Lucy Guzman? Adela had gone to school with her. Her father sent her to bed without her supper for a week just for not saying Su permiso, as was correct when addressing one's betters. That was the well-bred way, the proper way, the Spanish way.

Here she was, in her very own kitchen, with her very own husband, and she wasn't sure of what she could ask of him, expect of him, demand of him. After all, he was a stranger to her still, more so than on the island. He was not the Aníbal she had known. She wanted to ask Aníbal what was troubling him, if it was something with which she could help him. Felicidad pitied her new husband his troubles. What could have happened in a single month to change him so?

All evening Aníbal could hear his mother's voice telling him what he had done with Marta was mal hecho, that he should remember how she had suffered when his father went about his pocavergüenzas. She would say that he had a good girl for his wife and he needed to do his duty by her and leave the other one, la divorciada, alone.

That night in bed, Aníbal again heard his mother's voice, this time urging him to make love to his wife. Something held him back. Maricón, it couldn't be his conscience. Why the fuck should his conscience be bothering him when it hadn't earlier when he'd been with Marta? Shit, he was an asshole. It was like it had been before his marriage: one woman here, another there. Same old Aníbal. Whenever he had troubles, he tried to leave them inside a woman. Maybe making love to his wife might help him figure out the mess in his head, but damn, he couldn't do it. Something held him back, froze his thing to the size of his pinkie, and he lay awake, thinking, How the fuck am I going to get through the day at the factory, what the hell am I going to do with my wife? How the devil am I going to get rid of Felicidad or stop wanting Marta's big brown tits?

He recalled Felicidad's happiness at Comacho's, a little girl opening up her Christmas presents, and then, later, at the dinner table, the Felicidad he had first known back in her place. He couldn't just make love to the Felicidad from the island when it pleased him, he couldn't pretend to care about her and send her away a few days later. He had to think, to make up his mind what to do. No, he couldn't touch her, not that Felicidad, not the one from the waterfall, not the girl skipping down the aisles at Comacho's, not the Felicidad playing wife.

Felicidad moved in her sleep, and he propped himself on his elbow to look at her. She smelled so good, so different from the awkward girl who got off the plane stinking like the farm and la pobreza. This girl he could eat. This wife of his was a pretty girl, a lovely girl, a delicious girl.

He wanted to touch her, just a little, her shoulder maybe, but who knew where that could lead to. He was only a man, after all. She was like a cousin—no, a sister—yes, a sister. He turned his back to her and pulled the covers over his head, but he didn't think he was going to be able to sleep.

Aníbal hated the winter days most, not because of the infamous Chicago wind that cut his cheeks so that he forgot he had ever felt the warm caress of a Puerto Rican breeze, and not because of the long, gray days that lingered on in endless rotation; he hated winter most because he entered the factory in the black of predawn and left it in the shadowy gloom of a winter night. At the factory entrance, when he slid his time card into the machine and heard it click, he felt the click punching a hole in his dreams. For eight or ten hours a day, sometimes twelve, he was guided by the spirit-zapping power of fluorescent lights and the tick tick of the clocks and the din that is a factory full of men shuffling in their posts, turning and shifting and twisting and lifting and throwing. And then there was the stink of labor, the curses in Spanish and Polish and English and who knew what other languages he couldn't understand. He heard only the beat, beat of his heart counting down the seconds to break time then lunchtime then break time, then the blare of the horn calling out get-the-fuck-out-of-here time.

Some days he wondered how much longer he could bear it. Aníbal wasn't the man he wanted to be. In Puerto Rico he was a white man, puertorriqueño, sí, pero blanco. Here he was a man of color, brown or beige or blue. He could be any color, just not white. His hair was like a white man's hair, his eyes hazel, but he wasn't white. He could be standing in a group of ten white men and he was white until he opened his mouth to speak. His Eng-glesh came out of his mouth in chunks—two or three words mezclado, mixed together like rice and beans or arroz con gandules. Eng-glesh. He spoke Eng-glesh a la Español.

Over in California in his first job on the mainland, he learned English, mostly the names of vegetables and fruits he picked: tomatoes, apples, pears, blueberries, strawberries, lettuce, plus the names for the parts of a woman's body: ass, tits, boobs, cunt, pussy, slit, and such. He also learned automobile parts from his stint in Michigan: fender, headlights, grille, bumper, trunk, hood, radiator, battery, spark plugs, gas line, engine, ignition switch. From women he learned good, great, slow, faster, harder, there, yes, there.

Aníbal wanted to be like his father and work for himself, although he wasn't sure about being a businessman. All the businessmen he knew didn't mind cheating a customer out of a few dollars or even just a nickel. Like Comacho over at the grocery store. Aníbal had seen him putting his thumb on the scale along with the ham. If a customer called him on it, then the next time he was laid off or fired and money was scarce, Comacho said cash only. That was the way with these businessmen like Comacho, charging Aníbal's neighbor Doña Petra extra for a pound of gandules, just because his store was the only place walking distance a person could get comida criolla. Unless he could change from a decent man to a cheater, he wasn't too sure el negocio was for him.

When Aníbal first came to Chicago, he worked in the factory during the week and Saturdays he did collections for Paquito Hernández, Chago's cousin. Paquito had a jewelry store over on North Avenue, plus he sold jewelry door-to-door and at family parties—anybody's family, didn't have to be his own—and baptisms and such. People said he even sold a diamond ring at a velorio right next to the recently departed, lying in the coffin dressed in a brand-new suit that his family had bought on time. Paquito had no shame. Everything was on credit, so somebody had to collect the payments, and for one whole summer, Aníbal carried in his shirt pocket a notebook and little yellow envelopes marked with customers' names. They stayed mostly empty. Aníbal liked to say, "Me and el negocio don't make love."

Little old ladies who had no business buying earrings sent their grandbabies running for their handkerchiefs so they could cry into them the stories of their miserable lives for Aníbal's benefit. Their pockmarked daughters plied him with café con leche. Sometimes, he was lucky and it was a husband who poured him un palo de ron along with the promise of two dollars next week for his wife's gold necklace. Housewives invited him to bed if he canceled their accounts. He was nice about it, but he always said no, next week pay double. If he bumped into one of those damas on the street, he just might take up her offer if he were in the mood for fucking, but doing it for money, either for her or for him, he didn't do that. Sex should be just for sex, because it was fun, because a man wanted it, because it felt good, because he was horny, because he had a hard day, because he had a good day. Sex was sacred, a blessing from God, and exchanging it for money made it unclean.

Or perhaps he just didn't feel like fucking a woman so desperate she would be willing to give her body to a stranger for a few cents. But he didn't blame people for buying jewelry they couldn't afford from Paquito Hernández, who waved shiny objects in front of them when they were at their most vulnerable. Maybe it had been a while since the housewife had worn a pretty bauble or maybe she just found out her niece was fucking her husband and she needed a gold bracelet to make her feel better and why not give that maricón another bill to pay, he would just spend the money on the young slut anyway. Maybe la viejita just wanted to remember being young and pretty and the way silver earrings danced at her earlobes. Maybe Julio Torres couldn't get it up and that big pinkie ring made him feel like a man again. Maybe Paquito Hernández had said, "Don't worry, you pay little by little. Take the bracelet, consider me your compadre."

A man had to be a certain type to be a good businessman. He couldn't mind when people crossed the street because they didn't want to meet him or when they told their little kids to say they weren't home when he knocked on their doors. He had to be tough, he had to say, "But Mrs. Pérez, you said you would pay me last week and the week before that. You know the bill won't disappear, and then there's the interest. Pay something, Mrs. Pérez. You want to keep that ring on your finger, doncha?" No, he didn't think being a businessman was for him. Still, he didn't want to be one of those old guys slaving in the factory and having a young punk like that asshole Mackie telling him when it was lunchtime so he could go shit off the clock.

He didn't think he could hold off much longer from beating the crap out of Mackie. His compadres advised him to lay out for Mackie after work, wait for him in the alley. Aníbal told them he didn't think so, that that would make him a pussy just like Mackie. When the time came to fight Mackie, they would do it honest and clean with fists, no knives like Mackie and all the rest of the blancos thought. A man said he was Puerto Rican and he was asked, "Where you knife?" as if he were a butcher or a cook.

The people on the island thought that because on the mainland they had jobs, they were rich. His family didn't understand that he had to pay for rent, electricity, car payments, gasoline, food, everything. Back home his father had little money, but he didn't have to pay rent on the farm because it was family land. Aníbal's mother washed clothes for free in a galvanized tub or in the river. Aníbal didn't like the thought of Felicidad bent over the tub. He planned on taking her to the Laundromat.

No, señor, it wasn't so easy here in America. Daily he studied the English-language newspapers, keeping an eye out for the words *Puerto Rican*. He wanted to know what the American planned to do to him next. Nothing would surprise him. The United States was a country where the Puerto Rican was treated like a child who needed to be toilet-trained. Men were not men; the best of the blancos explained to them the simplest of tasks as if they lacked basic intelligence. When they did their jobs well, they patted them on the back like well-behaved children. If they screwed up, the white men muttered to one another, "Well, what can you expect?"

Puerto Ricans got off the plane full of energy and hope and, if they were lucky, went back home with their suitcases stuffed with clothing from Woolworth's. They told their relatives, "America is fine. Americans are buena gente. Jobs are easy and plentiful. The snow, the snow is God's blessing." And then the next batch of young, home-grown hombres y mujeres got on the plane to the promise of America, leaving behind their past for an uncertain future. But what the fuck choice did they have?

Aníbal planned to be somebody one day, to be the man he had dreamed he would be, respected by all and loved by some. He wanted to be a man like his father.

As a new bride, Felicidad spent the first days in the apartment in a dream-like trance. She washed the dishes, cleaned the stove, made the bed, polished the precious toilet and bathtub until she slipped when she sat on them. She couldn't decide which she liked more, which she was willing to live without if she were compelled to—the toilet or the bathtub? She spent hours looking out the windows, staring down at the street. She began to embroider tiny, perfectly stitched roses in earnest. Although she could embroider many other flowers, roses comforted her, reminding her of her mother and another, simpler, more innocent time. When Doña Petra admired her handiwork, she offered to add roses to her plain brown scarf.

Felicidad wished that she had some fabric and a sewing machine to make curtains for the windows. She was embarrassed to sleep in a room where the neighbors across the courtyard could peek in and see her sleeping with a man, husband or not. It was as bad as sleeping in her parents' house, where one night she had gone to bed and the moon was so bright it had streamed into the room through the cracks in the wood walls. She and her sisters had laughed at the light until she saw an eye peering through a missing knot in the wood. She screamed, sure that it was a Spirit. Papi had jumped from the bed and Vicente and the other boys joined in the chase. They found Tomás el Tonto squirming with fear in the bushes. Papi had chastised him and sent him on his way, saying poor nutrition made a man soft in the head.

Felicidad was rich now; she didn't have to worry about holes in the walls or young men with the intellect of children. She had her own apartment, a pantry full of food, a radio. The only other time she had ever felt so alone was when she was caring for Doña Carolina, the aunt's invalid mother. Now here she was, thousands of miles away from the island, looking out the window of a third-floor apartment and staring down into the street. She counted the cars driving down the boulevard; she counted the trees that lined the street. She took to watching for Doña Petra, her downstairs neighbor. She would run down and help her carry her basket of laundry. After the first time, Felicidad made the coffee while Doña Petra separated the clothes into piles—no starch, light starch, starch.

When Felicidad cleaned her apartment, she turned on the radio; it kept her from the silence of her days. She fell in love with Nat King Cole and Doris Day and Perry Como and Rosemary Clooney and Ella Fitzgerald. She listened carefully to the lyrics, picking up a phrase here and there. Often she thought a song was about heartbreak because of the singer's mournful voice, and she would dream of someone who loved her so much that he would sing about it. Sometimes her companion would be Aníbal, but other times it would be the Spirit Prince by her side. In the late afternoon she turned on all the lights in the rooms, vanquishing any thoughts other than those anticipating Aníbal's arrival and the hope that this would be the day that the Aníbal from the island would return to her.

If she woke in the middle of the night, Aníbal facing away from her, she felt the Spirit Prince watching over her. It made her feel less lonely yet a little ashamed to have him there while her husband was sleeping. She welcomed his companionship in those very first days when she waited for Aníbal to come home from work, days when she had nothing to do but housework, gray winter days that stretched out endlessly with only the arrival of her silent husband to brighten them.

Each day, Felicidad hoped it would be the day when her husband would talk to her, that he would be the Aníbal from the waterfall and she could be that Felicidad, too. Where was that Aníbal? How had she lost him here in America? How could she find him?

Aníbal took her to Chago and Ana's to celebrate Three Kings Day. Silver HAPPY NEW YEAR banners and 1953 streamers fluttered a welcome in the open doorway. Every puertorriqueño in Chicago was there: men in suits that would never be worn in offices, women spilling out of cocktail dresses so tight that the outlines of bras and panties were visible on those who wore them, and few did.

He steered her through the smoky living room filled with dancing couples making love with mambo. She liked the music and the racket of people laughing and talking over it, the children of all ages dressed in their Christmas clothes running around in packs, bumping into their parents or, if they were lucky, strangers who were less likely to yell or send them away with a little smack. Every man and woman moved in a path of scent and cigarettes. With each woman's kiss, Felicidad could imagine the woman spraying herself with her favorite perfume or dusting with a fancy puff, the white powder coating her skin and, to her hopeful eyes, appearing to lighten it a full shade. The men squeezed her hand, their palms and fingers cold from their drinks, their eyes assessing her physical attributes, their smiles welcoming another pretty face.

Music engulfed them even in the bedroom, where they added their coats to the piles on the bed. Aníbal stacked the presents they brought on the bureau, toys for the children and a box of chocolate-covered cherries for Ana. He knelt to remove Felicidad's galoshes.

"Felicidad! Since when did you start shaving your legs?" Aníbal ran his hands down her legs.

"Today," Felicidad said.

"I didn't give you permission," Aníbal said.

She admired her pretty legs. "They look so nice and clean. All the girls here do it. Doña Petra says her daughter does it. Don't you like it?"

Aníbal gave her that look a husband gives his wife when he would like to tell her a thing or two but knows his own temper and that he would be better off mute.

Out in the hallway he spoke close to her ear to be heard over mambo.

"Chago is more like my brother than my real brother, Diego."

"And Ana, is she more like your sister?" She wasn't nervous about meeting Chago, only Ana. How she wanted Ana to like her. How lovely it would be to have a friend.

"I never had a sister," he said.

Three women in movie-star makeup and low-cut dresses crushed spices and chopped loaves of bread at the kitchen table, their mouths moving as fast as their fingers. They offered garlic kisses and good wishes and left the kitchen in a trail of bread crumbs. Ana was at the stove turning over with a ladle the arroz con gandules cooking in a huge pot that sat on two burners. She embraced them and waved the spoon over them like a priest blessing the faithful.

"You did good," she told Aníbal, accepting the box of chocolates. "For a while there I was afraid you wouldn't do me proud." To Felicidad she said, "I was like a mother to your husband, or maybe a sister, because how could I be mother to this machote?"

They laughed at the idea of Ana, this woman in a dress with fringes that failed to constrain her restless energy and scattered electrical charges when she moved, ever being Aníbal's mother. Chago came in, kissed Felicidad and laughed, too, being one of those people who don't need to know the joke to laugh. They all leaned closer to hear him.

"People told me they had seen a pretty girl go into the kitchen but never come out. I thought I'd rescue Felicidad before Ana puts her to work," Chago whispered.

"Take Aníbal. He looks a little shaky, like he could use a highball. Felicidad and I will have a little chat." Ana urged her husband out of the kitchen with the spoon.

"We have presents for the children," Aníbal said.

"They're around here somewhere. Don't worry, they'll find you," Chago said.

Ana took Felicidad's arm and led her to the table. It took Ana ten minutes and one rum and Coke, Felicidad's first, to get her life story from birth to the present.

She set the teakettle on the stove to boil water for coffee. "Felicidad. What kind of name is that? I never heard of a Puerto Rican woman named Felicidad," Ana said. "Where did your mother find such a name?"

"I don't know," Felicidad said, wishing not for the first time that her mother had named her María.

Ana checked the rice, tasting a few grains. "Needs another ten minutes."

Next to the rice a tall stockpot boiled. Felicidad took a deep breath and breathed in Christmas. "Pasteles," she said. Every year, she had helped the aunt make the traditional meat pies to sell en la fonda.

"Nobody makes them as good as me. Probably not even your own mother." She smiled when she said it so Felicidad wasn't too scared of her. "Tell me you can cook."

"I can cook," Felicidad said.

"That's a relief. Some of these girls coming up nowadays from the island can't. They're too busy washing clothes at the river or whatever they do, so they can't cook. No excuses, a woman should know how to cook," Ana said.

Three little girls, fancy in lace dresses and Mary Jane shoes, pushed open the door, letting in laughter and music. They nodded respectfully then left, shutting Felicidad from the festivities.

"Are you madly in love with your husband?" Ana refilled Felicidad's glass. She made herself a cup of coffee.

Felicidad wasn't shocked that Ana was so blunt, not after all

the women from la panadería. Still, a little warning. She would
have liked to prepare her answer. Felicidad moved her fingers
up and down the glass, relishing the coldness on her fingertips. Normally, she didn't like her hands feeling cold, but now it
helped her to concentrate.

"I'm lucky to be his wife." She kept her gaze on her glass.
She didn't want this stranger discerning how her new husband
slept with his back to her.

"I'm glad you realize it, because your husband is a good man
with a generous heart, but you're going to have to work hard
to keep him home. He's not used to staying in one place with
one woman. He's lived like an alley cat, stopping here and there
wherever he pleased. You will have to become a wild woman
because a sweet, young thing like you will soon bore him," Ana
said.

Felicidad looked into Ana's eyes, which she had outlined
with black eyeliner so that the dark pupils seemed to penetrate
right into her heart. Felicidad wished that she could confide in
Ana. She wanted to make her husband happy, but ever since she
had arrived, Aníbal had avoided touching her except for just
now when he had run his hands down her legs, and that was just
because she had shaved them. It was too bad that she didn't have
anything else to shave.

Ana got up to refill her coffee cup. "Take my advice: Ani-
mate yourself. You saw those women here earlier? Any one of
them would be glad to take your husband off your hands, and
two of them are already married."

She kept looking over Ana's shoulder, wondering, Where
was Aníbal and how many shots of rum did a husband need
when his wife shaved her legs?

"Doña Ana, I—"

Ana's coffee spilled black on the white saucer. "Don't doña

me. That's for old ladies like my mother and mother-in-law. I'm not so much older than you."

Felicidad had been taught that to give an older, married woman the title of *doña* was to bestow the ultimate respect. "Forgive me, I didn't mean to offend you," she said.

Ana could see that this young wife of Aníbal's was quite the little jíbara. She touched Felicidad's hand. "Claro, you didn't. Listen, you need to wake up, to look around you and see what's what. You have to stop being a little girl and be a woman to your man. That's all I can say, and I say this with the love of a sister and not only for Aníbal, because I feel that you and I will become close as sisters."

Felicidad stared down at the Formica table, Ana's words a jumble in her head. What did she mean that she was like a little girl? And how was she supposed to be a woman to a man who obviously didn't want her? She wished that Aníbal would come and take her out to the party where, in the crowd of people, she could pretend to be the happy little wife.

Chapter Twenty-seven

February 1953

He wanted to fuck her.

Before Felicidad came, he'd counted the minutes until his shift was over at the factory, but since her arrival, he dreaded going home. It took all his control to walk through the door of the apartment and not make love to her. There was his wife in his green plaid shirt and all he wanted to do was to slide his hands beneath it. She would shiver from his cold palms on her breasts and he would quiet her squeals with his kisses. They would do it right there against the living room wall with his pants bunched about his ankles. Instead he kept his hands in his pockets to stop himself. It wouldn't be right, not when he was messing with Marta, not when he still didn't have a plan.

When he sat across from Felicidad at the kitchen table, he wolfed down his food, eager to leave the intimacy of the meal. He was careful not to let his gaze linger on her collarbone, delicate above the neckline of his shirt, or to think about his fingertips grazing the soft skin just below it. After a few attempts to draw him into conversation, she didn't speak, and for this he was grateful. Yet he was aware of her every movement, of her lips wet from her cup of coffee or glass of water, how she tilted her head so that her hair shielded her face. Later, when Felicidad sat next to him on the sofa laughing at the antics on *I Love Lucy* or entranced with the singing or comedy acts on *Toast of the Town,* he would look at her and realize that he was smiling. He told himself that it didn't mean anything; only that she was like a sister or cousin and he liked his relatives to be happy.

Most of the time he could almost believe that Felicidad was like a sister or a cousin. And that the reason it felt so unnatural to be alone in the apartment with her was that he didn't have sisters or close female cousins. He wasn't used to the intimacy of living with a young woman whom he wasn't fucking. In fact, he'd never spent so much time with any lover, not even Marta, so of course it was logical that it would be difficult living with Felicidad. It was to be expected, this awkwardness, this sense of waiting. Shit, each night he lay down next to a woman he couldn't touch. Or wouldn't. (It was a point of honor.) How unnatural was that? Yes, he had to continuously remind himself, she was like a cousin to him or a sister, yes, a sister.

But he couldn't kid himself when she took a bath. The bathroom was right off the living room and he could hear her singing softly. He found himself turning off the sound of the television and listening for the splash of water as she lowered herself in the tub. If he closed his eyes, he could follow the soapy washcloth on its journey over her body—the collarbone that inexplicably made him ache with its fragility, the crook between her neck and shoulders on which he'd last pressed kisses back on the island, her breasts that daily taunted him to hold them in his palms, her soft stomach and the belly button he had teased with the tip of his tongue once he'd found her ticklish. When Aníbal thought of her rubbing the washcloth between her legs, soaping up the dark curls, he feared he might go mad. He had to shove his hands inside his pockets to keep from busting down the door or worse—begging that she let him in.

He paced the living room, the TV flashing black and white, the newscaster's lips soundlessly moving, yet Aníbal knew he was mocking him for being an idiot, causing his own suffering. He couldn't help pausing in the tiny hallway between the living room and bathroom, waiting for what he knew was still to come, that moment when he would hear her pull the rubber stopper so that the water rushed down the drain. He stood perfectly still, holding his breath, eyes closed, seeing her stand up in the tub wet and shivering, beads of water on her flushed skin, her nipples erect, her pubic hair in a wet tangle, as beautiful as she had been that day at the waterfall when she had been his happy bride laughing at him for wanting to make love under the clear blue sky.

Fuck! Aníbal's throat was dry. He went to the pantry and took a swig of rum straight from the bottle. When he heard her enter their bedroom, he took another. He went to take a shower but the room was steamy from her bath. He had to get out and he grabbed his coat, putting it on as he ran down the stairs. It seemed that since Felicidad's arrival, he was always running somewhere. Aníbal sat in his car with the broken heater he hadn't gotten around to fixing, for once glad of the cold.

He couldn't help recalling how just two nights ago, he held her in his arms. They had gone over to Chago and Ana's for one of their get-togethers. Saturday night with a dozen of their closest friends, drinking a little rum and dancing a little merengue, pretending that they were back in Puerto Rico rather than fucking below-zero Chicago. Aníbal noticed that Felicidad had slipped off to the kitchen. That was all right with him. He didn't want her dancing with the other men, friends or no, not when he had to treat her like his cousin or his sister. Aníbal danced with Ana and the other women; mambo, merengue, guaguancó, cumbia, and then someone put on a Rafaél Hernández Marín record and dimmed the lights. It was dangerous to dance a bolero with another man's wife, even a compadre's.

Aníbal had another shot of rum while he contemplated dancing with Felicidad. A brother could dance with his sister, a cousin with his cousin. He was considering another shot before he went to find her when Ana called out to him to dance with his little bride. He found Felicidad at the kitchen sink, elbows deep in dishwater. Without thinking, he came up behind her and wrapped his arms around her waist. She leaned back into his arms and he was surprised at how right it felt.

Aníbal whispered in her ear. "Dance with me."

"I can't." She raised her hands; the soapy water glided down her arms.

"Dry them or not. I don't care," Aníbal said.

"I don't know how to dance," Felicidad said.

He kissed her hair. "It's like making love; it comes natural."

"Show me." She turned around.

He put his hands on her waist, drawing her to him, pressing her body into his. She looked up at him with those eyes of hers that said he was everything she ever wanted. He held her closer, thinking that just for this bolero, for this single dance, he would forget that she was his sister or his cousin. Just for this one dance, he would pretend that he was the man she believed him to be, the man he wanted to be, and that she was the only woman for him.

On this pitifully cold night, he recalled how he taught her to dance, how her wet hands on his shirt had sent shivers up his back, and how she felt so right in his arms.

He lit another cigarette and looked up at his apartment and tried not to think. Sometimes, it was better not to think.

Chapter Twenty-eight

When Marta came to visit on that fateful February day, Felicidad invited her to sit on her prized possession, the new red velveteen sofa protected in plastic that Aníbal had let her pick out. Marta sat sideways, showing off her sleek, shapely legs. She balanced her cup of coffee on her lap, which Felicidad had hurried to prepare while her honored guest made herself comfortable en la sala.

With the pride of a little girl giving her first tea party, Felicidad carried in crackers and white cheese and sweet, sticky guava chunks. She set the plate on the coffee table she had improvised out of a piece of cloth and a crate begged from Comacho.

Marta sat there all chichi drinking Felicidad's coffee and ignoring the food as if the offering were too provincial, too backward for it to touch her red, red lips.

When Marta swallowed, she tilted her head back so that Felicidad could better admire the cocoa smoothness of her throat and the generous mounds of her breasts. Marta was one of those mujeres who knew the power of her body, who knew her skin emitted a sexual odor that said, I like to fuck—an odor that only the dead or naive or too young can't identify. Felicidad was in the naive category.

Felicidad perched on the edge of the sofa, knees closed, feet together, a please-like-me smile on her face.

She felt satisfaction, pride, in fact, to be able to show off to another woman her own home. She wondered on what pretense she could ask Marta into the kitchen so that she could admire her beautiful turquoise refrigerator.

Books that Aníbal claimed were in the apartment when he'd started renting it filled the shelves. He thought they probably belonged to a long-ago tenant back when Americans lived on the block, before even los polacos. Felicidad had wiped off dead roaches and spiders and lined them by height. They were all in English except for a few volumes of Spanish poems—Neruda, Gautier Benítez, Lloréns Torres—but the books and authors meant little to her.

In school a favorite teacher, a Mr. Colón, liked to tease that he was a descendant of Cristóbal Colón. Mr. Colón always read a poem at the end of class, sometimes one by José de Diego or Gautier Benítez or another Puerto Rican poet. Fridays, he read in English, a sonnet of Shakespeare or a few poems of Emily Dickinson, his favorite. Felicidad had thrilled to the rhythm of the words, the song of the sentences. She ached for the beauty presented to her in Mr. Colón's sonorous voice. Now, years later, she recalled Mr. Colón standing in front of the class, cradling a book between his palms as if it were more necessary for survival than the bread and sausage he ate for lunch.

When she lived with the aunt, she had never had time for reading and never practiced the English words she learned in school. What mattered most to her now was the books' physical beauty, the heft and weight, the rich leather binding, the delicate, gilt-edged pages, and the feel of each volume in her hands. She loved to leaf through them almost as much as she enjoyed standing in her pantry and surveying her bounty. But she was neither curious nor motivated enough to read them, let alone decipher their meaning.

She was so grateful to have all these beautiful things surrounding her. And now she was entertaining her first guest like a bona fide ama de casa. Mami would be proud to observe the proper way she was conducting herself as hostess. Felicidad thought that even the aunt would approve.

At this point, Marta was still only Marta, her neighbor Doña Petra's daughter, la divorciada Marta, a woman to be pitied. How else could a decent married woman think of another of her sex cast off by her husband, a woman whom even her own mother knew had been used by more than one man as surely as if she had crowded around her bed and witnessed the matings, as if she had heard her screeches or the banging of the bed or the grunts of exertion? Her virginity, a woman's only gift, guarded and revered by her parents, her brothers, the community, the Church, and probably even the government, long gone. It wasn't only that her marriage had lasted but one year. It was much worse. Marta was also una mujer operada. All that female equipment down there, where sperm traveled by way of the sacred tunnel, had been chopped off. People whispered that it had been Marta's choice. Every other Puerto Rican had a sister or aunt, neighbor, or friend who'd had her tubes tied or, better yet, cut, just to be safe from pregnancy—but always after the multiple blessings of a handful of children. Marta didn't have any children, and now not even a husband.

Marta's allure captivated Felicidad. She was a girl in the

presence of a movie star, awed by such obvious glamour and sophistication. Felicidad tugged the skirt of her housedress, wishing she had known Marta was coming to visit so she could have changed her dress, put on nylons, maybe her red sandals. She envied without knowing that she envied the nerve Marta must possess to bleach her hair platinum blond, flaunting convention, and having the audacity to visit Felicidad's home, this woman branded USED AND DISREPUTABLE by her experience, rumors clinging to her skin.

In Puerto Rico, Felicidad wouldn't have been able to receive her; the aunt would not have permitted it. Marta might be admitted into the homes of close relatives, but only when the children were sent away to keep them from her bad example and possible contamination, and the men safe in the fields or toiling in another town.

All this was enough for Felicidad to shut the door on Marta's face. Aníbal might also have disapproved; he might know of Marta's bad reputation. But Felicidad wanted a friend so badly that she chose not to think of Aníbal's wishes. Instead she thought of Doña Petra, who was so sweet to her. And she thought of herself.

She was lonely. She spent her day waiting. She waited for Aníbal to finish his coffee and toast so she could buckle his boots for him and help him with his coat and hand him his lunch, preparing to send him off to work as if he were a soldier going off to war instead of a twenty-block car ride to the factory. She waited by the front window peering down to the street, waiting for Aníbal to clear the snow off his car, waiting for the car to warm up, waiting for him to go. And then she had a whole day to fill: How many hours could she stand at the window, how many hours could she embroider, how many times could she mop the floor or clean the bathroom, when could she run down to see Doña Petra, how many hours could she wonder when was her husband going to make love to her?

When Marta knocked on her door that day, she welcomed her as a fellow puertorriqueña, a woman to be a sister, an older sister from whom Felicidad could ask advice and guidance in her new world, someone she could talk to about her husband, someone who could tell her how to find the young man she had known in Puerto Rico, the young man under the waterfall. Marta had to be buena gente, forget what the chismosas said. After all, she was Doña Petra's daughter.

The rim of Marta's coffee cup shimmered red and wet with her kiss. She dug two fingers into the cleft between her breasts, groping in there for a cigarette and a pack of matches, the way other women search through their purses. Felicidad's own breasts began to tingle. She didn't know why.

Felicidad tried not to stare at Marta's breasts but she found herself fascinated by their shape, which reminded her of coconuts in their hard green shells.

Marta tapped her cigarette against the saucer with short jabs.

"You're so young, only twenty. Or is it fourteen? Such a sweet little wife for Aníbal. Are you woman enough for him?"

She decided Marta's breasts were more like eggplants. She had seen eggplants in the fancy grocery store where Aníbal had once taken her and she had marveled over their shape and deep purple color. Her own were the size of mangoes and as sweet, Aníbal had once said back on the island. He had taken their weight in his palms and squeezed them until she cried out with pain or pleasure, she hadn't been sure which. She was confused by all these thoughts of breasts. Was this normal for a married woman? Was she becoming one of those mujeres people whispered about?

"Felicidad." Marta drew the cigarette to her lips.

"Hmmm?" Felicidad admired how she could smoke her cigarette and still keep the cup and saucer balanced on her thigh just like a woman she had once seen in a film.

"Muchacha, are you back in el campo with the pigs and chickens?" Marta asked.

"Forgive me, Marta. I'm a bad hostess." Felicidad made to get up. "May I get you something else to eat?"

"Your husband." Marta sucked on her cigarette.

Felicidad was drawn to the puckered red lips, fascinated by the way the bright color contrasted with Marta's teeth, the beige of leche con café. She waited for Marta's laugh, signifying another joke, unsure if she liked the other woman's sense of humor. But she knew women like Marta, who enjoyed relaying crude comments about male and female genitalia (never in mixed company, of course, always waiting until the older damas left the room), making the married women laugh, the unmarried girls blush. They'd swear they could guess by a man's hand the length and girth of his penis: One man's penis was a green plantain, hard and thick around the middle, another's was sure to be as soft and limp as his handshake.

Marta tilted her head back, blowing smoke up to the ceiling, little puffs that heightened Felicidad's enchantment.

"Aníbal told you? About me?"

"About you?"

"About us."

Felicidad looked down at her feet, the spell broken. She was wearing the shoes she had worn en la panadería. Sturdy brown shoes better suited for a grandmother.

Marta flicked her cigarette over the ashtray. A speck floated on top of a chunk of guava paste. Often Felicidad had yearned for a piece while working for the aunt, only to have to wait until offered. Why, even today, she had served herself only a sliver. She was certain Marta didn't mean to show her any disrespect. Some people just didn't have any manners, no reflection on their mothers. She shouldn't let a little bit of ash annoy her so.

"Aníbal needs a woman, not a girl. A woman like me who knows how to do the things he likes," Marta said.

Suddenly she didn't see Marta quite clearly. Felicidad blinked, struggling to clear her vision, to regulate her breathing. Not even the aunt could criticize the evenness of her tone, her precise enunciation. Felicidad was grateful to have to labor over each word. It gave her time to comprehend Marta's revelation.

"I'm not sure what you mean," Felicidad said.

Marta pointed her cigarette at the door. "Your husband and I are lovers."

Felicidad understood now. This creature sitting on her sofa with her bleached-blond hair and her breasts struggling to break free of her blouse was the reason that her husband couldn't bear to touch her, the reason that Aníbal didn't want her now. Oh, the pain of it, the utterly numbing pain of yet again being unloved and unwanted, worse now, because he had sought her out and, for a time, if only briefly, he had loved her and she had belonged to him.

Later, she would recall jumping up and knocking Marta's cup and saucer into her lap and grabbing her arm and lifting her off the sofa, its plastic sheeting making a ripping sound as Marta's legs were torn from it. Felicidad had never before had the luxury of being an impetuous girl. She wondered if a Spirit had possessed her.

Felicidad shut her ears to the curses and the shattering

porcelain. She cared only about getting that puta Marta out of her house, her clean, little apartment, the four rooms plus bath that had been a dream fulfilled. That puta Marta's cigarette burned a tiny circle onto the plastic slipcover, testimony that her life with Aníbal had been only that—a dream.

She pulled Marta to the door, yanked it open, and pushed her out.

In the hall Marta wiped at the coffee dripping down her skirt. "Didn't you want to know, you stupid little jíbara? I was trying to do the decent thing," Marta said.

"Decent? If it weren't for Doña Petra, I would kick your big ass down these stairs." Felicidad could see Marta rolling down the wood steps like a ball of color, platinum curls, smooth brown legs, and red—blouse, nails, lips.

"Your husband likes this big ass." Marta placed her hands on her hips.

Felicidad slammed the door, trying to control her shaking. Never had she grabbed or pushed another human being. Felicidad found her own behavior deplorable and even childish. Perhaps she was wrong to act so to Marta, puta or no. She hoped that Doña Petra would never learn of it.

She didn't want to think of what Marta had said about Aníbal. She pulled at the laces of her shoes and kicked them off. One hit the wall and made a tiny dent. Barefoot, Felicidad walked to the sofa and turned over the cushion that Marta's cigarette had burned. She picked up the plate on the coffee table and ate a chuck of guava paste and then she ate another. Then for the first time since the day her mother stood on the roof, naked, Felicidad cried.

Felicidad would come to view her life in two parts: before and after that puta Marta.

In their bedroom Felicidad waited out Aníbal and the winter day. Light had long since slipped out of the apartment, along with the innocent, trusting Felicidad.

She leaned against the headboard of their bed, feeling queasy from all the sugar of the guava paste. She wore the beige house-dress Aníbal's mother had given her. It was ugly and too large, but she was ugly and unloved. She knew she would never wear the brown old-lady shoes again, not even if she had to walk barefoot in the snow.

While she waited for Aníbal, she thought about what that puta Marta had said about her husband. It came to her now that Ana had been warning her about Marta, counseling her to be more than a good wife. But what did that mean exactly? If he didn't want her then what could she do about it? Did he really prefer that puta Marta to her? Yes, Felicidad could see how he might. Instinctively, she knew that Marta would know what a man needed, and that she would give it to him.

Did Aníbal care about her even a little? And love, what about love? Did it matter to Felicidad so very much if he loved her? Felicidad had lived years without a mother's love and she knew that, yes, she could survive without love. But when her husband had loved her, those few enchanted days on the island, she had discovered that she liked loving a man and being loved in return.

She didn't greet her husband at the door to take his coat and hat and gloves as a good wife should. She heard him call out her name and then the click of the locks. His boots made a clump clump sound on the linoleum.

The fool was trailing snow on her clean floors.

"Felicidad. Felicidad!"

She didn't answer. Worry was the least he owed her.

He stood in the frame of the bedroom door, fat in his coat and scarf, the flaps of his hat hanging down like donkey ears. His gloved hands dangled her ugly brown shoes by their laces. She wanted to cry again, but laughed instead, a ghostly laugh of the girl splashing in the river, the girl who'd believed someone loved her.

"Mujer, what's wrong? You look kind of green. Are you sick?"

"No," she said.

"Then why are you in bed?" Aníbal dropped her shoes on the floor. "Why were your shoes lying around? I tripped on them."

"I served coffee to your puta Marta." For the first time in her life, she used the vile word that she had never dreamed she would ever call another woman.

Yesterday, if someone had asked her if she thought she knew her husband's character, she would have answered yes. Yes, he was a good man, kind and generous. She would have cited examples: giving her money for her sisters' teeth, or how when she told him Doña Petra was selling pasteles to pay the rent, Aníbal had paid double for theirs. He had asked Felicidad if she could get more so he could sell them to his compadres down at Tony's garage.

Yesterday she had hung on every word that came out of his mouth, grateful for all he cared to relay, hoping that the time would come when he would take her into his arms and love her. She wondered how she could have changed so much in a few hours.

She wanted to yell and scream at him. She wanted to hurt him the way he had hurt her. Before that puta Marta, Felicidad had meant to be wife, lover, mother, and sister to him. She had meant to give him sons and daughters. Before that puta Marta, she had believed that Aníbal was the one person who didn't want her just for what she could do for him.

So he had another woman. What of it? Aníbal hadn't done anything so unusual, only what other men did, like her uncles, her father's brothers, with their two families apiece: one legitimate, one por amor. Stupid her, she hadn't expected it from her own husband, not from Aníbal. After all, they were still newlyweds. Stupid her, just because he called her querida when he made love to her under the waterfall. All it had taken was one word from him.

She had to be cold.

Aníbal raised his voice, twisting his annoyance at being found out into anger at her falta de respeto. He was her husband and the head of the house and she was supposed to respect him, damn it. The gray hat with earflaps nested on his hair like a dead squirrel, making him look silly and young.

His thing with Marta was really her fault. "If you had come home with me, we wouldn't have this problem." Aníbal took off his gloves and dropped them on the bed.

Felicidad felt as if he had slapped her. Surely, he had understood? Yet he had been disappointed when she had told him that she wanted to stay with her family, but for the first and only time in her life she had done as she pleased. She knew if she were to poll her family, including her mother and the priest Padre Ocasio, Doña Petra even, that they would all admit that Aníbal had razón. She should never have let Aníbal, a young man not yet tamed into a husband, out in the world on his own. Not the way mujeres were these days, especially not women in America, women the island people scoffed at for being promiscuous and un-lady-like—atrevidas allá fuera.

"I'm to blame for Marta?" she asked.

"I'm a man." Aníbal yanked off his cap, tossed it in a corner. His hair was flat except for a single curl that stuck up on one side.

She thought, Why couldn't he hang anything up? Did he think she was his servant? Yet she knew that she had relished the little tasks she could do for him.

"I needed a woman," he said.

"You had a wife." Make me understand, she wanted to tell him. Ask me to forgive you. When you called me querida, was that a lie, too?

"But not with me." Aníbal thought about that night when he had returned from Puerto Rico, how he had been a man alone in a world filled with people. Marta had been there waiting for him. She hadn't worn panties. It had been one of those opportunities few men could resist. A normal man shouldn't be expected to resist it. When a woman wanted to have sex with a man, just sex, nothing more, what was he supposed to do? Say no, my wife wouldn't like it if I fucked you? Besides, he owed Marta something after running off and marrying Felicidad and, after all, it was Christmastime. He didn't want to admit to himself that maybe a wife could forgive that one night, but how could he justify after, like New Year's Day? Could Felicidad forgive that?

Clumps of wet snow dropped to the floor that Felicidad mopped un día sí, un día no. He hoped this wasn't going to turn into one of those big crying scenes. He was tired. It had been a particularly hard week, what with Mackie assigning him to Area B, which the workers called The Border because of all the immigrants, and then working evenings at Tony's garage.

Tonight Felicidad was no longer the timid girl afraid to question her husband, but a wronged woman determined to get the sordid details no matter how much it might hurt her. It was the only way she could think to punish him for breaking her heart and herself for not protecting it. When did it start? Did they do it in this very bed that she made each day, smoothing out each crease, each bump on the bedspread, plumping the pillows, fancy in the white eyelet pillowcases? How proud she had been to have her very own bed.

Aníbal sat on the edge of the bed and started to unlace his boots. At this moment, his affair with la puta Marta outweighed the oil stains from his work clothes that might seep into the white bedspread that Felicidad had transformed into a garden of embroidered roses.

"Felicidad, some things are better left unexplained," he said.

"Tell me," she said in a voice so reasonable and calm that she could have been asking Doña Petra for her arroz con dulce recipe.

Aníbal glanced down at his hands. His fingers were swollen at the knuckles, healed testimony to various factory accidents.

"The night I came back from the island without my own wife was the saddest day of my life. I was lower than the lowest dog," he said.

"And?"

"Marta was waiting for me. She made me coffee," he said, thinking it ridiculous that he was talking about coffee.

Felicidad couldn't help clutching at the bedspread. La puta Marta had seen her turquoise refrigerator before she had! Mujer, control. She had to close her eyes for a moment to gather up her strength.

"You have your wife with you now," she said.

Aníbal got up from the bed. He wasn't used to having his

actions questioned. If they continued talking he might start feeling guilty, and over what? Doing what men do? He stood, hands on his hips, as his own father had often done.

"This conversation is finished. The thing with Marta has nothing to do with you. I don't want to talk about it anymore." Aníbal walked out of the bedroom.

She heard him switch on the television. From the bureau, she took out Doña Petra's scarf and began stitching tiny pink roses.

Felicidad spent the evening alone in their bed embroidering and choosing not to think, both skills that she had begun to develop in childhood. Later, when Aníbal came to sleep, she wrapped herself in the bedspread and moved to the sofa. The plastic was stiff and made a crackling noise. She remembered the night Aníbal had carried in the television, laughing at his good fortune. He had bought it cheap from some fulano or another returning to the island. They had sat on this very sofa like a long-married couple watching other married couples on the small screen living their lives in English and black and white.

Her feet were so cold. She thought of how she had painted her toenails red to match her sandals, which had frozen to her feet that first night. Sandals bought to impress her new husband and her new country.

Winter air blew under the plastic sheeting tacked to the window frames filtering into the apartment. Moonlight glimmered through the stained-glass windows over the mantelshelf where she had lined up half a dozen candles. They were the kind in tall bottles, each embellished with a picture of a saint except for the last candle with Our Lady of Lourdes. Felicidad had chosen the saints with the prettiest bottles, Saint Peter yellow, Saint Dymphna green, Saint Michael the Archangel blue, and Saints Mary

Magdalena and Joan of Arc red. The Blessed Virgin came only in white.

She closed her eyes against the candlelight. She didn't want to think about saints or God or anything holy.

The image of Marta sitting on this very sofa, dragging her cigarette to and from her red lips, was as vivid in the room's darkness as it had been that afternoon. Those nights when Aníbal said he was working in Tony's garage, he most likely was with Marta. How could she compete with an experienced woman like Marta who had known her husband first and whom he obviously preferred?

Felicidad remembered the little girl hiding the wad of caramelos in the palm of her hand. She squeezed her eyes shut and then she opened them again and stared at the candles. What were her choices? She could leave Aníbal and go back to Puerto Rico if he paid her fare, but to where? Back to the aunt? Nunca.

Could she go to her parents' house? ¡Qué ridículo! There wasn't any room for her there; besides, she needed to earn money to help them.

It was very cold. Felicidad saw Aníbal with his hands on his hips telling her that Marta had nothing to do with her, that he was a man and could do exactly as he liked, as if it didn't matter that he had hurt her, as if she didn't matter.

The candles flickered on the mantelshelf; the radiators began to hiss and yield up steam heat and the sweetness of flowering hibiscus. Warm, it was so warm, just like on the island, just like it had been when she and Aníbal made love under the waterfall. She swept the bedspread off and unbuttoned her housedress with trembling fingers. She closed her eyes. She heard the rush of water and felt the warm breeze on her bare skin. There was a touch on her cheek, a caress on her bare shoulder, a trail of kisses on her breasts, a tongue teasing open her legs.

But not her husband's.

Felicidad held out her arms to her Spirit Prince.

"Love me," she said.

After Marta

Chapter Twenty-nine

Felicidad peeled off a bit of plastic sheeting from the window-pane and peered down into the street at her husband. The sky was beginning to lighten to that peculiar shade of gray that is typical of Chicago in February. She preferred it to the lingering black of night that recalled her childhood when she woke to make her father's coffee, running out in the predawn to gather twigs for building a fire in el fogón, roasting the coffee beans, machacando them into a fine powder in the special pestle and mortar that her father had carved from a tree trunk. Ten years later and she still looked back at those hurried mornings with a sense of loss.

There was Aníbal, her husband, dusting off the snow that had fallen during the night, trudging along the back of the car to brush off the taillights, smoke puffing from the exhaust pipe. Did someone go around teaching all the island transplants how to do this? There he went scraping the ice from the windows. She couldn't hear anything but she wished she could. How she yearned to be a part of ordinary, everyday life. The sounds of the radiators—the hiss of steam, the banging of the pipes gur-gling up wisps of heat—reminded her that she was alone in the apartment. There, there was her husband pulling out and stopping in the middle of the street to pick up the chairs and set them in his now vacant parking space.

Felicidad pressed her forehead against the icy windowpane. It froze her skin and she trembled, but she was glad to feel something other than numbness. Now that her husband was gone—now what? She wouldn't see him for nine, maybe ten hours. Yesterday she knew that she would clean the apartment, that she would wash some of his things in the tub, draping them on the radiators hoping that they would dry during the day. She had learned to place the clothing on a rag or old towel after the first time she had ruined a shirt of Aníbal's—stained with brown iron marks from the radiator. In the midafternoon, when long hours had ticked away, she permitted herself the most enjoyable part of her day, when she would reorganize her pantry. She would lovingly touch the labels of the cans, her fingers smoothing flat the small sacks of beans, enjoying the pebbly feel beneath her fingertips. There was the shiny toaster and the tins of sugar and coffee beans. She would pick up the coffee grinder and turn the handle just because it made her happy. She was saving some of her household money to buy one for Mami. Standing in the pantry, she would marvel at her good fortune and plan the meal she would cook for her husband, who was responsible for all of this bounty. What special dish could she create for him that would tempt him into becoming her lover rather than her benefactor?

But that was yesterday. Yesterday, before Marta, she could hope. Yesterday, a wish that her husband would love her seemed reasonable and she had believed with all her girlish heart that her wish would come true with time and the careful tending to his comforts.

She had been at the stove frying eggs when he came into the kitchen. He'd said good morning, she'd said good morning.

She'd served him coffee and eggs with toast. He drank his coffee, ate his eggs and toast, complained about the landlord and the lack of heat, then he had taken his lunch and left. No, How did you sleep? Not a single word about last night.

Felicidad picked up the bedspread. The sofa wasn't as comfortable as the bed, but it hadn't kept her from dreaming. In the dream she rushed about the kitchen dressed in her wedding suit and red sandals cooking every dish she knew how. She felt how frantic she was. Platters of fried chicken and pork chops covered the table and chairs and stove. Pots and pans filled with rice and beans were stacked on the radiator. And still she cooked, afraid that she would not prepare enough food. She kept looking up at the kitchen clock, worried that she wouldn't have everything ready for Aníbal. But in her dream, she knew that he would not come.

In the gray morning light of this cold February day, Felicidad knew it to be as true as it had been in her dream: Aníbal didn't love her. She buried her face in the bedspread, determined not to cry. She had cried plenty already. Felicidad was weary of not being wanted, of doing her best and it not being enough. Her cheek rubbed against the roses she'd embroidered with such expectation. She examined her handiwork, recalling all the hours she had spent embroidering while she waited for her husband to come home and love her. She had been living a girlish dream and now she hadn't any choice but to face reality. Felicidad went to the bedroom and she started to make the bed, then stopped herself. No, let Aníbal make it or Marta. She pulled out her empty suitcase. Except for the winter things—coat, hat, gloves, scarf, galoshes—she packed only what she had brought with her from the island. She picked up the flannel shirt Aníbal had lent her that first morning. Her eyes filled with tears, and she dried them with the soft fabric. Maybe she would take it to remember. Remember what? The coldness of her husband? His thing with Marta? How he didn't care what she felt? She was a stupid girl to cry over an ugly piece of plaid cloth, and she tossed it on the bed too.

In a corner of the bedroom she found the brown work shoes that she had kicked off in her fury about Marta. Aníbal had carried them into the bedroom by their laces; they were too ugly to cradle in one's palms. She put her galoshes on over the shoes. Poor girls didn't have the luxury of pride.

Felicidad went to the kitchen to turn off the lights. She saw the dirty breakfast dishes on the table and stacked them in the sink. She considered washing them, even picked up the dish-rag, but then put it down. She steadied herself against the sink. She would never do for her husband again, she would never sit across from Aníbal at the table, hoping that he would look at her the way he had on the island, his intentions clear, making her blush with eagerness for his touch. She had to accept that and move on.

At the door, she said good-bye to the apartment, to the Felicidad from the island. She wondered what she should do with the key. Felicidad didn't think Aníbal would like it if she left the door unlocked, for he was always warning her that she no longer lived in the Puerto Rican countryside. She paused outside Doña Petra's door, thinking that maybe she could leave the key with the kind lady, but what if Marta was visiting her mother and answered her knock? Or if la doña insisted on a cup of coffee, hoping to persuade her to stay until Aníbal came home? No, she would return the key some other time.

She ran down the stairs, pausing just outside the building. All that she had come to love about the apartment, from the clawed lion's feet of the porcelain tub to the pantry with its cans and sacks of food, was now testament to the naive girl she had been. A girl who had believed in fairy tales.

Now what?

It was snowing fat, thick flakes. She admired the snowflakes fluttering white on her dark blue coat that Aníbal had bought her the first week. Felicidad couldn't help feeling like a little girl when it snowed. She lifted her face up to the sky, and snow fluttered onto her cheeks and eyelashes and mouth. She brushed her face with her gloved hand. Cars drove slowly down the tree-lined boulevard. Snow draped the buildings in meringue and frosted the trees in spun-sugar crystals. She breathed in the cold freshness of falling snow, and she stood entranced until the wind flicked its cold hand across her cheeks—as if to say, Muchacha, are you crazy? It's February, it's Chicago! It's cold!—and she yanked up her scarf to cover her cheeks.

Even though the last person she ever wanted to think of was her husband, Felicidad was grateful to Aníbal for her winter attire. If not for him, instead of wearing a winter coat and galoshes, she would still have been the shivering girl dressed in a thin suit and sandals.

She started to walk, stepping firmly on the snow-covered sidewalk as if she had a purpose, a place to be. She had always enjoyed walking, especially back on the island when she lived in el campo. The wind snuck up her skirt, sliding icy fingers up thighs protected only by stockings. She quivered in her coat. Where should she go? She had met people through Aníbal, but she didn't think that she knew any one of them well enough to knock on the door and say, Please let me stay. Her steps faltered. She slipped a little on the sidewalk and walked a little slower. Was there a single person she could ask for help until she found work? If only she could get a job in a factory. She would even bake bread if that was what she had to do. Maybe if she went to Comacho's, Lupe, who had always been friendly, might help her.

Yes, she would go to Comacho's. Her suitcase bumped against her legs and, despite the wind, she tried holding it away from her body. Comacho's was only six blocks away, not too far to walk, even in the cold. She had spent the first half of her childhood walking and the rest of it standing in la panadería. She might not look it, but she was strong. She wasn't too delicate to work in a factory or to walk in the snow.

The door to Comacho's banged shut behind Felicidad. She touched her gloved hand to her nose as the smell of insect repellent mingled with the stale odor of fried foods from the alcapurrías and rellenos, yautía and green banana batter and potato balls stuffed with seasoned beef, island favorites that Lupe made and sold.

Aníbal's young bride brought speculation into Comacho's along with her suitcase. The men who hung around nodded to her. Smoking cigarettes, they gathered by the door ready to leave if they were in the way. Comacho was nowhere to be seen, for which Felicidad was grateful.

"It's not too cold for a walk?" Lupe came out from around the counter, pretending not to see the suitcase.

"I need to talk to you," Felicidad said, hoping the men wouldn't hear her.

"Is it snowing again?" Lupe helped Felicidad brush the snow from her hair.

Felicidad looked into Lupe's eyes and thought, This is a woman who has suffered and will help me.

The whole neighborhood knew of Felicidad tossing Marta out of the apartment. That blabbermouth Dora Matos from the first floor had been getting her mail and heard everything.

Yesterday afternoon, Dora didn't wait for her son Olando to come home from school, but went herself to Comacho's for a gallon of milk, hoping, if God was good, to meet acquaintances along the way so she could describe how she had trembled with fear that the two women might fall down the stairs and break a leg or an arm or crack a skull even. Ay bendito, she considered calling the police, but not even fear for her life could get her to call the law on her own people.

The customers at Camacho's agreed, you didn't call the police on the race, but, coño, it couldn't be true that Aníbal had them at the same time? Yes, Aníbal was one maricón.

Everyone knew, except for Doña Petra, who had been out delivering her ironing (white shirts, light starch on hangers) and whom no one had had the nerve to tell about el revolú. Some things it was better for a mother not to know.

Lupe busied herself moving some cans around on a shelf. The men in the store looked away. Enjoying your neighbors' misfortunes with a nice little bit of chisme was a delicious treat, but getting involved with a husband and his wife, especially when his woman happened to be little more than a girl and a beautiful one at that, no señor, anybody with any kind of sense knew better than to get mixed up in that.

Felicidad's suitcase grew heavy. She dropped it with a thud. Lupe and the men looked up against their will.

"Why don't you ask me why I'm here with my suitcase?"

"Oh, yes, your suitcase. I didn't notice," Lupe said.

Felicidad couldn't help the quaver in her voice. What if Lupe wouldn't help her?

"Lupe, I've left Aníbal," she said.

"You don't say!" Lupe squeezed Felicidad's hand in sympathy. Felicidad looked away. "It's too shameful."

"Nothing is too shameful between a man and his woman."

Lupe laughed as she said this and the men murmured quietly among themselves. After all, Felicidad was so young, without the years of experience that teach you that you can stand more than you think you can.

"May I stay with you for a little while?" Felicidad leaned on the counter. She couldn't help noticing that the tiles were cracked and could use a good scrubbing. The aunt had prided herself on having a spotless counter, a tidy shop. Felicidad had seen to it.

"I wish you could, but Comacho wouldn't allow it. He's not generous that way," Lupe said. "Why don't you go back home? If you go now, Aníbal will never know you left."

Felicidad shook her head. What could she say, what could she do to persuade Lupe to change her mind?

"Aníbal is not a bad man," Lupe said.

"No, Aníbal is not a bad man," Felicidad said. How could she make Lupe understand that it wasn't a matter of her husband being good or bad but a matter of being wanted?

Felicidad touched Lupe's arm. "Have you ever been in a place where you're not wanted?"

"I'm sure you're exaggerating," Lupe said. Did the girl not have eyes in her head? Could she not see that she, Lupe, was the kind of woman few men would want?

Felicidad picked up her suitcase. The floor was in need of a good mopping. Muddy shoe prints had dried on the linoleum. A dirty mop in a bucket stood in a corner behind the counter. She looked down the rows of canned and packaged goods, only four rows—no, five—but once it had seemed the land of plenty.

"Con permiso, señora. Do you have any money?" one of the men asked.

"A few dollars," Felicidad said, surprised, for the elderly man had never spoken to her.

He reached into his pocket and took out the only bill in his wallet—a ten.

"Oh, no, thank you," she said.

"Vicente Valentín, a sus órdenes," the elderly man said with a little bow. The ten-dollar bill floated on top of his palm, from which rose the history of his ancestors, of the family coffee plantation that had once been, of his childhood and young manhood tending coffee trees and picking coffee berries under the shade of plantain and banana trees and now, in his old age, the aroma of the coffee he brewed each morning.

Lupe took it and curled Felicidad's fingers over the ten-dollar bill. "Don't be proud. You'll need money for bus fare and such."

Lupe opened a paper bag and began to fill it with things she found handy. Later Felicidad would find a pack of Wrigley's spearmint gum and another of Marlboros, although she didn't smoke, along with a can of evaporated milk and a tin of guava paste.

"Why don't you try Ana, that friend of Aníbal's? She's the kind of woman who can help you," Lupe said.

The men nodded respectfully to Felicidad as she left, the smoke from their cigarettes curling into the words of comfort and encouragement they wished they could say to the beautiful girl. The wind was a steady wail, whipping the snow against the shop's glass door. They spoke of the girl carrying her suitcase and brown bag through the snow-covered streets, the wind bitter against her delicate cheeks. Ay, that Aníbal was one stupid maricón.

"She's only a young country girl," Don Valentín said. "She deserves better."

"I, too, was once a young country girl. Now look at me," Lupe said.

The men looked away, intent on the cigarettes between their

fingers, smoke signals forming in the heated room. Lupe moved about, rearranging this and that, hiding the gaps made by the items she had given Felicidad. No one spoke. The men contemplated what a tragedy it was against the Puerto Rican race and womanhood in general for a beautiful girl to be wandering the bitter cold streets of Chicago alone. Lupe was thinking the girl was lucky, even if she didn't know it. Much worse to be ugly, for few ever loved an ugly woman. She could testify that it was better to be alone and beautiful than to be alone and ugly.

If Felicidad had had the misfortune to be born a plain girl as she herself had been, she, too, might be like Lupe, shaming her family by living with a married man. When she paid her yearly visit home, Felicidad, too, would have to hang her head in vergüenza when she sat among her pretty, light-skinned sisters. No one ever mentioned that it was Lupe's money that paid for the milk and food that helped her sisters grow up with straight spines and good teeth. Yes, as far as Lupe was concerned, if it was a curse to be beautiful, then she wished that she had been so cursed. At least she might have found a man who would love her, instead of being grateful for any man's interest, married or not, respectable or not, knowing that it would be all she could expect.

Twice, Felicidad lost her way, as she was unfamiliar with Chicago streets—Aníbal had driven her everywhere. On the bus she slouched down as much as she could with her suitcase on her lap. She was sure that the lurching of the bus was causing the pangs of nausea that came and went and that her hands were shaking because of the cold.

She endured the curiosity of the other passengers, the disinterested glances of the half-asleep high school students, their jaws working wads of gum, the looks of the other women, disdainful or sympathetic. Worse were the blatantly appraising stares of the men on their way to the factory or the higher-status jobs of security guards or office clerks.

Each man wondered about her situation—so young, so beautiful, so alone, so shy that she kept her gaze cast down on her suitcase, such a girl would be lonely and bound to be grateful for a few kind words and a helpful hand—and fantasized about exploiting it to his advantage. Fuck the factory, fuck the security desk, fuck the mailroom. Fuck the wife and children. Ah, for such a girl to warm one's dick on such a fucking cold day.

Walking from the bus stop to Chago and Ana's apartment, she was careful not to let her suitcase brush against her frozen legs. Aníbal's friends lived in one of the first-floor apartments of a monstrously ugly brick building that took up half a block. Ana liked the convenience of the first floor for carrying up groceries or laundry. It was so handy to be almost at street level. In the summer she could stick her head out of a window and call out instructions or reprimands to her children playing on the grassy courtyard. She could toss a few coins to her son Chagito and send him to the corner store to buy milk. She could chastise Anita for playing baseball with her brother or chasing the little neighbor boy. Better to play with her doll and tea set like a good girl should or better yet come up and help wash the dishes or make your brother's bed. That's what a girl should do, not play dodge baseball or dodge soccer or dodge whatever. As for chasing after boys! Yes, young lady, march yourself right upstairs or else.

Felicidad had to knock twice, the second time pounding on the door a little louder than absolutely necessary to be heard above the radio, Ana being one of those women who could not live in silence.

Ana yanked the door open. She was wearing an apron and a kerchief over her hair. Whatever she had been about to say caught in her throat at the sight of Felicidad. Felicidad looked down at her suitcase because it was easier than staring into Ana's eyes, which even so early in the day she had outlined in black.

"Muchacha, what are you doing here?"

Felicidad heard the surprise in the other woman's voice along with a hint of exasperation for the interruption of her routine and the certainty that she was to be asked for a favor because why else would Felicidad be here carrying a suitcase and looking so pitiful? She shook in her coat and hat and gloves and galoshes. The other woman put it down to the girl not being used to the cold winter weather, but it was actually from fear that Ana might laugh at her for being so foolish as to leave her husband. Naturally, Ana's loyalty would be first to Aníbal, who was her friend, while Felicidad had no claim to such friendship. What if Ana turned her away? Then where would she go?

"Doña—"

"¡Doña!" Ana gave a little shriek. "Your brains must be frozen to call me that."

"I'm sorry—" Felicidad thought she might faint, just collapse right here on Ana's doorstep from the weight of her winter attire, from the fear that she had again insulted Ana and ruined any chance she might have had to appeal to her as one woman to another.

Felicidad's suitcase slipped from her fingers. Maybe she would faint. Yes, faint. Why not faint? Just a single moment of oblivion. She could close her eyes and not have to think or be afraid. And Ana would take care of her.

Ana grabbed her by the shoulders and shook her. The girl was not going to pass out on her doorstep—not when she still had the breakfast dishes to do and all the ironing before the children came home for lunch.

"Felicidad. None of that now. I don't have time for hysterics."

She pulled Felicidad into the apartment. In a corner of the living room, Ana had set up a makeshift altar crowded with candles for different saints and Spirits, including one for Saint Barbara, and four special candles, each a different color, representing the four winds. There on the altar she kept snapshots of all her loved ones. Heat rose in a strong, steady hiss from the radiators. Felicidad took a deep breath and smelled Pine-Sol and freshly brewed coffee. She knew that she would like living here if only Ana would allow it.

"Take off your galoshes." Ana pointed to the old towel that served as a doormat. "I mopped the floor and I don't plan on doing it again."

Felicidad took them off.

"Ay bendito, those are damn ugly shoes." Ana shook her head over Felicidad's feet. She wondered if the girl had a problem with her feet and had to wear orthopedic shoes. How was it that she hadn't noticed before? She felt a little satisfaction that one so young and beautiful should have such a deformity. Her own feet were finely formed with shapely toes. She had often been complimented on her pretty feet in Puerto Rico, where she had always worn sandals to flaunt them. The compliments were more prized because they came from other women, as most men didn't waste time looking at feet. And women were selfish with their compliments. Ana kept the toenails painted red—refreshing the polish every week—and the heels soft by massaging them nightly with olive oil before donning socks.

"They're from la panadería," Felicidad said.

"La panadería? You're not making any sense," Ana said. How could shoes come from a shop that sold bread? The girl was obviously disoriented, still in a state of shock over whatever catastrophe she had suffered. The sooner she sat her down and gave her some black coffee, the better.

"I wore them at la panadería," Felicidad said.

"They're not orthopedic shoes?" Ana tried to keep the disappointment from her voice.

Felicidad stared at her, uncomprehending.

Ana resisted the temptation to shake her again. "Come, you need some strong coffee," she said.

Felicidad stared out Ana's kitchen window. Her passive demeanor reminded Ana of Three Kings Day, when she had given the girl her first rum and Coke. How she had envied that Felicidad for being so young, for her beauty, and, not least of all, for having that gorgeous hunk of a husband with whom to crawl into bed at night.

Even now, with the girl slumped over her kitchen table, she envied her. She was tempted to say, Snap out of it, Felicidad. You're only nineteen or is it twenty? Nothing can ever be so bad at twenty. Try being thirty-four like me with the best times of your life already lived. Try forcing yourself to get out of bed every morning when all you have to look forward to is the drudgery of housework, to listening yet again to your husband's lame jokes delivered in a permanent whisper, and the tedium of one day being exactly like another. Try that for a few years, Señora nineteen-year-old island blossom, then cry me your sad story.

Instead, Ana poured more black coffee in Felicidad's cup, urging her to eat a second slice of hot buttered bread. She insisted that the girl eat it, she didn't want to hear again how she didn't care for bread. What person didn't like a nice piece of bread? It was childish to dislike food. She herself did not permit her own children to do so. She bet that Felicidad had been hungry more than once in her life and would have done anything for such a big piece. Besides, she could tell that Felicidad had had a shock of some sort, and hot coffee and buttered bread were good for shocks.

Ana brought her own coffee cup to the table. She brewed endless cups of coffee throughout the day to keep her nerves steady.

"Is it Marta?" It was obvious that she would have to yank the story out of the girl.

"He's not even sorry." Felicidad didn't ask how Ana knew. She stirred the coffee with her spoon.

Ana shrugged. "He's a man."

Felicidad looked up. "I wanted to be a real wife to him."

Ana gasped. "You never—?"

"Never," Felicidad said.

"Ever?"

"Well, yes. In Puerto Rico when we got married."

"That's a relief. We couldn't have you running around Chicago all virginal and pure. It would be like saying to all the portorros, Come give it a try."

"I don't understand," Felicidad said.

"Don't worry about it." Ana reached across and touched Felicidad's arm. "Look, go back to the apartment before Aníbal gets home from work."

Felicidad shook her head.

Obviously, the girl was too ignorant to realize her limited choices. What, she wanted to work in a factory?

"He'll never have to know that you left," Ana said.

"He probably won't even realize that I'm gone," Felicidad said.

"Don't make a big drama about it. Of course he'll know you're gone," Ana said.

Felicidad giggled.

Ana hoped that she wouldn't have to slap her out of hysterics. Except for one young man, a certain Juan Martinez who had reached under her blouse while he was kissing her (she had allowed herself a minute or two to enjoy his hands on her breasts—the first time a man had touched her), she had never slapped anyone. Her father, may he rest in peace, had been a firm believer in a daily slap or flick of the belt. Ana did her best not to follow his example, although she had to admit to being tempted once or twice.

"He married you in the Church," Ana said. That was one of the things Ana regretted, marrying Chago in the Church. Why hadn't she just lived with him as his common-law wife as her sisters had done with their husbands? Because his mother had insisted, that was why. Ay bendito, she didn't want to think about how she might one day explode out of these five rooms and a bath. Better to concentrate on the girl's situation.

"I don't know what he was thinking when he married me," Felicidad said.

Ana rose to wipe down her stove. If she wasn't careful, she would find herself feeling sorry for the girl and who knew where that might lead.

"I have a favor to ask," Felicidad said.

Ana kept her back to her, scrubbing at a permanent spot of rust.

"I realize that you don't know me very well and that Aníbal is your friend." Felicidad stared down into her coffee cup as if she could read her future in it.

The rag dangled from Ana's fingers. "Listen, Felicidad. I know what you're going to ask me, but I don't believe in bringing a young, good-looking woman into my house, not with a healthy husband. Dios libre." Ana might have said more, such as, I admit that Chago annoys me sometimes, but muchacha, I have a husband with a job and believe me, I'm grateful.

"But Aníbal lived with you and Chago when he first came to Chicago," Felicidad said.

Ana turned to look at her. Didn't the girl see how impossible it was? "That's different. A woman can control herself if she wants to. A man can't."

"Lupe said no, too," Felicidad whispered.

"Don't whisper!" Ana shouted.

Felicidad stared at Ana, frightened.

"Sorry," Ana said. "Maybe you should go back to the island."

"No one wants me there," Felicidad said.

The girl spoke in a normal voice. Ana felt calmer.

"You're one depressing girl," she said. "I might start crying in a minute."

"But it's true." Felicidad couldn't suppress a smile.

"I can give you a few dollars," Ana said. "For bus fare to someplace."

"A nice man at Comacho's gave me money."

"You took it?"

"A very nice elderly gentleman."

"Others saw?"

"Of course."

To take money from a strange man? And in front of witnesses? Ay bendito, by tonight Aníbal would know it and his mother in Puerto Rico, too.

Ana couldn't help laughing. "Maybe you should stay here for a day or two. You're too stupid to be out on your own."

Felicidad jumped up from her chair and hugged Ana, who pushed her away, ashamed by Felicidad's gratitude.

"It's only for a few days. I can't have you wandering around and freezing to death on my conscience," Ana said. "And from now on, you don't take money from a man unless he's your husband, you hear?"

"He was an old man, Ana," Felicidad said. "He was one of those old types from the island, a gentleman, a caballero."

"Old men are the worst," Ana said. "All men expect something in return for their money. You're not too young or stupid to understand that."

"Whatever you say, Ana," Felicidad said.

"And one more thing," Ana said. "Never, ever whisper. You don't know how it gets on my nerves."

Ana showed Felicidad the cot on rollers, which was closed and hidden under a tablecloth. The extra sheets and blanket were stored in boxes under the children's bunk beds. Felicidad asked permission to keep her suitcase in a corner of the dining room. Ana took pity on the girl and instructed her to hang her dresses in the children's closet. Felicidad was so touched by every concession that Ana realized that here was a girl unused to kindness. She felt the stirring of something for Felicidad. She wasn't quite sure what, maybe mere admiration for the girl's stoicism or perhaps a sisterly concern—not motherly, Dios libre! Pobrecita, Ana surprised herself by pitying a beautiful girl.

The girl was looking at her wide-eyed, the way her own daughter did when she was overwhelmed by the task at hand and unsure how to proceed. Ay, she could see that she would have another burden to bear. Well, she would help her get through this first day, but, tomorrow, Felicidad would have to start figuring out things for herself.

"Why don't you rest on Anita's bed? I have ironing to do," Ana said. "And if I don't start before the children come home from school, I'll find a reason not to do it. It's so boring."

"Let me do it," Felicidad said. "I'm very good at ironing and I'm too nervous to lie down."

Not do a week's worth of ironing! Ana wasn't one of those women who refused a good offer out of politeness.

"Well, if you're sure," Ana said. "But save a little energy for tonight. I think you'll need it because your husband will come looking for you."

"I doubt it," Felicidad said, "unless he wants his housekeeper back."

Ana nodded approval. Better to face the facts quickly, however ugly they might be.

"Let me show you where to set up the ironing board," Ana said. The girl might as well get to the ironing before she left.

Chapter Thirty

Aníbal lifted a hundred-pound sack and threw it on the flatbed. He picked up a second sack and threw it on the flatbed. He was resigned to the fact that thinking wasn't required, only breathing. Fantasizing about women or remembering his childhood in Puerto Rico was the only way he could make it through eight hours of lifting and throwing.

When the foreman came around assigning an extra hour or two of overtime, he was tempted to pick up a sack and bash it over the man's head. Not even that fantasy helped much these days. He was desperate for a change, for a reason to get up in the morning, something to justify working like a mule. Life had to be more than rice and beans and a roof over one's head.

Every day he punched his time card was another day he lived with the knowledge that there wasn't any future en la fábrica for men like him, uneducated men who wanted to succeed, who knew that they could if given the chance. But it was more than that. He was disheartened that he wasn't the man he'd thought he would be when he first came to America.

Aníbal used to have dreams of being somebody. He had thought himself destined for something special. He was smarter, better looking, more charming even, than other men. Everyone said so. That had to count for something. He used to believe that if he came eager to work, started early, stayed late when needed, if he did all this, somehow he would get ahead. Maybe make supervisor.

Aníbal didn't kid himself anymore. This was the third factory since he had arrived in Chicago and, before that, he had worked at another in Michigan and before that, he picked vegetables and fruit in Kenosha, Wisconsin, and, before that, in California. The problem was that he wasn't grateful anymore to do whatever work he could get to earn a living the way he had been when he had first arrived, happy even to pick peaches and apples for he had thought it boot camp for the American Dream.

He couldn't recall exactly when he had become dissatisfied. Was it because he could speak English better now and didn't feel quite so helpless? It hadn't happened overnight. It had taken weeks, months, maybe years, the days passing without his noticing, the way days do when one is working at a job just to pay the bills. Now it was all he could do to get to work on time and punch his time card.

Thinking about sex with different women had once helped ease the boredom, and then after Felicidad came, he dreamed about fucking her. Ay bendito, but he couldn't do that unless he wanted to be a brute. He couldn't do that and send her back to the island.

That was what Aníbal had decided to do. When he got home from work, he would tell her that she had to go. He would look down at the floor or read the paper so he wouldn't see the disappointment in her eyes. He was lucky she wasn't one of those women who screamed and broke things. Why, one time a woman came after him with a knife! No, he had to send Felicidad away. It was better for him and for her. Last night, after she found out about Marta, she left their bed, taking the bedspread with her, leaving him a thin sheet. He had lain awake shivering from the cold and thinking about his problem of one too many women—one of them a naive little wife easily hurt. As painful as it might be, sending her back to the island might be the best solution. He tried not to dwell on how the aunt and others would treat her.

He was sorry that she had to go back. Very sorry, he was surprised to realize. She was so pretty to look at and they had begun to settle into a companionable relationship of sorts—watching TV together, driving to Comacho's and the Laundromat, visiting friends—all times he was careful to remind himself that she was like a sister to him. One of the things that he appreciated about Felicidad was that she made no demands on him. He awakened each morning to the smell of freshly brewed coffee and came home to a warm, delicious meal and she never complained or asked anything of him. What else could a man want? He would not think of her taking a bath or how sometimes he watched her sleep, how he could see in the curve of her cheek, the little girl she had been. It had made his heart ache in a way that was unfamiliar. He took it to be pity. It was better that she go, it would be worse later if he kept carrying on with Marta. Yes, he couldn't make Felicidad any promises about that. He was the man and could do as he pleased.

There she was the next morning, all docile and quiet like the previous night had never happened, like she didn't know about Marta, there she was pouring him his cup of black coffee, frying him up a couple of eggs. She apologized for the icy utensils, but she had warmed up the plate and coffee cup in the oven. Aníbal had almost told her then, but she appeared so fragile in his flannel shirt and he knew his news would break her into tiny pieces. He had stared at the plastic-sheeted window, noting the thick layers of frost on the glass panes. The room had an unpleasant wetness. Steam rose from the pots of water boiling on the stove. Vapor clung to the walls and lingered in a haze over them. The smell of gas overpowered the fragrance of fresh-brewed coffee. A blast of heat surged from the opened oven door. He glanced down at it, surprised. There was Felicidad trembling in his flannel shirt. This was no way for people to live, especially for island people unused to bitter cold. He started ranting about the landlord, that maricón, and gulping down his coffee and eggs so he could get away from the pitiful sight of his wife in his too-big shirt. For the first time that he could remember, he was glad to go out into the still dark morning.

It eased his guilt some to know that once she returned to Puerto Rico she would no longer be cold. Being a husband was a responsibility, a commitment that he couldn't embrace. Marriage made him feel like one of the old guys—like Chago or Tony or one of his other compadres. It added to his disappointment in himself, to his dissatisfaction as an unskilled and uneducated factory worker, and to his increasing disenchantment with the American Dream. He was beginning to believe that working in a factory was the most he would ever achieve.

When he came home at night, there would be his wife wearing his flannel shirt, cooking his dinner—his wife always seemed to be at the stove. Instead of her smile easing the disappointment of his day, he felt burdened by it and forced to face the truth of his failures. He was not the man he wanted to be. He was ashamed because her adoration was unearned and that made it unbearable.

Aníbal didn't want to be like Chago, who only aspired to a steady paycheck. He didn't want to worry about shoes for the children or discuss at length why real milk was better than powdered for strong bones. He didn't want to check the children's teeth, praying that they wouldn't be bucktoothed when he didn't even believe in prayer. He didn't want to have only a couple of dollars in his pocket for gas and the occasional beer. Worse still, he dreaded the day might come when nothing more was expected of him than a paycheck, not even from himself.

He wanted to be the old Aníbal, the one before Felicidad. The Aníbal who could fuck a woman until he got tired of her and then move on to someone else. He wanted to be the Aníbal who with every new woman and each shot of golden rum convinced himself that, yes, he was somebody.

He wanted to be a man who knew where he belonged. Aníbal wanted to be a man like his father. A man whom all respected, if not loved, a man proud of his heritage, who came from a culture where the man ruled the family and the woman served and nurtured it. This was the Spanish way, the way of his father, and his father before him. It didn't matter that it was 1953 and he was living in another country, this was the only way Aníbal knew. His father's way, Aníbal's way, the Puerto Rican way. And when Papá had to deal with some unpleasant business, whether it was his wife thinking she could tell him what to do or an obreo who was not harvesting as much as he should, he didn't waste days or weeks mulling over what he would do as Aníbal had done.

When the quitting bell rang, Aníbal dropped the sack he was carrying. He ran to get his coat and shove his time card into the machine. He pushed past four or five men to the head of the line, something that was wrong to do with men he worked with, men who were in a hurry to get out of the factory, too. He rushed out without explanation, without apology. He was a man who had something important to do, distasteful even, and he felt the need to get it over with as if his life depended on it.

Aníbal drove like a madman down the streets slippery from

the recent snow. The car glided of its own volition down the boulevard to his parking space, where someone had already parked his car. Aníbal's chairs lay on the snow-covered ground. He swore before doing the same to someone else, sparing only a fleeting thought for the etiquette of the snow-filled city streets.

When he got to the apartment, he called out Felicidad's name, expecting her to greet him as she had before last night. He was disappointed when she didn't. Always, there were the sounds from the radio or of her cooking—the clicking and clacking of pots and pans or the banging of the oven door, which had loose screws or something. Tonight it was eerily silent. He raised his voice, thinking that she might be in the bedroom and unable to hear him. But still, no answer. It reminded him of the strangeness of his arrival the evening before, how she had been waiting in their bed to confront him about Marta. And just like then, he trudged through the dark apartment, oblivious to the icy footprints his boots left on Felicidad's clean floor.

He switched on the light in the bedroom, expecting he might find her curled up like a child under the bedspread of roses. He was surprised to find the bed unmade and his flannel shirt tossed on top of it. He knew then that she had left him.

Aníbal reached for the shirt. The soft material reminded him of Felicidad and of his first days in Chicago, how one Saturday he had bought a dozen or two of the very same flannel shirt— blue and red and green—over on Maxwell Street, thinking that he could make a few dollars selling them from the trunk of his car. The shirts were good as work shirts and as another layer of protection against the sparks of blowtorches and chemical spills. He had sold them to his fellow factory workers but had made little profit because almost everyone he knew could go to Maxwell Street and buy for themselves. In the end, he not only lost the urge to sell out of his car, but got stuck with half a dozen shirts.

A puddle formed on the bedroom floor from his work boots; he pressed the flannel shirt Felicidad had worn to his cheek. He smelled her—Ivory soap, coffee, the gas from the stove, the Old English Furniture Polish she favored. He tossed the shirt on the bed.

Aníbal shoved his hands in his pant pockets. His wallet. His keys. He patted the pockets of his jacket. Empty. He could really use a cigarette.

Everything about Felicidad annoyed him, he decided. She had embroidered roses on their only bedspread without asking him. Maybe he didn't want to sleep in a bed of roses! And she still acted like a child, waiting for him to make all the decisions as if he were her father or something. Coño, why didn't she just take control once in a while like Marta did? Why did she always have to wait for him to decide everything? She looked at him with those big brown eyes of hers that were so trusting and hopeful at the same time. He wasn't God or a saint or even a Spirit, shit, he couldn't even say that he was a good man. Coño, what did she want from him?

But she *had* decided. She had left him before he could tell her to leave. He felt deflated, let down somehow. He had planned to ease the harsh finality of his decision with sincere words of regret, to accept all blame if anyone was to blame in these situations. He would promise financial support as best as he was able for as long as she needed. He would offer nothing less and she could expect nothing more. And now she was gone.

The door to the pantry was open and he glanced at all the cans and boxes organized in perfect symmetry. Who cared if the labels faced forward and that the sacks of beans—red kidney beans with red kidney beans, pink rosadas with pink rosadas, white beans with white beans—had their own stacks? This wasn't a fucking grocery store.

It irritated him to see it so organized and he swept his hand over the shelf, knocking down a container of salt and boxes of crackers and pancake mix. A sack of garbanzo beans caught on a nail and tore. Hard round beans rained down the shelves and floor.

"Shit," he said, stepping on them, hearing the crunch beneath his boots.

He reached up for the bottle of rum that Felicidad kept on the top shelf next to a few bottles of Coca-Cola and the bottle of Spanish olive oil. He knocked that down, too, ignoring the sound of shattering glass.

Aníbal drank rum in front of the television straight from the bottle. Another benefit to not having a wife: You didn't have to pretend to have manners. The rum helped him to think clearer. Shit, he was one lucky maricón. How many men didn't even have to tell a woman to get lost? Except for her airfare and clothes and what he had put toward the furniture, she hadn't cost him too much. And the goddamn woman had the decency to leave without a whimper, without yelling or tossing about recriminations and blame so that it got so that a decent man's conscience bothered him until he couldn't sleep without meeting the night with a bottle of rum. Not a single tear. That girl was something.

Everything was going to be exactly as it had been before he had ever known her sad story and had tried for a few days to make a happy ending. And he *had* tried those first days in Puerto Rico, no one could say he hadn't. Not only had he tried but he had liked saving the beautiful girl. She had looked at him like he was a sun god or something and so he had felt like one. Once in a while, a man liked to be a sun god. Was that so wrong?

The more he drank, the clearer it all became. Yes, in Puerto Rico, he had been a sun god, but, here in America, he was just another factory worker. A mule carrying sacks from one spot to another. Some sun god. This situation was really all her fault. If she had come home with him right after their marriage, he would have sent Marta away that first night. What a lío that would have been! Felicidad the campo girl meeting Marta the city woman waiting for him outside his door. A woman didn't wait for a man at night except for a particular reason, one that would be obvious to anyone, perhaps even a campo girl. What explaining he would have had to do! He took another swallow, the liquid scorching his throat, making him feel like a man. There was nothing better than rum for a Puerto Rican man. He didn't understand why the guys from work were so enamored of beer. Give him some rum any day.

Shit, it was burning his stomach. He hadn't eaten since lunch. It had been nice to have someone to pack his lunch of ham-and-cheese sandwiches and fill his thermos with hot coffee. He was hungry, but no wife, no dinner. If she had told him she was planning on leaving he would have stopped off at a diner or at Chago and Ana's, where he had eaten when he was a single man.

He wondered where she had gone. Should he worry? She didn't know anyone really except for Chago and Ana but she'd only met them a few times and Ana had overwhelmed his young bride, so he couldn't see her asking Ana for help. Doña Petra? Shit, she wouldn't have gone to Doña Petra. Marta's mother! He was a little drunk and laughed at the thought. The wind rattled against the windows and cold air seeped into the apartment through the plastic-covered glass panes. The radiators were silent as was usual this time of the evening, but Aníbal didn't notice, encased as he was in the warmth of rum. The wind made him think of Felicidad shivering in his flannel shirt. Where the hell was she? What if she was wandering the frigid streets of Chicago looking for someone who spoke Spanish, some kind person to help her? Anything could happen to her. She was so naive. So trusting. So beautiful. Shit, it was February! ¡Maricón! The girl could be dead or something.

Aníbal set the bottle of rum on Felicidad's makeshift coffee table and went to get the brown work jacket he had tossed on the bed. He picked up the flannel shirt. He had no choice but to go looking for her. His conscience told him that he should have done it an hour or two ago.

Aníbal knocked on Doña Petra's door. He would have given anything not to do it—his right arm, his television set, the turquoise refrigerator. He could only hope that Marta wasn't visiting her mother, but that Felicidad was there in la doña's kitchen waiting for him to come get her.

Doña Petra opened the door. She stared up at him in the dim hall light, wrinkling her nose at the distinct smell of alcohol and the swagger of a man who is drunk.

La doña was looking at him strange-like as if he had been drinking or something. He labored over his enunciation to prove to her that he hadn't.

"Buenas noches, Doña," he said. "Is my wife with you?"

"Your wife? Felicidad?"

"Of course Felicidad," Aníbal said. "A man can have only one wife."

"Isn't she home with you?" Doña Petra fingered the blue glass rosary that she kept tied to her apron.

"Why would I be looking for her then?" It was annoying

talking to old ladies. A young macho like he should never ever have to talk to old ladies.

"You're drunk."

Aníbal chafed under her accusation. What right did the old woman have to accuse a man who chose to drink after a hard day's work?

"A man is entitled to a little rum when he gets home from work," Aníbal said.

La doña gave him a look that he would have had to be a lot drunker to misunderstand. A look that blamed him for all the problems of the world, for his wife gone missing, for drinking rum, for being a man.

Mamá had taught him to respect his elders. When he spoke again, his tone was as deferential as he could manage.

"Is she here or not, Doña Petra?"

"Of course not," Doña Petra said. "It's so late. And she's not home?"

Aníbal ran down the stairs. He didn't have all night to be talking to old ladies. He'd never noticed before how dim-witted Marta's mother was. Then again, maybe it was just old age.

He yanked open the entry door. The wind swept over him in a blast of bone-piercing air that knocked the rum's golden high right out of him. He looked up and down the boulevard into the expanse of white. A stray dog peed under a tree. Down the corner, illuminated under a streetlight, he saw a couple of men smoking and talking, as if it weren't winter. Aníbal was tempted to shout, Coño, it's fucking cold, maricónes!

Someone had placed chairs on the hood of his car, and he tossed them in the snow. The aluminum frames hit the ground with a loud clang in the quiet night. He started swearing. The men stopped to look at him and then resumed talking. If later he found scratches on the paint he would look for whoever owned those chairs and make him pay! True, he shouldn't have taken the spot that someone else had shoveled, but shit, another maricón had taken the space he had cleared. What was a man to do?

Aníbal waited for the car to warm up, thinking, Now, what the fuck? Where the hell could she have gone? He needed a cigarette. He opened the glove compartment, finding the car title, a pack of gum, a black bra. Marta's. He couldn't remember how that had gotten there. Shit, he was lucky Felicidad hadn't found it. No cigarettes. He would get some at Comacho's. See if Felicidad had stopped off there. By the time he arrived at Comacho's, he was certain she would be there waiting for him. It all made sense to him now, how she would be there, looking beautiful—because she always looked beautiful—and pitiful, with her little suitcase clutched in her tiny hand and like any other woman expecting him to drop to his knees and beg forgiveness. Like he would ever do that, and in front of Comacho and the others, too! Just being a beautiful girl wasn't enough to get Aníbal Acevedo to drop to his knees—not to beg forgiveness—no señor, and if she wanted to learn it in front of a bunch of cigarette smoking, rum-drinking island transplants, well then, so be it.

There was Comacho leaning on the counter next to a half-full bottle of rum, expounding on what he would do if he got lucky and won la bolita like some guy he knew. Three or four men Aníbal didn't know downed rum at twenty-five cents a shot and listened to Comacho's growing list of riches as if they, too, would have a share in it. Comacho paused in the description of the great coffee plantation he would buy on the island.

He leaned forward to shake Aníbal's hand.

"Aníbal! What brings you here this time of night?"

"A pack of Camels," Aníbal said. He thought, Mierda, why was Comacho pretending like nothing was wrong when it was obvious he knew something? He wished that he didn't have to ask about Felicidad in front of strangers. Although what did it matter if he asked him in private when Comacho would be blabbing everything he said with each sale? Gathering and spreading chisme was one of the main pleasures of owning a grocery store for men like Comacho, men who on the island held court in little country stores built with wood planks and zinc roofs or shacks assembled from sheets of tin. Men who passed out small favors as they saw fit. Always, the handy bottle of rum at the ready for the cane worker who stopped in to fortify himself for the long walk home or for the campesinos gathering to talk politics or share complaints of the day almost sure to include women or the governor. These storekeepers were thrifty with their rum and credit, although sometimes a particular one or his wife was known to be generous to a poor widow and her brood of barefoot, starving children.

Comacho passed him the cigarettes.

Aníbal gestured for a shot of rum. Comacho poured it. Aníbal drank it.

There was no easy way to ask. Better after a shot of rum than not. "Has my wife been here today?"

"She was here," Comacho said. "I didn't see her, but Lupe did. She came in while I was in the back with the man from the meat company. You know that they raised prices and still expect me to take any meat they want to give me, even with great ribbons of fat? I think it's because I'm Puerto Rican. I had it out with the salesman and I said—in English, you understand, because you have to talk to these maricónes in their language for them to respect you—I said that when I wanted to buy lard and fatback—that's English for tocino—I would buy it and not have to cut it from my own meat."

The men lurking in the dark corner murmured approval.

Aníbal wanted to say, Listen, Comacho, I don't give a damn about your meat problems. You'll find a way for your customers to pay. What about my wife? He was tempted to grab Comacho by his shirt collar and say, I don't give a fuck about tocino!

Instead he lit a cigarette like he didn't give a shit. "What did Lupe say?"

Comacho was disappointed not to finish his story. He thought it a particularly good one. It showed him up not only as an astute businessman who wasn't afraid of those Italians from the North Side but as a competent speaker of the English language, which everyone knew was difficult as a son of a bitch.

"Lupe said your pretty little wife was looking for a place to stay," Comacho said.

Aníbal knew that when Comacho stopped talking it was because he wanted you to tell your business and your mother's business and your father's business. So he smoked his cigarette in silence.

After a while, Comacho said, "And she wanted to stay with us."

Felicidad stay with Comacho? ¡Carajo! Aníbal peered at him through the smoke of his cigarette, waiting.

"I would have said yes if I had been here, but Lupe said no," Comacho said, holding up his hands as if to say, You know how women can be. Uncharitable to each other.

Someone was looking out for her. Maybe Lupe. Comacho was a man who always expected to be paid. Better for Felicidad to be out there frozen and friendless. Yes, someone was certainly looking out for Felicidad.

He set down his shot glass with a little tap. Comacho filled it. Aníbal drank. "What then?"

"One of the caballeros"—here Comacho pointed to the men

in the shadows—"gave her some money." Comacho smacked his lips over the word *money*.

Aníbal peered into the darkness, wishing to discover who had the nerve to give his wife money. The men kept their heads down.

"Money for bus fare," Comacho said. "I guess she didn't have any."

One of the men coughed. No one spoke but Aníbal felt himself judged and found wanting. To let his wife be so destitute that she had to take money from another man for something so basic as bus fare was reprehensible.

Aníbal almost fell into Comacho's trap. He was tempted to defend himself, to explain his situation, to point out how she had left him of her own volition.

"Lupe sent her to your friends—Chago and Ana," Comacho said.

Aníbal took a drag of his cigarette, trying to hide his relief.

"So why is your wife wandering the streets of Chicago? What could cause a sweet thing like that to leave a man?"

Aníbal thought Comacho lucky to have a counter between them, lucky to have witnesses. He took out his wallet, distracting Comacho by the show of dollar bills. Aníbal was gone before Comacho could weasel his secret out of him and then lecture him on the stupidity of letting a girl like Felicidad get away, whatever the reason. Women like that weren't born very often. Some people didn't know what to do with their good fortune—to have a wife like Felicidad and a woman like Marta and to be young and strong.

Carajo, he just didn't like Aníbal. He didn't know why, he just didn't like him.

"That maricón," Comacho said. "He deserves whatever he gets."

Aníbal wished he had taken one more shot of rum at Coma-cho's to take the edge off his nerves. He couldn't figure out why his hands trembled on the steering wheel. He looked up at Chago and Ana's apartment. Did he expect to see Felicidad at the window? Maybe Chago to head him off and suggest the bar instead? He had to circle the block a few times before someone pulled out of a space not reserved with chairs. He didn't know why he was here or what he expected. Maybe he just needed to know that Felicidad was safe so that he wouldn't feel like an ass-hole and he could go back to being the old Aníbal, the Aníbal before Felicidad.

Chapter Thirty-one

Ana blocked the doorway. "There you are, sinvergüenza. It's about time," she said. "You ought to be ashamed of yourself."

He made to kiss her cheek; she turned her face.

"Is Felicidad here?"

"What do you care?"

"Ana, be reasonable."

"Reasonable? You're telling me to be reasonable?"

Any other man would have stepped back from the glare of her dark eyes. Even Aníbal was relieved to see Chago come up behind his wife, pushing her out of the doorway.

"Shh, mujer, Aníbal is our friend," he said in his customary whisper. "Come in, hombre."

Aníbal stumbled over the threshold.

"You're drunk!" Ana said.

"I had a few on an empty stomach," *Why did women keep saying he was drunk?*

"Don't expect me to serve up some rice and beans." Ana placed her hands on her hips.

"Woman, serve Aníbal some rice and beans," Chago said, expecting her to obey.

"Huh! Not until I hear his story," Ana said.

Aníbal wiped his feet on the towel on the floor. He knew the last thing Ana would excuse would be dirty footprints on her floor.

"Is Felicidad here?" He glanced around the room.

"And where else would she be when her own husband doesn't want her?" Ana asked.

"I'm glad." Aníbal sat on the sofa.

"Oh, you're glad? You're glad that your wife had to leave her own house and go about in a strange country looking for a place to stay? That's very pretty." Ana looked at him with such disgust that Aníbal felt ashamed.

"That's not what I meant—" Aníbal said.

"Oh, no? What did you mean?"

Chago held out his hands in a placating gesture. "Ana, let the man talk. How can he tell us what has happened if you don't let him talk? Remember, Aníbal is our friend."

Ana tilted her head as if to say, Well, let this friend of yours have his say, but he's not going to tell me anything that is going to change what I think of him.

"Does Felicidad need anything?"

"Ha! What she needs you won't give her." Ana arched her eyebrow. It was obvious to both men what she meant.

"Coño, Ana, you don't understand," Aníbal said.

Chago shook his head, embarrassed. "That's not really our business."

"And whose business is it? Not Aníbal's. He doesn't think it his business to fuck his wife." By this time, Ana was standing over Aníbal. For a moment, he feared he might have to defend himself, at least to raise his hands to block any pescosas.

Chago laid a calming hand on his wife's arm. "¡Mujer! Go get Aníbal some dinner and send Felicidad here. You want to see her?"

"Does he want to see her—" Ana raised her voice.

"Quiet!" Chago held up his hand. He was the man of the house and his wife would do what he said.

Ana stopped talking, but she said everything she wanted to say with her black-lined eyes.

Did he want to see Felicidad? His friends expected it. He didn't know what good it would do. He had only wanted to assure himself of her safety.

"Send her to me," he said.

"If only I were a man." Ana thrust her fists in her apron pockets. The men suppressed their laughter until she left. Ana should be laughed at—but not too loudly, because one knew how angry women could get, and Chago still had to live with her.

Chago pantomimed *A little drink,* then Aníbal was alone, wondering what he would say to his wife.

Felicidad heard Aníbal's voice all the way in the kitchen where she was drying the dinner dishes. Oh, she didn't hear him exactly—not the words he spoke nor Ana's, either, and certainly not Chago's—but she knew her husband's voice. Now she strained to listen over the pounding of her heart.

He had come for her as she hadn't dared to hope that he would. He had come to take her back and this time, it would all be different. She would be a true wife to him and he would be a true husband. A plate slipped from her fingers and she caught it as it fell. The pots and pans were still unwashed on the stove, but she would tell Ana that she was sorry she couldn't finish. Her husband had come for her.

She dried her hands on a dish towel and went to the bedroom where the children were doing their homework. Anita asked Felicidad what six times three was because her brother wouldn't tell her, and Felicidad told her. The children were sweet, especially Anita, who had hugged her the moment she came home from school. Chagito was in the sixth grade and dumbstruck by this beautiful girl whom his mother said was staying a few days. He could only stare at her and hope that Felicidad would never address him directly.

Felicidad fussed with her hair.

"You look pretty." Anita touched a curl.

Felicidad kissed her. She wanted to say: You really think so? Do you think my husband will think so, too?

She hurried to the living room, bumping into Ana in the hall.

"That husband of yours is here," Ana said.

Felicidad embraced her and fled to the sala where Aníbal awaited her. She was so happy. Tonight she could kiss anybody, hug everybody. She heard Ana call out to her, but she didn't stop. Her husband had come for her.

Aníbal stood over Ana's altar with the saint statuettes. He had a framed photograph in his hands, which he set down when Felicidad came into the room. He hadn't changed out of his work clothes or removed the jacket that she had mended for him, but she thought him as handsome as he had ever been on the island.

"Here I am," Felicidad said.

"There you are." Aníbal turned to look at her.

He had come for her. Felicidad couldn't help smiling at him. *Embrace me, husband. Take me in your arms and kiss me. I don't even care if you say you're sorry. Lo que pasó, pasó. From now on, we'll belong only to each other. Kiss me.*

"I heard you took money," Aníbal said.

She shivered. Ana had lent her a sweater and she huddled deeper in it.

Her husband's voice was harsh, the words clipped. Where was the honeyed voice she longed for? Where were the sweet words of love?

"They told me at Comacho's you took money. Is that true?"

"I went to see Lupe—"

"And the money?"

If he would just let her explain. "A nice caballero gave me ten dollars for bus fare," Felicidad said.

"Ten dollars! For bus fare! Who was it?"

"Some old man. He was just being kind." Why was Aníbal angry? Why be angry when he had come to take her home?

"Don't take money from men. If you need money, then ask me."

Aníbal patted the pockets of his jacket and brought out a pack of cigarettes. He fumbled opening it. She wondered if he was nervous, too. Felicidad waited while he took out a cigarette and lit it. He reached for something green on the sofa.

"You forgot this." He held out the flannel shirt.

She took it. He did care. He had remembered how she was always cold. She knew that if only he kissed her they could start over.

Look at me, Aníbal! Look at me, your wife. Why wouldn't he look at her? Didn't he want her? Hadn't he come to get her? *Kiss me.* When he didn't, when he continued to smoke his cigarette without looking at her, without speaking, she brought the green plaid shirt to her cheek. The fabric was cold. It smelled of home, of their apartment. She hoped she would not cry.

Chago came in empty-handed. He thought, Good, Aníbal had come to his senses and would take his wife home with him where she belonged.

"Sorry about that drink, Aníbal, but Ana wants you to come eat," Chago said.

"I can't stay, compai." Aníbal crushed his cigarette in an ash-tray shaped like a palm tree.

Chago looked from one to the other. "Stay. Eat."

Aníbal stood so close that she could smell the rum on his breath. He looked beat, a weary version of his normal self. She held her breath. This was it. He would ask her to go home with him. If only Chago would go away again, but it didn't matter. Soon they would be alone in their sweet little apartment.

"I was very comfortable when I lived with Chago and Ana. Isn't that right, Chago?"

For the second time that day, she thought she might faint. She couldn't faint. Ana wouldn't like it and Aníbal wouldn't care. Felicidad tilted her head, her hair cascading, veil-like.

"Ana and Chago are buena gente. You won't find two better people." His breath teased her hair.

Was he still talking? It didn't matter to him that she would be imposing on his friends whom she barely knew, who were only letting her stay out of pity. He didn't care what happened to her as long as he didn't have to be bothered.

They stood in the middle of Chago and Ana's living room, not talking, each lost in thought, feeling something shift between them that left husband and wife bereft. Neither under-stood that their sadness was for the loss of who they had once been on the island—for the Aníbal who rescued a pretty girl, wanting to give her a happy life, and for the Felicidad who had once believed that he was everything she had ever dreamed.

Chago coughed.

Aníbal took out his wallet. "Chago, I want to give you a few dollars for Felicidad's keep."

Chago protested, Aníbal insisted.

"You're doing me a big favor, taking her in," he said.

Felicidad turned away.

Ana had come into the room drying a frying pan with a dish towel. "Aníbal, I served you. Your food will be cold and I have better things to do than to keep warming up food for someone who is not my husband."

"Aníbal has to leave," Chago said.

"What?" Ana's glance took in the situation. Felicidad held herself so still Ana knew the girl was doing all she could to hold on to her dignity. Chago was taking money from that idiot Aníbal. To bring a girl to another country and then change your mind about wanting her? A nice girl, too? No, señor, she was not going to have that sinvergüenza in her house one more minute.

"Get the *hell* out of my house, Aníbal," she shouted.

"Ana!" Her husband struggled to say her name above a whisper but it came out a squawk. His wife felt no pity for the strain on his vocal cords.

"Chago, if you know what's good for your friend you will get him the hell out of my house before I take this frying pan"—here Ana raised the pan—"and bring it down on his empty head!"

"Ana, please. Don't." Felicidad dropped the shirt on the floor.

"You're crazy, Ana," Aníbal said.

"I'm crazy?" The nerve of him! Of all the conceited machos that Ana had ever known—and she had known her share of Puerto Rican men thinking it their right to stick their dicks wherever they pleased—Aníbal was the worst.

Ana advanced with the frying pan raised like a club.

The children came running. "Mami! Mami! Why are you yelling at Tío Aníbal?"

"Tío Aníbal, what did you do to Mami?"

"Go to bed!" Ana shouted.

"Aníbal, you'd better leave," Chago said, embarrassed by his wife's behavior, outrageous by most people's standards. But Ana was brava—one of those women who was too temperamental, too high-strung, too volatile, capable of anything—a woman who acted before she thought things through, one prone to violent likes and dislikes. Chago, formed from calmer, gentler matter, had learned after years of marriage to such a woman to step out of her way and let her rant until she spent herself. He and the children knew all was well when she sat at the kitchen table drinking her coffee.

Aníbal didn't move. It was a tragedy that his best friend couldn't control his wife, but no woman was going to chase him out with a frying pan. What would people say? He was a man. He had his pride.

Felicidad tugged at Ana's arm. "Give me that, Ana."

"Only if you use it," Ana said.

Felicidad almost smiled.

"Aníbal, you should leave," Felicidad said to the frying pan. She decided that she would not look at her husband. "Thank you for your concern, but as you can see I am among friends now."

"Come, Felicidad, I'll make you some coffee to steady your nerves," Ana said with a toss of her head. "You kids want some?"

The women left the room arm in arm, the children followed, the men stared.

"What the hell?" Aníbal said. There was his shirt on the floor. One of the children had kicked it in a corner.

Chago shook his head. "Women," he whispered.

The Aníbal who drove home was still a little shaky. He thought maybe he had drunk too much rum. When Felicidad had come into the living room smiling at him like that, he had to reprimand her to keep from returning her smile. She had looked so beautiful, so glad to see him, the way she had looked on the island. He'd had no choice but to be cold. It was better for her and for him.

When he got to his block, he couldn't find a parking space. On both sides of the street, chairs had toppled on the snow-covered ground like dominoes.

"Maricón," he said, driving on.

Chapter Thirty-two

Ana sat on the cot next to Felicidad, who was dressed for bed in her granny nightgown. She had been staring out the window at the apartment across the courtyard, where a man and woman sat at the kitchen table smoking and playing cards.

"Those are the Robles," Ana said. "They play cards every night. I've lived here five years and there hasn't been a night when they haven't played."

Felicidad envied the Robles, who couldn't spend an evening apart.

The two women sat on the cot where Felicidad would sleep for much longer than she could that night imagine or dread. Felicidad berated herself for smiling at Aníbal like a little idiot girl from the country.

"It won't do any good pining for him," Ana said.

How well she knew. These weeks of living with him, Felicidad had done nothing but yearn for her husband's love, and it had gotten her a cot in someone else's house.

"I would keep myself busy," Ana said.

Busy. Yes, if there was anything Felicidad knew, it was how to keep busy. Hard work helped you wear yourself out so that at night when you closed your eyes you had only a moment or two to remember how lonely you were, how much you wanted someone to hold you, someone to love you. And then you fell asleep and, if it was a good night, you slept the dreamless sleep of the exhausted. Yes, she would work and eat and sleep. She would be again that worker girl who had earned the respect of others with her labor. She would be Felicidad la trabajadora. If she was lucky, she wouldn't have to work in a bakery.

The two women looked across the courtyard at the Robles, Felicidad wondering if she would ever be so lucky and Ana thinking Chago's whispering would get on her nerves.

That night with the memory of Aníbal's impersonal touch still more than she could bear, Felicidad called her Spirit Lover to her. Later she fell into a dreamless sleep.

The next day Chago took Felicidad to make the round of factories. Ana woke her at five o'clock in the morning and helped her choose her factory worker uniform.

"That dark skirt will be just fine. And a white blouse. That one." Ana pointed to one of two Felicidad had laid out on the cot.

"This one? But it's so plain. No ruffles or embroidery," Felicidad said. "I meant to trim it with roses."

"It looks like something a jamona would wear and that's what you want," Ana said. "We have to make you look plain. Business-like."

Felicidad turned around for Ana's inspection.

"I guess we'll settle for business-like," Ana said. "Wear your panadería shoes. If ever anything said *Factory worker,* it's those shoes. And don't forget your birth certificate. You might need that to prove you're a citizen. Does your birth certificate have your correct birth date?"

Felicidad glanced up from tying her laces.

"Don't look at me like I'm babbling," Ana said. "My own birth certificate is two years younger than I am. Papi didn't like to trouble himself for only one child. I had to wait until my sister was born."

"How unlucky," Felicidad said.

"Unlucky! You mean lucky," Ana said. "Not only am I two years younger but I am not a José Luis." She passed Felicidad her cup of coffee. "One year my uncle went to register his new baby and people here and there bought him shots of rum. When he finally got to town, he wrote down José Luis."

"What's wrong with that?"

"My cousin was a girl."

Felicidad laughed.

"It gets worse. My uncle already had a son named José Luis," Ana said.

When she was leaving, Ana gave her a sack lunch. It reminded Felicidad of the lunches she used to make for Aníbal.

"Why so sad? It's only bologna and cheese on white bread," Ana said.

In the car Felicidad strained to hear Chago over the noise of the heater.

"Remember to call the men *mister* and the women *miss*. And look everybody in the eye. That's very important, Felicidad. I lost a job or two when I first left the island because I didn't look people in the eye. Americans think you're lying or hiding something when you don't look them in the eye. You understand?"

"Look everyone in the eye," Felicidad said. She had to stop herself from laughing hysterically. All the years of training on the proper behavior of civilized people, and especially that of a young woman, and now she was supposed to forget it all.

"If anybody asks you if you can do anything like work some machine or type or something, say yes," Chago whispered.

"Type? On a typewriter? I can't type," Felicidad said.

"There's always somebody around who will teach you," Chago said. "If only you had some skill."

"I can embroider. And sew," Felicidad said.

"I know somebody at a factory where they make clothes," Chago said. Even a whisper couldn't hide his relief. "We'll try there first."

Eight hours a day, twenty-minute lunch, five-minute break at the clothing factory. Felicidad got a paid break because she was an American citizen. Las Mejicanas, the Mexican women, were illegals and did not. At lunch las Mejicanas ate a homemade tortilla or two wrapped around a spoonful of frijoles and hot peppers. The other women—the Puerto Ricans, a few Negroes, one or two whites—ate sandwiches or rice and beans from last night's dinner. The women shoveled tortillas, beans, rice, and bread in their mouths without pausing in their conversations about men, sex, babies, money, men, life, and men. Felicidad kept quiet. What could she say? Once I had a husband and my own home but now I think it was all a dream?

At the end of the week, Felicidad stared at her paycheck, disappointed at the amount, until she thought about her Mejicana co-workers, paid two dollars to her three. In the panadería the aunt paid her eight dollars a week. Here she earned thirty dollars, but had taxes and who knew what else. El Bosso said the Mexicans were paid less because they didn't pay taxes, but everyone knew it was because they couldn't do anything about it. The Mexicans worked ten hours each day to the others' eight. El Bosso didn't pay overtime.

When she started working in the clothing factory, Felicidad complained to Chago and Ana one night during dinner about El Bosso's treatment of the Mexicans. Was there anyone she could tell? Surely someone cared that these women were being singled out and mistreated, maybe someone in City Hall?

"This is Chicago. Unless they're Irish, the mayor isn't going to care," Ana said.

"They're still human beings like everyone else." Felicidad wondered why the Irish were so special.

"It happens everywhere," Chago said, shaking his head.

"¿De verdad? Do you think it happens where Aníbal works, too?"

"You need to stop thinking about that man." As Ana set down her coffee cup, it clicked against the saucer.

Felicidad wanted to say to her: Do you think I haven't tried? Instead, she said, "We should tell someone."

"¿Estás loca, mujer?" Ana got up to make more coffee. "Then those women won't have jobs, plus they'll send them right back to Mexico. They don't have papers. Why do you think they tolerate it?"

Felicidad pushed her plate away. "It's not fair."

"It's worse for the men. In one factory I worked in, the bosses docked you if you took a piss. One young guy took a leak in his pants, but he didn't stop working," Chago said in his usual whisper.

Felicidad was ashamed to laugh.

"The only thing that saves us Puerto Ricans is that we're citizens," Chago said.

"Felicidad, eat your dinner and forget about what we can't change," Ana said.

Felicidad stared down at her rice and beans, thinking, If only it were so easy.

★ ★ ★

El Bosso didn't like the women getting up from their benches. He liked to hear the roar of the machines, the clatter of scissors dropped into wire notions baskets, the swish of fabrics.

Felicidad lowered the needle and drew the green thread from the bobbin, picked up a blouse the green of the thread, inserted it under the presser foot, and fed it to the machine.

The fluorescent lights hurt her eyes and she was tempted to sew the straight seams with her eyes closed, except the supervisor Nena León might see her and show her no mercy, no special consideration. They should be comadres, two young women so far from the island. Felicidad knew El Bosso needed legal workers in case of an inspection. He would say, "These are my special girls. It's hard to find ones who can sew and speak American."

El Bosso always knew when the factory would be inspected. He had a connection down in City Hall, but it was possible that he might have the bad luck of getting an inspector whose hand he couldn't grease enough, or even an honest inspector, although Chago had told her that that was unlikely.

Her shoulders ached from eight hours of leaning over the hot sewing machine. Her thighs were sore from sitting on the hard wood bench and her feet hurt from pressing the pedals. The women stooped over their machines, fingers quick and nimble, beads of perspiration splashing down on the fabric. It was winter, but inside the factory, the heat reminded Felicidad of the aunt's house. Floor fans were scattered throughout the warehouse, but not close enough to make much difference. Some women placed wet washcloths on the backs of their necks or kept jars of water next to them to sprinkle on their faces like holy water.

This was not work for the fainthearted. The roar of the machines drowned the occasional cough or sneeze. It was a race to beat the clock, to finish the required number of pieces. It wasn't a time for daydreams or worries; only concentration and cooperation between mind and body could achieve the quota. For this, Felicidad valued the work—because she couldn't think about anything, not if she wanted to meet the quota.

After she had been working at the factory a few weeks, Awilda Ortiz, one of the Mexicans, had an asthma attack. El Bosso ordered Nena to drive Awilda to the hospital. He shoved ten dollars in Felicidad's hand and told her to go with them. "Pay the doctor. Say you're her sister. One Spanish girl is the same as another."

Nena let Awilda and Felicidad out at the entrance. In the emergency room Felicidad pretended to be Awilda's sister. She was more humiliated at not having enough money to pay Awilda's entire thirty-dollar emergency room bill than ashamed of her lies.

The next day El Bosso fired Awilda.

Felicidad said, thankful for the mandatory English in Puerto Rico's schools, "Give her one try. It no her fault."

"She's a liability. She's gotta go," El Bosso said.

Felicidad didn't understand *liability*. Perhaps El Bosso was just saying Awilda was an asthmatic. She couldn't let him fire Awilda, not when she still owed the hospital twenty dollars.

Felicidad looked El Bosso in the eye. "El doctor say where she sick. I say el doctor nada."

El Bosso crossed his arms over his chest, his pale skin a playground for heat rash. The last thing he needed was a health inspector nosing around, kicking up a fuss about the furnacelike temperature or the roaches hatching in the walls and the rats that colonized the dark corners of the warehouse.

"I'll move Awilda over by one of the fans. Tell her to drink lots of water. I heard that's good to do," he said.

"She drink, she go toilet," Felicidad said. "No finish twenty."

"She gotta go, she goes. Is that all right with you, FeleeDad?"

She smiled. El Bosso was human after all.

"Who would have thought a pretty thing like you would have a good brain. Learn yourself some more English and you can help me and Nena with the orders. Maybe get you a little raise," El Bosso said.

She looked at Nena standing behind the boss mumbling under her breath, possibly chanting some spells. Felicidad knew of one having to do with a lock of hair and a photograph. Maybe she should start wearing her hair in a bun.

Felicidad's life slipped into a tolerable routine: Monday through Friday, she worked in the factory, taking two buses to and from Chago and Ana's apartment. She ate the dinner Ana had prepared, afterward insisting on washing the dishes. Saturday, Ana shopped at Comacho's for comida criolla, but Felicidad feared running into Aníbal and preferred to stay and finish Ana's ironing.

Later friends dropped by to play dominoes, drink a little rum, dance a little merengue. Music and laughter carried through Chago and Ana's apartment as it had that night when Aníbal came into the kitchen and danced with her. If she closed her eyes and stood very still, she could feel his arms around her and hear him whispering in her ear: "Right, left, right, left," until she got the hang of it. She felt his breath on her hair, imagining that he pressed a kiss on it.

Felicidad preferred to cook for Ana's parties, to fall back into the role she knew so well. She was not a servant, but neither was she a member of the family, and therefore it was important that she earn her friends' continued benevolence by the depth of her helpfulness.

Yet she risked Ana's displeasure by refusing to attend Mass

on Sundays, choosing to stay alone in the empty apartment, the radio on for company. Ana judged Felicidad's absence as a form of truancy. She had even managed to persuade Chago to go to Mass, but Felicidad was firm. The certainty that the chismosas they had in common would stop their incessant clacking of the rosary beads to take apart her dress and demeanor and talk about the disintegration of her marriage was more than Felicidad could yet endure. Even worse, she feared she might hear gossip in the vestibule, bochinche about her husband consorting with Marta or some fulana or another.

Mostly, in her spare time, she embroidered—roses on Ana's tablecloths, bedspreads, pillowcases, towels, Anita's dresses, but when even Chagito began sporting roses on his pajamas, Ana took Felicidad aside.

"Listen, mujer, you have got to find yourself something to do. Get yourself a lover, take English classes, work some overtime, something, but don't turn my son into one of those fulanos that people talk about. You know what I mean. Every town had some. I'm sure there were a few of them even on the mountain," Ana said.

Felicidad didn't tell Ana that every time she stitched a rose she recalled the happy days of her childhood, but she could see that the roses were straining Ana's nerves. She took her advice and began taking English classes.

Dios, but it was hard to get through the day. The best part of it was when she slid her time card in the machine in the morning, for she knew that eight and a half hours would have to pass before she could think about Aníbal. When lunchtime came, Felicidad's heart beat a little quicker knowing that she was halfway through her workday. At quitting time, when the buzzer set the women off in a stampede for their coats, she stared down at the garment in her hands, wishing, despite the pain in her shoulders and the ache in her thighs from the wood bench, that the workday was just beginning.

Felicidad imagined she saw Aníbal everywhere. If she glanced out the bus window, there was sure to be a car like Aníbal's following. Sometimes she thought she saw his car in the neighborhood—how that would infuriate Ana if it were true. Felicidad kept these sightings secret from her friend. Ana would think her an idiot and not be afraid to say it. Worse were the nights she heard Chago and Ana making love in the next room, forcing her to flee to the living room. One such night, she paused in front of Ana's altar. The candles that were always lit flickered inside their saint bottles. Felicidad picked up a framed photograph of Ana in her wedding dress smiling at Chago.

She stood at the window, parting the curtains and splaying her palms against the glass pane. She offered up a prayer to the full moon, as she had often done to the stars when she lived on the island. Felicidad thought she saw Aníbal's car cruise down the street and pause. She held her breath until it drove on, the red glow of taillights fading into the night, taking her hope with it. These were the nights Felicidad was most grateful for her Spirit Husband. They made love quietly because Chago and Ana's bed was on the other side of the wall.

It was April and the winter's last snow melted from the city's dirty sidewalks. Felicidad noticed that Ana had little patience for Anita's tears over a friend's slight or Chagito's obvious infatuation with Felicidad, although she conscientiously tended to their well-being. She cooked hearty meals, cared for their clothes, devoted herself to the home. Ana didn't mean to yell at her children, but what did it matter if she yelled at them? They would get over it; they were only children, after all. To settle her nerves, Ana drank coffee. She felt her mood begin to change the moment she opened the bag of coffee beans. She breathed in the aroma that began and ended her day, which promised her the rich, black warmth that would soon soothe her throat and gentle her nerves. Her fingers were steady as she poured the beans into the grinder. She turned the handle, listening to the beans rattle, her heartbeat slowing to a normal beat. Smiling, she scooped coffee into el colador, admiring its dark brown color, thinking that nothing smelled better than coffee just ground. Next she poured water that she heated in the teakettle. Ana knew that the modern women of television—the I Love Lucys and Our Miss Brooks—brewed coffee in stainless-steel coffeepots, but she couldn't imagine any coffee tasting better than that which she filtered through her little piece of cloth (stained dark brown from frequent usage), stitched over a wire circle. This was the way her mother had done it. When she drank a cup, she knew that she could make it through another day, or at least until the next cup.

Coffee. Coffee was Ana's addiction, her love, her reason to get up in the morning, what held her together another day. She could never drink too much of it. When she wasn't drinking it, she was brewing it. Ana couldn't live without coffee. She gladly admitted it. Housework got done thanks to coffee. Chago's whispering didn't annoy her when she had a cup of coffee in her hand. She could tolerate anything as long as she had coffee.

One day Chago said something about seeing Aníbal at the bar and how he was drinking too much. Did she think he should mention it to Felicidad?

"Don't you dare," Ana said, taking a calming sip of coffee instead of telling her husband that he was out of his mind.

Ana enjoyed Felicidad's company and appreciated her sweet nature, her helpfulness. The girl was really no trouble, and the money she contributed each week went to pay for the new TV.

The problem with Felicidad was the roses. She couldn't stop embroidering them. Felicidad was clean, respectful, more a sister to her than her own sisters. But those goddamn roses were getting on her nerves.

Ana went to fill the teakettle with water. She took off the cover decorated with roses. Goddamn roses.

Chapter Thirty-three

Aníbal expected to forget Felicidad as he had forgotten most of the women he had enjoyed, although he might give one or another a fleeting thought, relishing the memory of a certain encounter or the feel of a particular pair of breasts in his hands. But this time it was difficult. He blamed it on the roses. Felicidad had embroidered roses on the towels, tablecloth, sheets, and the goddamn bedspread, which was the only one he owned. Even roses on the motherfucking sofa cushions. Why hadn't he noticed any of this when Felicidad was around? It was like when he returned to Puerto Rico and wondered, Was the sky always this blue? Had the mountains always been so steep?

How Marta had laughed at the roses.

"Hombre, what the fuck! Was your wife a fucking gardener or something?" Her fingers picked at a rose.

He couldn't do it with Marta on the bed what with the bedspread and embroidered sheets and such. He felt too much of a maricón. Plus, he couldn't get hard, not that he confessed this to Marta. She teased him enough already, calling him a pendejo for being so squeamish, but he just couldn't screw another woman among his wife's things.

He found that being with Marta annoyed him in ways he hadn't noticed before. She didn't like to stay home and watch *I Love Lucy* with him like Felicidad did. Marta said Lucy was una mujer loca and why didn't Lucy and Ricky just go dancing every night? A little mambo, a little chachacha would shake them up. They were in New York, weren't they? And why were they friends with those boring old landlords? Marta always wanted to go dancing or drinking even if it wasn't the weekend. She didn't care that he was exhausted from lifting hundred-pound sacks. She also was unwilling to do things for him as Felicidad had done. When he asked Marta to run his bath, she said, "Coño, you must be out of your mind. Do I look like your criada?" Aníbal didn't like her saying that about criada. He thought it a reference to Felicidad growing up a servant girl in the aunt's home.

Mornings, when he got up, there was no coffee and no eggs and ham, no lunch, either. When once or twice he had stayed over at Marta's and he asked her to make him some coffee and eggs, she said, "Fuck you. You know where the coffeepot is. Make *me* some fucking coffee. And by the way, I like my eggs over hard."

Often Aníbal would arrive at work with an empty stomach. It made him less tolerant of doing what he called mule work. One morning he sought out Mackie, the fucking foreman who always assigned him to The Border with all the immigrants. Aníbal reminded Mackie that he had promised him a job in another section, possibly on one of the machines.

"One of these days," Mackie said.

Aníbal had swallowed his pride and gone back to work, keeping to himself what he had wanted to say to Mackie and taking out his anger and frustration on the sacks.

That day, there was a letter from Puerto Rico. A rush of love flowed through him when he recognized his mother's beautiful penmanship. How he yearned to hear his mother's voice, to be guided by her counsel. Then he thought, Maricón, am I crazy! It had been his mother who had started the whole Felicidad situation. Aníbal set aside the letter. He wasn't in the mood for his mother's schemes.

Aníbal didn't understand why he couldn't just slip back into his old life before Felicidad. When he sat on the sofa watching television, he found he had to have a bottle of rum to keep him company since he didn't have Felicidad sitting alongside him embroidering her roses. After a couple of nights of too much solitude and even more rum, he stopped watching television. He found himself pacing the living room floor and recalling how the woman had tortured him with her baths without even knowing it. The rose-covered bedspread smelled like his wife's Ivory soap and he was glad that it was spring and he put it away. Why was everything so different now? He had lived alone before and never felt so lonely.

He began to avoid the apartment. He drove around aimlessly, parking in an empty lot when he tired. Twice, a cop had rapped his knuckles on the car window asking him his business, suspicious even after he shone his flashlight into the empty backseat. He went to the bar Friday nights when Chago was there, hoping he might volunteer how Felicidad was getting along. But Chago didn't, and Aníbal didn't ask, confused as he was as to why he should care so much. Weekends, which used to be his salvation, were now the hardest to endure—so many hours to fill. Before Felicidad, there was always a woman or two to take up his time, but now there was only Marta and they had only one use for each other. Aníbal found that sex with Marta was not enough anymore, that although momentarily he would be satisfied, soon he would be as restless as when he first arrived at her apartment.

It was in early April that the night came when he'd had enough of Marta. It all began with her complaining about his recent performance. Aníbal had been staring up at the ceiling, thinking that Marta should talk to her landlord about the crumbling plaster. One day it just might fall on top of them while they were in bed.

Marta was stepping into a slip when she said, "Maricón, you don't fuck like you used to."

Was she saying he hadn't satisfied her? Impossible! In the past he'd had women thank him! But there might be some truth in what Marta said; these days he found his attention wandering. Still, it annoyed him that she called him maricón and he flung the sheet off while hunting around for his pants. He found them in a pile of Marta's dresses. On more than one occasion, he had teasingly asked Marta if she knew what clothes hangers were, or a washing machine, for that matter. He wasn't one of those men who took much notice of tidiness, but he had to step on piles of clothes to get to her bed. And it was difficult to ignore the smell of dried sweat and past sex that sometimes washed over him when he was in bed with Marta.

"Where do you get this maricón mierda? No other woman has ever called me that," Aníbal said.

"Maybe not to your face." Marta brushed her hair in front of the mirror. He recalled its softness without feeling the urge to touch it as he once had.

Aníbal made a sweeping gesture with his arm. "Maybe if you cleaned this place up, I could get into it more."

"Fuck you!" Marta threw the hairbrush at him. He ducked and it landed in a pile of her shoes.

"We used to have such fun, Aníbal," Marta said. "What happened?"

"I don't know." He sat back down on her bed, suddenly tired and unsettled.

"I do," Marta said. "Maricón, I think you love your wife."

He and Marta had kissed good-bye like civilized people—no hard feelings, it was fun while it lasted. Aníbal had sat in his car thinking that the intense sensation in his gut was just an overwhelming relief to be finished with Marta and all her drama. Aníbal leaned his head against the steering wheel. No, that wasn't it. It was what Marta said: He was in love with his wife. He was unsure how it had happened, but there it was. He didn't think it was only because Felicidad was beautiful; he had known other pretty women. Aníbal was twenty-three years old and women had always wanted him for one thing, which he had always willingly performed to the best of his ability. Why had it taken him so long to realize that Felicidad was different? After a long day at the factory, she had been glad to see him, as if she had waited all day to serve him his dinner, to make conversation, to relax next to him on the sofa. And if he hadn't been such an idiot, Felicidad would be waiting for him right now. She'd be sitting up in bed embroidering those damn roses and wearing that damn granny nightgown until he took it off her. Then, after they made love, at least twice to make up for lost time, she would lie in his arms while they talked. There was a lot that Aníbal didn't know about his wife and that she didn't know about him. He had never been one to talk much, but now, inexplicably, he wanted someone to talk to about his day and what dreams he might have. He wanted to hear what she had to say; maybe she had her own dreams (although he thought this unlikely). He wanted to show her things, to do things for her, with her. Aníbal realized that he'd rather be with her than with anyone else. Was this love? He thought it might be. But what did he know about love? Sex, he knew about, but love? And then it came to him, a whisper in the night. She loved you. Felicidad loved you.

Next day, at the factory, he approached Mackie with as much politeness as he could muster considering Mackie was a son of a bitch. He had decided that if he wanted to be a real husband to Felicidad, then he had to do more than be a mule for hire. A man had to give his woman a reason to be proud of him, but first he had to take pride in himself.

Aníbal said, "El job, Macki. Juw promiss."

Mackie said, "Listen, Anneball. I'm pretty tired of your lip. All you immigrants always complaining about something, not knowing how to be fucking grateful. Go on back to your sacks where you fucking belong."

Aníbal walked toward Mackie, intending to show him how grateful he was. Mackie picked up a wrench and waved it at Aníbal shouting, "Get the fuck out!" Aníbal considered saying good-bye with his fists—wrench or no wrench—but instead he went to the office to pick up his paycheck. He would find work somewhere else. He was young and strong and determined, and that had to matter, even in America.

He went looking for Chago. It was Friday and he was sure to be at the bar. Aníbal wanted to find out when would be a good time to come get Felicidad. No need to mention Mackie.

Steep spiral stairs led down to Lucky's. Nightly, men rushed over to get one of the tables by the stairs or tipped the bartender to save one so they had a clear view of every pair of legs coming and going. It was an accepted fact that the type of woman who came to the bar was the type of woman who wanted men to look up her skirt. Aníbal had never thought it right to shell out money for the opportunity. He liked to shoot pool and, except for a curious glance now and then, especially if the guys were howling, he would rather be eyeing the cue ball.

Chago was at the counter. He pointed to his shot of rum. "You look like you could use one."

Aníbal motioned to the bartender to leave the bottle. He lifted his glass.

"To endings and beginnings," Aníbal said.

"Endings?"

"I'm through with Marta."

Chago nodded as if he had expected this news.

"Who is the new woman? Not that cashier at Woolworth's? That very pretty German girl? Greta something or other," Chago said, leaning in so his friend could hear him in the noisy bar.

"It's my wife. I'm coming to get Felicidad."

"You've got to be out of your fucking mind," Chago said.

"What?" Aníbal set down his shot glass with a little thud.

"She's a good girl," Chago said. "Too good for you to use and discard when you get tired of her."

Aníbal struggled to control his temper. Chago was his friend, his compai!

"Who the fuck are you to tell me about what I can or can't do with my own wife?"

"I'm her friend. I care about Felicidad and that's more than you ever did. Screwing around with Marta while your wife was at home cooking your dinner." Chago pushed the bottle of rum toward Aníbal.

"That's none of your fucking business," Aníbal said.

"Maybe not before, but Felicidad is living in my house and what happens to her now is my business," Chago said. "So stay away from her."

Aníbal stared at his friend, thinking he was not hearing him clearly. That sometimes happened because of Chago's whispering.

"I heard you got fired," Chago said. "What good is a man to a woman without a job?"

Aníbal stood up quickly, knocking down the bar stool and grabbing his friend by the lapels of his jacket. The other men turned around to look; even the guys playing pool put down their cue sticks and glanced over with halfhearted interest. Nobody bothered to intercede. The bartender moved the bottle of rum. Chago brushed off Aníbal's hands, shoving him against the bar. Later, neither could say exactly how Aníbal ended up with a black eye and Chago with a bloody nose. All Aníbal could recall clearly was Chago lying on the floor with blood splattered on his jacket, his hand over his nose. Chago, his friend—no, more than his friend, his compadre—more than that even, his brother, yes; Chago was like his older brother. Chago, who had taken Aníbal into his home the same day he had arrived in Chicago, knowing no one, but sure he could make his living with his young, strong body. Chago, whose wife had fed him rice and beans like Mamá's, which helped him to forget his homesickness even as he remembered his mother's cooking. Chago, amigo, compadre, hermano.

"¡Cabrón!" Chago whispered from the floor.

Aníbal gave him a hand and helped him up.

"I'm sorry," he said.

"Fuck you," Chago said.

"I love Felicidad," Aníbal said.

Chago accepted Aníbal's handkerchief and pressed it to his nose. It quickly spotted red. He gulped down a shot of rum behind it.

"What is love to you, Aníbal? What you call love? Two weeks? Three? Marta was around for what—seven, eight months? And you married for half that time. That's sex, my friend, not love. That's lust." Chago drank a second shot. "You know what love is, Aníbal? It's going to work even when you're sick because if there's no money for the rent, the landlord throws your stuff onto the grass in the courtyard, and I wouldn't be much of a man if I let that happen to my wife and kids. Love is staying with a woman for fifteen years because you believe in your heart that she still loves you. Even though you can't open your mouth without her yelling at you. That's love, my friend. You don't know fuck about love." Chago massaged his throat; he wasn't used to giving long speeches.

Aníbal stared at Chago, surprised, shocked even, at his outburst, the contempt for his own behavior unmistakable. Aníbal downed a shot of rum. He found that he missed cañita from the island. A man forgot his troubles a lot quicker with homemade ron caña.

"Why are you being so hard on me, compai? A man can make a mistake," Aníbal said.

Chago got up to leave, tossing a few dollars on the bar and squeezing his friend's shoulder. "You're not thinking straight, compai, because if you were, you would realize that the best thing for Felicidad is for you to stay away from her."

He watched Chago leave, Chago, his brother. He stayed until closing time; there was nothing waiting for him at home.

Aníbal placed the bottle of rum on top of the roof of his car and leaned back against the hood. He peered up at his apartment through a half-closed eye; the empty rooms filled him with dread. He fumbled in his pockets for a cigarette but found none. He hadn't yet gotten into the habit of buying them regularly. What did the neighbors think, seeing him outside at night skulking under a streetlamp when he had a perfectly good apartment? For sure, that bochinchera Dora Matos was peering at him behind the curtain, imagining how she would describe him the next day at Comacho's. He should be glad his misery was providing entertainment for somebody.

Chago's words had shaken him. If even your compadre thinks you're no good, you have to consider it.

¡Coño! Could Chago be right that he was no good for Felicidad? He allowed the possibility that it was too late to prove otherwise. Aníbal looked up at the sky and asked the stars if it could be so. That first night when he had carried Felicidad in the snow because she wore sandals, Aníbal had reveled in his body, his strong arms. He had believed that he was as indifferent to the woman in his arms as he was to one of the sacks he lugged at work. How wrong could he have been? He laughed at himself; it rang hollow in the night.

The moon lit his way on the sidewalk. He tucked the bottle of rum under his arm and felt the weight of his neighbors' prying eyes. He hunched his shoulders and ducked his head. Whatever his neighbors said about him, he deserved.

Aníbal met no one on the stairs. Inside the apartment, he threw himself on Felicidad's sofa without even removing his jacket. He was going to finish off the bottle of rum and, with any luck, drink himself into oblivion.

Midday sun streamed in through the curtainless windows. Aníbal groaned. For a minute, he couldn't remember where he was. One eye was swollen and difficult to see out of. Something hard lay on his chest. A bottle. Maricón. He had fallen asleep with the bottle of rum clutched in his hand. Carajo. Rum had spilled on his shirt and jacket and even on Felicidad's sofa. He made to get up. The stiff plastic crackled. He wondered if someone had bashed his head with the bottle of rum—when he moved, it felt brittle like crushed glass—but there was the bottle in his hand. He set it on the floor and raised both hands to his head, gingerly feeling for bumps or bruises. Nothing. After a minute or two, he felt able to sit up.

His throat was dry, the rum bottle empty. He stumbled to the kitchen and stuck his head under the faucet, letting the cold water splash over him—easing his throbbing eye, if doing nothing for his head.

Coffee. He needed coffee. Fucking coffee.

Aníbal had avoided the pantry since that first night when he discovered his wife had left him. He had slammed the door shut and every morning had gone without coffee rather than enter Felicidad's kitchen where the shine of the turquoise refrigerator reminded him how much his wife had loved it.

Aníbal yanked open the pantry door and pulled on the ceiling light cord.

"¡Coño! ¡Carajo!" He had forgotten that the pantry was a fucking disaster. Boxes and cans knocked down, salt had spilled from an overturned container, beans everywhere—scattered on the shelves, spread out over the floor, garbanzos gleaming on the sandy salt like big, round pearls. He stepped around pieces of glass. Felicidad's bottle of Spanish olive oil had shattered, olive oil that she had treasured as some women do perfume. A puddle of the golden liquid had hardened, a cockroach petrified in the pond. Aníbal stared at the chaos, thinking it was the work of a crazy man. Everything was such a mess. Felicidad's pantry, in which she had taken such pride.

It had given him pleasure to be able to buy her food. It made him think better of himself like he was making up for her miserable childhood. But if he were honest—and on this day when he could see clearly out of only one eye—he could recall that there had been something in Felicidad's eyes that had enthralled him. He could have left her on the island even after reading the priest's letters. She would have met some other man. She was a beautiful girl and there was always a man for a beautiful girl. This unwelcome thought shot a jolt through his aching head.

He realized that the pantry had been a symbol of what she had hoped their life together would be—a life of plenty, filled with delicious food she would prepare with love, the love that she had expected they would one day share.

Aníbal closed his eyes and pinched the bridge of his nose. Ay carajo, he had been such a fucking bastard.

He went to get a paper bag and began to clean the mess he had made. He squatted down on his haunches, tossing the empty salt container into the bag. Aníbal pricked his finger on a shard of glass from the bottle of olive oil, but he didn't stop to bandage it. That he might bleed a little was the least he deserved.

Aníbal decided that he didn't give a shit what Marta said or what anybody else said, including Chago and Ana, he only cared what Felicidad would say when he asked her to come back to him. But he had to show Felicidad that he was no longer a maricón, that he could be a good husband.

He made the round of factories and could only find the kind of work that he had always done, work that only required his youth and muscle. He didn't want that anymore. Felicidad deserved a man who was more than a body, who used more than his body. Finally, in late April, he found a job as an apprentice welder at a tool-and-die factory way over on the South Side. He had to commit to taking a welding class twice a week. He was glad of this—two evenings that he wouldn't be sitting alone in an empty apartment where embroidered roses reminded him of what might have been. He decided to take English classes to fill up two other nights. It would help with his welding course and, also, he was ashamed for Felicidad to learn that he knew so little, he who had once bragged to her that he knew as much English as was necessary. But that was the old Aníbal. One day he would take the GED test and that would really impress her. Now the only way he made it through the school's front entrance was imagining another time when he might carry Felicidad's books to class, hurrying to open the school's heavy door, trailing her down the corridor's long tunnel, the heels of their shoes clacking on the old floors. Felicidad would probably stop outside each classroom, admiring the teachers' construction paper displays, the children's paintings, the stories written in pencil, all a blotch of scribbles to him.

Aníbal was glad that the teacher had managed to secure a sixth-grade classroom with normal-size chairs. The first week they had been assigned a kindergarten classroom and only Claudia Rodriguez, who was stick and bones and four feet tall, had managed to be comfortable, while the rest of them had to squat down on the round area rug.

Students took turns reading from the English textbook. Ashamed of his heavy accent, Aníbal never volunteered to read. Mr. Cochran liked to choose students to partner him in little skits he wrote for each class. Once, he chose Aníbal to play a waiter, he the customer. Aníbal was so nervous that he slurred the phrase "May I help you?" three times and the teacher had said good job and chosen someone else. Aníbal tried to follow Mr. Cochran's advice to concentrate on how the lips and tongue formed each individual word. He said that each word had a certain texture, a different shape or color, each weighed more or less than another, that he imagined it was the same in Spanish.

Aníbal had second thoughts about the class. How could any words, Spanish or otherwise, be more than mere sounds? Words were exactly that: just words, nothing more, nothing less.

He felt a fool studying another man's mouth, he who had spent countless hours tending to the lips of many a woman. If he were one of those funnies like Hernando Hernández over at the factory maybe he could do it, the way that Hernando tossed those sacks. Oh, Hernando was strong and all that, as strong as any of the other men, Aníbal included, but he arched his back and stood on tiptoe. Everybody knew that wasn't normal.

If Mr. Cochran was a pretty Miss Cochran, then he could concentrate on her lips, especially if she was sticking her tongue out to pronounce a word. He would be happy to stare at her tits and ass, too, while he was at it. No harm in that. But to hang on another man's every word the way a woman does when she's about to come and a man has to keep telling her she's beautiful for it to be good, no, he wasn't going to do that.

"Mr. Acevedo."

Claudia Rodriguez poked him with her bony elbow. The teacher was talking to him.

"Sorri, Mister Cochran." Aníbal stood up. He kept forgetting he didn't have to do that in America.

"You don't need to roll your *r*'s in America." Mr. Cochran waved him back in his seat. "You said that you read the newspaper?"

"Jess."

"Yes."

"Yess."

"Very good." Mr. Cochran twirled his pointer. "Everyone should follow Aníbal's example and read English daily and speak it always. You'll be surprised how quickly you'll master the language." He turned back to Aníbal. "Maybe one of these evenings you would care to share something of interest from your reading."

For the rest of the class, Aníbal concentrated on easing his pounding heartbeat back to normal and copying down Mr. Cochran's twice-weekly list of necessary English phrases, such as Excuse me, Officer, but I appear to have lost my way. Excuse me, miss. May I inquire as to the price of that refrigerator? Pardon me, madam, but you happen to be stepping on my shoe.

He wished that it was Felicidad, not the stick-like Claudia Rodriguez, who sat next to him.

Sometimes, late at night, Aníbal would drive past Chago and Ana's apartment, slowing down when he got to their block, holding his breath as he drove past, wishing that he would see Felicidad. The night came when he glimpsed her at the window, moonlight and streetlight passing through her, casting a nimbus of light about her. Shaken by the vision, he took his foot off the gas pedal for a heartbeat before recalling himself and driving home. He sat in his car smoking and staring up at his dark apartment.

He began to drop by Comacho's for a pack of cigarettes whether he needed one or not. He was quick to offer a smoke to others just to get rid of them. Half-full packs littered his car. Surely one day Felicidad would accompany Ana to Comacho's. Women liked to go about together, didn't they? He would brave even Ana if he could see Felicidad.

Comacho enjoyed Aníbal, this gran macho who had once been so cocky, coming into his store and fooling no one with his cigarette-buying self. Aníbal would take a quick look down the aisles, searching for his wife. Comacho was tempted to laugh at his dashed hopes, but not stupid enough to do it to his face. Aníbal was one of those young men quick with his fists and, also, better for him to buy cigarettes there than somewhere else. Later, when he would tell Lupe about Aníbal, she would purse her lips, nodding, as if this, too, she could have foreseen.

Chapter Thirty-four

Summer 1953

Week in, week out, Felicidad worked at the factory, attended night school, came home, ate, washed dishes, slept. Nights, when she was most lonely, she called her Spirit Husband to her and, only then, in his arms, could she sleep. By July she wearied of living without expectation. It reminded her of living with the aunt, when she had been so ready for a handsome stranger to walk through the doors of la panadería and carry her away from the endless hot humid days and uneventful nights. And then one day, when her head was aching from the smell of freshly baked bread, in walked Aníbal, and she had a glimpse of what her future could be.

One Saturday night, Felicidad was at the sink when Ana and several of her friends pranced into the kitchen in a mist of highballs and rose and gardenia perfume, hips swaying as if still on the dance floor, high heels clicking on the linoleum, dazzling in costume jewelry and flashy dresses with rustling skirts that called attention to their legs. They carried in empty platters and bowls once piled high with arroz con pollo and habichuelas guisadas and mountains of fried plantains, both the golden sweet maduros and the crunchy salty tostones.

Felicidad was elbow-deep in soapy water.

"Mujer, leave those dishes. I'll get you a rum and Coke," Ana said. "Maybe two."

Felicidad shook her head. "I like it at the sink."

"You *like* it at the sink?" Ana repeated the phrase as if it were a scandalous revelation.

Laughing, the other women left, charm bracelets jangling, but not before giving Felicidad pitying looks.

"You're not a servant. You don't have to work so hard," Ana said.

Felicidad stared at her, taken aback. No one had ever told her not to work hard.

One of the glittery women pushed open the door and called out to Ana, who waved a cheerful good-bye at the silent Felicidad.

Felicidad looked down into the sink. The bubbles had mostly popped, and she could see the dirty dishes in the murky water. She thought of her parents' house where she had washed dishes in la palangana, using only a spiky leaf that the family had named hoja de fregar after its purpose. It had been so laborious, lugging the five-gallon cans from the well and washing in cold water without the luxury of soap.

She felt a sudden yearning to see her mother. She wanted to sit next to her and embroider while listening to her stories. Any of them. All of them. The tales about the Spirits that roamed the mountains even. But mostly she wanted the mother who talked about flamenco dancers, who saved her part of her own lunch, the mother who had loved her. Felicidad wanted the happy days before her sister died, before her mother became ill.

And she wanted those few days with Aníbal on the island.

Hot tears fell on her cheeks, and Felicidad raised a soapy hand to wipe them. She was not quite sure why she was crying.

She had so much now. A job, her own money to send to her family, friends who cared about her, plenty of food to eat, a nice place to live. Independence.

She recalled Three Kings Day when she had been in the kitchen with Ana, drinking her first rum and Coke, feeling American with her smooth, shaved legs. She'd hoped that the Aníbal she had known on the island would soon return to her, and thought it only a matter of time when he bought things to please her—the bounty at Comacho's, the sofa, the thread for her embroidery. When they had watched television together, it had been so intimate, sitting alongside him in the near dark, trying to figure out the English phrases, laughing along with him, that she had dared to hope. She raised her hand again to wipe her face.

Ana came in, carrying a stainless-steel carafe. "I have to make more coffee," she said. Something in Felicidad's stillness gave her pause. "Are you all right?" She set down the carafe. "Are you crying?"

Felicidad tilted her head so her hair hid her face. Ana was having none of that. She smoothed back Felicidad's hair.

"You *are* crying!"

Felicidad threw herself on Ana, water dripping on the floor and on Ana's dress.

"My dress! Careful with those wet hands." Ana handed Felicidad a dish towel embroidered with roses.

"Please forgive me," Felicidad said.

"For what, mujer? Don't be a tonta. There's nothing to forgive. It's only a little water. It'll dry." Ana led Felicidad to the table piled with unwashed serving bowls and platters. She sat down next to her.

"What is this nonsense?"

Felicidad looked into Ana's black-lined eyes and wondered why she had ever been afraid of her.

Ana touched her hand. "Felicidad, you can trust me."

She looked down at Ana's hand clasped in hers, at the long fingernails painted bright red and the gold wedding ring that Ana had said wasn't even real, that Chago had bought for only five dollars when that was all the money he'd had in the world. Their hands were different shades, Ana's darker. Here was a woman who had fought for her, who had taken her into her home. Here was a woman who would understand.

"Ana, when I was a child, my mother became ill and had to go away. When she came back, my parents sent me to live with my uncle and the aunt. They were so poor and the money from my uncle helped so much," Felicidad said.

"Ay bendito," Ana said.

"I didn't think my parents loved me."

"Pobrecita." Ana squeezed her hand.

"I know that they did what they thought best, but Ana, I never belonged, even though it was my uncle's house and I loved my cousin Adela," Felicidad said.

"No me digas." Ana nodded as if all was clear to her.

"And yet, if I hadn't gone, I wouldn't have been able to finish school or to help my family. I wouldn't have my own teeth," Felicidad said.

Ana gave a little laugh.

"Don't laugh. It's true." She looked down at their hands again and said, "And I wouldn't have met Aníbal. One day, Aníbal came to my uncle's panadería and he was so beautiful. I thought I would do anything if he asked me," Felicidad told her.

"He's been known to have that effect on women." Ana's sarcasm was lost on Felicidad.

She was back on the island, looking into a pair of caramelo eyes.

"He said, 'Come with me,' and I went. He said, 'Marry me,' and I did," Felicidad said. "The way he looked at me!"

"Is this what the tears are about? Aníbal?"

"Oh, Ana, I've tried to forget him." Felicidad sank her head into her hands. She had left her husband to live a life that demanded little of her heart.

Ana went to the stove to make coffee. "You're not that little girl who was sent away. You're grown now. You can do anything you want."

Felicidad stared at Ana openmouthed. She felt her heart beat faster. Could it be so simple?

"Listen, your husband is not my favorite person right now. Especially not since Chago came home with a bloody nose," Ana said. "I'd like to give *him* a bloody nose."

Felicidad didn't doubt that Ana meant it.

"But you have a right to your own home." Ana turned on the faucet to fill the kettle. "And you need a man to love you."

Felicidad recalled how as a little girl, her mother had warned her that wanting something desperately was dangerous because the Spirits were always there to confound things. What if Mami was right.

"I want a man to love me too," Felicidad dared to say.

Ana scooped coffee beans into the grinder.

"Well, you're not going to find him in my kitchen and certainly not in the dishwater," she said.

Felicidad watched Ana turn the handle of the coffee grinder and listened to the rattle of the coffee beans. She realized that she was trembling. Ana was right. She wasn't that little girl anymore who had been sent away. She could decide things for herself.

Chapter Thirty-five

He drove to Comacho's after spending the morning working at Tony's garage. He was late. He knew that Ana finished her shopping before noon, but Aníbal hoped that this would be the week when she would shop later, that this would be the day when she would bring Felicidad. When he saw Chago's car, he was so relieved that he could have kissed it. He drove half a block farther for a parking space; he hurried down the sidewalk.

Everybody was at Comacho's. Factory workers and amas de casa spending Friday's paycheck buying comida criolla. Hair tonic and cologne—one always had to look good even for a trip to the grocery store—perfumed the air, adding sweetness to the greasy odor of the cuchifritos and empanadas Lupe had fried that morning. He would buy Felicidad a cuchifrito or an empanada, or both, if she wanted it. Aníbal exchanged greetings with the three or four of his countrymen smoking cigarettes and dodging housewives. Comacho was in a happy mood from all the dollar bills that had passed through his hands. He was leaning on the counter where a pretty woman was laughing at one of his jokes. Aníbal stared. *Felicidad! His*

Felicidad! She was here. But no, it couldn't be his wife enjoying herself with another man while she haunted him with her absence.

He would get her away from Comacho, protect her from him. Men moved out of his path, women glanced up curiously from shelves crammed with overpriced cans of beans and vegetables, fingers pausing on dusty jars of Spanish olives, instinctually sensing a possible revolú. Aníbal was oblivious to the whispers gathering force and migrating to the back of the store where Ana was chatting with Lupe and swirling over to Chago, who was watching the butcher wrap a pound of chorizo while discussing the best way to roast a pig in America.

Aníbal had eyes only for his wife. Her hair fell in waves about her shoulders, and the neckline of her dress embroidered with tiny roses framed the creamy smoothness of her collarbone. He was back on the island waiting to order bread from the pretty girl en la panadería.

Something happened to Aníbal that had never happened before—he opened his mouth to speak but not a single word came out of it. He shuffled his feet on the dirty tile floor like a teenage boy wishing a girl would notice him and dreading that she would.

Mala suerte, Comacho saw him first.

"Señora Felicidad, look." He pointed to Aníbal, who registered that Comacho called her señora, which indicated that he hadn't crossed the line and taken improper confianza, so he wouldn't have to punch him.

Comacho tossed a pack of Camels on the counter.

"Hello, Aníbal," Felicidad said.

The words that Aníbal had wanted to say to her these past weeks were stuck in his throat.

"How have you been?" she asked him.

Felicidad's lips were red and he wanted to kiss them.

Comacho made some joke about Comacho's being the store where one could find anything boricua, even wives.

"Chago and Ana are here," Felicidad said.

Carajo. Chago and Ana. He had forgotten about them. He glimpsed Ana and Lupe marching down the aisle toward him like sentinels and he managed to squeeze a few words out of his mouth.

"Come with me?" He had never felt so unsure, so nervous. "We can go for a drive? I've got my car."

"Aníbal, you bought yourself a new car? Is it a Cadillac?" Comacho said, smacking his hands on the counter. "¡Coño!"

He felt foolish. Comacho could see right through him and was making fun of him. But he didn't give a damn what Comacho said, he only cared that Felicidad would give him a chance to show her how much he had changed.

Ana was calling Felicidad's name.

"Please, Felicidad?" He went outside, hoping she would follow.

When Ana got to the counter Comacho told her how Aníbal had come to take Felicidad for a ride in his new car, a Cadillac.

Outside, Felicidad looked up at him with those eyes he'd dreamed about, those eyes that had once believed in him. What could he say to convince her to come back to him? He stuck his hands in his pockets to hide his nervousness, afraid that he wouldn't meet her expectations.

He said, "Why so nice to Comacho?" Why had he said that? He was such an idiot.

"He's always been very kind," Felicidad said.

"I'm sure he has, especially with you laughing at his jokes like that." What was he doing? He should be telling her how beautiful she was and how much he'd missed her, but he couldn't help himself.

A mother with three young children came out of the store and walked to a waiting car.

They stood on the corner, she staring up at the sky, he at the passing cars. They might have been strangers exchanging comments about the weather. A little breeze ruffled Felicidad's dress, and she crossed her arms. It was July; she couldn't be cold. Aníbal remembered his shirt tossed on the floor.

"Carrying on like that and you, a married woman." He had to stop. How would she know that he had changed, that he was sorry for hurting her, that he loved her?

"Am I?"

Felicidad looked him in the eye.

It wasn't right, the way she looked at him, challenging him like that. He knew then that, whether or not he liked it, the Felicidad who would have done anything he told her belonged to the past.

"You've changed, Felicidad," Aníbal said.

Felicidad's fingers played with the strap of her purse.

Two women came out of the store carrying groceries. They walked slowly, their gazes measuring the distance between the couple, noting how Felicidad held herself aloof and how Aníbal kept his head down, looking as miserable as any boy moored in unhappiness of his own making.

An unbidden thought came to him. What if this new Felicidad didn't want him?

Several of the men who had nothing better to do than loiter around Comacho's came out for some fresh air and, finding their corner occupied by Felicidad and Aníbal, crossed the street and smoked cigarettes, politely looking away from the couple.

He needed to let her know that he wasn't the old Aníbal, the maricón who fooled around with Marta, the one who changed his mind about her the moment he left her back on the island.

"I'm not the man I used to be, Felicidad," Aníbal said. Any moment, Chago and Ana might come out and take Felicidad away. "I'm not seeing Marta anymore."

She stopped playing with her purse.

"I have a new job and I'm going to school now, too." He wished he dared touch her. "I'm not seeing Marta. Or anybody else either." Had he already said that?

"Do you care?" That pleading voice couldn't be his, not the voice of Aníbal Acevedo who had prided himself on never being concerned about what any woman thought of him.

She was so still. If it hadn't been summer with the sun hot on their skin, he would have thought her frozen to the ground on the corner of Mozart and Augusta.

"Felicidad, do you?" Of course she still cared, he thought. Coño, she had to care. Fuck, what if she didn't?

She brushed her hair from her face, and he thought he saw a smile.

Chago and Ana came out of Comacho's. Ana's eyes narrowed, assessing the situation. She stepped between them. She wasn't going to make it so easy for Aníbal; after all, she hadn't heard an apology for her husband's bloody nose. And if he wanted to see Felicidad, he knew where she lived. Let him come up to their apartment like a decent man, not accost her on the street. Next thing you knew, some chismosa would be sending a letter airmail to another chismosa in Puerto Rico and pretty soon anybody who had ever met Aníbal or Felicidad would know that Aníbal was exposing his business to the whole world in the middle of the sidewalk back in the United States.

"Go take a ride in your Cadillac," Ana said, taking Felicidad's arm and leading her away.

Aníbal held out his hand to Chago, who shifted his groceries to take it—what was a bloody nose or black eye between compadres? He could hear Ana asking about the Cadillac, but Aníbal could only wonder if he had really seen Felicidad smile.

Chapter Thirty-six

A glimmer of morning sun peeked in between the pair of curtains—white chintz with red cherries that reminded Felicidad of coffee berries. She and Ana had made them one evening, sewing and trimming the curtains with red ric rac.

Felicidad had spent the night thinking about what Aníbal had said and how he had looked when she peered at him through her hair. She hadn't been surprised to see him at Comacho's. She had told Ana that she wanted to return the money that the old caballero had given her, but she could have sent the ten dollars on with Ana. After these months apart from Aníbal, she had felt ready to face him, confident that she could meet him in a crowd and act like he was just another man to her.

She had been talking to Comacho, laughing at some joke that hadn't been particularly funny. Then her husband walked in, looking the way he had that first time en la panadería.

He asked her to come outside with him and so she went, not because she had to, but because she wanted to, was excited and nervous about what he might say. When he started in about Comacho, she thought it just a pretense to get her angry, to prepare her for the bad news he was to give her about Marta—that he was in love with her. When he said he wasn't seeing Marta her heart had begun to beat so quickly, she had to stand very still to steady it. He'd looked at her the way he had on the island, asking her if she still cared. But she couldn't tell him how she felt right there in the middle of the sidewalk in front of everyone and she was glad when Ana came out.

Ana's voice jarred Felicidad out of her reverie. Chago and Ana were lying in bed on the other side of the wall.

Felicidad was ashamed to hear her friends' private conversation and she covered her head with her pillow, but it did little to shut out Ana's voice.

"Aníbal said that? Why didn't you tell me this before?"

Silence. Chago must be talking.

Ana's muffled laughter. "Ay bendito, sometimes life is fair! After all these years as a picaflor, he's getting what he deserves."

What did Aníbal deserve? Felicidad moved, wincing as the cot squeaked.

Felicidad worried that they had fallen back asleep.

"Of course I feel sorry for Aníbal! I'm not a heartless woman! But the maricón did it to himself, let's not forget that," Ana said.

Ay bendito, if only Chago could speak above a whisper! What had Aníbal said?

But Felicidad didn't really need to know. Aníbal had asked her a question and she needed only to answer it.

Aníbal had driven around aimlessly all day. What was there for a single man to do on a Sunday when he wasn't interested in drinking or chasing women? Ay carajo, why hadn't he asked Felicidad straight out yesterday to come back to him? Maybe Marta had razón when she called him a pendejo. Why had he wasted precious minutes accusing her of flirting with Comacho when he should have taken her into his arms and begged her forgiveness between kisses al aire libre right there on the corner of Mozart and Augusta in full view of every Puerto Rican in Chicago.

Maricón, if he ever got Felicidad all to himself again he would tell her exactly how he felt about her. He parked his car and sat in it for a minute, gathering his strength for the long walk to the lonely apartment—thirty feet—street, sidewalk, building, and then the three flights of stairs to climb. He locked his car and leaned against it.

The grass was green and dry, flowers were blooming and the trees were crowned with foliage, but it could have been the middle of Chicago's bleak, cold winter for all the notice he paid the charms of a midsummer's night. Aníbal didn't hear the birds in the trees calling out their good nights or the clamoring of the crickets and cicadas hiding in the grass. He was oblivious to the dozens of neighborhood children running around in packs, their mothers sitting on stone stoops sharing recipes and gossip. He didn't even see the men playing dominoes at the card table set up on the grass. One of the men offered him a beer but Aníbal didn't hear him. He hunched his shoulders against the evening breeze, blind to the reds and magentas of the setting sun. His thoughts were of Felicidad. Had he lost any chance he had of getting her back? Aníbal took out a pack of cigarettes, staring into the half-empty package as if in it he would find a reprieve from his misery. He took out a cigarette, then stuffed it back in with impatient fingers. He was sick of cigarettes, sick of days and nights driving around without direction and so filled with longing for his wife that his stomach churned with the pain of it. And he was hungry, too. He cursed himself for being too stupid to pick up a hot dog or something. He'd seen only a dozen places where he could have eaten. Coño, he didn't feel like getting back in the car.

Aníbal stuck his hands in his pockets and looked up at the apartment, expecting to see it shrouded in darkness as it had been every night since Felicidad left. But tonight there was a light. A light! Was it his imagination? All the nights he'd dreamed of just this. He squinted, moving to see if perhaps the light was a reflection from something or other—he didn't know, the setting sun, from the building next door—but no, it was a light inside the apartment.

He ran. He ran around a car that had just driven up and was parking. The driver honked and shouted something. Aníbal jumped over the metal tubing that protected the building's lawn, his feet crushing the grass. He pushed open the entry-way's heavy wood door, taking the stairs two at a time. Aníbal fumbled with the key. ¡Carajo! Finally, he managed to open the door and lock it behind him.

The fragrance of frying pork chops greeted him. The lamp was on in the living room, the saint candles lit on the mantel. He heard music coming from the kitchen. Was it a dream?

"Felicidad. Felicidad!" he called out, his voice catching in his throat. Ay carajo, if he could be so lucky, he would never ask for another thing. He hurried to the kitchen, hoping he wasn't dreaming.

The table was set with a cloth and serving bowls of lettuce and tomato salad and rice and beans.

She was at the stove humming along to the radio. An appari-tion in red and white, some kind of gauzy apron peppered with tiny roses at her waist.

"Felicidad," he said, wanting to say so much more.

She looked up from the pork chops she was turning. Her fin-gers smoothed her apron.

"I came to answer your question," she said.

"Question?" He wanted only to kiss her.

"What you asked me at Comacho's," she said.

What about Comacho's? He couldn't remember. All he cared about was that she was here in the flesh. Two steps and she would be in his arms.

Felicidad gave a little laugh. "Don't you want to know the answer?"

He remembered. He held his breath; the clock on the wall counted off the seconds.

Felicidad stood with the window behind her. She had peeled the sheeting from the glass and laid it folded in a neat square on a chair, a measuring tape on top of the plastic.

They were oblivious to the falling darkness. Aníbal knew only that when she looked at him, he believed that he could be the man he wanted to be. One step, two.

"Querida," he said, kissing the tears on her face.

They didn't notice the pork chops burning in the pan.

Book Club Questions

1. Early in the novel, Felicidad's parents made a difficult decision that changed the course of her life. Do you think that it was the right decision under the circumstances? How did it color her view of herself? Did Felicidad gain more than she lost?

2. The aunt assigns Felicidad many duties and says to call her *señora,* yet she takes the trouble, as she does with her own daughter, to teach Felicidad the proper way of señoritas. Would you say that Felicidad was ill treated? Can any of the aunt's actions be justified?

3. How does Felicidad's "Spirit" serve to free her from the gender identification of her culture and that assigned to her by Aníbal?

4. Consider the different ways in which *spirit* is used in the novel. Discuss these and why the realm of spirit is as important as the realm of physical reality.

5. Aníbal takes Felicidad from the island for reasons other than love. What are these reasons? What must he give up to truly love Felicidad? What does he gain in the process?

6. *Respeto,* meaning "respect," is very important in the Spanish culture. Mackie's behavior toward Aníbal is a falta de respeto, a lack of respect, and adds to Aníbal's growing frustration with his inability to be a man like his father. Do you think that hampers Aníbal's ability to get on in America? Is it easier today for someone from another country to achieve the American Dream?

7. Aníbal says that he might look like a white man but his accent makes him brown. How is this reflective of society even in today's world? Does your accent or race or religion set you apart from your associates? Or have we evolved to a point that none of the above matters?

8. Do you see any correlation between Aníbal and Felicidad's immigrant story and that of people you might know—your parents, grandparents, friends, or perhaps even your own story?

9. Is infidelity ever excusable?

10. How does Marta serve to clarify the main characters—Aníbal and Felicidad? Is it fair to call her a puta, a whore?

11. Chago and Ana become Felicidad's surrogate family. Ana feels constrained in her marriage to Chago, and her addiction to coffee helps her get through her days. Is this malady typical only of the 1950s because of the traditional male/female

roles in marriage and the Puerto Rican culture, or is disillusionment and lack of fulfillment also common today? What resources do women have today that they might not have had in the 1950s?

12. Throughout the novel Felicidad is placed in uncomfortable situations and foreign settings. How do these serve to bring out her true identity?

13. How does Felicidad's personal history allow her to accept her own spirit and eventually transform her identity?

14. The novel makes the point that transformation must be earned, sacrifices made to overcome insecurity and character flaws. Discuss the sacrifices made by Felicidad, Aníbal, and other significant characters in the novel.

About the Author

Marisel Vera wrote *If I Bring You Roses* to claim her Puerto Rican heritage by discovering it. *If I Bring You Roses* is inspired by her jíbaro roots, her awe of her ancestors and their island, and of her parents and their migration to the United States. Born in Chicago, Illinois, Vera was raised in a large, traditional Puerto Rican family. Growing up during the 1970s when women and minorities were fighting for equality and human rights—sometimes to the point of violence, as in the infamous Humboldt Park riots in Vera's own neighborhood—sparked both her quest for equal rights in her family's patriarchal culture and her need to learn more about her Puerto Rican ancestry.

One of six children, Vera graduated from Chicago's Roberto Clemente High School and was the first in her family to earn a college degree: a BA in journalism from Northern Illinois University. She has worked in public relations and advertising.

Vera studied with Paulette Roeske, Margaret Gibson, Jonis Agee, Rosellen Brown, and Cristina García. She won the *Willow Review* literary magazine's fiction prize for two of her short stories: "The Liberation of Carmela Lopez" (2000) and "Shoes for Cuba" (2003).

Vera lives in a Chicago suburb with her husband and two children.

If you enjoyed *If I Bring You Roses,* then you're sure to love these emotional tales of self-discovery—

Now Available from Grand Central Publishing

The Realm of Hungry Spirits

Lorraine López, award-winning author of *The Gifted Gabaldón Sisters* (GCP, 10/08), returns with a novel about a woman who craves solitude, only to find family more fulfilling.

Try to Remember

"Lyrical, poignant, and smart, as compassionate and hopeful as it is heartbreaking...a novel you will never forget."
—*New York Times* best-selling author
Jenna Blum

Tell Me Something True

"*Tell Me Something True* is a bittersweet journey about coming to understand and forgive the indiscretions of one's parents through the simple act of living one's life."
—*Miami Herald*

Look for future books from Leila Cobo.